# KANSAS WEDDINGS

# KANSAS WEDDINGS

*Three Brides Can Never Say*
*Never to Love Again*

## KIM VOGEL SAWYER

BARBOUR
PUBLISHING

Published by Barbour Publishing, Inc., P.O. Box 719, Uhrichsville, Ohio 44683, www.barbourbooks.com

*Our mission is to publish and distribute inspirational products offering exceptional value and biblical encouragement to the masses.*

Member of the
Evangelical Christian
Publishers Association

Printed in the United States of America.

Dear Reader,

Welcome to Kansas, home of my birth! In my 40-some years of life, I have lived all but one year in the heart of America's Breadbasket, and I can't imagine living anywhere else. Creating my own Kansas town and peopling it with special friends has been a great deal of fun.

The character John was inspired by a man who attends my church. John's favorite seat is the bench right in front of our sound booth. It gives him a straight view to the minister's pulpit, and from the choir loft, I've had a straight view of John. Every emotion can be read in John's face, and his sincere, heart-felt worship has moved me to tears on more than one occasion. He's taught me a great deal about throwing off one's inhibitions and praising God with the whole heart, so it gives me great pleasure to share John with you in these stories.

I hope you enjoy this visit to Kansas as much as I enjoy living here. Please feel free to visit my Web site at www.KimVogelSawyer.com and drop me a note—I love to hear from readers!

May God bless you richly as you journey with Him,
Kim Vogel Sawyer

# DEAR JOHN

# Dedication

For Kaitlyn, whose loving heart is open to everyone.
And with gratefulness to John, for showing me how to truly worship.

# Chapter 1

Marin Brooks blinked twice and stared at her aunt. "Excuse me. What did you say?"

"I said"—Lenore's stiff lips barely moved—"I hope you will finally do the sensible thing and have John put in some sort of home."

Marin shook her head. Why would she bring this up now of all times? Marin's parents were dead only four days, the funeral was barely over, and already Aunt Lenore was hollering to "put John away."

This conversation had been played before, but it had always been Marin's mother on the receiving end of Lenore's opinionated comments. Her heart ached as the loss of her parents hit her again. In fact, she felt as if a boulder sat on her chest. Why couldn't Lenore give her time to heal before beginning that tiresome tirade about John?

"Aunt Lenore, you know how Mother felt about—"

"My sister spent every day of that boy's life taking care of him." Her aunt cut her off abruptly. "She worked herself into an early grave trying to make him more than he had the ability to be. Now she's gone—God rest her soul—and that responsibility falls to you." Lenore clutched Marin's arm, leaning in and whispering harshly. "Do the sensible thing, Marin. Put him in a home and get on with your life. Don't waste your life as my dear sister did."

Marin stared in amazement as Lenore released her arm and strode away, her chin held high, a fake smile plastered on her wrinkled face. The voices of visiting relatives and bereaved friends seemed to fade into the distance as Marin turned to focus her attention on John. He appeared so forlorn sitting in the middle of the sofa, his palms on his thighs, his face drooping as he watched the milling people who talked around him as if he weren't there. The boulder pressed harder. John was her responsibility now.

How she loved him.

And pitied him.

Sometimes the two emotions were so intermingled it was hard to choose one over the other. Her earliest memories involved John. How could she do what Aunt Lenore suggested? And how could she not?

Marin shook her head again, trying to clear it. She would have time to think of that later. Time when the funeral was officially over, people had gone home, and she and John were alone. Then they could talk. Then she could think. There was too much noise, too much consoling, too much. . .sorrow. . .to add more to it now. There would be time. Because from now until her dying day, John would be her responsibility.

~ঔ

"Marin, where are Mom and Dad?"

Marin looked up from her morning newspaper and offered a sad smile. "Remember, John? We talked about this. Mom and Dad are in heaven. They had an accident, and they went to heaven with Jesus. Remember?"

John nodded, his thin blond hair falling over his high forehead. His hazel eyes, flecked with gold and green, caught Marin's attention as they always did. John's every thought could be read in his almond-shaped eyes. She read fear and uncertainty now, and pity rose in her chest.

"You don't have to worry. Mom and Dad are happy and well with Jesus."

John's lower lip quivered. He poked at the toast on his plate with a stubby finger. "I miss them, Marin." His clipped, concise way of speaking seemed more pronounced in his sorrow. As always, his pronunciation of *r* came out like a *w*, making him sound much younger than his thirty-one years. Marin felt maternal as she reached across the table and took his hand.

"I know. I miss them, too."

"I will not see them again."

Marin tugged his hand. "Yes you will. We'll both see them again, when we get to heaven."

John's eyes lit up, the smile changing his countenance. "Can we go today, Marin? Can we go to heaven today?"

Marin felt tears prick her eyes. How she missed her mother! She had always known the best way to explain things to John. She could make him understand without hurting him. Marin was completely out of her league.

"No, I'm sorry, but we can't. You see—"

John threw her hand away, anger pursing his face. "You are mean, Marin. You are mean not to let me see Mom and Dad. I do not like you when you are mean." He rose and stood glowering at her.

Marin rose, too, reaching her hand to him. "John, it isn't that I don't want you to see Mom and Dad. I want to see them, too. But—"

John covered his ears and squinched his eyes. "No! I will not hear you, Marin. I will not listen!"

Marin sighed, and the tears that had threatened earlier now slipped free and rolled down her cheeks. *I can't do this, God! I can't take care of John. I don't know how. . . .*

Her father's voice slipped into her memory. "Marin, when your mother and I are gone, you will be all John has. We're counting on you to care for him." How many times had she heard those words? Countless times. But had she ever believed it would happen? Never. Their parents had been so healthy, so vital. Marin had heard the statement, agreed to it, but never once had she believed she would be twenty-three years old and left to care for her brother. Resentment built, but responsibility squelched it. She wouldn't let her parents down. She wouldn't let John down.

"Marin?"

John's voice intruded into her thoughts. She lifted her face to find that he had dropped his hands. His eyes now glittered with tears.

"Marin, being in heaven means dead." John's chin quivered as he waited for her to respond.

Marin wished so much she could deny the truth of his statement. She fought the sobs that pressed against her chest as she slowly nodded, tears raining down her cheeks.

John's anger dissolved, and he reached for her. "Do not cry, Marin. I am sorry."

"Oh, John—" Marin rounded the table and enfolded her brother in a hug. He clung, in need of comfort.

The problem was, Marin needed comfort, too. But the hug was all one-sided. John took comfort, and Marin gave it. And that was how it would be.

—◦—

Marin signed the last of the papers on the lawyer's desk and then leaned back with a sigh. "I assume you will handle the funeral expenses and all my parents' final bills, then send me a check for the balance of Dad's insurance?"

Mr. Whitehead nodded, his snow-white hair shining in the sunlight that poured through the large plate-glass window behind him. Had the situation been less somber, Marin might have giggled. *Whitehead* fit the man so well.

"That's correct, Miss Brooks. Your father was quite an astute businessman, and he left you very well provided for. Financial worries should be few." He linked his fingers and rested the heels of his hands on the edge of the highly polished cherry desk. "Would you like for me to arrange for the sale of Brooks Advertising?"

Marin set her chin. "No. I intend to run the advertising firm myself. I have my business and graphic arts degrees." A stab of pain struck as Marin remembered why her parents had been on the road the night of the accident. She shoved the memory aside—she didn't have time for that now. "I am qualified to step into Dad's shoes, and I intend to keep the business running. Of course"—she offered a shrug and a smile—"I'm counting on his employees to stick with me. If they bail, I might have a problem."

Mr. Whitehead returned her smile with one of his own. "In my estimation, your father's employees were loyal to him and would transfer that loyalty to you. They are not eager to search for another place of employment." Then his expression turned serious. "But I do have a small concern. You are quite young, Miss

Brooks, and the two top men in your father's employ have much more experience. You might consider, for your sake, making them partners in the business and leaning on their expertise. It would lighten your load considerably, which would be to your advantage, considering. . ." His cheeks mottled with pink as his voice drifted off.

Marin understood. "Considering I have John to care for, as well?"

The man nodded, looking away. His cheeks blazed red now. Bringing back his gaze to meet Marin's, he continued in a gruff voice. "Miss Brooks, if I may be honest. . . ?"

Marin held her hand outward, inviting him to share his thoughts.

"You are a young, attractive, intelligent woman. Your father often shared his pride in you. He also shared his concern about his son. I believe your father would understand if you chose to find a suitable placement for John. Between the insurance settlement and the business, you will have adequate financial support for both yourself and your brother. If you would like for me to make inquiries about facilities that cater to the disabled, I would be more than willing to assist you."

Marin shook her head. "Mr. Whitehead, I appreciate what you're saying. Believe me, you aren't the only one who has expressed this thought." Marin's ears still rang with Aunt Lenore's daily harangue. "But I promised my parents I would care for John, and I intend to do so at home, just as Mother did. There really is no other option. John would never understand why I was removing him from his home. He's lost Mom and Dad." Her throat tightened. "I won't take away his home, too."

Mr. Whitehead sighed. "I understand your position. But if you should change your mind. . ."

"I won't." Marin stood on that firm announcement and held out her hand. "Please let me know if I need to sign any other papers. I've left John too long. I need to be going now."

The lawyer rose and shook Marin's hand firmly. "I will be in touch. Good luck to you, Miss Brooks. And again, my condolences on your loss."

Marin nodded and left the office. She moved through the echoing hallway to the elevator and, alone behind the sliding doors, allowed herself a couple of minutes of sorrow. Condolences on her loss, Mr. Whitehead had said. Did anyone really understand everything she had lost? Her parents, her best friends, her encouragers, her Christian examples. . .and her short-lived independence.

How Marin had enjoyed college! The freedom to stay out late, to giggle with friends, to flirt with the handsome boys on campus. . . Only the family picture on her desk had intimated that Marin was different from the other girls. She had finally found the freedom to be young and carefree during the years at college, away from home and away from the responsibility of being the protector and teacher of her older brother.

"Young and carefree" had now abruptly ended before she was ready for it. *Why, oh, why did Dad have to pull out in front of that semi?* she wondered again. *Mom and Dad weren't old enough to die. . . .*

The elevator came to a halt, and the doors slid open. A glance at the numbers confirmed that Marin still had four floors to go. She stepped to the corner as a tall man entered and reached toward the buttons. Then he smiled in her direction. "Oh, both heading for the lobby. Good." He leaned into the opposite corner, the warm smile still lighting his face. "You look familiar. Have we met?"

Sounded like a pickup line—one she wasn't in the mood to entertain, no matter how handsome this stranger. She didn't smile in return. "I don't believe so."

The man shook his head slowly, his brown eyes narrowing below thick, arched brows. He stood a good ten inches taller than Marin, and she stifled the urge to shrink into the woodwork. "No, really. You look very familiar. I know I've seen you—" Then his eyebrows shot high in recognition. "Is your father Darin Brooks?"

Now it was Marin's turn to raise her brows. "Y–yes. How did you know?"

He chuckled—a low, throaty sound that seemed comforting for some odd reason. "I knew I'd seen you. The pictures on his desk—a regular portrait gallery. You're Marin, right?"

Marin nodded. She gave the man a quick perusal. He didn't seem the executive type usually seen wandering through the Branson Building. Worn Levis, a plaid shirt open at the collar—no tie—and brown hiking boots made up his attire. His brown hair was rather shaggy, longer at the collar and curling up around his shapely ears. He gave the rugged appearance of a lumberjack. What could he have been doing in Dad's office?

"I'm Philip Wilder. Your father helped me with some brochures for my business." The elevator doors slid open to the lobby, and Philip gestured for Marin to precede him. He followed her out and flashed another white smile. "He did great work. Tell him thanks again for me, will you?"

Before Marin had a chance to explain that his request would be impossible, he turned and trotted toward the double doors leading outside and disappeared. She felt somehow deflated by his departure. It was the first normal conversation she'd had since her parents' deaths. The first exchange that hadn't included condolences or John. It had felt good.

Sighing, she walked slowly to the exit. Maybe her only normal conversations would now come from strangers. It was a depressing thought.

⟡

Philip Wilder paused at the curb, looked both ways, then dashed across the street to his waiting motorcycle. "Hello, sweetheart," he greeted, running his hand along the sleek curve of the gas tank before popping open the small trunk and retrieving the cobalt blue helmet—the same shocking color as the cycle itself. He loved the bright blue balanced with the abundance of chrome that decorated the classic cycle. The bike was his pride and joy—and he treated it like the child he would likely never have.

Echoes from the meeting on the eighth floor of the Branson Building replayed in his mind. The lawyer's voice explaining, "The account is unavailable, Philip. No explanation from the bank. I'll keep trying. If something changes, I'll be in touch." In the meantime, how would Philip pay the bills and keep his business running? He had another month's expenses squirreled away, but after that... His heart beat erratically as he considered the number of people relying on him.

*God, You have a plan. Hope You'll reveal it to me in time. So much is riding on it.* Strapping on his helmet, he glanced toward the building in time to see his elevator mate exit. He watched her, observing how her head hung low, her shoulders slumped as if carrying a weight too heavy to bear. He wondered whom she had been visiting. Whoever it was must have given her some bad news. *The Bad News Branson Building*, he thought with a measure of disdain. Then he shook his head, determined to find a positive on which to focus.

Pretty girl, he acknowledged. But he'd thought that when he'd seen the arrangement of pictures on the corner of Darin Brooks's desk. Unpretentious, but attractive—wholesome. That appealed to him. He considered calling her name, giving her a wave, but then he wrapped the errant hand around the handlebar of the cycle to keep from giving in to that urge. What was he thinking, encouraging contact with Marin Brooks? Despite her despondent appearance right now, she'd no doubt be smiling and laughing soon—Darin Brooks would see to that. The man obviously idolized his daughter. A girl like that had the world by the tail—she surely wouldn't be interested in someone like him. He'd discovered long ago that his life calling didn't appeal to most folks. No, it was best to put aside his desire for a family. His family would be the workers at New Beginnings. They were about all the responsibility one man could handle.

His helmet secured, he swung his leg over the bike. The engine revved to life with a thrust of his foot against the kick start. As he backed out of his parking space, he sent a glance skyward and spoke aloud. "Okay, God, remember what I said. I need a plan—and quick. Start thinking, and when You've got it worked out, fill me in. Thanks."

# Chapter 2

"Marin, I am going to sort my job now." John stood in the doorway of their father's den. He refused to step over the threshold despite Marin's invitation.

Marin admitted she felt like an interloper sitting in Dad's soft, black leather executive chair behind the massive antique banker's desk with a towering credenza behind her. Dad had always looked so at home in this setting—Marin probably looked ridiculous, dwarfed by the size of the furnishings. But she needed to become accustomed to the feel of sitting in Dad's chair. She needed to learn to fill his shoes.

"Your job?" Then Marin remembered. "Oh, you're going to sort the bottles and cans."

John nodded, his face shining. "Yes. It is my job. I will do it now for Mom." His chin dropped, the sunny expression clouding over. In slow motion, he shook his head, his thin hair flopping across his forehead. "No. I will not do it for Mom. Not anymore. I will do it for you, Marin."

Marin's heart turned over in her chest. John was transferring his affection for their mother to her—accepting her as his caretaker. She found it touching. And scary. "Thank you." Her voice sounded tight. She swallowed and gave her brightest smile. "Do you need any extra bags?"

"I will find them. You stay here." John waved his stubby hand at her and disappeared, his slogging steps fading away as he made his way to the kitchen.

Marin sat and listened to the noises—cans clinking, water running, the creak of a milk carton being crushed. John fully understood the recycling. She smiled. He took such pride in it. The telephone rang, and she snatched it up. "Hello?"

"Marin? This is Lenore."

Marin stifled a sigh and slumped back into the chair. Not again. "Aunt Lenore. What can I do for you?"

"Not a thing. But I can do something for you." Lenore's authoritative voice boomed through the lines. "I did some calling today. Did you know there's a facility in Harper that takes Down syndrome people?"

Marin felt heat building. "Aunt Lenore, you know Mother never liked you to refer to John as a 'Down syndrome person.' He's a person first. He simply has a disability."

"Yes, a disability that consumed your mother's life." Her aunt's tone was hard, unforgiving. "And now you're going to carry on in her stead. Well, young woman, I will not stand by and see another life ruined by that—"

"Stop!" Marin wished she could throw the phone across the room. She took a deep breath, praying silently for control before speaking again. "Aunt Lenore, I know you love me, and I know you think you're doing what's best for me, but you aren't helping me at all by trying to shuffle John off to some institution where he'd die of loneliness. If you really want to help me, why don't you offer to take John for a couple of afternoons each week? I'm going to have to make some sort of day care arrangements for him. If he were with you, at least he'd be with family part of the time." The silence at the other end was deafening. "Aunt Lenore?"

Finally her aunt's voice came, breathless and full of disbelief. "You want me to take—? Marin, you must be kidding."

Marin released a brief, humorless snort. "Yes, I suppose I am. That wouldn't work at all, would it? You probably don't even recycle."

"What?"

With a sigh, Marin shook her head. "Never mind. Listen—I appreciate your checking in, but I really must run. I'm trying to go through Dad's accounts and see which have precedence. I'll talk to you later, okay?" She didn't give her aunt a chance to reply. "Good-bye." She placed the phone back in its cradle then sat staring at the telephone for several minutes, certain it would ring again. When it didn't, she heaved a sigh of relief and went back to her file. But just as she got focused, John reappeared in the doorway.

"Marin? I am all done." In his excitement, he expressed himself with sign language in addition to verbal words. "I put the bags in the gaw–gaw—" Impatiently he chopped out the sign for *garage*, unwilling to form the tricky *r* in the word.

"Good," Marin praised him, surprised by how much her voice sounded like her mother's. "Thank you."

John beamed, wringing his short fingers together. "I will take my bath now. And then I will want my toast."

Marin nodded, familiar with his nighttime routine. "Fine. You take your bath. And when you're in your pajamas, come and get me, and we'll have toast together."

John wagged his head up and down, smiling. "Yes. Together we will have toast." He disappeared from view once more, and before long, the spatter of water against the porcelain tub could be heard, followed by John's cheerful, off-tune singing.

Marin leaned her chin in her hand, listening, a fond smile tugging at her lips. She could almost hear her mother sighing, "Dear John. . ." Mother had always stood outside the bathroom door and listened as John sang. Somewhere he'd heard that people sang in the shower. He hated showers—the splash of water in his face upset him—but he loved his bath and would always sing at the top of his lungs as he scrubbed himself clean.

"Dear John. . ." Mom would sigh as she stood in his doorway and watched him sleep. "Dear John. . ." with pride shining in her eyes when he learned something new, like tying his shoes at age nine.

"Dear John. . ." Marin heard herself release the words, and a bubble of sadness welled in her chest. Had her mother ever stood outside Marin's room, watching her sleep, murmuring, "Dear Marin. . ."? How Mother had loved John! Marin could never remember a time her mother had been impatient with John. Always she had been giving, tender, full of wisdom. She seemed to know instinctively what John needed and never hesitated to meet his needs. At times, Marin had envied their relationship—she never felt as if she mattered as much to Mom as John did.

At the same time, she had always wondered if Dad truly loved John or was simply resigned to taking care of him. Her father had never been brusque or uncaring with John, but his relationship had been somehow distant. Sometimes she'd seen her father sit and watch John with a pained expression on his face. She wished now she had asked him what he had been thinking as he silently watched his only son.

Marin dropped her gaze to the file on her father's desk. Dad had been meticulous in his record keeping. It would be easy for her to step in where he had left off. But it would take time to acclimate to the office, to get to know the staff, to discover the needs of her clients. Time she didn't have unless she found someone to care for John.

The thought worried her. Mom had never wanted John to be with strangers. But unless a relative stepped forward and offered to keep him, Marin would have no choice. Just during the days, though, she told herself. Never what Aunt Lenore suggested—an institution or home where other people with handicaps were shuttled away from their families. Mom would turn over in her grave, and Marin would never be able to live with the guilt of sending John away. She sighed again. "Tomorrow I'll make some calls—maybe Aunt Chris will have some suggestions." Dad's sister was much less abrasive than Mom's sister.

"Toast now, Marin!" John stood in the doorway in his pajamas, his wet hair slicked down, a huge grin on his face.

As always, the sight of John in his pajamas gave Marin a start. His behavior was so childlike that it seemed odd to see him in men's two-piece pajamas and a plaid robe. Shouldn't he be wearing flannels with trains or puppy dogs printed on the fabric? Marin lifted herself from the chair and met John in the doorway, linking arms with him.

"Toast," she agreed. "With butter and sugar, right?"

"Butter and sugar, right." John nodded, easily pleased.

Marin hoped the accommodations she found for John's daytime hours would please him as readily as the promise of buttered toast with a sprinkle of sugar.

Because she didn't know what else to do with him, on Wednesday morning of the first week following her parents' deaths, Marin loaded John in her car and took him with her to Brooks Advertising. Before entering the building, she gave him a bright smile. "Okay, here's the office. I know you've been here before, right? Remember, the people here are working, so we can't stop and talk to everyone we see. But you can wave and say hi, okay?"

John gave her one of his looks—squinty eyes, pursed lips, chin pulled down until it doubled. "I am not stupid, Marin. I know I cannot bother people who are working."

Marin squeezed his hand. "I know you're not stupid. I'm sorry if I sounded like I thought you were. I'm just a little nervous."

John's expression changed to one of surprise. "You are nervous, Marin?" His hands formed the sign for *nervous* as he spoke.

Marin nodded, nibbling at her lower lip. "Yes, I am." But she didn't expand on the reason. Would Dad's employees accept her leadership, or would they see her as the boss's little girl trying to be a big shot? She wanted Dad's business to continue being the success he had made it—and she would need their help. Would her planned speech help them see how much she needed their cooperation without making her sound like an inexperienced kid?

Marin nearly snorted. Had she ever been a kid, in the true sense? Not really. "Are we going in, Marin?"

Marin gave a start, having drifted away in thought. She shot a glance at John, waking up, then nodded. "Yes. Let's go."

She swung open her car door and John followed suit, ambling around the hood of the car with his hand extended. She knew what he wanted. Obligingly she handed him the automatic lock and let him push the button.

At the "beep" indicating the doors were locked, he beamed. "All is safe!"

Marin smiled, wishing her emotions could be so easily safeguarded. She took the keys back and dropped them into her purse then led John into the offices. Brooks Advertising was located in the older part of downtown Petersburg, Kansas, and still retained the appearance of its 1920s beginning. Marin liked the sense of stability the redbrick building with its ornate plaster scrolls and window casings projected.

Inside, hardwood floors shone with a high polish, and the twelve-foot ceiling bore pressed tin panels. The plaster walls were painted a soft mauve above beaded wainscoting. A beautiful border that resembled a burgundy swag separated the paneling from the painted wall. The soft colors were at once welcoming and relaxing. Dad had done a great job of maintaining the tradition of the structure without sacrificing today's style.

John immediately waved to the receptionist, Crystal Brown, and Crystal gave a hesitant wave in return. Marin had learned early to detect when someone was uncomfortable with John's disability. Crystal tried to hide it, but her frozen smile and stiff gestures gave her away.

"Is everyone in the meeting room?" Marin asked, pausing at Crystal's desk, which was a 1920s soda counter reconstructed to meet the needs of a secretary.

"Yes, all in and accounted for, Miss Brooks." Crystal's gaze darted to John as if worried he would do something unusual and she might miss it.

"Great. I'll talk to you later." Marin turned to John. "John, do you want to sit out here and look at the magazines? I'll be back in a few minutes."

John nodded and padded to the reception area where a large oval rug held a circle of upholstered chairs and a low table arranged neatly with a variety of magazines. He picked one up and held it out to Marin with a huge smile. "Cars, Marin! I will look at the one about cars!"

Marin gave him the thumbs-up sign. "Great choice. Back soon." She turned and clicked her way to the meeting room, her heart rate increasing with every step. Before entering the room, she ran her hands over the slim skirt of her jade green suit and touched the collar of her white blouse. Dad had always dressed to the hilt when coming to the office, and Marin had tried to emulate his appearance in her feminine way. "The clothes make the man," Dad had always said. Marin hoped her professional appearance would help hide her inner nervousness.

Swinging the paneled door open, she offered a big smile to the employees seated at the round meeting table. Dad had insisted on a round table to make everyone feel equal—just like King Arthur's round table. One seat was open— Dad's. Marin swallowed a bubble of sorrow as she moved to that chair and rested her hands on its high back.

"Good morning, everyone," she greeted them, letting her gaze rove around the group, offering a smile to each person. They smiled and offered greetings in return, but she could sense their unease, as if waiting for a shoe to drop.

"First of all, I want to thank all of you for being so dedicated to my father in the years you've worked with him. He always spoke highly of his staff, he considered you his friends as well as his employees, and I know he'd be pleased you were all here, ready to continue with his business." Marin paused, fighting the urge to cry. She would not cry! She had to be strong! Swallowing, she forced a smile she didn't feel.

Taking advantage of a moment to gain control, she pulled out Dad's chair and gingerly slid into the wooden seat. Folding her hands on the edge of the table, she continued. "I'm sure you have lots of questions about where the company will go from here. I assure you, I have some, too!" She laughed lightly and felt relief when answering smiles broke across their faces. "But I do know one thing—Dad's company will continue just as he would intend it. Brooks Advertising has built a reputation of integrity and quality. That will not change. The only difference is essentially a consonant change in the ownership—from Darin to Marin. It's what Dad wanted, and I will do my best to be the kind of leader my dad was—fair, approachable, and knowledgeable."

The oldest of the employees, Dick Ross, raised his hand. "Miss Brooks— Marin—I appreciate your statement and your desire to keep the business running. But"—he glanced around the table, and Marin got the impression whatever he was about to say had been discussed between the employees before she got there— "with all due respect, your father had been in this business for years. You are newly graduated from college without experience in running a business. Are you sure you are up to the challenge?"

Marin felt the familiar swell of guilt that came with the mention of her graduation. Resolutely she pushed it aside to ask in an even tone, "Up to the challenge? I believe so, Dick." She intentionally used the man's first name, knowing her father would have addressed him in that manner. "I realize you haven't seen me in these offices a great deal, but Dad and I often conferred in his office at home. He kept me up-to-date on his accounts, explained why he chose one design over another, brainstormed with me. . . . He made me a part of Brooks Advertising because he knew one day I would *be* Brooks Advertising."

A sad smile tugged at the corners of her lips. "Of course, our hope was we would work together for several years before he handed over the reins. But that wasn't to be. So I'm going to make the best of our current situation."

She paused, unlinking her fingers to place her palms flat against the thick oak table top, gathering strength from the solid surface at which her father's hands had so often rested. "But I can't do it alone. I will depend on each of you"—she let her gaze rest on Dick's face the longest—"to assist me in this transition. Please communicate with me, keep me abreast of what your clients want, attend the morning meetings, just as you always did with Dad. Be patient with me as I learn to fill Dad's shoes. We all know they are big shoes to fill."

Tears threatened, but she blinked, keeping them at bay. Tears had no place here. "I will do my best, but this company has always been a group effort—Dad's name is in the title, but all of you are essential if Brooks Advertising is going to function the way it has for the past twenty years. I hope your commitment to the company will remain strong."

"You can count on me, Marin," Randall Stucky inserted, his blue eyes meeting her gaze head-on. "I had a great deal of respect for Darin Brooks. He gave me my first chance to prove myself in advertising. I won't let him down."

Marin smiled warmly. "Thanks, Randall. I appreciate that."

"You said we'd be having our morning meetings, just as Darin led them," Hannah Dutton said.

Marin nodded in her direction. "Yes, that's my intention."

Hannah flushed slightly but raised her chin and continued. "Your father always began our morning meetings with a word of prayer. Will that be a tradition you follow, Marin?"

Marin froze momentarily, unsure how to answer. She knew Dad had been a firm believer in prayer. He'd prayed with her often at home. Marin had accepted Jesus into her heart as a little girl as a result of her parents' gentle guidance. But prayer had been Dad's arena—he was the spiritual leader in the home. She hadn't considered assuming that role. It left her frightened and uncertain.

Hannah and the others waited for an answer. She had to say something. She opened her mouth and heard herself admitting, "To be honest, I hadn't processed that far. I've never seen myself in that kind of leadership position." She squared her shoulders. "But it was important to Dad to build this company on the Bible and on the premises of his faith, so I will continue in Dad's tradition there, as well."

The others nodded as Marin's throat tightened. *Help me do this, God!* Marin had prayed that simple prayer dozens of times since the phone call telling her of the accident. *Help me do this, God*, as she'd planned her parents' funeral. *Help me do this, God*, as she'd dealt with Aunt Lenore's pressure. *Help me do this, God*, now as she bowed her head to offer a prayer.

"Heavenly Father. . ." Marin heard the quaver in her voice as emotion rose. Tears stung behind her closed lids. *Help me do this, God.* "We come before You today with heavy hearts because someone we cared for—someone we've depended on—is gone. But, God, we are all aware of what Dad wanted when he built Brooks Advertising. He wanted to build a company that reflected Your face to every person who walked through the doors. Help us continue Dad's company the way he intended. Give us the knowledge and wisdom to meet the needs of the people who call upon our services. Help us bond as a group; help us learn to work together without Dad's gentle leading. Help me be the best leader I can be. Bless each of these employees seated around this table—thank You for their dedication to You and to Dad. Thank You for being here with us. Let us feel Your comforting presence as we move forward. In Jesus' name, we pray. Amen."

Marin raised her head to find a glimmer of tears in the eyes of some of the people seated around the table. She offered a quavering smile. "Thank you. I won't be able to stay today, but I'll try to be back tomorrow—I hope for the entire day—and we'll have a chance to get caught up on everyone's projects. In the meantime, I know I can trust you to finish the work you were doing before Dad's. . .death." It still hurt to say the word.

Everyone stood and filed out, stopping to touch Marin's shoulder or shake her hand, to offer another word of condolence or a "welcome" message. Dick was the last to leave, and he paused, his head down, obviously deciding how to approach whatever was on his mind. Marin waited patiently.

"Marin," he finally said, his gaze averted, "I've been with your dad a long time, and I loved him like a brother. I'll be honest—I'm concerned about how things will go now. You're young. I know you mean well, and I'm sure there's plenty of Darin in you to give starch to your spine, but you're going to be carrying a mighty load, keeping up with the responsibility of this company as well as your. . .responsibility. . .at home."

Marin felt warmth climb her cheeks. John again. For a moment, she wished she could dive back into the elevator of the Branson Building with the tall stranger, the one person who'd spoken to her in the past several days and not mentioned her brother.

Dick's face was set in a grim expression, but Marin could see sympathy in his eyes. "Darin had Mary to take care of home. Your name might be a combination of *Darin* and *Mary*, but you can't be both people, Marin. No one could be both people—it's too much. As harsh as it sounds, you're going to have to do something with John."

At that moment, Marin heard a movement at the door, and she looked over her shoulder. John had opened the door a crack and was peeking in, one hazel eye crinkled with smile lines. Without effort, she smiled back. "I'll be there in just a minute, John." The door closed.

She turned back to Dick. "I know what you're saying, but there is no way I can do what you're suggesting. You're right that my name is a combination of my parents'—and each of them bestowed in me the best of their hearts. Mom loved John with everything she had. Dad took care of him by providing financially. They would never forgive me if I didn't continue caring for him with the same dedication. Somehow I will make this work. I promise you that."

Dick shook his head, his glasses reflecting the overhead light and hiding his eyes from view. "I admire your spunk, Marin—reminds me of Darin—but I still think you're biting off more than you can chew."

"Then pray for me," Marin challenged, surprised at her boldness. She heard a giggle from behind the door. She added in a grim tone, "I'm going to need all the prayers I can get."

# Chapter 3

Marin slammed down the phone and clasped the hair at her temples. She hadn't realized it would be so difficult to find day care arrangements for John. Every place she'd located in the yellow pages had a waiting list. If she heard "If you had called six months ago. . ." one more time, she might scream. If she'd known six months ago that her parents would be dead and she would be the sole provider for her brother, maybe she would have called! The statement was ludicrous, given her circumstances. Marin fought the urge to lay her head on the desk and bawl.

It was getting late, but maybe she could make one more call. She heaved a huge sigh, then looked in the phone book again. The next listing was New Beginnings. Although the information was scanty, she resolutely punched in the numbers and waited for an answer.

On the third ring, she heard the receiver being lifted. "Hello, New Beginnings!" The masculine voice seemed vaguely familiar.

"Yes, I'm seeking a day care arrangement for my brother who has Down syndrome." Marin began her spiel, feeling as if she could recite the words by rote. "He is thirty-one years old, and—"

"What level?"

Marin stopped, confused. "Excuse me?"

The voice at the other end laughed. "I'm sorry. Let me rephrase that. You said your brother has Down syndrome, right?"

"Yes."

"Okay. So is his disjunction, mosaicism, or translocation?"

Marin rubbed her chin. "I–I'm not sure."

"Well, then, don't worry about it. But levels of the retardation seem to vary among the different types, so knowing that can help me place him initially."

Marin's heart lifted at the end of his statement. "You mean, you might be able to provide day care services for my brother?"

Another low chuckle was emitted, and Marin was sure she'd heard that sound before. "Well, I gotta tell you—this isn't exactly a day care. This is a job placement service."

Marin's heart fell. Job placement? "I'm sorry. I didn't realize. . . . I don't think you'll be able to help me after all." Marin started to hang up, but she heard a frantic voice calling from the telephone receiver.

"Wait! Wait!"

She placed the receiver against her ear. Impatience with her helplessness and pressure of her need came through clearly in her tone. "What? My brother is thirty-one years old, and he's not been out of our house for more than outings. Job placement is ridiculous. It would never work. I appreciate your time, but—"

"Now just hold on." The voice took on an authoritative tone. "You say your brother has never been out of the house, except for outings, in thirty years?"

Marin flumped back in the chair and crossed her legs. "That's right."

"So what has he been doing all that time?"

Marin blinked. Doing? "Well, he's been with my mom. Helping her, I guess. I've been away at college, so I really am not sure how he's spent his days." Marin turned her ear to the living room, where the stereo suddenly came on full blast. Thumping noises told her John was dancing. She'd need to get off the telephone soon.

"And he isn't helping her anymore?"

Marin pinched the bridge of her nose. "No. My mom was killed in an accident a little over a week ago. So I need to find someone to take care of John while I'm at work."

"Oh." The voice carried a hint of sympathy now. "I see. And your dad can't help?"

Marin swallowed hard. It was so difficult to go over this, especially with a stranger. "He and Mom were together in the accident. Neither survived."

"Hey, I'm sorry." Marin could tell by the gentle tone he meant it. "You've really inherited a responsibility, haven't you?" She didn't reply, just held the phone tight against her head, relishing the understanding that came through the phone line. "Listen—I'd like to help you out, but—"

Marin suspected she knew where this was going. Before someone else could disappoint her, she cut in. "I thank you for your time and concern, but it's obvious to me that my brother and your work program are not a good match. Good-bye." She hung up before he could respond.

She sat at the desk, staring at the phone book. The only other listing was a group home in nearby Garden City—and Marin didn't want to put John in a group home. She gave in to the earlier urge and let her forehead rest on the phone book while tears welled again. *Oh, please help me, God. What am I going to do?*

⸻

Philip traced over the telephone number he'd recorded from the caller ID. Since it wasn't in his phone's memory bank, he had no idea to whom he had just been speaking, but his heart ached for the hopelessness he'd heard in the young woman's voice. He didn't know if he'd be able to help her—if the brother had been at home with the mother, without schooling, for thirty years, it was possible it was too late.

In his years of working with people with disabilities, Philip had learned that much rested on the formative years. A twenty-point increase in IQ could be made if the parents simply exposed the child to the same activities as one would do with a "normal" child. *If there is such a thing,* he thought with a brief laugh.

He'd found that when a child with disabilities came into a family, the family often rallied around to protect the child. Not that he could blame them. Philip knew valid reasons existed for forming a protective barrier. But when it was carried to the extreme, the protective barrier could hinder learning. But if the mother of this man had sent him to school, if he had learned basic self-help skills, then there was a good possibility Philip could work with him. He wanted to try.

He was certain the woman wouldn't call again. She'd sounded as if she was at the end of her rope, however, and he wished he'd had the foresight to ask her name before she hung up. He ran the pencil lead over the final digit, darkening it more than the other six numbers in the telephone number. So she wouldn't call him. Didn't mean he wouldn't call her. But he'd really like a name to go with the voice before he spoke to her again.

Suddenly an idea struck. "Hey! Thanks, God!" he said, giving the credit to the One he was sure planted the thought. Flipping open his telephone directory, he began scanning the list of numbers.

—☙—

Marin turned off John's light and whispered, " 'Night, John. Sleep tight."

" 'Night, Marin," came his sleepy voice in return. No doubt worn out from his dance session, he should sleep well tonight.

She closed his door and took one step toward her bedroom when the telephone rang. She frowned. Who would be calling at ten o'clock? She sighed. She hoped it wasn't Aunt Lenore. A glance at the caller ID confirmed it wasn't, but she didn't recognize the number. For a moment, Marin hesitated. But she was afraid the incessant ring would bother John, so at the fourth ring, she snatched it up.

"Hello?"

"Is this Marin Brooks?"

For a reason she didn't understand, Marin's heart began to pound. "Yes. To whom am I speaking?"

"Philip Wilder—New Beginnings."

It took Marin a moment before a picture of the man from the Branson Building elevator—his tall stature, warm smile, and relaxed apparel—appeared in her memory. It gave her an odd feeling, but now she understood why his voice had seemed familiar.

"Listen, Marin—I'm so sorry about your parents. I didn't know. When I talked to you on the elevator and told you to tell your dad..." He paused, the silence heavy. His voice sounded husky as he finished quietly, "I wish I'd known."

"It's okay." Marin finally was able to form words. "How did you know it was me who called?"

Another pause. Then, almost shyly, his voice came again. "Well, I had your number—it came through on caller ID. So I got out the phone book and started hunting. Only 23,500 names—not that big of a deal." That low, throaty chuckle sounded again; only this time, it held a hint of self-consciousness. "But it sure helped that you're in the *B*s, or it would've taken a lot longer."

Marin dropped onto the couch, the phone still pressed to her ear. He had gone through the telephone book? "But why?"

"You hung up on me before I could finish what I was saying," he said. "I know we aren't a day care facility, but we still might be able to help your brother. What did you say his name is?"

"John," Marin answered automatically. "His name is John. But as I told you, he's never been involved in any kind of employment. I can't imagine he'd be of any use to you there."

"You'd be surprised. So many people look at the disabled, and all they see is a disability. I like to see the ability in the person."

Marin digested this. She liked the way it sounded.

Philip continued. "Tell me about your brother. What are the things he enjoys?"

Immediately Marin pictured John dancing around the room—swinging his hips and snapping his fingers to a Steven Curtis Chapman CD. She smiled. "He likes music. He enjoys dancing, although he isn't very good at it by most standards. Different sounds seem to capture his attention—rings, beeps, squawks. He has a fascination with noises. I have to watch him. If an appliance makes an unusual sound, he'll take it apart to see what's doing it."

A light chuckle came through the line. "What else? Does he have chores around the house?"

"Chores?" Marin shrugged. "Well, yes, I suppose so. He makes his own bed, keeps his bathroom clean, clears the table after dinner. And his job is recycling."

"Job? You said he didn't leave the house."

Marin heard his confusion. A light laugh escaped her lips—the first since her parents' death. Amazing how good it felt to release it. "He calls it his job. Actually he rinses all the recyclable items and sorts them in the garage for pickup."

"He categorizes them?"

Marin felt surprised by the enthusiasm she heard in his tone. "Yes. Puts the plastics together, the glass, so on. It isn't complicated."

"No, but what you're telling me is that John is able to sort items—categorize them according to common characteristics and put them away without guidance."

"That's what I'm telling you." Marin still could not see any significance in what she had shared, but it was obvious that Philip was excited by her words.

"That's wonderful! Did John go to school?"

Marin leaned back into the cushions of the couch and hugged a throw pillow to her. Her comfortable position invited a lengthier conversation. "Yes. He attended special education classes."

"EMH or TMH?"

"EMH, I believe. I can't be sure. John is eight years older than I am, so I was still in elementary school when he finished his education."

"Marin, if John attended classes for the educable mentally handicapped, then he definitely qualifies for job placement through New Beginnings."

Marin sat up straight. "You're kidding? On the basis of sorting recyclables?"

Philip laughed. "I do have some placements for the trainable mentally handicapped, but most are for EMH. I could work with John here at New Beginnings and eventually place him at any number of locations—a school to do custodial work or a fast-food restaurant clearing tables and mopping up. Maybe even—"

"Whoa, hold on!" Marin threw the pillow aside. This was going too fast. "You want John to be in a regular workplace—not at wherever you're located, which I assume is a protected environment, but out where he'll encounter all kinds of people."

"That's exactly what I shoot for."

"Then we're not interested." She stood, the pressure building in her chest again. She had hoped—but no, John couldn't handle it. Marin couldn't handle it if something happened to him out there.

"But why not?" Philip didn't sound angry, just curious.

Marin sighed. "Philip, it isn't that I don't appreciate your taking the time to track me down and tell me a little more about your program. But you don't understand my needs. All I need is a place for John to 'hang out' while I'm at work—a safe place for him to spend the day. So I'm sorry, but I'm going to have to look elsewhere."

"There is no elsewhere, Marin. Not unless you want him in an institution."

A stab of pain struck. That's exactly what she wanted to avoid. Anger billowed, and she took her frustration out on the man at the other end of the telephone line. "Why do you have to be so negative?"

"I'm not being negative. I'm only telling you the truth. There are basically two options: Put the disabled away where we don't have to see them or acknowledge their presence, or somehow integrate them with our world. I prefer the latter. I thought you did, too. After all, you called me looking for help."

"I do need help! But I don't want John to be hurt!"

"Good. That means we have the same goal."

His calm reply deflated Marin's anger. Why was she yelling at this man who was only trying to offer her a solution to her problem? When she didn't say anything in response, he began speaking again in a hushed tone that invited complete attention.

"Listen, Marin. I think I told you your dad did some advertising brochures for me. In our conversation, I got the impression he was a Christian. Am I right?"

"Yes. Dad was a strong Christian."

"And are you?"

Marin considered his question. She had accepted Christ, but she didn't see herself as the spiritual giant she perceived her parents to be. Still, there was no other accurate answer. "Yes."

"Then you believe God has a plan for each life, don't you? I believe that, too. God put a seed in my heart a long time ago, when I was still a boy. Something. . . happened. . .to make me see a need existed for people with disabilities and people without disabilities to learn to work together and accept one another. That seed coming to fruit is New Beginnings. I opened it four years ago to help people like your brother find a way to feel as if they belong in society. With God's help, lives have been changed."

Marin clutched the telephone receiver with both hands. "That's all very well and good—and I admire your stand—but I'm still not sure it's a good fit for John." She swallowed hard, lowering her voice to a whisper. "Philip, we've always kept John away from public places. Not completely, of course—he's attended church with the family, and he goes out for dinner or shopping. But whenever he's gone out, he's been with my parents—never by himself. Mom didn't trust people with him. John is so open to everyone, so loving, that he's a prime target for cruel jokes. I don't think my mother would approve of my placing him in a program that would intentionally put him in the public eye."

"I do understand your concern, Marin." Philip's voice held compassion. "Believe me, I have the same concerns. That's why this program is carefully monitored. I'd be happy to give you some names of families who have made use of New Beginnings and are glad they did."

She wavered. "I don't know. . . ."

His voice came again, strong in his conviction. "Marin, I don't think it was an accident that you and I met in the elevator at the Branson Building. And I don't think it was an accident that I happened to be in the building three hours later than my normal schedule, making it possible for you to talk to me rather than my answering machine when you called here tonight. New Beginnings is here to help you, but New Beginnings is useless unless people like you trust me enough to *let* me help them."

Marin sighed, sitting back down. She rested her chin on her hand. The idea of John in a public workplace, where people might laugh and point and— she shivered—do worse things, did not set comfortably. But Philip was a good salesman. He had her thinking. She hedged. "Could we visit? Maybe see what you do?"

"Sure!" She could almost feel Philip's smile come through the line. "That would be great. Would nine o'clock tomorrow morning work for you?"

Marin considered this. She had intended to go to the office tomorrow, to become familiar with the routine there. But until she found a place for John, she wouldn't be able to go to work anyway. They'd have to go another couple of days without her. "Yes. I can make that work."

"Wonderful! Do you have the address?"

"Yes, it's in the phone book."

"Good. I'll see you then. And, Marin?"

The way he spoke her name left her feeling tingly under her skin. "Yes?"

"Don't coach John before you come. Let him be himself."

Marin frowned. Didn't she always let John be himself? "Okay."

"I'll see you and John tomorrow. Sleep well, Marin." The phone line went dead.

Marin sat for a moment, staring at the buzzing receiver. Then she carefully placed it in the cradle. *Sleep well, Marin*, he had said. He'd sounded like a friend—like someone who cared. Marin needed all the friends she could get right now. She hoped this Philip Wilder proved to be as good as he sounded.

# Chapter 4

Philip hung up the phone, then leaned back in his squeaky, secondhand desk chair, propped his heels on the edge of the scarred desk, and linked his fingers behind his head. He smiled, remembering the attractive girl from the elevator. Then the smile drooped as he recalled her bearing when she left the Branson Building as well as her defeated tone on the telephone. *She must feel as if she's carrying the weight of the world right now*, he mused, *losing both of her parents and having to assume so much responsibility*.

Philip understood the weight of responsibility. He ignored the jumble of papers on his metal desk, keeping his eyes aimed toward the ceiling. He'd stared at the figures long enough earlier in the evening to know if something didn't change quickly, New Beginnings would be just a memory in a very short time. Maybe he was foolish, bringing in new clients when the fate of New Beginnings was so uncertain. What else could he do, though, but trust that somehow things would work out? His Bible told him all things worked for good to those who were called according to God's purpose. Wasn't he serving God's purpose by reaching out to those who were often rejected? He knew without a doubt New Beginnings was God's plan for his life.

His thoughts drifted back a dozen years, to that beautiful April afternoon that had turned suddenly ugly—the afternoon when the difference between disabled and nondisabled had become all too clear. He shook his head, pushing away the memory. It stung even after all this time. The guilt still weighed on him like a millstone around his neck. He had to keep New Beginnings running—he had to do now what he hadn't done then.

Bringing his clasped hands to his chest, he bowed his head and prayed—asked for forgiveness again. Asked God to remove the burden of guilt. From there, he offered a prayer for Marin's peace and then asked God to help him find the best way to help this young woman and her brother. Each time he helped a person with a disability find a way to belong in society, it helped appease his guilt.

His prayer finished, he kept his eyes closed and thought back to the day almost five years ago when he'd visited Brooks Advertising with the purpose of putting together some brochures that would let people know what New Beginnings was all about. Not once had Darin Brooks mentioned he had a son who could benefit from the services New Beginnings offered. The only hint—and it hadn't carried real significance until now—the man had someone close to him who was disabled was the fact that, when Philip went to pay, Mr. Brooks had refused to take his money.

"No, son," he'd said, "I choose two accounts each year to do pro bono. I'd appreciate it if you'd accept being one of them."

Philip had been thrilled. Relying on donations and a small government stipend to get the services up and running, the money he'd set aside for brochures could be used a dozen different ways. He'd accepted Mr. Brooks's kind offer with a lump in his throat.

Philip rocked his chair, pressing his memory. Funny, when Philip had been in Darin Brooks's office, he had seen only pictures of Marin, not of John. Philip wondered about that now. Was the man ashamed of his son, or was he afraid of people's reaction to his having a handicapped child? Philip would never know for sure since the man was now gone. He hoped John hadn't been kept hidden away from people as much as Marin had implied. At thirty-one, it would be hard to change him if he'd never had social interaction. Not impossible, but hard. And Philip was running out of time.

Scowling, he dropped his feet with a thump against the concrete floor and buried his face in his hands. He wished he'd hear from the lawyer to know whether or not New Beginnings would be able to continue. There were so many needy people, and Philip believed from the depth of his soul that God had led him to help. He *had* to help—his own personal worth depended on it. "I'm in need of a miracle here, God," Philip said, speaking to the high, echoing ceiling. "You're the God of miracles. You've always met my needs in the past. Have no reason to doubt You now. But I do wish You'd hurry up a bit, because I have to admit, I'm starting to get nervous."

—❦—

The cowbell hanging above the metal door clanged loudly, signaling the arrival of guests. Philip lifted his gaze from the mop, which Anita, one of his clients, was attempting to wring, and his heart leaped into his throat.

Sunlight slipped in behind the couple framed in the doorway, creating a halo of the woman's shining blond hair. She looked fragile next to the bulky build of the man who stood next to her—obviously her brother, John—but Philip knew that *fragile* wasn't a word one would use to describe Marin Brooks. The young woman had a great deal of inner strength—he was certain of that. John stood with shoulders hunched forward, his almond-shaped eyes warily glancing right and left, his stubby hands clasped against his chest. The pose didn't inspire Philip's confidence.

"Anita, I'll be right back," he said, touching the woman's shoulder. He waited for her nod of acknowledgment before jogging across the floor to greet Marin and John Brooks officially. "Marin, you made it." He stuck out his hand, and she placed her small hand within his.

Her narrow fingers with neatly manicured nails rested there for the length of two slight pumps before she withdrew them. She didn't return his smile. "Yes, we're here. Philip, this is my brother, John."

Philip turned his brightest smile on the man who stood only a couple of inches taller than his sister. John's thin blond hair was neatly combed, his clothing unrumpled, with the red and blue polo shirt tucked into his jeans. White leather sneakers covered his feet. It pleased Philip that John was attired like any other "normal" person. Some families didn't see fit to dress their children with handicaps as neatly as their nonhandicapped children. The unkempt appearance only added to society's disdain.

"It's nice to meet you, John," Philip said as he extended his hand.

John slowly brought his right hand forward and placed it in Philip's palm. But he didn't grip.

*Lesson number one*, Philip thought. "Hey, buddy, let me show you something." Philip pulled his hand back and flexed his fingers. "Can you close your fingers like this?"

John tipped his head, examining Philip's hand. He brought up his hand and imitated the movement.

"That's right, just like you're grabbing an ice cream cone or the stick on a corn dog."

John grinned shyly. "I like ice cream." He pronounced each word carefully.

Philip could easily understand the man's speech. That was a plus. Philip winked. "Me, too, buddy." He lowered his hand, offering it again. "Now this time when you take my hand to shake it, pretend you're taking hold of an ice cream cone and give me a firm grasp, okay?"

John wagged his head up and down twice and followed Philip's instruction.

"Now that's a handshake!" Philip praised as John smiled broadly. He gave John a light clap on the shoulder. "Anytime someone wants to shake your hand, you grab firmly, okay? Makes a good impression."

Again John nodded, still smiling. "I will make a good impression, Marin."

"I know you will," Marin confirmed in a warm tone.

Philip let his gaze drift back to Marin. Her eyes appeared as wary as her brother's had been. She wouldn't be as easily won over as John.

"So what do we do here?" Marin lifted her shoulders in a graceful gesture of query. "Do you give us a tour, do we fill out some paperwork. . . ?"

Philip chuckled, pinching his chin between his fingers. "The paperwork can wait, Marin." He noticed John imitated his stance, and he hid a smile. "I'll show you around, but mostly I want to get acquainted with John this morning—find out what he likes to do, what his strengths are. It will help me find the best situation for him."

While Philip spoke, John rocked back on his heels, letting his gaze rove from Philip's head to his toes. Suddenly he burst out, "You have big feet!"

Marin turned bright pink. "John, that isn't very polite."

But Philip laughed and put his foot next to John's. His own brown work boot dwarfed John's leather sneaker. "You're right, John. I do have big feet. I wear a size 14. What size do you wear?"

"Size 8 shoe. Wide." John recited the list in a monotone. "Size 34 pants. Thirty length. Size 16-and-a-half shirt. Sometimes a medium, sometimes a large if it does not have buttons. And 32/34 shorts." John leaned forward and finished in a whisper. "Undershorts. White only. I do not like colored ones."

Marin looked almost purple by now. Philip bit down on the inside of his cheeks to keep from laughing. He liked John already, but he knew if he laughed, Marin might assume he was making fun of her brother. He was also aware that while he found John's candor endearing it made him an instant target for cruel people. It was best not to encourage him by laughing right now.

"Well, I bet you're great when it's time to go shopping. You know just what to look for." Philip clamped his hand on John's shoulder. "But you know, buddy—when it comes to undershorts, it's okay to keep that size a secret. Most folks are only interested in the clothes they can see you wear on the outside."

John's hazel eyes crinkled as he gave another face-splitting smile. "Okay. I do not wear undershorts on the outside."

"Nope, no one does," Philip agreed. He dropped his hand and turned to Marin, pleased to see her face returning to its normal color. His heart turned over in sympathy. How difficult this situation had to be for her. He wished he could give her a hug of support, but he suspected she would rebuff him. She seemed to hold herself firmly aloof. That was probably best, too—her sweet face and tenderness toward her brother were already tugging too much at his heartstrings. He couldn't let himself get too involved.

"Would you like to make the rounds, see what others are doing, while I visit a bit more with John?" Philip asked.

Marin's eyes—hazel like her brother's, but without the gold flecks—widened. "Leave John?"

Philip stifled a sigh. This letting-go process was tougher for some than others. He could see that Marin was going to have a difficult time. But she would have to learn, and this was a good place to start. "John will be in shouting distance." He waved his arm. "New Beginnings isn't that large." He felt gratified when she offered a small, self-conscious smile. "Why don't you sit down here"—he pointed to a molded plastic chair—"and read the brochure of all the options for job placement? We'll be back in a few minutes to talk with you. Okay?"

Still appearing somewhat dubious, Marin seated herself in the chair he had indicated and took the brochure from the table beside it. "Okay." Looking at John, she added, "I'll be close by, John. Don't worry."

"I will be okay. You do not worry, Marin."

Philip grinned. John had more spunk than Marin was willing to accept, he'd wager. He threw his arm around John's shoulders. "C'mon, buddy. I've got some people I'd like you to meet."

⟿

It didn't take long for Marin to read through the brochure—she recognized the Brooks Advertising logo on the back—and she was impressed with what she saw. Philip had done a commendable job of putting together a variety of programs to meet the needs of physically as well as mentally disabled individuals. She still wasn't convinced it was the right type of arrangement for John, but she did have to admit Philip seemed to know what he was doing.

She glanced around the warehouse-type building. Nothing fancy, but everything was clean. People seemed to be divided into four groups, and it was obvious that two of the people in each group were not disabled. They must be the trainers, she decided. With each trainer were no fewer than four people with some sort of disability. Marin didn't watch any group for long—she didn't want to give the impression she was staring. It made her uncomfortable when people stared at John.

Over the years, she'd learned to split people into four categories, with varying degrees of each level. First were the gawkers, who openly stared without compunction, either fearful of or fascinated by John. Next were the ignorers. They looked past John as if he didn't exist, talked over or around him, and left Marin wondering if her brother were invisible. The third group—who meant well, at least—were the sweethearts. They spoke to John the way one would a small child. Although it was better than the previous two, it still set Marin's teeth on edge—he was a grown man. Last, the smallest group by far, were the normals. She admired the few normals who were able to treat John like any other person they encountered. Philip was definitely a normal, and she appreciated his warmth and acceptance.

She lifted her gaze toward the high, metal-beamed ceiling. A large banner hung on the north wall, bearing the Bible verse from Ephesians 2:10—"For we are God's workmanship, created in Christ Jesus to do good works, which God prepared in advance for us to do." She'd never really considered that God had a plan in place for His children in advance. The thought warmed her. Did God have a plan for John, too? Was New Beginnings part of John's plan?

"Marin, guess what?" John's happy voice interrupted Marin's musings. She turned her head to see both John and Philip approaching. John beamed from ear to ear, and Philip seemed pleased, too. "Philip says I am very good at organizing. This is a good thing, Marin."

Marin rose and hugged John when he held out his arms. "That's terrific."

"Hey, John." Philip's voice captured John's attention, and he pulled loose from Marin's hug. "Do you remember the snacks room?"

John nodded, eyes shining. "Yes. A girl named Anita was eating a chocolate chip cookie." He grinned at Marin. "She is pretty."

Marin carefully refrained from showing worry. In many ways, John was like any other young man—he recognized a pretty girl and wanted to show attention to her. But in other ways, John was different. Marriage and family weren't possibilities, given John's limitations, and Marin didn't want to see him hurt.

Philip threw back his head and laughed. "Ah yes, buddy, Anita is a pretty lady. And she's nice, too. Would you like to go have a cookie with her while I talk to your sister?"

John turned his eager gaze in Marin's direction. "Could I go have a cookie with Anita, Marin?"

Marin swallowed the lump that rose in her throat. It felt strange to have Philip witness her giving her older brother permission. "Sure. Go ahead. But not too many, huh? Lunch isn't that far off."

John nodded and headed away, his swaying gait emphasized as he hurried toward the break area. Marin watched him until he disappeared behind a six-foot-high partition. She heard his giggles and released a sigh.

A hand descended on her shoulder, and she turned to find Philip watching her with concern in his eyes. "You're going to give yourself wrinkles if you don't quit that scowling," he said in a teasing voice.

Marin took one step sideways, away from the warm hand. "If you had a brother like John, you'd worry, too." Before he could reply, she asked, "Do you think you'll be able to find a place here for him?"

Philip gestured to the plastic chair she'd sat in earlier. After she seated herself again, he yanked another one from beneath a nearby table and sat down close to her knees. "I could find many placements for John. Marin, he's really very bright—high functioning for Down syndrome. He's personable, follows directions easily, and remembers them well enough to repeat them a few minutes later, and he has a desire to be with others." He crossed his arms, giving his shaggy head a slight shake. "I'll be honest. From what you described on the phone last night, I didn't expect him to be easy to work with. Obviously your mom didn't just follow him around and take care of him—she taught him to do for himself. That's great."

"So you'll be able to use him here." Marin leaned forward, her brows pulled down.

"Marin, as I told you before, New Beginnings isn't a day care. Our goal is to place our clients in jobs—and those jobs are out there." He gestured toward the door. "John is a prime candidate for placement."

"No."

The abrupt reply brought Philip's brows into a sharp V. He rested his elbows on his knees and leaned forward, bringing his face close to hers. Lowering his voice, he offered a gentle reprimand. "Loving people means doing what's best for them, even when it's hard. Keeping John cooped up away from people isn't what's best, Marin."

Marin felt anger building. This man didn't know her or her brother. He didn't know the hurt they'd encountered. How could he sit there and tell her what was best for John? She picked up the brochure and held it up. "This says, 'Meeting needs where they exist.' I interpret that to mean you provide a service to families in need of one. The service I need is day care. Can you or can you not provide that for me?"

Philip sat up straight, his mouth set in a grim line. "If it came down to it, I could. I have eight employees who are here every day, all day, working with clients, preparing them for their placements. John could stay here, helping out with cleaning and participating in the training classes with the others."

"Good."

Philip held up his hand. "*But.* . .that doesn't mean I will."

Marin released a huff of aggravation. "Why not?"

"Because that isn't the goal of New Beginnings. I don't want to keep my clients shut away from the world. I want them to become a valuable part of the world. I want the nondisabled to see them as valuable. That can't happen if they are kept apart from one another."

"I don't want him out there."

Philip shook his head. "You must be the most stubborn mother I've ever worked with." His smile softened the words. Without warning, his large hand snaked out to capture her fingers. Although she tensed and tried to pull away, he continued to hold her hand, stroking her knuckles with his thumb.

"Marin, believe me—I understand your concern. There are people who take advantage of those with handicaps—who are even intentionally cruel. But don't you see—the perceptions that people with handicaps are unworthy of fair treatment can never be changed unless a relationship is established between the handicapped and nonhandicapped. That's what New Beginnings is all about— bridging the differences that exist between the disabled and nondisabled. John is so friendly—he needs interactions with others."

"He can get that here, with your employees and with your other clients." Marin jerked her hand away. Her knuckles tingled from his gentle touch.

Philip sighed and opened his mouth, but before he could speak, Marin rushed on.

"I looked carefully at the brochure, but I didn't see a fee. What is the charge for your service? Whatever it is, I'll double it if you'll allow me to bring John here during the day while I'm at work."

Philip scratched his chin, examining her from beneath lowered brows.

"Doubled, huh? Well, that's pretty easy to figure, even for a mathematical wizard like me. Nothing times nothing is nothing."

Marin dropped her jaw. Had she heard correctly? "Nothing? You don't charge?"

Philip crossed his arms and grinned. "That's right. New Beginnings is non-profit. I don't charge my clients. The clients eventually are placed in a job situation where they draw a wage, so they stand to gain something; but I don't put a dollar amount on my service."

Marin's gaze swung around the building, taking in once more the tools and supplies and partitions and furnishings. "How do you keep this place going?"

"I receive a government stipend each month. The businesses that hire my clients pay a small percentage of the clients' salary to New Beginnings. But most of my resources come from private donations. People who believe in what I'm doing contribute." He frowned for a moment, worry creasing his brow, but then he seemed to deliberately relax the scowl lines and offered a small smile. "So you see—you can't bribe me."

"I'm not trying to bribe you." Marin used her sternest tone, although she was finding it increasingly difficult to be cross with this very likable, giving man. "I'm trying to persuade you. There's a difference."

Philip laughed, showing white even teeth. She liked the sound of his laugh and the crinkle lines on the outside of his brown eyes. He shook his head at her, still grinning. "A difference. Right, Marin. Look them up in a thesaurus—bet you'll find them side by side."

She ducked her head, trying not to smile at him. When she felt controlled, she raised her gaze and found him waiting, a sweet expression on his handsome face. Her heart caught in her throat. Swallowing, she started again. "Philip, I understand the purpose of your program. I admire it, and I can see you are sincere in what you want to do. But please understand where I am coming from. My parents wanted John protected. We all know too well how cruel the world can be. You're right that John is friendly. He'd talk to anyone. He'd *trust* anyone. And too many people aren't trustworthy." She took in a deep breath then blew it out. "If I were an employer hiring one of your clients, what would I probably pay an hour?"

Philip shrugged, seeming startled by her change in direction. "Average hourly wage is $6.50."

"How many hours a week does the average client put in?"

"Usually no more than thirty." Philip leaned back, giving her a speculative look. "Where are you heading with this?"

Marin held up her hand. "I'm an employer, willing to pay $10 an hour for forty hours a week. I want to hire my client to be one of your helpers. That comes to roughly $1,700 a month. That's what I'm offering you to allow John to become one of your employees at New Beginnings."

Philip's gaze narrowed. She didn't waver, just waited for him to decide. If this was a nonprofit organization, no doubt he struggled as much as any other to keep the place afloat. She hoped her offer would be impossible for him to refuse.

It seemed as if hours passed before Philip finally straightened in his chair and opened his mouth to speak. "Marin, I want you to know I never intended New Beginnings to be a day care facility. It goes against everything I believe in to keep your brother locked away from the world. God has a purpose for John, but if he's never allowed to experience anything beyond these four walls, he may never find his purpose. To me, there's nothing sadder than a person who falls short of God's glorious plan for his life."

Marin felt her chest tighten. Philip's tone was gentle, but it hurt nonetheless.

"But right now I'm not seeing John as the real person in need. I see you as the one who is needy. So—*temporarily*—I'm willing to allow John to come here, just like any other employee, and be a custodian. But I'm emphasizing 'temporarily.' I want you to pray—pray hard!—about what is best for your brother. I'll allow him to remain here for one month." He held up one tapered finger to underscore his word. "At the end of John's month, you're going to have to make a decision—either allow me to place John in a job outside this warehouse, or you'll need to find another place for him to go."

# Chapter 5

Philip watched from the window as Marin and John Brooks made their way to the sporty car parked at the curb. He smiled as Marin handed John the keys and John aimed the keyless remote at the vehicle. John's pleasure in opening the locks was easily seen in the lift of his chin and the jaunty flip of his thumb on the button. Then he tossed Marin the keys. She caught them, threw her arm around John's shoulders in a quick hug, and brother and sister climbed in on opposite sides of the car. In moments, they pulled away.

Marin was good with John, Philip acknowledged with a lift in his heart. He'd encountered many siblings whose own personal embarrassment at their brother's or sister's limitations led them to be stilted or, worse, harsh. He admired Marin's ease in talking with John as if he mattered a great deal to her. Yet frustration built at her stubborn refusal to allow him to be with other people. Closing him off wasn't what was best—why couldn't she see that?

The memory surfaced, a wave of guilt rising with it. *God, I'm making up for that. Please take the memory away.* The prayer came automatically, a natural extension of the remembrance. Pushing himself off with his palm on the window frame, he headed back to the custodial corner. Anita would be starting at Burger King in three more days. They still had work to do.

After only two weeks, John was as settled in his new routine as if he had followed it for years. At supper, he jabbered nonstop about "Philip this" and "Philip that," interjecting snippets about Eileen or Gregory or Andrew, some of the adult trainers who were employed by New Beginnings. Not once did John balk about going but cheerfully put breakfast on the table each morning—bowls of cornflakes with chopped bananas—to help hurry Marin along. She wondered sometimes how he could have so quickly forgotten Mother and Dad and the old routine he'd shared with them.

This morning when she'd dropped him off, Marin had mentioned how easily he had adjusted, which was not typically in character for him. Philip had smiled and said, "Then it must be a God thing."

"A God thing," Marin now reflected aloud as she angled her car into her parking space at Brooks Advertising. She'd never heard the term before. In a way, it almost sounded too casual to be appropriate for referring to the omnipotent Lord; yet it seemed natural coming from Philip. He firmly believed God had a hand in everything that came along life's pathway.

*Well*, she thought as she unlocked the front door and headed inside, *I hope Philip will see John's "employment" at New Beginnings as a "God thing" and keep him for more than a month. I haven't had time to make any other arrangements.*

Marin had slipped into her role as commander-in-chief of Brooks Advertising with a bit less ease than John had managed his change in routine. She sighed, the responsibility pressing like a knife between her shoulder blades. All of the employees were helpful and cooperative, but she felt she needed to stay two steps ahead to maintain her status as "boss." Being new to the role, it was more difficult than she could have imagined. How she wished she'd had an opportunity to ease into this position, but Dad's untimely death had changed everything.

But she didn't want to dwell on that again. Determinedly she pushed thoughts of Dad and Mother aside and focused on the here and now. She unlocked her private office, leaned her leather briefcase against the desk, then sank down in Dad's executive chair and picked up the "to do" list waiting in the center of the large desk calendar. The list seemed a mile long. With a groan, she dropped the paper and lowered her forehead to her hands.

"Marin?"

She popped upright, feeling a heat climb from her neck to her cheeks when she spotted Dick Ross hovering in the doorway. "Oh! Dick—I didn't hear you come in."

"I gathered that." He offered a smile and stepped completely into the office. His shoes echoed on the wooden floor. "You're here early."

Marin pushed her hair behind her ears and grimaced. "Yes. John was so eager to get to 'work' this morning that I couldn't slow him down. Something about its being Donut Day." She laughed lightly, shaking her head as she remembered him sitting in the car with his nose to the glass, watching for her to come out. He certainly enjoyed his time at New Beginnings.

"So that placement is working out well?" Dick's voice interrupted her reverie.

Marin lifted her gaze to meet Dick's. "Yes—yes, it's working out very well. But—" She broke off. She didn't need to share personal issues with Dick Ross. Why would he care that the placement would only last another couple of weeks? As she recalled, he had been one to encourage her to put John away somewhere. She had no desire to start that conversation again. Aunt Lenore was adversary enough on the issue!

Dick waited on the other side of the desk, his head tipped and brows angled high. She cleared her throat and crossed her arms, leaning back in the chair. "I'm sorry. Did you need something?"

"Yes, before the morning meeting, I wanted to go over. . ."

Dick pulled a chair up to Marin's desk and explained a problem he had with the amount of information Jefferson Landscaping wanted to include in a forty-five-second commercial. While they discussed how to present a compromise to the potential client, the front door opened and closed several times, signaling the arrival of the other employees.

At promptly eight thirty, Marin and Dick walked together to the conference room. By ten fifteen, she was back in her office, determined to work her way through the first three items on her list before noon. At eleven thirty, the telephone interrupted her concentration, and she spoke distractedly into the receiver. "Yes, Crystal?"

"Hi, Marin. I was wondering if you might be free for lunch today."

She gave a start. That wasn't the receptionist's voice on the other end. She pulled the receiver away from her ear, stared at it dumbly for a moment, then brought it back. "Who is this?"

A familiar chuckle rumbled through the line. "I'm sorry. I thought the receptionist introduced me. It's Philip Wilder."

At that moment, Crystal appeared in the doorway, a frantic look on her face. She mouthed the words, "I'm sorry," and gestured broadly, obviously trying to explain something.

Marin shook her head at Crystal, scowling, unable to interpret the gestures.

"Marin? Are you there?" Philip's voice sounded in her ear.

"One minute, please," she told him then punched the mute button on the phone. "Crystal, what do you need?" She hoped her tone didn't sound as harried as she felt.

"I just wanted to apologize. I had two other calls when his"—she pointed at the telephone—"came through, and I accidentally sent it to you without checking with you first."

Marin waved her hand in dismissal. "Don't worry about it. It's fine." The front desk telephone rang shrilly, and she suggested, "Better go answer that." Crystal scuttled away. Marin dropped her head back, sighed, then released the mute to get back to Philip. "Hello? Are you still there?"

Another chuckle. Strange how that sound managed to soothe the edges of her frayed nerves. His voice followed. "Having a rough morning?"

"Not rough exactly, just busy," she clarified.

"So could you use a break?"

In the background a giggle erupted then was firmly shushed. The giggler was John. It followed that the shusher was Philip. She frowned. What was Philip up to? "What did you have in mind?" she asked cautiously.

"Well, John's done so well around here that he's earned a free lunch. He thought you might want to join us."

Of course John would want to include her. Of course it wasn't Philip's idea. For some reason disappointment niggled, but she firmly squashed it. She glanced at her wristwatch. "I suppose I could get away for a quick lunch. Where does John want to go?"

"He wants a Big Mac and french fries. Is that okay?"

The local McDonald's was only a few blocks from the office. That would mean less time away from work. "That's perfect," she said.

"Great! We'll see you at twelve?"

Another giggle could be heard, and Marin felt a pleased smile building. John was certainly comfortable with Philip. "I'll be there." She hung up, shaking her head. *A God thing.* It seemed Philip Wilder's friendship was a God thing, too. He and John were quite a pair.

⤳

"Now remember, John," Philip repeated, leaning across the table to speak earnestly. "Let *me* bring up the job idea. If it's going to make Marin mad, I'd rather she was mad at me, okay?"

John wagged his head up and down. His almond-shaped eyes sparkled behind the wire rims of his glasses. "I will let her be mad at you. I will eat my ice cream and not say a word." He placed a thick finger against his own lips.

Philip winked his approval. John had done so well at the New Beginnings warehouse that all the employees felt he should be given the opportunity to take a community position. Marin had made clear her feelings on the matter, but Philip was willing to go to bat for John. Working as a custodian in this very restaurant was one of Philip's clients—a man only two years older than John, also with Down syndrome. If Marin saw Curtis successfully at work, surely it would help convince her John was just as capable.

Suddenly John exploded with giggles, pointing to the doors. "Here she is! Here she is!"

Philip leaned back to assume a casual pose, which was difficult with John chortling from across the table. He watched over his shoulder as Marin scanned the busy restaurant until she spotted them. He gave a quick wave, and she moved in their direction, the full skirt of her creamy two-piece dress swirling around her shapely ankles. He admired her appearance, which was always of professional elegance.

"Whew! It's crowded in here," she said by way of greeting. Sliding into the booth beside her brother, she nudged him with her shoulder. "What's so funny?"

John covered his mouth with both hands, which muffled his giggles, but his crinkling eyes proved the mirth was not controlled. Marin looked at Philip. "Have you two been telling jokes?"

John looked ready to explode, and other patrons were beginning to stare. To Marin, Philip explained, "I think he's just excited." Philip reached across the table and tapped John on the forearm. "Hey, buddy, no more giggling now, okay?

You can't giggle and eat at the same time."

John dropped his hands to reveal pursed lips forming a huge, distorted grin.

Philip stifled an inward groan. John's theatrics, while somewhat humorous, were not timely considering the purpose of this meal out. How would he convince Marin that John was mature enough to handle a public employment situation if he couldn't get through a simple lunch without giggling like a child? Philip shrugged, sending Marin a weak smile. "Should we order?"

Marin raised her eyebrows, looking askance at her brother for a moment before answering. "Yes. Let's do."

They got in line behind three elderly women who smiled warmly in response to John's friendly hello. In the line next to them, however, was a young couple who openly stared at John as if he were a circus sideshow. Marin turned her back on the young couple, her jaw set, and Philip's heart turned over in his chest in sympathy. John appeared oblivious to the stares—he animatedly described what he planned to order, his stubby hands signing the words as he spoke—but Marin's discomfort was palpable.

John smiled broadly at the young cashier. The cashier kept her gaze angled toward the keyboard, which showed the menu options, while John cheerfully requested a Big Mac meal with super-sized fries and a soda. Marin leaned over and suggested he get the regular-sized order instead.

"But, Marin," he protested in a booming voice, "I like McDonald's french fries very much. I want lots of them."

The cashier, her chin still low, shifted her eyes to look curiously at John.

"There are lots of fries in a regular order, too, John. It's always been enough," Marin countered evenly.

"No, it is not enough. I want super-size today!" John thumped his fist on the counter.

The couple next to them snickered, and the cashier jumped slightly. All seemed focused on the interaction between John and Marin. Philip, listening, wondered if he should try to help Marin out, but he suspected she would resent his intrusion. Besides, he needed to see if John would allow this issue to be resolved. So he remained silent as Marin's cheeks flamed pink with embarrassment and John glared at her.

Marin glanced at her watching audience, offered them a weak smile of apology, then took a great breath, which seemed to calm her. Leaning toward John, she spoke in an even voice, barely above a whisper. "John, you may have super-sized fries *or* ice cream, but we can't do both. So you decide."

John rocked back and forth on his heels, a finger beneath his chin, deep in thought. Finally he huffed and announced, "Regular fries. And a hot fudge sundae." His voice carried over all the other restaurant noise.

Marin made another quick glance around before nodding to her brother.

"Good choice." She quickly gave her order then stepped back to allow Philip to move forward. His chest swelled with pity. John had settled down, but people still watched, as if expecting an encore. Marin's hazel eyes looked unnaturally bright, and he feared she might break down and cry. As he reached for his wallet to pay for their food, he suggested she and John go sit down while he waited for their order.

By the time Philip returned to the table, tray in hand, Marin and John had apparently made their peace. They were visiting quietly, and no sign of John's earlier tantrum was seen in either face. The moment the tray touched the table, John reached eagerly for the wrapped food items.

"I will hand things out," he said, beaming. "I remember what you ordered." With great ceremony he placed Marin's chicken sandwich and iced tea in front of her then gave Philip his burger, fries, and soft drink. His tongue poked out as he took his own items and popped the lid off the sundae. Stretching his hands toward Marin and Philip, he said, "Pray."

Philip took John's hand then reached for Marin's. She flushed slightly but placed her hand in his. He gave it a quick squeeze before bowing his head and offering a simple blessing for the meal. At the "amen," John pulled away immediately, but Marin wrapped her fingers around Philip's hand and held tight for a moment. He tightened his own grip, offering his understanding, and at last she pulled away.

John gobbled his food, and Marin leaned over to whisper in his ear. He slowed his pace. Marin smirked and snitched one of his fries. He grinned as she dipped it in ketchup and raised it to her lips. After she swallowed, she turned to Philip. "What did John do to earn this meal out?"

She had given him a perfect lead in. Philip took a sip of his drink before answering. "The clients earn points by following directions, finishing tasks within a specified time limit, staying on task—those types of things. If you're going to have a job, you've got to be able to stay focused from beginning to end, right?" He pointed at her with a french fry. "John earned as many points in two weeks as many of our clients earn in a whole month. He's done a great job."

Marin smiled at John. "That's terrific! I'm proud of you."

John lifted a spoonful of drippy sundae and slurped it. Speaking around the biteful, he said, "But I cannot tell you what will happen now. You will get mad. Right, Philip?"

Philip sucked in a breath as Marin's gaze spun in his direction. He watched her brows come down—in curiosity or irritation? Tipping her head, she fixed Philip with a stern look that made him wish he were someplace else.

"What exactly has John been instructed not to share with me?"

*Lord*, Philip prayed inwardly, *help me choose my words here.* He pushed aside his burger and rested his elbows on the edge of the table. "Well, Marin, I hoped to talk to you about—"

At that moment, Philip felt a hearty clap against his shoulder. Marin's gaze shifted sharply, and Philip turned his head to find a familiar face smiling down at him.

"Hi, Philip!"

Philip forced a smile, his gaze skittering between Marin and the newcomer. He swallowed. "Hi, Curtis."

From the look on Marin's face, no further explanation would be needed. She knew.

# Chapter 6

Marin wadded up the paper wrapper from her sandwich and dropped it on the empty tray. She wanted to throw it—hard—at Philip, but ever mindful that she was setting an example for John, she kept a rein on her temper.

A setup. This whole lunch had been a setup. Nothing more than a way for her to see one of Philip's clients in action so she would bow to Philip's discretion in placing John in such a job. Well, it wasn't going to work. She was not so easily manipulated, and Philip Wilder better learn that right now!

Ignoring Philip's contrite look, she gave John a quick peck on the cheek, grabbed her purse, and rose to her feet in one fluid motion. Smoothing her skirt, she said stiffly, "Thank you very much for the lunch, Mr. Wilder." Turning to John, she added with a bit more warmth, "I'll see you around five, John." And she spun on the heel of her off-white pump and marched out of the restaurant without a backward glance.

Fury filled her chest, increasing with every staccato step that led her back to the office. She had walked—it wasn't far, and it was such a pretty day. Now she was grateful for the opportunity to dispel some of this frustration before she returned to the office.

Who did he think he was, filling John's head with notions of jobs and working? Hadn't she made it perfectly clear that John in a workplace was a subject not open for discussion? She paid dearly to have John in the protected environment of New Beginnings, and as long as Philip took her check each week, he would follow her rules!

She stopped at an intersection and squinted against the sun, impatiently waiting for the red light to change to green so she could continue her stomping progress. Though her feet stilled, her thoughts raged on. Philip hadn't been around John long enough to make a determination about his readiness for a job. Of course John did well at the warehouse—all the success elements were in place: few people around, a secure setting, lots of attention. Most of the time, John did well at home, too, but even there, he had his moments.

The light changed, and Marin stepped off the curb, her face hot as she remembered the embarrassment of John's brief tantrum in McDonald's. At home with no audience, she felt equipped to handle John's erratic moments even if she'd prefer not to. In public, it was a completely different ball game.

She relived the snickering and curious glances. A knot formed in her stomach. Philip had surely been aware of how John's behavior had captured everyone's attention—the sympathetic pressure on her hand as he'd prayed made clear he felt compassion for what she had experienced. But what Philip didn't realize was that John could stir that kind of reaction simply by walking into a room—he didn't have to throw a tantrum for people to snicker and stare.

And that was why John didn't belong in public places. Not on his own. Not without Marin to act as a buffer. Sadness battled with the anger, seeking equal footing. Her steps slowed. Philip had obviously wanted her to see his client—what was his name? Curtis?—in action. Well, instead Philip got to see John in action. Now maybe he would understand why it wasn't possible for John to take a job in public. John was. . .unpredictable. And people were. . .morbidly curious. She would not allow him to be gawked at like an animal displayed in a zoo cage. Today the reaction didn't go beyond a few rude sniggers and open stares. But she knew real cruelty could sometimes follow.

Marin reached Brooks Advertising and paused outside the doors, taking big breaths to calm her unsteady nerves. *Philip Wilder will have to be made to understand that John is not to be taken to public places without my permission*, she determined. *And I better start hunting right now for someplace else for him to go.*

She felt a prick of guilt—John enjoyed New Beginnings so much. It would be hard for him to leave. But, she reminded herself as she stepped into the cool reception area and headed for her office, if he adjusted to this change, he could adjust to another. He would have to.

―⁓―

Philip slapped the ledger closed with more force than was necessary. Across the room, the lone remaining employee, Eileen, raised her gaze from rinsing the sink and queried, "Problem?"

Philip sighed. "Eileen, would you come over here? Maybe you can help me with something." He had tried to keep his financial woes secret from his employees—no need to scare them into seeking other employment—but Eileen had been with him from the planning stages of New Beginnings. He knew he could trust her to keep a tight lip but also be a support.

She snatched up a cotton towel and carried it with her, drying her hands as she crossed the floor. Early sixties, chunky but solid, with tight gray curls, compliments of a home wave, Eileen looked like anybody's grandma. Philip smiled as she settled her bulk in the plastic chair next to him and flopped the damp towel on the corner of his desk.

"You looking all long-faced there because of Marin Brooks?"

Her question caught Philip off guard. He raised his brows. "Huh?"

Eileen smirked and pointed at him. "You haven't fooled any of us. We've been watching you." She linked her fingers and rested her hands on her belly.

"You're a personable man, Philip, and you're friendly to everyone. But it's different with this Marin Brooks."

Philip felt his heart begin to clamor. Cautiously he questioned, "How so?"

Eileen shrugged. "Little things. The smile in your eyes when she drops off or picks up her brother. The quicker step you use when she's at the door, like you're hoping to gain a little more time with her. The extra few minutes you spend just chatting with John." She laughed, picking up the towel and flapping it against his arm. "Stop looking so stricken. Being interested in a pretty girl isn't the end of the world. You're a young man—a handsome one at that. I'd say it was high time you expressed that kind of interest."

"But you don't understand," Philip protested. Eileen and the others weren't aware of his arrangement with Marin. His additional interest in her was due to the short amount of time he had to convince her to allow John to remain in his program. Wasn't it?

Eileen interrupted his thoughts. "She seemed upset tonight. Something happen?"

Philip replayed Marin's cool reception to his attempt at conversation when she retrieved John that afternoon. Upset was an understatement. She had appeared to simmer with controlled fury. He feared he had messed up things permanently. But she hadn't said she wouldn't bring John back, so perhaps there was still hope.

"Philip?"

Philip realized Eileen was waiting for an answer. He sighed again and leaned back in his chair. "We had a little. . .setback. . .when I took John for lunch. Marin came, too—at John's request." Eileen smirked at that, but Philip ignored her and went on. "John wanted a super-sized meal, and Marin suggested he stick to regular-sized. John got a little upset." He realized he was downplaying the outburst, but Eileen had worked with people with disabilities long enough to understand the picture without his outlining every detail. "Stirred things up for a bit, but he settled down pretty quickly. Marin was embarrassed, though, and I think she's irritated that I took him out."

Eileen frowned. "Seems odd she'd be angry at you if it was John who created the uproar."

Philip dropped his gaze, running his thumb over the edge of the desk. "Well, she's mad because I kind of pulled a sneaky trick."

"You?" Eileen draped the towel across her knees and leaned forward, her eyes bright with interest. "A sneaky trick?" Her tone indicated she didn't believe Philip capable of underhandedness.

Philip nodded, sheepishly meeting her gaze. "Yeah. See, Marin is really opposed to John taking a position in the public eye."

"Then what is he—?"

Philip held up his hand, interrupting her flow of words. "She's worried about how people will treat him. But you know Curtis is doing real well at McDonald's, so I thought if she saw Curtis at work she'd realize John could be just as successful." Shaking his head, he finished ruefully, "But John threw a hissy fit, and half the restaurant stared as if they'd never seen anything like it before. Then Curtis came to the table before I had a chance to say anything to her, and I could tell by the look on her face she knew she'd been had. I really blew it."

Eileen clucked. "Oh, now, Philip. She'll get over it. She was probably still feeling uncomfortable about the way people reacted to John's outburst. I know from experience how that can discombobulate your sense of self-esteem. But you'll see. When she comes in tomorrow, she'll be her same sweet self. So stop fretting."

Philip released a brief huff of laughter. "To be honest, Eileen, I'm not fretting over Marin. Somehow I'll work that problem out. It's. . ." He scratched his head, wondering if it was fair to dump this on Eileen. She loved working here—with her husband dead and all her children grown and moved away, the New Beginnings clients were a surrogate family to her. How would she react to the possibility of losing it all? Yet he needed a sounding board.

"Go ahead, Philip. Spill it."

Eileen's brisk, no-nonsense tone was the deciding factor. He flipped the ledger open and pointed to the last numbers in each of the columns. Eileen leaned forward, reading along the lines, and her graying brows formed a sharp V. She pointed to each number with a work-roughened finger, her lips pursed in obvious concentration. At last, she looked up, disbelief coloring her expression. "Are these numbers accurate?"

Philip nodded. "I'm afraid so." He closed the ledger again, an attempt to shut away the problem. "My biggest contributor stopped contributing. No explanation given, but the account was closed." He tapped the cover of the ledger book. "There might be enough funds for full operation for one more month—maybe six weeks if I batten down the hatches and don't take any new clients. But beyond that. . .?"

"Oh, Philip. . ." Eileen's sympathetic tone touched Philip's heart. They sat for a few minutes in silence, digesting this information. Then suddenly Eileen straightened in her chair and slapped her palms to her thighs. "Well, then, we've got work to do, don't we? We need to brainstorm. Come up with some ways to bring in more funds." She grasped Philip's hand and shook it. "But first we need to pray. Close your eyes."

Philip closed his eyes and listened as Eileen petitioned the Lord in a clear, sure voice. Emotion pressed at his chest as he silently echoed every word of her request. Part of a verse from John's Gospel flittered through his memory: *"Ask and you will receive. . . ."* In the quiet building, with Eileen's warm palm pressed to his, her confident voice raised in communication, he felt the Lord's presence.

She finished, "Thank You for working this out to Your glory. Amen." Giving his hand another firm pat, she said, "Now no more fretting. Look again at the verse you have painted on the banner and remember that the Lord prepared you for this work. He won't let you down."

Philip offered a smile, his gaze moving to the words boldly displayed over the work area. He did believe in Ephesians 2:10—every person was created to perform good works, and he knew without a doubt God had placed this work on his heart. Eileen was right—somehow his financial problems would be solved. "Thanks, Eileen. You're a good friend."

Eileen snorted, but she smiled at him. "Yes, well, right now my cat is probably wondering why his good friend hasn't come home to feed him. So I better *git*." She stood and headed toward the door at a brisk pace. Before she left, however, she looked back over her shoulder and added, "I'll be praying that Marin gets over her mad, too, because I don't figure you'll be able to concentrate on much of anything else until you're on the rights with her again."

"Go home, Eileen," Philip ordered dryly. His cheeks twitched with the effort of controlling his smile.

She hooted with laughter and stepped out the door, sealing the warehouse in silence.

Philip propped his heels on the desk next to the ledger and allowed his gaze to return to the painted words displayed over his head. He read aloud, " 'For we are God's workmanship, created in Christ Jesus to do good works, which God prepared in advance for us to do.'" He scowled for a moment, recalling that despite God's preparations many did not choose to do good works. Rocky immediately came to mind, and his heart clenched as he wondered what his brother might be doing these days.

But he really didn't want to think about Rocky. Keeping New Beginnings going was top priority, and that's where he would keep his focus. Thumping his feet to the floor, he announced, "New Beginnings was formed to do good works, and somehow it will continue to do good works." *Maybe saying it out loud will help it be true.* He scooped up the ledger, opened his top drawer, and dropped the book inside. Shutting the drawer firmly, he rose and went through the lockup routine by rote. With the building secure, he straddled his motorcycle and turned his thoughts toward home.

But suddenly, as if by their own accord, his thoughts changed course. A second problem required immediate attention. Marin and John. Somehow he had to find a permanent placement for John before his self-imposed time limit. He had no time to waste.

He made a snap decision. Instead of going to his own home, he'd go see Marin and John. They didn't live far from the city park where he had spent summer hours during his growing-up years. The Bible admonished believers not to go to bed angry, so he'd just help Marin not break that biblical demand. With a twist of his wrist, the cycle engine throttled to a steady hum. He aimed the bike in the direction of Park Street.

# *Chapter 7*

Marin sat on the front porch, the cordless phone pressed to her ear. The early evening breeze felt pleasant against her bare legs, and she stretched them out to catch the last of the waning sun. Behind her, through the open screen door, she could hear John thumping around in the kitchen, organizing the recyclables, as Michael W. Smith crooned from the radio. Across the street, a half-dozen grade school–age boys kicked a soccer ball back and forth across the yard, cheering each other on. Sometimes she had to strain to hear the soft voice of Aunt Chris, but she refused to give up her pleasant perch.

Marin answered her aunt's question. "Yes, John loves going there. That isn't the issue. The issue is that it isn't a day care facility, and the owner has made it clear he won't allow John to stay there longer than a month."

"Are you sure he wouldn't reconsider since it's working out well for John?"

Marin scowled, remembering Philip's ploy at noon. Her tone turned hard. "I doubt it. He's already making noises about it, and John's only been there two weeks."

"Well," came Chris's reasonable voice, "maybe you should consider what he suggests."

Marin nearly swallowed the telephone. "Consider it? Aunt Chris! You know how protective Mother always was with John! Why, she'd turn over in her grave if I even thought about letting him take some sort of job."

A goal was made in the soccer game, and the boys jumped in a circle, screeching in joy. Marin pressed the phone tighter to her ear to hear. All she caught was, ". . .was necessarily best for John."

"I'm sorry—what did you say?"

She was thankful the noisy throng across the street dropped to the grass to rest so she was able to hear clearly.

"I said, although I know Mary did what she thought was in John's best interests, Darin didn't always agree it was necessarily best for John."

Marin felt stunned by this. Her father had never indicated he wanted anything different done with John. At least he'd never voiced it to her. "How do you know that?" she asked as she toyed with the frayed edge of her denim cutoffs.

Marin could almost hear the smile in Chris's tone as she answered. "Marin, darling, your father and I were very close. He shared a great deal with me—his pride in you, his worry for John, his love for Mary. He understood your mother's fears, and he also understood she and John had a tighter bond than the one that existed between him and his son. So he allowed Mary to make the decisions where John was concerned."

Reeling, Marin pressed, "So do you think Dad wanted John put in some—some institution?"

"Absolutely not!" Aunt Chris's adamant tone carried through the line. "Never an institution. John is too high functioning to require that type of placement, although it's perfectly acceptable and even desirable for some families. But I know at one time he did look into some group homes. Your mother was very much opposed, though, so he dropped the idea."

"But Dad always told me I'd be responsible for John when he and Mom were gone."

"Marin, you do realize being responsible doesn't have to mean giving up your whole life for him, don't you?"

No, Marin hadn't realized that. She'd always envisioned herself assuming her mother's role, maintaining the home, caring for John. She didn't know how to respond.

Aunt Chris spoke again. "Listen, honey, whatever you decide, I know you'll pray about it and make an unselfish decision with John's best interests at heart. I have confidence in you, just as your dad did. And whenever you need to talk, you remember I'm just a phone call away."

Tears pricked behind Marin's lids. How she appreciated her aunt's support. If only Aunt Lenore, who lived blocks away rather than states away, could be so helpful. She uttered a brief, silent prayer for Aunt Lenore to somehow become more like Aunt Chris. "Thanks, Aunt Chris. Oh, by the way—"

A distant growl intruded, and Marin lifted her head, seeking the source of the noise. The boys across the street also turned as a group, and their faces lit with delight as a bright blue and chrome motorcycle turned the corner and roared onto their street. To Marin's surprise, the cycle slowed in front of her house and pulled directly into the driveway. The rider killed the motor then reached up to remove his helmet. Marin felt her heart skip a beat when she recognized the rumpled brown hair of Philip Wilder emerging from beneath the shimmering helmet.

"By the way, what?" came Chris's voice.

"Aunt Chris, I've got company. Can I call you later?" They said their good-byes, and Marin placed the phone on the porch, rising as Philip swung his leg over the bike.

"Hey, mister," one of the boys called from across the street, "that's a neat motorcycle! Can we come see it?"

Philip grinned and waved his large hand. "Sure, come on over."

With a rush, the boys raced across the street to surround Philip and the cycle.

Marin stood on the porch, watching him interact with the boys, listening to him answer their boisterous questions, wondering why he was here. The screen door opened, and John emerged. When he spotted Philip, he broke into a huge smile.

"Philip!" John ambled down the porch steps in his awkward gait. "You came over!"

The boys saw John, and their withdrawal was immediate. It nearly broke Marin's heart to see how their expressions became wary, uncertain. John was harmless—why couldn't these children see it?

The one who had asked permission to come over gestured to his buddies. "Well, thanks, mister, but we gotta go. Come on, guys." Marin heard one of them mutter, "Didn't know a retarded guy lived over there." The group headed back to their own yard and disappeared behind the house. The parting words stabbed like a knife in Marin's chest.

If John heard the comment, he was too excited to care. He pounded Philip's back and jabbered, unconcerned. "Philip, I like this motorcycle! It is very blue and shiny. Is it yours?"

Philip draped his arm around John's shoulders. "Yep, it sure is, buddy. Maybe someday I can take you for a ride."

"Today?" John leaned toward Philip eagerly. "We can go for a ride today?"

Philip shook his head. "Not today, John. I didn't bring my extra helmet, and you should always wear a helmet when you ride a motorcycle. But if it's all right with Marin, I'll bring the bike back and we'll go for a ride one evening soon, okay?"

John hurried to where Marin remained perched on the top step, her bare toes curled over the concrete edge. "Marin, will that be okay? Will it be okay for Philip to take me for a ride? When he has his extra helmet?"

Marin smiled. "Sure, John. Philip and I will work it out." She came down one step, putting herself on an equal level with John. "Did you get the recycling finished?"

He shook his head. "There is more."

"Well, the truck comes tomorrow," she reminded him. "Better finish up."

John looked forlornly toward Philip and the cycle. "But Philip is here."

Philip now stepped forward. "I'll be here for a while, John. Go ahead and finish up. I'll wait till you're done; then we can visit before I leave."

Satisfied, John padded into the house. Philip crossed the sidewalk to stand at the bottom of the porch and look up at Marin. He squinted as the rosy sun slanted across his face. "I hope it's okay that I just dropped by. I wanted to talk to you."

Aunt Chris's revelations still in her ears, Marin wasn't sure she was emotionally prepared to listen to anything Philip had to say. She grasped the porch railing for support. "What about?"

"Lunch. And why I invited you."

Marin shifted her gaze. His brown eyes were too sincere, too penetrating. He had a very unsettling effect on her emotions. "I think it was fairly clear. And there really isn't anything to discuss."

"I think there is."

She slowly brought her gaze back around. He waited patiently, a slight smile tipping up the corners of his lips. He held his helmet against his hip, causing his light jacket to hang open. His green T-shirt fit snugly against his chest, which appeared defined, as if he lifted weights. Although he stood two steps below her, his height put him almost even with her. Altogether he created a pleasing package. She was suddenly acutely aware of her ratty jean shorts, stretched-out T-shirt, and bare feet. What must he think of her scruffy appearance? Her tummy trembled slightly as she realized it mattered what Philip thought of her.

He lifted one booted foot and placed it next to her toes. In a near whisper, he asked, "Will you at least allow me to apologize?"

Marin suddenly discovered she was holding her breath. She released it in a *whoosh* then waved her hands in dismissal. "You don't need to apologize. It was just a—a mess with so many people crowding around and John getting upset, and I'd already had a very busy morning, which made me rather short-tempered, so—" She broke off as he burst into laughter. Well! She was trying to set things right, and all he could do was laugh about it. "What's so funny?" she demanded.

He swallowed, obviously trying to gain control. "I'm sorry. I wasn't really laughing at you, but when you said you were short-tempered. . ." He smirked. "Really, Marin, if that was your best shot at being short-tempered, I'd say I have nothing to worry about."

Despite herself, she had to smile. She had been so irritated with him, had felt almost betrayed by his blatant attempt to change her mind—but standing here in the splashes of sunlight that brought out the golden highlights in his tousled hair, she found the anger dissolved. All that remained was a slight discomfort. And right now, she couldn't completely identify the source of that discomfort.

Philip smiled again, lifting his shoulder. "Come on, Marin. Let's sit down here and let me try to explain something to you." As if certain of her acquiescence, he turned and seated himself on the third step. He rested his helmet on his left knee and cupped one broad hand over it to hold it there. Looking up at her, he added, "Please?"

She sighed. Philip Wilder was a difficult man to resist. She scooted to the opposite end of the steps and perched sideways, her back against the wrought iron railing. She pulled her bare heels close to her hips and wrapped both arms around her legs. The position gave her a measure of security. "I'm listening."

"Good." Shadows from the oak tree in the yard veiled his features as he began to speak softly. "First of all, I want you to know I understand and respect your feelings about keeping John safe. I've worked with people with handicaps long enough to know the world isn't always a welcoming place for those who are different."

Marin nodded. "Like those boys just now," she blurted out. The hurt was still fresh. "You saw how they all disappeared when John came out. He's no monster." She heard the defensiveness in her tone, but she couldn't seem to hold it in.

"Of course he's not," Philip agreed. "He's John—gentle John. We know that because we know him. And if those boys took the time to know him, they'd find it out, too. But chances are, they will never get to know John. Partly because of their own misconceptions about disabilities, and partly because. . .you won't allow it."

Marin tightened the hold on her knees. "That isn't fair, Philip. You don't know what my family has been through with John. Believe me when I say we have our reasons for keeping him away from people like those boys."

"I don't doubt that," Philip countered. "I'm sure you've been hurt over and over again by people's misconceptions."

"It's not just misconceptions!" Marin burst out, the hurtful comment made by the boy leaving her yard replaying itself in her memory. "It's out-and-out meanness! And it hurts so much when people—" She broke off, abashed, as tears formed and spilled down her cheeks. She dashed them away with shaking fingertips, but not before Philip had seen them.

His brown eyes softened with understanding concern. "I'm so sorry you've been hurt, Marin. I wish I could change what's happened. I can't do that—I can't rewrite the past." His face clouded for a moment, his forehead crinkling as if struck by a sharp pain. Then the expression cleared, and he added, "But I believe we can make the future better, if we work together."

Marin affected a harsh tone to control her sadness. "How?"

"By changing people's perceptions."

Again she barked one word. "How?"

Philip leaned toward her, his deep voice assuming a whisper softness. "Think about it, Marin. It's only our perception of being retarded that makes it a negative thing. Consider music—the retards in music give a different feel. The music becomes restful, relaxing, welcoming. People have taken the word *retarded* and turned it into something bad. But really, retarded simply means slowed down. Being relaxed, rested. Most retarded people are so loving and welcoming—they just reach out to you. How can that be a bad thing? In itself, it isn't. It's our reaction to it that makes it negative.

"So there's my goal—to educate others on what it means to be retarded. To help them look below the surface to the soul of the person. Maybe I can build an understanding empathy, and people will become more accepting of their developmentally delayed peers. It can happen, Marin. I believe it."

"But how, Philip? How can it happen?" When she asked this time, it wasn't with anger or defensiveness but with a real desire to know the answer.

"It can happen when people like John spend time with people like you and me, and they discover just how much alike they are."

Marin shook her head. "It sounds wonderful, Philip, but it isn't realistic. How can I expect 'the world' to accept John when people in my own family—people who've known him his whole life—can't accept him?"

Philip leaned against the railing and looked at her with his eyelids lowered. She felt as if he were trying to peer below the surface of her skin and see what was underneath. After a long time of silence, while crickets took up their night chorus and the sun slipped behind rooftops, he finally spoke. "You're scared. I see that. I even understand it—more than you know, I understand it. But someday, Marin, you're going to have to release that fear and let John go. Because a life shut away accomplishes nothing, and I can't accept for even one minute that 'nothing' is what God has in mind for your brother."

Before Marin could respond, the screen door swung open and John stepped onto the porch. "All the recycling is done," he announced. "Now I can visit." His hands chopped out the sign for *visit* as he plunked himself in the wedge of space between Philip and Marin.

Marin quickly rose. "Yes, you two visit. I'll be inside." She stepped into the house before Philip could say anything else. She walked through the dark hallway to Dad's office, turned on his desk light, and sat in his chair. Propping her chin in her hands, she stared at the family picture on the corner of the desk. How she wished her parents were here in person rather than merely captured on photo paper.

"Dad," she whispered, "did you really want something more for John?" Tipping her head, she examined her father's warm smile. "Why didn't you ever talk to me about John? What else didn't I know about you, Daddy?"

Marin had always gravitated toward her father. She knew this was partly because Mother was always so involved with John and partly because she and Dad shared so many common interests. But now, to her great regret, she realized she and her father had never discussed the most important things. "Maybe you thought we'd have time. . .later," she said to the portrait.

She reflected on the day of her college graduation. Mom and Dad had left John with Dick Ross's family, so for the first time, she'd had their full, undivided attention for an entire weekend. She'd relished those moments, basked in their pride, anticipated the evolving relationship that included friendship. When they'd gone to supper after the graduation ceremony, Dad had toasted her with iced tea and announced, "To Marin, the future of Brooks Advertising!" Then he'd lowered the glass, smiled at her indulgently, and added softly, "Ah, Marin, what plans I have for you. . . ."

They had fully intended to discuss those plans when Marin returned home the following week, but the opportunity was lost. Only a few hours later—Mother was eager to return home, to John—Dad pulled in front of a semi, and their lives were finished. And Marin's life—the life she had planned for herself—was finished, too.

Resentment pressed upward.

Regret mingled with it.

A hoot of laughter carried from the porch to the office.

Resolve pushed the other emotions away. For whatever reason, God had chosen to take her parents home, and John was now her responsibility. She would never know for sure what her father had planned for his son, but she had no doubt in her mind what her mother wanted. For now, she would continue what her mother began.

The motorcycle rumbled to life, and she crossed to the window, peeking between the wooden slats of the blinds to see Philip on the bike. Dark strands of hair curled around the bottom edge of the bright blue helmet, and Marin thought, *He needs a haircut.* John hovered close by, nearly dancing in excitement. In the yard across the street, two boys stood, obviously imitating John. Marin clenched her jaw.

Philip's head turned toward the house, no doubt seeking her, but she remained unmoving even while her heart tugged at her to go and say good-bye. As soon as he pulled away, she went to the door and called, "John, come on in now."

John ambled up the driveway, humming an aimless, off-tune melody. As he entered the house, he gave her an impulsive hug. "I love you, Marin."

Marin felt the sting of tears. "I love you, too, John." She did. She really did.

Humming again, John released her and headed toward his bedroom. He shut the door, leaving Marin alone. She stayed in the doorway, considering marching across the street and taking those boys to task for their rude behavior. But then she heaved a sigh. What good would it do? She closed the door and turned to the empty room.

More than any other time since her parents' death, Marin wished she had somebody else in this house to talk to. Someone with whom she could share these tumbling emotions. Someone who would just listen and not tell her what to think or feel. Philip's face appeared in her memory—his open, handsome, friendly face. But she pushed the thought aside. He would certainly do more than listen—he would tell her what he thought she should do, and she didn't want to hear it.

Dropping onto the couch, she brought up her knees and wrapped her arms around them. She closed her eyes and whispered, "Oh, Mom and Dad, I miss you so much."

# Chapter 8

Rays of early morning sunlight crept between the slats of the blinds and inched their way across Marin's rumpled comforter. She lay, propped on pillows, and watched the golden bands creep ever closer until a shaft of light assaulted her eyes. With a groan, she pulled the sheet over her head and wiggled a little lower on the mattress, knowing if the sun's rays had disturbed her slumber they had no doubt disturbed John's. And he would expect company when he awakened.

Sure enough, as if her thoughts could make it happen, a light tap sounded on her bedroom door. She sighed. "Come on in, John."

The door swung wide, and John appeared, his sleepy eyes wide with confusion. "How did you know it was me, Marin?"

She stifled a laugh. "Well, who else is here?"

He blinked twice, digesting this. "Only me," he finally said. He stepped closer to the bed. "It is Sunday."

She yawned. "I know."

"It is pancakes day."

Marin nodded. She knew. "Give me another minute or two, would you, please?"

He turned complacently but paused in the doorway. "One minute or two minutes?"

Marin shook her head. John would stand in front of the kitchen clock and count down the seconds, reappearing in either one or two minutes, whichever she decided. She threw back the covers. "I'm getting up."

He grinned. "I will be in the kitchen!"

━━⟋⟍━━

Philip tossed back the sheet and bounced out of bed, reaching into an all-over stretch the moment his feet hit the floor. Shivering—he'd left the window open last night—he crossed to the sliding glass doors that led to a small concrete patio outside his bedroom and peeked out at the new day. The yard, which fell west of the apartment complex, still lay in full shadow, but he spotted two robins pecking for worms in the sparse grass. He scratched his chin, reminding himself that he hadn't gotten around to dumping that fertilizer he'd bought to help thicken the grass cover.

Well, he wouldn't be doing it today. Today was the Lord's Day.

And this Lord's Day was his first day of teaching Sunday school. A smile tugged at his cheeks as he considered the prospect. He'd been a Sunday school attendee for years, but teaching? Not something he figured he'd do. When Rev. Lowe had asked him, though, he hadn't been able to say no. It meant a change in routine—normally he slept in on Sundays then attended Sunday school and the late church service, but now that he was a teacher, he felt the need to attend the early service and be fed before he tried to feed his own little flock.

Rubbing his hands together in anticipation, he chose his clothing, including a tie, which sported sheep grazing on a grassy pasture—*to remind me of my little flock*—then hopped into the shower. While he stood beneath the jets of steaming water, he reviewed the lesson he had planned for the junior high boys. He hoped the boys would be as enthusiastic about learning as he felt about teaching. He smiled, remembering the teacher who had led him to the Lord when he was a troubled eighth grader. He owed a huge debt of gratitude to Mr. Spence, and he hoped to repay it by being as good an influence on his students as Mr. Spence had been on him.

Only forty minutes after rising to greet the day, Philip was behind the wheel of his battered pickup truck, heading to Central Community Church. He pulled to the farthest corner of the parking lot. Only a handful of cars decorated the expansive parking area, and Philip chuckled to himself. *Guess I was more excited than I thought—I beat nearly everyone here.* He gave a shrug, whistling, as he strode across the asphalt and up the sidewalk leading to the worship sanctuary. *But it'll be great for me to hear the early sermon before I teach the boys.*

He shook hands with the greeter, accepted a bulletin, then found an aisle seat in one of the first few rows of pews, his heart already looking ahead to what Rev. Lowe had prepared to share.

⸺૭

"Marin, why on earth do you let him sit there by himself?"

Aunt Lenore whispered in deference to their surroundings, but her strident voice carried beyond Marin's ears. The row of teenagers in front of them turned to peek over their shoulders. She raised her eyebrows at them, and they turned back around.

John loved sitting in the pew directly in front of the sound booth. It rested at the foot of the center aisle of the church and gave him a straight view to the pulpit and choir loft. He claimed it was the best seat in the house, and Mother had always allowed him to sit there. Marin saw no reason why she should change the arrangement just because Aunt Lenore didn't approve. Aunt Lenore approved of nothing where John was concerned.

Leaning close to Lenore's ear, she explained quietly, "He enjoys sitting where he can see everything. He and Mother called it his 'special pew.' The sound-booth technicians don't mind—it doesn't hurt anything."

Aunt Lenore shook her head, clicking her tongue against her teeth. "I think it's asking for trouble, leaving him completely unattended."

Frustration welled. Aunt Lenore was Mother's twin, but Lenore had none of Mother's gentleness and compassion. Marin wanted to poke her aunt hard in the ribs and tell her to mind her own business, but church was not a place for confrontation. Instead she forced herself to whisper calmly. "He's fine. Trust me."

Marin sent a glance in John's direction. He sat quietly, a bulletin in his stubby hands, his ankles crossed. When he spotted Marin looking at him, he gave a little wave. Marin smiled and waved back with two fingers.

She turned her focus to the pulpit where Rev. Lowe began his sermon. Only five minutes into the delivery, a mild commotion broke out behind her. Assuming a small child was wrestling with his or her parent, she kept her eyes facing forward, but Lenore turned around. She emitted a gasp and clamped her hand painfully on Marin's knee.

"Marin, do something!" Lenore hissed.

Marin looked over her shoulder to see John standing in front of his pew, waving his hand and beaming broadly. "Hello! Hello!" His raspy voice, while a whisper, carried clearly.

"Make him sit down!" Lenore ordered through clenched teeth. Her neck and cheeks were mottled with anger.

Marin, her face hot with embarrassment, gestured to John. He looked at her, but instead of settling down, he became more animated. Now that he had Marin's attention, he pointed with both hands and laughed out loud.

Lenore nearly pushed Marin out of the pew. "Get him out of here before he ruins the entire service!"

Marin stumbled into the aisle, regained her footing, and went to John as quickly as her high-heeled sandals would allow. Though she kept her gaze straight ahead, she could feel the curious looks following her progress, and she was certain her face was as red as the dress she wore.

"Marin, it is Philip," John said when she reached him.

Without responding, she looped her arm through his and directed him toward a set of double doors leading to the foyer.

"It is Philip right over there," John continued, too excited to remember that talking aloud in church was against the rules.

Once they were in the foyer, well away from the doors, Marin wheeled on her brother. "John, what got into you? You know better than to create a scene in church! Mother and Dad would be so disappointed in you!"

John's smile faded, and his shoulders drooped. "But—but I saw Philip."

"You couldn't have seen Philip. Philip doesn't attend our church," Marin argued, her embarrassment displaying itself in anger. "But even if you had, you know better than to stand up and wave and talk. You won't be able to sit in the special pew anymore if you can't stay quiet."

Tears glittered in John's eyes. "I am sorry."

His genuine remorse completely dissolved Marin's anger, but it couldn't remove her humiliation. "I know you are, John, but Aunt Lenore is really mad. You can't stand up and talk in church."

John nodded, his expression sad. "But I only said hi to Philip."

Marin blew out a breath. "That's not the point, John. You can't talk *at all*."

At that moment, the doors from the sanctuary opened again. Marin cringed, anticipating Aunt Lenore's thundering presence, but her jaw dropped when she saw who it was.

A huge grin split John's face, and he held out his arms. "Philip!"

Philip whispered, "Hi, John." He strode across the carpet to join them.

John opened his arms for a hug, which Philip returned; then Philip kept his arm around John's shoulders.

"So I guess we caused a ruckus, huh?" Philip asked, giving Marin an apologetic look.

His aftershave, a scent of spiced oranges, filled Marin's nostrils. Clad in tasseled loafers, pleated blue trousers, a white button-down oxford shirt, and a tie with—of all things—grazing sheep marching up and down, he looked nothing like the man who greeted her each day at New Beginnings or rode that blue and chrome motorcycle. She took a step backward, gaining control of her senses. "So he *did* see you."

"And you look like you've seen a ghost."

Marin watched John happily pat Philip's shoulder and beam upward. She stammered, "I—I'm just surprised, that's all. I didn't realize you attended here."

"Is this your home church? Funny I've never seen you. I transferred my membership here about a year and a half ago, but this is my first time at the early service." He straightened his shoulders, his height becoming even greater with the action. His brown eyes sparkled. "I start teaching a junior high class today, so I figured I'd be better off getting here before Sunday school."

Marin nodded dumbly. Well, that explained why Philip hadn't seen John here before. Being an early riser, John had always attended the first service. Because there was no class to accommodate John's special needs, Mom and Dad hadn't stayed for Sunday school. Of course, with Marin away at college, it had been several years since she'd attended this church regularly.

John asked, "Can I go to Sunday school with you, Philip?"

"No," Marin answered bluntly. John in a room full of junior high–age boys? That would be asking for trouble. At Philip's puzzled look, she added gently, "Remember, John? We go to Aunt Lenore's for lunch after church. So we can't stay for Sunday school."

John pulled a face. "I do not like Aunt Lenore. She is bossy." He signed the word *bossy* with relish.

Marin agreed, but the subject wasn't up for debate. "Sorry, John, but we have to go."

John sighed but didn't argue.

"We could still catch most of the sermon if we head back in there," Philip suggested. He looked down at John. "Want to sit with me, buddy?"

John immediately lit up. "In my special seat?"

Philip looked at Marin, his eyebrow raised.

"The pew in front of the sound booth," Marin explained. "He likes sitting there."

Philip nodded. "Sure, John. I'll sit there with you."

Marin nearly wilted with relief. If Philip were with him, John would surely behave. And Aunt Lenore couldn't complain about John being unattended.

"Come on," Philip told John, heading him toward the doors to the sanctuary. "But we have to be very quiet so we don't disrupt."

John placed a stubby finger against his lips and tiptoed beside Philip. Marin followed the two of them back into the sanctuary. Philip and John settled side by side in the middle of John's pew, and Marin crept down the aisle to rejoin her aunt. Aunt Lenore, her face pinched, glanced toward John's pew. When she spotted Philip with him, she gave a brusque nod of approval then turned back to the Bible in her lap.

Marin kept her gaze to the front, but she felt very aware of Philip's presence behind her. She supposed she should be grateful for his assistance with John; yet, if she were honest with herself, grateful wasn't the feeling he evoked.

# Chapter 9

Monday morning as Marin pulled up in front of New Beginnings, she discovered her palms were moist and her stomach fluttered. And she knew why. Since yesterday, when Philip unexpectedly appeared in the church foyer to assist with John, she had been unable to get him out of her mind. Seeing him at church, away from the New Beginnings setting and his "job," he had turned into a "real person." While she couldn't define why it had impacted her so, she could not deny that she was seeing him with different eyes.

"Come on, Marin. Let's go in." John nudged her with the heel of his hand, waking her from her reverie.

"Um, John," she hedged, wrapping her hands around the sturdy plastic steering wheel, "can you walk in by yourself today?"

John's hazel eyes widened. "You always walk me in."

Marin resisted the sigh that longed for release. John was such a creature of habit. If she disrupted his routine, it might upset his whole day. There wasn't much choice—she'd need to walk him in. *But maybe,* she thought as she stepped out of the car and walked with John to the door, *Philip will be occupied elsewhere, and I won't have to speak to him.*

That hope was immediately squelched with the opening of the door. While Philip did appear to be occupied—he held a clipboard and spoke earnestly with an older, smiling woman—the moment the door creaked, he turned in their direction and broke into a huge smile. "Good morning, John and Marin!"

Marin felt a prickle of regret that he'd greeted John first. *Stop it!* she berated herself. She raised her hand for a quick wave and turned to leave as John trotted across the floor to embrace the woman.

"Marin, wait!"

Freezing, her hand on the doorknob, her gaze on the doorjamb, she waited until Philip came to a jogging halt beside her.

"Hey, I wanted to share an idea with you. I got a request on the answering machine for someone to help out at Barks, Squawks, and Meows, the new veterinary clinic that just opened on Fourth Street, and I wondered how you'd feel about—"

Marin felt her blood pressure climb. All warm feelings toward Philip fled. She spun and interrupted. "Don't even suggest it. Not now, not ever. I've made it perfectly clear that John is not here to learn to go—out there." She flung her hand outward, indicating the outdoors. "He's here to have a safe haven. You told me he could stay for a month, and there's another week left of that month, so don't make any more noises about jobs. Honor your agreement."

While she raged, Philip took a step back and lowered the clipboard to his side, his expression changing from welcoming to woeful to weary. He nodded, his brown eyes clearly displaying regret. When he spoke, his voice was soft yet held an undercurrent of hurt. "Fine, Marin, for one more week, I'll keep my silence, as we agreed." He leaned in. "But at the end of the week—then what?"

She had no answer, so she stood in stony silence.

He nodded, as if he knew her options were limited. "You might ask John what he'd like to do. It is *his* future, you know." And he turned and strode to John and the woman, ignoring Marin.

Marin careened out the door, slammed herself into her vehicle, and dashed away as quickly as safety allowed. While she drove across town, her heart pounded and her ears rang. She wished so much someone else were dealing with these issues. She wished she'd never met Philip Wilder, who was entirely too handsome and smart and left her emotions in an upheaval when she needed her world to be quiet and ordered. She wished she could keep driving and driving and driving until she was far, far away.

But whom was she fooling? She couldn't keep driving. She had responsibilities. Her home, Brooks Advertising, and John. Even though she had moments—like now—when she wanted a break, she could never leave permanently.

She pulled into her parking area, shut off the ignition, and lowered her forehead to the steering wheel. Closing her eyes, she prayed inwardly, *Lord, as much as I hate to admit it, Philip is right. I don't have other prospects for John's care. And John should have a say-so in what happens to him. But how much say-so? What can he really handle, God? I don't want to burden him.* The Bible verse displayed on the banner at New Beginnings played through her mind. *What good works do You have planned for John? How I wish I knew. . . .*

With a sigh, she raised her head and peeked at herself in the mirror. Her cheeks were slightly flushed, but other than that, she appeared composed. Under the surface, however, emotions continued to rumble. If she got busy—focused—she could find a measure of control. That determination made, she headed into Brooks Advertising.

─∽─

After the morning meeting, Crystal followed Marin to her office. She held out a manila envelope. Her expression seemed apprehensive. "Miss Brooks, I probably should have given this to you the first day you came in, but Mr. Ross thought it would be best to wait and give you time to settle in."

Marin pulled her brows down, her stomach churning in sudden trepidation. "What is it?"

"The bank statement for April. Your dad would have taken care of it, but—" She broke off, shrugging helplessly.

Marin nodded, understanding. The accident had changed many routines. She took the envelope and offered a sad smile. "Well, you're right that I probably should have dealt with this awhile back, but I understand the reasoning behind holding off. Thanks for giving it to me."

She walked to her office, closed the door, and spilled the contents of the envelope across the desk. This distraction was just what she needed to bring an end to her John worries. Pulling out the executive checkbook register, she began the balancing process. All fell neatly into place with the exception of one debit. No reference was applied to it in the register—only the initials R.H. and only a routing number on the statement. She backtracked in the checkbook records, discovering the same amount had been automatically withdrawn from Dad's account the thirtieth of each month for as far back as the register showed.

*What is R.H.?* she wondered. It was a sizable enough amount to warrant concern. She pushed the intercom button. "Crystal, could you have Dick come in here for a minute, please?"

In moments, Dick appeared. Marin gestured for him to sit then swung the checkbook register and statement in his direction. "Dick, do you have any idea what this is?"

Dick examined both documents, his brows furrowed. "R.H.," he mused. "No, that doesn't ring any bells with me."

Marin flipped through the register. "Look. There's a similar notice of withdrawal all the way back to December of last year. I imagine if I check previous checkbook registers, I'm going to find it goes back further than that. But there's nothing here to tell me what it's about. A bill of some sort? Payment on a loan? Do you have any ideas?"

Dick leaned back and shrugged. "I don't know, Marin. Darin always handled the financial end of the business—the rest of us were creative staff, so I can't tell you what it is. But maybe—" He broke off, his expression thoughtful.

Marin tipped her head. "What?"

Dick scratched his chin, releasing a light chuckle. "Well, this might sound far-fetched, but your dad was a strong believer in not letting your left hand know what your right hand was doing. Maybe that R.H. means right hand, and he was making some sort of charitable contribution."

Marin nodded slowly. "Dad was adamant about tithes and offerings. He said God gave us much, and as good stewards, we should share. You could be right, but why would he keep it so secretive?" She scowled, frustrated. "I made a commitment to carry on Dad's work, but if *my* left hand doesn't know what *his* right hand was doing, how can I keep doing it?"

Dick gave another shrug. "Check with Mr. Whitehead? As far as I know, he was Darin's only legal advisor."

"Yes. . .yes, that's a good idea. Thanks, Dick."

After Dick left, Marin flipped through the file of telephone numbers until she located Mr. Whitehead's number. When his receptionist answered, she spoke briskly. "This is Marin Brooks. I need to schedule an appointment with Mr. Whitehead as soon as possible, please. Would he have some time late this afternoon perhaps?"

Five fifteen. Philip felt his stomach clench when he noticed the time. Marin would be arriving to retrieve John within the next five minutes. After this morning's run-in, he wasn't eager to see her. She was wrong. He knew she was wrong, but he didn't know how to make her see it without alienating her. He'd be doing some heavy-duty praying in the next few days to find a way to reach her.

In the meantime, he turned his attention to the older couple across his desk. Their son had suffered brain damage from a severe allergic reaction to penicillin when he was still a toddler. He had always been cared for at home, but as the couple aged, they realized they needed assistance. Their initial plea for help had been similar to Marin's, but Philip believed they would be open to a job placement once they realized it would meet their needs.

While he shared the different job opportunities available to New Beginnings clients, he kept one ear tuned to the door. His heart picked up its tempo the moment the knob turned and he heard John greet his sister. But he didn't turn his head—he remained focused on the couple. John hollered a good-bye, and he responded briefly, sending John a quick smile, which also swept over Marin; then he returned his attention to the man and woman across the desk.

The door closed again, and he heaved an inward sigh of relief. *Can't let her boggle my mind so much*, he thought with determination and continued his explanation to Mr. and Mrs. Jeffers. When he'd completed covering all the work options, he admitted, "I must be honest with you—New Beginnings is encountering some financial difficulties right now."

The couple exchanged a worried glance, and the man said, "My wife and I are on a fixed income—"

Philip held up his hand. "No, no, I wasn't asking you for money. As I said earlier, New Beginnings is strictly nonprofit. I do not require a fee from any of my clients. I only mentioned it to let you know I'm uncertain how much longer the services will be available. I want you to know that if I must close I will do everything I can to find comparable services for your son. I won't leave you high and dry."

The woman's eyes glittered. She pointed to the Bible verse. "Mr. Wilder, did you put that up there?"

Philip nodded.

"Then you're a Christian?"

Again Philip nodded. "Yes, ma'am. I am."

She took his hand. "Then the Lord will provide. He takes care of His own—I know that. All these years, He's given me the strength to care for Randy. He guided us here to you when we needed help. He'll give you what you need to keep this wonderful place going. I will join you in prayer."

Philip's heart swelled. This confirmation was just what he needed. He squeezed the soft, wrinkled hand that rested in his. "Thank you, Mrs. Jeffers. And I'll do whatever I can to help you with Randy."

The couple stood to leave, and Philip walked them to the door with a promise to start working with Randy in the morning. After closing the door behind them, he leaned against it and heaved a sigh.

"Lord, You heard Mrs. Jeffers. She believes You'll provide. I believe it, too. I just don't know how. Would You please hurry up and tell me? And while You're fixing things, please help me find a way to reach Marin."

John sat quietly next to Marin as she showed the bank statements and checkbook register to Mr. Whitehead. "I don't have a clue what this is for, but Dick Ross thought it might be a charitable contribution. Can you tell me what it is?"

Mr. Whitehead gave a short glance, then nodded. "Of course I know what it is. One of your father's 'right hand' dealings." He smiled. "You know, Marin, your father was one of the finest Christians I've ever had the pleasure of knowing. His ideas of stewardship would put most of the rest of us to shame. He gave several onetime offerings to various organizations, but this one—this one was extra special. He donated to it consistently for nearly three years."

Marin raised her eyebrows. "Three years? That same amount?"

Mr. Whitehead nodded. "Yes. He fully supported this organization's work." The man shrugged. "Of course, now that you're in charge of Brooks Advertising, it's easily changed. He made the arrangements monthly, so it automatically stopped with his death. It does not need to resume."

"But I want it to resume." Marin leaned forward. "If it was important to Dad, I'd like to continue giving, just as he did. But I don't know who he gave it to!"

Mr. Whitehead's forehead furrowed. "Well, that leaves me in a rather awkward position, Marin. Your father wanted this transaction kept secret—from the receiver of the funds and from his family. I feel as if I would be breaching a confidence to share the name of the organization."

Marin leaned back, thinking. Was it important for her to know who was receiving the money? She knew she could trust Mr. Whitehead to funnel the money for her—Dad had trusted him unconditionally. While she was curious, it was more important to her that Dad's work continue. She gave a nod, her decision made. "Mr. Whitehead, if you can set up an automatic transfer of funds to this organization without divulging its name to me, I'd like for you to do that."

The man smiled. "That could be arranged."

"I know Dad went month by month, and because of that, a month was skipped. I don't want that to happen again, so let's set it up for twelve months. At the end of that time period, please contact me, and I'll renew for another year." Marin paused, frowning for a moment. "That is possible, isn't it?"

Mr. Whitehead gave a light laugh. "With today's computer systems, it's a simple matter to set up such transactions." His eyes shone with approval. "Darin always spoke highly of you, Marin, and he felt very confident you would continue his work with diligence. It would be easy for you to let this slip aside—no one would ever know since Darin kept it private. I'm proud of you for being willing to follow your father's spirit of giving."

The words warmed Marin. She stood and held out her hand. "Thank you, Mr. Whitehead. Let's restart those transfers on the thirtieth, just as Dad had done."

# Chapter 10

Philip could hardly believe how quickly the month had flown by. With summer in full swing, John had started wearing knee-length walking shorts and sandals in place of jeans and tennis shoes. Eileen teasingly called him Spanky after *The Little Rascals* character, and John always responded with a laughing protest—"Oh, Eileen, I am John!"

The two of them were now in the housekeeping center with another client, Bobby, doing cleanup after a session of cooking. Everyone else had left for the day. The mumble of their voices kept Philip company as he paid bills at his desk. He heard Eileen say, "Okay, John, now back to work," and he smiled, certain that right now John was wrapping Eileen in one of his famous hugs.

John knew the routine of New Beginnings so well that Philip was positive he'd be great in a work placement. But Marin remained stubbornly determined to keep him sheltered. In fact, it seemed deeper than stubbornness. There was a real fear. Fear was not of God, and Philip wanted the opportunity to tell her that.

Each day of the past week, he'd tried to get a moment alone with her to approach the subject, but she'd managed to sidestep him. She wouldn't be able to do it tonight, though. This was the last day of his stipulated one-month period, so the issue must be faced. Marin would face it if he had to tie her to a chair and make her listen.

He finished writing a check to pay the utilities bill, scowling a bit as he realized how low his bank account was getting. Before worry could set in, he reminded himself of last night's Bible reading. Philip had sought comfort in the Psalms, and in chapter 32 he'd found it: *You are my hiding place; you will protect me from trouble and surround me with songs of deliverance. I will instruct you and teach you in the way you should go; I will counsel you and watch over you.*

Nothing had changed. His bank account held only enough funds for another two weeks of full operation. But the psalm promised deliverance. Already he'd found a measure of deliverance. He and Eileen had brainstormed ways to keep providing some services within the confines of his lesser income. Even if he had to use other agencies, his clients would be all right. But he feared he would have to cut two employees because his income would no longer cover their salaries.

"John, the dishes are dry so stack them on the shelf, please. Bobby, use some cleanser on that sink and scrub, scrub, scrub!"

Philip turned an ear toward the housekeeping center, listening as Eileen gave directions. Her gravelly yet warm voice carried over the partition. He smiled, envisioning the scene in the minikitchen. Eileen was wonderful with the clients. If he had to drop someone from the payroll, she would be at the bottom of the list.

He slapped his checkbook closed, slipped the check and bill into an envelope, then opened his drawer to dig for a book of stamps. His arm was buried to the elbow in the drawer when the front door opened and Marin entered. He tried to stand, but his sleeve got caught on something; he flumped back into his seat with a muffled "Ooph!"

Marin covered her mouth with her fingers, obviously trying to hide a smile, but she didn't shield her eyes. He could see the smile in their hazel depths from the distance of twenty feet. The smile warmed him, and he couldn't help but respond with one of his own.

"Yep, caught me in my most graceful moment." He disentangled his sleeve and pulled himself loose. On his feet, he rounded the desk and called over his shoulder, "John! Marin is here."

Eileen stuck her head around the partition and flapped her hand in their direction. "John's finishing up. He'll be out in a minute. You two talk." She disappeared again.

Twisting her hands together at her waist, Marin gave a slight shrug. "We probably do need to talk. This is it, isn't it?"

Philip knew she referred to her month being up, but to him, the words held a deeper meaning. "I guess so," he said, "unless something changes." His reply held a double meaning, as well.

Marin sucked in her lips, looking up at him with an unreadable expression in her eyes. She tucked a strand of hair behind her ear then gestured toward the stacking chairs in the corner. "Could we sit down for a moment? I—I do have something I'd like to discuss with you."

Philip's heart pattered. He pulled out a chair and set it down. "Here you go." She seated herself, arranging her skirt over her knees. He yanked out another chair and straddled it, facing her, with his arms stacked one over the other on the backrest. "I'm all ears," he prompted.

Linking her fingers in her lap, she offered a small smile. "I want you to know how much I appreciate all you've done for John. He loves coming here, and he thinks of you as a friend."

"I am his friend." Philip leaned forward and added, "Yours, too."

She looked away for a moment, as if embarrassed, and when she turned back, he noticed two tears shining brightly in the corners of her eyes. "Thank you." She blinked several times then continued. "It will be hard for me to tell him he can't come back. I know you said one month, and I'm not going to ask you to do this indefinitely, but—as our friend—I hope you'll be willing to do a favor for

John and me." She paused, looking at him expectantly.

He threw his hands outward. "Well, what is it?"

She released a light, self-conscious laugh. "I hoped you'd say yes first."

"Can't till I know what it is," he said, his tone teasing. "You might ask me to rob a bank or something."

She laughed again but with less reserve. "Not likely."

Philip erased the teasing from his voice as he encouraged, "Marin, whatever it is, if I can help you and John, I'll do it. Okay? Now quit procrastinating and spit it out."

Marin tucked her hair behind her ears once more—an unnecessary gesture because her hair stayed neatly in place—and drew in a big breath. "You see, I have John on the waiting list of two different day care facilities, but neither has an opening—yet. I called everywhere after Mom and Dad died"—she grimaced slightly then drew herself up and continued—"but they said all they could do was put me on a list and call when they had an opening. So far no one's called, and I don't know what to do on Monday."

Philip nodded, guessing the favor. "You want John to continue coming here."

Marin nodded quickly, licking her lips. "Not forever. Just till I hear from one of the day care facilities."

Philip didn't bother to tell her forever might not be possible even if he were willing to continue providing day care for John. "You know my feelings about keeping John cooped up here."

"I know, but as I said, it won't be for much longer." Her voice rose with desperation. "Surely someone will call soon."

"And if they don't?" Philip watched her expression change from desperate to defiant.

"Well. . .well. . ." She squared her narrow shoulders and pinned him with a fierce gaze. "Matthew says today has trouble enough of its own without worrying about tomorrow. I'll just worry one day at a time."

Philip couldn't help it. He burst out laughing. "Marin, you are priceless," he finally managed to say.

She didn't look amused. "I'll keep paying you," she said, "just as I've been doing. Will you allow John to come here a few more weeks? Please?"

Philip forced himself to control his laughter. He knew she was not trying to be humorous, but if she could only see herself, sitting so sweetly in a butter yellow dress with the sun shining on her hair, her little face set with such determination. Such a small package, yet ready to take on the world if need be.

"Marin, I would love to continue working with John. He's a joy—really he is. We all have grown to love him, and I think he's grown to love us." At that moment, laughter erupted from behind the partition, proving how happy John was. "But it isn't fair to him to keep him here day after day. He needs new interactions, new challenges to grow. Think about a rose plant that's kept in a closet—it never blooms. It needs sunshine and rain to bloom, which can only happen outside." Philip reached over the chair to place his hands over Marin's, which were now closed into fists. "He'll never bloom, Marin, unless you allow him to venture into the world."

"Outside, roses get trampled. Blooms get battered by the wind." Her voice sounded tight, controlled. Anger was beneath the surface, but Philip decided to forge ahead anyway.

He squeezed her hands and said softly, "But they live to bloom another day, stronger and more hearty from the experience."

She yanked her hands away and stood. "So you won't let him keep coming?"

Philip sighed and rose, too. He looked down at her, his thoughts tumbling. If he said no, she'd have no one to turn to. If he said yes, he'd be enabling her to keep John confined. If he said no, he might never see her again—suddenly a very disturbing prospect. If he said yes, he'd have more opportunities to see her, talk to her, convince her to allow John to spread his wings.

"We'll take it a week at a time," he found himself saying.

Her face lit up. "Really?" The relief was evident.

"A week at a time," he repeated, as much for himself as for her.

She hugged herself. "Oh, thank you, Philip. You are a godsend."

*A godsend? Maybe just a big chicken.* Sternly he reiterated, "Remember—a week at a time."

John puttered around the corner to give Marin a hug.

"John, say good-bye to everyone. We'll see them again on Monday," she prompted.

" 'Bye, Philip. 'Bye, Eileen and Bobby," John recited dutifully. "I will see you Monday."

Philip watched them turn, hand in hand, and head for the door. As Marin reached for the doorknob, he impulsively called out, "Wait a minute."

Marin turned as John went on out. "Yes?"

"What are you doing tomorrow night?" His heart pounded at his own brashness. If he was going to take this a week at a time, he'd better make the most of it.

Marin's fine brows came down. "Nothing. Why?"

He hooked his thumbs in his rear pockets to hide the trembling in his hands. "I thought I might bring the cycle over—take John for a ride, as I promised. And then visit. . .if that's okay."

Marin seemed to examine him for hidden motives. When she answered, her voice held uncertainty. "Yes. I suppose that would be fine."

"Good. Okay." He backed up a step, tripping over one of the chairs. Catching himself, he added lamely, "I'll see you tomorrow night—seven thirty?"

She nodded then slipped out the door.

Philip sank down on the offending chair and buried his face in his hands. A tap on his shoulder brought him bolt upright. Eileen stood smirking at him.

"If you're going to ask a girl for a date, you need to do it with more confidence."

"I wasn't asking her for a date," he blustered. "I just need a chance to talk to her—about John."

"Mm-hmm," Eileen said, her expression knowing. She crossed her arms. "If you'll need someone to stay with John while you take her out, give me a holler. I'd be glad to do it. I'll even bring my cat."

Philip groaned. "Eileen—" But then something struck him, and he jumped to his feet. Wrapping his arms around her sturdy bulk, he swung her off the floor in a mighty hug. "Why, you sweetheart, you!"

"Yes I am, but put me down!" she demanded, thumping him on the shoulders. He released her, and she continued to grumble, straightening her shirt. But he noticed her eyes sparkled. "What was that all about?"

"It doesn't matter," he said, the smile still splitting his face. "Can you be ready by seven? I'll pick you up—and make sure you bring your cat."

# Chapter 11

At 7:25 Saturday evening, the doorbell rang. Marin remained in the kitchen, mixing a pitcher of lemonade, and allowed John to answer it. For some inexplicable reason, she felt shy about seeing Philip. She heard John exclaim, "Eileen!"

Eileen? She rounded the corner to see the older woman from New Beginnings step into the living room. A pet carrier dangled from the woman's hand.

John pointed to the plastic cage. "What is in there, Eileen?"

Eileen smiled, her bright eyes surrounded by wrinkles. She angled the opening of the cage in John's direction. "In here is Roscoe the Wonder Cat." She chuckled. "So named because it's a wonder he puts up with me. Would you like to meet him?"

John clapped his hands. "Marin, look! A wonder cat!"

Marin was baffled. What was this woman doing here? And where was Philip? A loud squeak followed by a *clunk* and *thump* sounded from outside, and Marin peeked out the window. There she spotted Philip unloading his motorcycle from the back of the most disreputable-looking pickup truck she'd ever seen. She turned to Eileen. "Did Philip bring you over?"

Eileen set the pet carrier on the floor. John immediately crouched in front of it, poking his finger in at Roscoe the Wonder Cat. Eileen straightened and turned her smile on Marin. "Yes. He thought you might like a ride, too, and I said I'd be glad to keep John company." She glanced down and chuckled. "Although it looks to me like he won't be bothering with me at all."

A look at John confirmed his fascination with Roscoe. Marin shook her head indulgently. "Well, I'll go out and check on Philip," she said, knowing she was leaving John in good hands. She stepped out on the porch as Philip put the cycle's kickstand into place.

He turned and grinned. "Will the neighbors complain about having such an eyesore on their street?" He patted the side of the rusty, dented pickup.

Marin laughed. "That's the ugliest thing I've ever seen."

Philip ran a loving hand across the hood as he walked toward her. "Well, beauty's in the eye of the beholder. I happen to love ol' Dixie."

"Dixie?" Marin crossed her arms, unable to squelch a smile.

"Didn't you know trucks run better when they have a name?" He made a face as if to say "Women!"

Marin just chuckled. She pointed over her shoulder. "So you brought a baby-sitter, too, huh?"

"Yup. I figured you'd feel more comfortable going for a ride if someone was here with John. He and Eileen are great friends." He propped his foot on the lowest step and smiled up at her, his brown eyes warm. He must have driven with the windows down; his hair was wind ruffled, and his cheeks looked ruddy which only added to his rugged attractiveness. Marin immediately tried to stifle that thought.

"But I thought you were going to give John the ride," she reminded him.

"And I will. But that doesn't mean you can't take a ride, too."

Marin looked at the bike. She imagined sitting on the back of it, riding through town with the wind teasing her hair, her arms around Philip's middle. Her tummy did a flip-flop. "It does sound like fun."

He gave a crinkling smile in reply.

"Come on in," she invited.

They entered to find John on the floor, his legs widespread. In the V of his legs, a fluffy yellow and white cat lay on its back and batted at a piece of yarn which John held.

Philip nudged her and offered a smile that set Marin's heart into overdrive. How she appreciated his open acceptance of John.

"Hey, buddy," Philip greeted, "ready for that cycle ride?"

"Not now." John's gaze remained on Roscoe. "I am playing with the wonder cat."

Philip looked surprised, but he recovered and shrugged. "So—is it okay if I take Marin for a ride?"

"It is okay." John jerked the yarn up and down. "You go ride, Marin."

Marin looked at Eileen, who waved her hand in good-bye. She turned to Philip. "Let's go then."

They donned helmets and climbed onto the bike. At first, Marin felt self-conscious with her hands on Philip's waist, but after a few minutes, she got caught up in the freedom of the open ride—the tug of the wind, the rev of the engine, and the feeling of being one with the cycle. He took a lazy route through town that ended at the city park. He pulled to a stop near the fountain and shut off the bike. It seemed quiet after having the growl of the engine fill her ears.

Philip offered his hand and helped her dismount. She gave a little bounce to recover her footing then removed the helmet and shook out her hair. He put her helmet in the small trunk and placed his on the padded sissy bar. With a grin, he asked, "Did you have fun?"

"Oh yes," she said. "It's a great bike."

He smiled his approval. "Want to walk a bit?"

She nodded, and they fell into step. They walked in silence, enjoying the gentle sounds of a summer evening in the park: children's voices, the quacking of ducks, the hum of locusts. After a few minutes, a lawn mower revved to life somewhere nearby, and unconsciously Marin cringed.

Philip must have noticed because he peered down at her with a puzzled look. "Why the scowl?"

"Oh, someone is getting ready to cut their lawn." She gave a slight shiver. "I don't care for the smell of fresh-cut grass."

"But it's the smell of summertime." Philip pointed to a bench off the walkway, and they sat. He turned sideways and bent his elbow, resting his wrist on the edge of the wooden backrest. His fingers hung beside her shoulder, not touching her but close enough that a slight shift in her position would bring them into contact. The thought sent a tingle down her spine. "You don't like the smell of summertime?"

Marin considered his question. Cut grass was not the smell of summertime for her—it was an unpleasant reminder. Just the thought of that spicy, fresh odor brought forth a wellspring of remembrances, and she tightened her shoulders, willing that particular afternoon's events to be driven far from her mind.

"Marin?" His concerned tone brought her chin up. She met his gaze, and the tenderness in his eyes nearly took her breath away. "You're uptight—I can see it. It seems you hold yourself at a distance from me. Do I frighten you?"

She found the question odd. Who could be afraid of Philip? Despite his size, which could be intimidating, he was obviously a kind, warmhearted person. John trusted him implicitly—but then John probably wasn't the best judge of character. Still, she'd watched Philip with her brother, and she believed he would never do anything to hurt John or anyone else. It wasn't part of his nature. She answered honestly. "No, quite the contrary. I probably trust you more than anyone else I've met—outside of my family, of course."

His smile warmed her from the inside out. "Good." He stroked her shoulder with his pinky finger—one light touch—before bringing his hand away again. She felt a sense of loss with the removal of that simple contact. "Then please tell me what you're thinking about now. I can see something is bothering you."

To her embarrassment, she felt tears well in her eyes. She turned her face away to hide. Strong yet gentle fingers cupped her chin to bring her back around.

"Marin, please. I want to help you, but I can't if you won't talk to me."

Philip's tender tone was her undoing. The tears slipped free and ran down her cheeks. Philip wrapped his arms around her, pulling her snug against his chest. His chin on the top of her head, he whispered, "Talk to me, Marin. Tell me how to help you."

Her cheek pressed against the warmth of his shirtfront; her senses filled with the essence of his aftershave. She felt more secure than she'd felt since the day of her parents' funerals. She remained still for several minutes, allowing the

comfort of his embrace to give her the courage she needed to share her deepes
hurt. Finally, while nestled in his hug, she whispered, "Someone was cutting gras
the day—" Her voice cracked, and she swallowed hard.

Philip brought his hands to her upper arms and gently set her aside. H
maintained contact by slipping his hands to either side of her neck, his thumb
resting lightly on her collarbone. "The day—what, Marin?"

She took a shuddering breath. "The day everything changed." Marin lifte
her gaze to meet Philip's. "It was spring, not summer. Someone was cutting grass
and John was listening to the motor. He said it was a riding mower—the engin
was too strong for a push mower. He knew his sounds."

Philip's thumbs drew lazy circles. "What were you doing besides listenin
to the mower?"

"Walking home. We—John and I—had walked to the grocery store. Mon
needed eggs, butter, and bread." She organized the sequence of events in her mind
She pulled down her brows, struggling against the memories. "It was such a pretty
day that I asked if I could ride my bike. It was only a few blocks to a little conve
nience store. But John wanted to come, too." Marin clenched her jaw for a mo
ment, remembering how she'd fussed about having to take him. "I wanted to go
alone. As I said, I wanted to ride my bike, and I knew I'd have to walk if John came
He couldn't ride a bike. I didn't want to be bothered with John's poking along."

"That sounds like a typical sister," Philip commented, his sweet smile en
couraging. "How old were you?"

"Ten." Marin released a short huff. "Ten, but still older than John. I didn't lik
having to be responsible for him. He was the older brother—it wasn't natural fo
me to be responsible for him. I really struggled with it at that age." She dropped
her chin. She had never admitted that to anyone before.

After a moment, she brought up her gaze and continued, bolstered by th
comforting feel of Philip's hands on her shoulders. "Everything went fine on
the way to the store. I bought Mom's things, and we took turns carrying the
sack home. I forgot about my resentment. John was so happy to be with me—
couldn't stay mad. He held my hand, and then he started singing."

She felt a smile tugging, a fondness filling her chest. "John's always loved fif
ties music, and he was singing 'Rockin' Robin'—and kind of jitterbugging as we
walked. I laughed and sang with him. A fun time. . ." Her smile wilted as a chil
crept through her veins. "And then John saw the baby bird."

The pain stabbed as hard as if it had happened yesterday. Her nose stung
as she fought back tears. "A baby bird—a sparrow, I think—had fallen from its
nest. It was under a tree. John saw it first, and he leaned over to look at it." Marin
was aware that Philip's thumbs suddenly stilled. "I crouched down to see, too
We were both focused on the bird when we heard someone behind us say, 'Hey
ree-tard, what are you doing?'"

Marin swallowed, and Philip's hands jerked away. His emotional response to her words didn't surprise her—Philip was so empathetic to the plight of people who were mistreated. She didn't look at his face but instead kept her gaze on his clenched fists, which now rested in his lap. "I stood up. There were three boys—probably all John's age—high schoolers, for sure. Two of them stood right behind us; the third one stood off on the sidewalk, just watching and listening. John pointed at the bird and told them a baby bird had fallen out of its nest. I knew he hoped the boys could help us put it back.

"But the boys didn't offer to help. Instead the tallest one poked his friend and made fun of the way John talked. He repeated, 'A baby biwd,' and the two laughed. I grabbed John's hand and told him we needed to go, but John wouldn't budge. He was too worried about the bird. He asked if the boys would help."

Marin paused, and Philip cut in, his tone stiff. "Of course they didn't help."

She shook her head, pushing her hair behind her ears. "No. They told John to try scaring the bird. Said if he scared it enough it would fly up to its nest. I knew that wasn't true, and I tried again to get John to come with me, but he wouldn't listen to me. He asked the boys how to scare it. 'Stomp at it,' they said."

A sob caught in Marin's throat. "So John did. He lifted his foot to stomp at it. And the tallest boy pushed him. John lost his balance, and when his foot came down—"

Philip's harsh voice interrupted. "I already know, Marin. Don't say it."

Marin lifted her gaze to look at him. His face appeared blurred through her tears. "Oh, Philip, the look on John's face when he realized what he'd done. He was devastated. John would never intentionally hurt anything, and he'd killed the little bird. He covered his face and dropped to his knees. Then he began wailing—a horrible cry. The worst sound I've ever heard."

"And the boys just laughed." Philip's tone was flat.

Marin nodded, affirming his guess. "Yes. They laughed, called John clumsy, said, 'Look what you did, ree-tard. What a ree-tard,' and they walked off like nothing of importance had happened. I wanted to run after them, to knock them down, to hurt them as badly as they had hurt my brother." Her voice quivered with indignation, amazed at how fresh the anger still felt after all the years that had passed. "But I was just a little girl. I couldn't protect John. All I could do was take him by the hand and lead him home. He cried all the way. He cried himself to sleep that night. It was months before he could look at a bird without getting upset again. It was so awful."

Marin swept away her tears. "I was so angry at those boys. They made me feel so helpless. Later, when I replayed the whole thing in my mind, I found that I was especially angry at the one who stood off to the side and watched it happen. I was too small to do anything, but that boy was as big as the others. He could have stopped them, if he'd wanted to. Yet he did nothing. Just watched and did nothing."

She sighed. "So many people do that. They don't actively involve themselves in the mistreatment of people with handicaps, but by their silence, they allow it to happen. There are more silent people than those who are openly cruel. What if all those silent people spoke up? Wouldn't things change?"

Philip stared straight ahead, his fingers clutched so tightly his knuckles glowed white.

Marin was touched that he appeared upset. It proved how much he cared for John. She shook her head, finishing her story. "That was the end of John going out anymore, unless Mom or Dad was with him. Mom never trusted people with him again. She kept John close to her for the rest of her life. At least he was safe with her."

"Safe. . .and locked away. Friendly, personable John, just locked away. . . ." Philip's tone sounded as if he'd drifted off somewhere and was talking to himself. Then he seemed to give a start and brought his gaze around to meet hers. "Have you been able to forgive them?" The question came out low, pained.

Marin knew without asking that he referred to the boys. "It was so hurtful. It changed so many things for us. I suppose I should forgive them. It would be the Christian thing to do. But to be honest, no—I probably haven't." She waited for Philip to begin a lecture, to remind her that Christ instructed His followers to forgive just as His Father forgives. Instead he voiced another question.

"If you were to meet up with those boys today, what would you say to them?" His voice sounded strange, hollow. Her story had obviously affected him deeply.

Marin had considered that question before. "If I had the chance to talk to those boys, I would ask why they did it. John wasn't bothering them. There was no reason to be mean to him." A wave of hurt and anger swelled in her chest. Then she shrugged. "But what good would it do? They obviously didn't care about John's feelings. People like that—I guess I don't have any respect for them."

Philip nodded slowly. His face seemed pale, his muscles tense.

Marin frowned. "Philip, are you okay? You look kind of funny."

"Actually, Marin, I am feeling rather—odd. Maybe I should head for home."

Concern immediately replaced the other emotions. "Are you okay to ride your cycle?"

He nodded again, but he appeared to have difficulty controlling his movements. His neck seemed stiff. "Yes. Thank you for worrying, but I'll be fine. Let's go."

Instead of the winding route they had taken earlier, he drove directly to her house and helped her off without saying a word. She watched as he propped his helmet on the backrest and dug in his pocket. He held out a set of keys. "Would you give these to Eileen and tell her she can keep Dixie? I'll ride to her place and get it later."

His change in demeanor caused a lump to form in her stomach. She reached for the keys, but she clamped her hand around his fist. "Will we see you at church tomorrow?"

"Yes." He stared off to the side. "Would you like me to sit with John in his pew?"

What had happened to the warm tone he always used with her? He seemed like a stranger. "Yes, if you wouldn't mind. He's very excited about sharing the best seat in the house with you."

A slight smile—almost a grimace—flashed across Philip's face. "I'm glad I can do something right. . . ."

Marin frowned. He was acting so strangely! "Philip?" She tugged at his hand.

He finally looked at her, his brown-eyed gaze seeming to search below the surface, and he opened his mouth as if to say something important. But then his jaw snapped shut, and he pulled his hand away. "Thanks for giving Eileen those keys. Good night, Marin."

The stiff, formal bearing made Marin's heartbeat rise in alarm. Something was wrong. Her voice faltered. "No problem. Thank you for the ride."

He nodded, his gaze now aimed somewhere off to the side. Without another word, he strode to his cycle. Leaving the helmet on the backrest, he swung his leg over the seat, started the engine, and roared away. He didn't look back to wave or acknowledge Marin's presence in any way.

His abrupt departure left Marin feeling as if a cold wind had blown around her heart.

# Chapter 12

Philip clenched the handlebars of his cycle, resisting the urge to drive recklessly. His heart pounded, the blood rushing through his ears. Tears formed in his eyes, but the force of wind in his face dried them before they had a chance to run. He glimpsed his helmet in the rearview mirror. It spun on the backrest. He should stop and put it on his head. But it was too much effort. He twisted his wrist, giving the cycle a surge that caused the powerful machine to leap forward as he aimed the bike toward a country road outside town.

Marin's story repeated itself in his brain. He could picture it all—the little blond-haired girl crouching beside the tree, her bulky brother leaning forward in an awkward pose. The intruding strangers teasing, taunting, then a pair of hands applied to John's back. Even over the wind in his ears, Philip could hear the anguished cries that poured from John's soul when the baby bird lay dead beneath his foot.

"Oh, why did I allow it?" he mourned, remembering how he had remained on the sidewalk, watching, wishing his brother would just come on and leave that poor boy alone. But Marin was right—he hadn't said a word. Fear had kept him silent. Fear of Rocky, older by four years and so much stronger. He had never stood up to Rocky. How he wished he had. That choice—that choice to stay silent while his brother played a cruel trick—had forced Marin's family into hiding.

Philip was hardly aware of the empty, stretching landscape, the cows grazing beneath a sky of robin's egg blue tinted with pink. Beneath his bike, the asphalt rushed by, the faded white center lines becoming a blur as he pushed the cycle faster and faster. But he couldn't escape the guilt that pressed upon him.

If he had stepped forward, if he had tried to defend John, how differently the story would have ended. Marin would have gone home to say, "Mom, some boys tried to hurt John, but another boy stopped them." And Marin's mother would have known that kindness existed in the world—she would have had no need to shut her son away out of fear.

"I'm sorry, Marin. I'm so sorry. . . ." The wind carried his words away. If he said them to her, would she accept his apology? Would she know he was sincere? Would she forgive him? The family had paid the price for his mistake—more than a dozen years of hiding. How could he make up for that?

A hard thud, followed by several tings, sounded behind him, and he looked in his rearview mirror. His helmet bounced two more times before spinning into the weed-scattered shoulder. He slowed the bike, turned it around, then pulled onto the side of the road and killed the engine. Anger billowed as he stomped to the fallen helmet. He scooped it up, sucking his breath through his teeth when he saw the series of deep scuffs left from the sliding ride across asphalt.

Philip ran his fingers over the lines of scratches, his chest tight and tears pressing once more behind his eyes. The helmet would never be the same—forever scarred. Just as he'd left John and Marin—forever scarred inside. Raising his face to the sky overhead, he cried out, "I'm sorry! I'm so sorry for what I did. Please, God—please let them forgive me."

The only reply was the whisper of the wind and the distant cry of a songbird.

—

Philip pulled his pickup into his designated spot in the apartment's parking area, unloaded the cycle, and rolled it into his storage area. He took another look at the helmet. In the dim light, the damage was barely visible, but when he rubbed the back of his wrist against the scuff marks, he could easily feel them. He released a sigh of deep sadness then gently placed the helmet on the backrest. After securing the padlock on the shed door, he headed to his apartment.

Inside, he tugged off his boots and hung his jacket in the tiny entry closet. Flipping on lights as he went, he moved through the narrow foyer to the kitchen. On the counter, the blinking red light on the answering machine signaled that someone had called. He considered ignoring it but decided it could be one of his clients. He leaned his elbow on the counter and pushed the button.

"Philip, this is Brad Carlson," came the voice of his lawyer. Philip punched the volume button twice to increase the sound and leaned closer to the machine, his heart pounding. "Good news. I got a notice from the bank today. A deposit was made for three thousand dollars into your business account. Apparently the donor is active again. Thought you'd want to know. I'll talk to you Monday."

The line went dead. Philip stood, relief washing over him. If the donor truly were active again, New Beginnings would be able to function at full capacity. *"You will protect me from trouble and surround me with songs of deliverance."* The words from Psalms replayed in his memory.

He closed his eyes and breathed a prayer. *Thank You, Lord, for this deliverance.* What a comfort it was to know his clients would be cared for and no employees would need to be let go. His burden should have been lifted with this news. Yet he still felt as if a great weight pressed on his chest.

He sank onto a bar stool, covering his face with his hands. What of the problem of Marin and John? The money, no matter how welcome, could never solve that problem. Marin would continue to keep John tucked away, and it was all his fault.

"How can I make it up to them, Lord?" He felt so hypocritical now for the flowery speeches he had made to Marin about letting John go. It had been his action that had sent her family into hiding in the first place. *Well,* he corrected himself, grimacing with the memory of Marin's painful story, *it was Rocky's action and my lack of action.*

Philip had told Marin he wasn't able to change the past. How he wished it were possible. If only he could turn back time, start that day again, and stand up against Rocky's cruelty. Philip understood Rocky—their father had been a hard, unyielding man who had ruled the household with an iron fist. Rocky had found ways of making himself feel powerful by bullying smaller or weaker children. Philip understood it, but he'd never liked it. Rocky had bullied him, too, and fear of retribution had kept him silent that day.

Suddenly restless, he got up and walked to the window that overlooked the backyard. A streetlight gently illuminated the area. All appeared quiet, peaceful. Philip's thoughts were anything but.

That day and John's anguished response to Rocky's bullying had changed everything for him. He'd never again run with Rocky and his friends. Instead he'd started hanging out with a new boy on the block—David Phelps. David's family had invited him to church, and he'd met Jesus. The Phelpses had become like a second family to Philip, and even after they moved away, their influence remained strong. He'd understood the meaning of gentle strength after being with David's father, and he had tried to adopt the same characteristic in his own life despite Rocky's endless teasing.

If only he had met David earlier, maybe he wouldn't have been with Rocky the day he encountered Marin Brooks and her older brother. Philip closed his eyes, trying to forget the fear and desperation in the child Marin's eyes as the bigger boys tormented gentle, unresisting John. Those hazel eyes had looked at him, silently begging him to help, but he had stayed still and silent on the sidewalk, doing nothing. Not even when the baby bird lay crushed and John had fallen to his knees in distress had Philip intervened. He'd merely followed his brother on down the street, on to the Tasti-Freeze for a soda with vanilla flavoring—his favorite drink.

He released a mirthless huff. Somehow, after that day, soda with vanilla had never again tasted good. Just as the smell of grass tormented Marin's nose, the taste of vanilla soda was like bile to Philip's tongue.

He spun from the window and stood in the middle of the living room, his heart aching, deep regret filling him. He wanted to escape it, but there was no way to get away from himself. The only solution, he knew, was to seek Marin's forgiveness. If she could forgive him, perhaps he'd be able to set aside the memory, to release the burden of guilt and shame.

What had she said when he'd asked her if she had been able to forgive the boys who hurt John? He pressed his memory, seeking her exact words. And then they came, uttered in a pained, hopeless tone. *"People like that—I guess I don't have any respect for them."* People like that—people without compassion or tolerance. That's how she'd seen him that day. The pain stabbed. Maybe she'd see him that way again if she knew he had been the one standing aside, unwilling to help.

Marin had been right when she said there were more silent people than intentionally cruel people. But ignoring a wrong was the same as involving oneself in it—he knew that. He'd tried not to be silent against wrong after that day. He'd vowed never again to stand by silently and watch someone be abused simply because he was different. He'd promised God and himself that he'd make a positive impact on the lives of those whom society often mistreated whether through deliberate cruelty or casual indifference.

The problem was, his determination had come one event too late. He'd been fooling himself for years. It didn't matter how many lives he impacted for good with New Beginnings. He could never change the impact he'd made on John and Marin Brooks and their parents. Nothing would make up for that.

He groaned, drawing his hand across his brow. How would he ever face them again now that he knew what he'd done to them?

———◦———

Marin sat with John in his pew, watching for Philip. Philip had said he would be here—it wasn't like him not to keep his word. Yet the service would start in only a few minutes, and he was nowhere in sight. John fidgeted, twisting his head back and forth to check both sets of doors every few seconds. Marin knew he was as concerned as she about Philip's absence.

"Philip is not coming," John whispered as the man who made morning announcements stepped up to the podium.

Marin patted his knee. "Something must have come up, John. Don't worry."

John shook his head, his hazel eyes sad. "He is not coming. He will not sit with me today."

Marin's heart turned over in sympathy at his bereft appearance. "Do you want me to sit with you?"

He shook his head.

"Are you sure?"

"You sit with Aunt Lenore. She will be lonely by herself."

It was typical of John to think of someone else's feelings. Marin squeezed his knee and whispered, "Okay. I'll get you after the service." She crossed quickly to the pew in which Aunt Lenore sat. Another couple had scooted in next to her aunt, so Marin had to step over them. She settled herself between the couple and her aunt, leaning close to whisper in Lenore's ear, "Philip didn't come, so John's alone."

Aunt Lenore's eyebrows drew down in worry. "You did tell him to behave, didn't you?"

Marin nodded, irritation rising. Why couldn't Aunt Lenore be sympathetic to John's feeling about being left to sit alone? But she only said, "We talked over breakfast about staying quiet."

"Good."

Surreptitious glances in John's direction through the announcements, chorus singing, and offertory convinced Marin that John would be fine today. The sadness still showed in his eyes—he obviously felt hurt that Philip hadn't come—but he remained quiet and respectful in the center of his pew.

A soloist stepped to the front, and an accompaniment track began to play. Marin recognized the introductory notes and settled back, eagerly anticipating the delivery of one of her favorite songs. She became lost in the message of the song and almost didn't hear Aunt Lenore's horrified hiss.

"Oh no. What's he doing now?"

Without asking, Marin knew she meant John, and her heart accelerated in nervous trepidation. She cranked her head around until she could see him in his familiar spot. He was at his pew, but not sitting. Instead he'd risen to his feet, his face turned toward the ceiling, his hands over his head.

*Oh no, John. Please sit down!* John's love for music had probably brought him to his feet, but when he became lost in his own pleasure, he could forget where he was. What would Aunt Lenore do if he began dancing up the aisle as he often danced through the hallways at home? What would the others in church think? A pressure built in Marin's chest, worry and protectiveness combined.

A sharp elbow jabbed into Marin's ribs, and she nearly leaped out of the pew. "Marin, make him sit down! He's making a fool of himself!"

Marin swung her gaze quickly right and left. Trapped in the center of the pew, how could she get out without causing more of a scene than John's arm waving could create? Yet disobeying Aunt Lenore's command was out of the question.

The singer at the front of the church broke into a wonderful chorus—her eloquent voice carrying the melody on sweet notes of praise. A glimpse around the congregation showed all were focused on the song. She was thankful no one appeared to have noticed John.

Marin felt caught. If she sneaked out and John wouldn't cooperate with her, they would pull attention away from the ministry of the music. She couldn't decide what to do.

Aunt Lenore poked her again. She gave Marin no choice. Marin turned in the pew, ready to rise; but then she looked at John once more, and her heart nearly stopped.

John still stood, still moved, but now Marin could see that his motions weren't wild actions of improper behavior. He was signing the words to the song! She sat mesmerized, watching as the next verse began. John listened intently, his gold-flecked, almond-shaped eyes alight with pleasure as his hands perfectly formed the heart-stirring words. Suddenly his image was blurred as tears filled her eyes. He was worshipping. There was no doubt.

Marin swept the tears away and glanced at the singer. John was right in her line of vision—was he distracting her? Her serene expression convinced Marin that John hadn't negatively impacted her concentration. In fact, at a small break in the music, she even seemed to smile in his direction.

Behind the singer, the choir members all appeared to be focused on John. Marin let her gaze rove across each face. From the sheen in many of their eyes, it was evident they were touched. No one looked upset or bothered by John—they seemed to be captivated by his sincere involvement. Tears stung again as Marin realized the singer and choir members were seeing John as she saw him. A great lump of love and gratitude filled her throat.

Aunt Lenore pulled back her arm to wham Marin again, but Marin put her hand on her aunt's elbow and whispered, "Aunt Lenore, he isn't throwing a fit. Look at him. Really *look* at John."

With a moue of displeasure, she swung her head to the side and looked. And her shoulders stiffened. John crossed his stumpy hands, which each formed the letter L, in front of his rapt face and brought them in a wide arc to his sides—*Lord*. His flat face shone with the glory of the word.

"Oh, my–y–y. . ." Aunt Lenore's vein-lined hand rested on her bodice, and Marin could see it quivering—with revulsion, anguish, or embarrassment? Lenore's gaze remained riveted on John until the end of the song.

At the final refrain, John placed one hand on his forehead and dropped to his knees, his head bowed low, his other hand reaching for the heavens.

At that moment, Marin heard a strangled sob. Aunt Lenore. She must be mortified beyond tolerance. Marin's heart clutched. Appropriate behavior in church was so important to her aunt. How would Marin defend John after his emotional display had wrought such a reaction from her?

Aunt Lenore turned to look at Marin. Tears coursed down her wrinkled cheeks, but there was no anger or recrimination in her normally icy expression. Squeezing Marin's hand, she whispered, "Let me out, Marin."

Marin tipped her head, puzzled.

"I want to sit with my nephew."

Marin pulled her knees back and allowed Aunt Lenore to step past her. She watched, amazed, as Lenore went directly to John and placed her hand on his shoulder. He lifted his gaze to her, and Marin could see him cringe. But then Aunt Lenore held out her arms. With a huge smile, John stepped into her embrace. After the hug, the two sat side by side on John's bench.

Marin brought her gaze forward again, hardly able to believe what she'd just witnessed. Philip had been right. Somehow, seeing John's response to the song had changed Aunt Lenore's perspective. Somehow it had allowed her to see the

John underneath—his tender, loving heart that had been invisible to her all these years. And if Aunt Lenore could change, then maybe. . .

The lump returned to her throat, and she swallowed hard. *Then maybe*, her thoughts continued, *others can change, too.* She could hardly wait to share this amazing transformation with Philip.

# Chapter 13

Philip felt ridiculous crouched behind the partition, listening as Marin greeted Eileen. But he couldn't face her. Not knowing what he'd done twelve years ago. And not after leaving John alone in his church pew yesterday. He was too ashamed to see her. So he remained in his hiding spot, secretly eavesdropping.

"Well, will you tell Philip I'd like to talk to him when I pick up John today?" Marin's voice carried to his ear. He detected a thread of controlled excitement in her tone. "Something happened I want to share with him."

"I'll tell him," Eileen said, her voice firm and determined, and Philip grimaced, imagining Eileen's expression. "Believe me, I'll tell him."

"Thank you. Good-bye, Eileen. Good-bye, John. Have a good day." The door clicked, signaling her departure.

With a sigh, Philip straightened and came around the partition to find Eileen, her arms crossed, glowering in his direction. He felt heat build in his cheeks. She held her tongue while John greeted Philip—to his relief, John didn't mention Philip's lack of appearance yesterday—and puttered off to the corner with Andrew and Bobby. But the moment John was out of earshot, she erupted.

"Well, isn't this a pretty day when my duties include espionage."

Philip forced a laugh. "Now, Eileen, you were hardly spying on anyone."

"Well, whatever I was doing, I didn't like it, pretending you weren't here when you *were* right here, no doubt listening to every word." She pointed at him, scowling fiercely. "You *did* hear what she said."

Philip nodded. "I heard."

"And you *will* take the time to talk to her at the end of the day. No more hiding."

It was a command, not a question, and for a moment, Philip felt resentment. Eileen was one of his employees, not his boss. But he knew she was right—his behavior hadn't been professional, and he would need to talk to Marin. His stomach fluttered so badly he was sure bats had taken to flight within his middle. He gave a brusque nod. "I'll talk to her."

"Good." Eileen immediately dropped her stern pose and stepped close, putting a hand on Philip's forearm. Her entire countenance softened. "Now—do you want to tell me what happened Saturday night on that motorcycle ride? You hardly said two words to me when you picked up Dixie. I have two good listening ears, if

89

you want to make use of them."

Philip offered a smile and patted Eileen's hand. Warmth toward this crusty lady filled his middle, dispelling the bats. The temptation to share his burden pressed at his tongue. But he shook his head instead. Eileen thought so highly of him, had praised his work here so many times. He couldn't bear her disappointment if she knew what he'd done. "Thanks for the offer, Eileen. I appreciate it. But talking won't change anything."

Eileen's lips drooped into a disappointed frown. "You mean nothing's going to happen between you and Marin?"

Philip's brows came down. "What do you mean by that?"

Eileen gave his arm a squeeze and smiled wisely. "You know what I mean. I've worked with you for four years now, and I've gotten to know you pretty well. I've never seen you look at anybody the way you look at Marin. You care for her, you silly man. And I'd bet my last dollar that she cares for you."

Philip shook his head slowly, denying her words. "Eileen, you're imagining things."

She huffed. "I'm not so old I've gone senile. No, you two have the makings of something special cooking." She released his arm and stepped back, fixing him with a stern expression. "But you'll mess it up if you don't repair whatever got broken on Saturday. You can't hide from her forever—she brings John here every day."

"Maybe not," Philip inserted, remembering Marin's message. "She said she had something to tell me—maybe she's found a day care placement for John so she won't need to come here anymore."

"Well, I'm gonna hope not," Eileen said firmly as she turned and strode away, " 'cause if ever two people fit together, it's you and Marin."

No matter how hard he tried, Philip could not set aside Eileen's parting comment from the morning. All day long, he kept wondering, did he and Marin fit? Could it be God had brought Marin to New Beginnings for more than to find assistance for John? He had given up praying for a wife long ago. He'd convinced himself that no woman would want to involve herself and her children—because Philip would want children—in his life's work.

But Marin wasn't like most women. Her experience with John made her different. Her kindness to John made her different. Maybe. . .

But no—he tried again to push the idea away. Once Marin knew of his involvement that April day, she'd never look at him the same way again. It was best to end it now, before his feelings were as obvious to her as they had been to Eileen.

He turned his attention to his ledger, refiguring his budgets. The deposit from his unknown donor made such a difference. July would beam brighter, thanks to the end of his financial worries. He breathed another prayer of thankfulness for the money. Then, curious, he impulsively picked up the telephone and dialed Brad Carlson's office. Once he had the lawyer on the phone, he said, "Brad, thanks so much for getting this donation business straightened out. Any idea why it didn't come through in May?"

The sound of papers shuffling was heard before Brad answered. "From what I understood, the original donor—who preferred to be anonymous—was killed in an accident in late May. Hence he was unable to make the transfer of funds. But his beneficiary—who also desires to remain anonymous—recently learned of the transactions and chose to resume them. According to the bank statement, these deposits are set up to occur on the thirtieth of each month until next June, so you won't need to wonder from month to month what will happen."

Philip sat, stunned. The word "accident" played in his head over and over. His throat felt tight, but he managed to say, "This is great. But—you're sure you don't have a name? I'd really like to thank this—individual." His heart pounded.

"No, I'm afraid I don't, Philip. The lawyer representing the donor was adamant that it be kept anonymous. Something about right hands and left hands. I don't understand what that meant, but I do understand the word 'anonymous.' I'm sorry. I'll send your thanks through the lawyer, if you'd like."

"I would. Thank you." Philip hung up the receiver with a hand that shook. Could it have been Darin Brooks donating to New Beginnings all this time? And if it were, then that meant now Marin— Philip pressed his fists to his forehead, reeling. That meant Marin was now giving money to the man who had so badly hurt her family. How could he continue to accept these funds from her? And how could he not accept them? New Beginnings depended on that money. If Philip declined its receipt, his clients would suffer.

The event had haunted Philip for years. It was clear to him he would never be free of the consequences of that afternoon's choice.

Marin skipped the final two steps leading to the front door of New Beginnings. The entire day, she'd had a lightness in her heart. She was finding her stride as the owner of Brooks Advertising. Aunt Lenore's change in attitude toward John eliminated the problem of where he would spend his days. Mr. Whitehead had started the contributions to Dad's mysterious charity again, which made her feel as if she were truly following in Dad's footsteps. Everything was falling into place.

And she wanted to share all of these happy thoughts with Philip. She paused for a moment, her hand on the doorknob. Why was it so important for Philip to be the one to celebrate these happenings with her? Her heart tripped. She knew why. Suddenly eager, she swung the door wide and bounced through.

Her gaze swept the area, taking in the neat arrangement of centers and the happy busyness of the few people remaining. Eileen and John sat at a table near the back corner. When she came in, they looked up and Eileen gave a wave.

"Good afternoon, Marin! John and I have been rolling silverware, but I think he's bored with it. He'll be glad to go home today, right, John?"

John nodded, as if in slow motion, then pushed himself to his feet. He ambled across the floor to Marin as Eileen bellowed, "Philip! Marin is here!"

Philip appeared from behind the partition, which Marin knew defined the break area. He approached as slowly as John had. Marin found herself feeling impatient with both of them. This was a happy day! Why did they appear so gloomy?

The moment Philip was in listening distance, Marin began to bubble. "Philip, you'll never guess what happened in church yesterday." She paused, tipping her head. "By the way, where were you?" Then she waved her hands. "Oh, never mind, it doesn't matter right now. You weren't there so John sat by himself, and he gave the most incredible performance of sign language."

She paused to put her arm around John's shoulder and give him a quick smile. He felt warm. "Whew, John, you must have worked hard at rolling silverware—you're all sweaty." She dropped her arm and turned back to Philip. "Aunt Lenore watched it, and—oh, Philip"—she felt tears form in her eyes—"it happened. She saw John—the real John—and just as you said, her perception changed. It was the most amazing thing."

Impulsively she stepped forward and embraced Philip in a hug of gratitude. She hardly gave Philip time to respond before stepping back and continuing excitedly. "After church, we had dinner with Aunt Lenore, as we usually do, and she volunteered to have John spend days with her until I find other arrangements. Isn't that wonderful?"

Philip smiled, but she saw no happy sparkle in his eyes. "Yes, Marin, I'm happy for you. I know you've been concerned."

Marin felt impatience building. What had happened to the Philip she'd known for weeks? A stranger had stepped into his skin on Saturday, and it seemed that stranger still remained. She put her hands on her hips. "Honestly, Philip, I'd think you could get a little excited with me here. After all, you're the one with the goal of changing the world. I thought it would please you to know one small corner of it made a huge change!"

Philip lowered his gaze for a moment, slipping his hands into his pockets and rocking on his heels, much the way John did when he was contemplating something. He finally lifted his head to meet her gaze again, and the smile appeared more realistic. "I am pleased you can count on your aunt, Marin. That's a real answer to prayer. So—when will John start going there?"

Marin shrugged. "I thought I'd let him finish the week here, give him a chance to say good-bye to everyone, and we'd start at Aunt Lenore's next Monday."

Philip nodded and opened his mouth, but John interrupted.

"Will my job be at Aunt Lenore's house?"

Marin gave a start. "Job? Well, John—you'll hang out with Aunt Lenore the way you used to hang out with Mom. You'll stay with her and keep her company."

John pulled a face. "That is not a job. I want a job. Everybody gets a job."

Philip seemed to watch this exchange with interest.

Marin gave Philip a helpless look then turned back to her brother. "I don't know what you mean."

John blew out a snort. "Everybody gets a job here! Anita got a job, Lloyd got a job, Bobby got a job—I have not got a job yet. I want one. That is why I am here. To get a job."

"But, John, you'll be with—"

John covered his ears with his hands and squeezed his eyes shut. "I will not listen, Marin! You are not being nice. You will not let me have a job. You think I am stupid. Stupid! Stupid!" He coughed.

Marin grabbed his hands and pulled them down. "John, stop it. I don't think you're stupid." She tugged at his wrists, her voice gentling. "John, please look at me."

John opened one eye.

"John, you know I don't think you're stupid."

Both eyes opened, and he coughed again, pulling one hand free to cover his mouth. When he'd finished coughing he asked, his eyes sad, "Then why can I not get a job, Marin? I want a job, too."

Marin looked at Philip. She saw sympathy in his expression, and she asked for help with her eyes. He must have understood, because he put his hand on John's shoulder and took over.

"John, most of the people here go *out* and work. But you've been working *here*. New Beginnings has been your job all along." John gave him a dubious look. Philip went on enthusiastically. "Sure it has been. You've helped Eileen, and you've helped Andrew. You helped Bobby learn how to load the dishwasher. You've done a great job, John. We're all proud of the job you've done."

John shook his head sadly. "It is not the same." He coughed again, longer this time.

Philip frowned. "Hey, buddy, are you feeling all right?" He turned to Marin. "You know, John's been dragging all day."

Marin touched John's forehead, and her pulse raced in alarm. "John, do you feel sick?"

"I am very tired," he said. His shoulders drooped, and his hazel eyes didn't hold their usual sparkle.

"Well, we'll have to discuss this job business another time. I think you've got the summer flu. I'm taking you home and putting you to bed." She turned to Philip. "He's got a fever. We probably won't be here tomorrow."

"Can I do anything to help?" he asked, his brows pulled down in concern.

Marin shook her head. She could handle things. "Thanks, but we'll be okay."

Philip touched her arm. "I'll say a prayer for John."

Her heart lifted with his sweet words. *Philip Wilder, you are almost too good to be true.* She forced a light laugh. "Might pray for me, too. I'm not the best nurse."

He nodded, his expression serious. "I always do."

Marin thought her heart might burst through her chest. She took John's arm before she did something foolish, like give Philip Wilder a kiss right in front of Eileen and John. "Come on, John. Let's get you home."

# Chapter 14

Marin was awakened by the sound of coughing. She squinted at the alarm clock on her nightstand, her vision blurry. It read 3:04. With a sigh, she threw back her covers and padded down the hallway. Turning on John's bedside lamp, she saw his face was flushed. She touched his forehead and cringed at the heat.

John opened his eyes and gave her a bleary look. "I am sick, Marin."

"I know, John. I'll get you some more aspirin." She hurried to the kitchen, got two tablets, and poured a cup of apple juice, then returned. But when she tried to get John to sit up and take the aspirin, he turned cranky and pushed the cup away, splashing his sheets with apple juice. His crankiness increased when Marin forced him out of bed so she could change the sheets. She shifted him to the sofa, covered him with a quilt, and allowed him to stay there even after the bed was ready rather than move him again.

She sank down on the blue floral padded chair that had been Mother's favorite spot and watched John sleep. His breathing seemed labored, his chest rising and falling in an abnormal rhythm. Without taking her eyes from him, Marin prayed silently. *Lord, please let this illness pass so he can feel better again.*

Philip's words came back to her—his offer to pray for John and his indication that he always prayed for her. Was Philip awake right now, praying, too? The thought comforted her. She yawned, settling back with her head nestled in the corner of the chair. She remembered the feeling of being nestled in Philip's arms on the park bench when she'd told him about the boys who had traumatized John. It had felt so good, so right, to be held there.

Closing her eyes, she imagined the sturdiness of his chest beneath her cheek, the strength of his arms around her back, the gentle way he had prodded her to share her hurt so he could help. Then her eyes popped open, remembering how he had changed after she'd told him what had happened that day so long ago. He hadn't been the same since.

She frowned. She wasn't surprised the story affected him—it was Philip's goal to keep those kinds of abuses from happening to people like John. But why it made him treat her differently she couldn't understand. Yawning again, she realized she was too tired to puzzle it out now. She needed to think about tomorrow, about caring for John. First thing in the morning, she would call Dick Ross and let him know she wouldn't be coming in to the office. And she should call Aunt Lenore—she might know of something that would help John feel better. And she'd need to. . .

Her thoughts drifted away as sleep claimed her once more.

⸙

"Marin. . .Marin. . ."

The word finally filtered through Marin's foggy brain and registered. She sat bolt upright and sprang from the chair, then dropped to her knees beside the couch. Touching her brother's hot forehead, she said soothingly, "Yes, John, I'm here."

John tossed his head. "Hurts. . . Chest hurts. . ."

Fingers of early morning light slipped through the lace panels covering the picture window, gently illuminating John's features. His lips appeared bluish in tint! Her heart immediately set up a clamor. "Oh, John." Tucking the quilt beneath his chin, she promised, "You'll be okay. I'm going to get help for you. Hang in there." Tears pressed behind her lids as she dialed 9-1-1. "Operator, I need an ambulance. It's my brother—he's very sick."

⸙

Philip strode through the hospital corridor, checking room numbers. His chest felt tight as he recalled Marin's panicked phone call an hour ago. Guilt assailed him—he should have been more aware of John's behavior yesterday. John had been droopy, had coughed off and on all day, but Philip had been caught up in his own worries. He had admitted as much to Eileen when he had called her to see if she could man the fort for the day.

"How could I have been so oblivious? I know people with Down syndrome are susceptible to respiratory illness. I should've paid more attention."

Eileen had been firm in her response. "Now that's enough, Philip. I spent most of the afternoon with John, and I didn't for one minute believe he was that sick. All the worrying in the world yesterday wouldn't have changed this outcome, so stop fretting." Then she'd added, "I can handle New Beginnings today. You go to the hospital and be with Marin—she'll need your support."

Philip wanted to be with Marin—to be her support. If he was honest with himself, he wanted to be her support for the rest of her life. *But, God, will she reject my friendship when I tell her the truth of my involvement that day?* Philip had determined over the course of the last hour he would not be able to live with himself if he didn't confess it was he and his brother who had terrorized John. If Marin turned away from him, he would have to deal with it, but he wouldn't keep it a secret from her. She had to know.

His gaze lit on number 424—John's room. The door was slightly ajar, and he tapped on it before pushing it open and stepping through. Strange sounds filled his ears—a gentle, rhythmic *whoosh-thump* and a soft whistle. A curtain hid most of the bed from view, but he saw Marin in a plastic chair against the wall, her eyes closed. He cleared his throat. At the sound, she looked up, and her white face took on an expression of great relief. She rushed at him, arms outstretched. "Oh, Philip, I'm so glad you're here!"

He wrapped his arms around her, lowering his head to rest his cheek on the top of her head. It felt wonderful to hold her so close. "How is John?"

Marin pulled back to look up at him, her eyes flooding with tears. "He has bacterial pneumonia. Most times it isn't serious, but with John. . ." Her voice trailed off. Philip knew what she feared, and he offered another hug.

She pulled away again, and he saw her expression change to firm resolution. "When he's better, I'm going to let him have that job. I haven't been fair to John, keeping him to myself. He's such a special person, Philip—he really is. He shines. Even Aunt Lenore knows it now." She swept away the tears that coursed down her cheeks. "Does that vet office still need someone? John would love to be around animals—he's talked over and over about Roscoe the Wonder Cat, and I think it would be good for him to have something to look forward to."

Philip nodded, pride filling his chest. He knew how hard it was for Marin to let John go. "I haven't filled it. I was hoping you'd come around."

"Good." She nodded, stepping away from his embrace but keeping hold of his hand. "Let's tell John." She tugged Philip around the curtain.

Philip's heart turned over in sympathy when he saw John lying in the railed bed. He appeared much smaller and older. A plastic cup covered his mouth and nose, apparently feeding oxygen. A narrow tube led to his arm, a steady drip delivering fluids and antibiotics. Philip found tears in his own eyes as he took John's hand.

"Hey, buddy," he said softly, and John's eyelids fluttered. "I wanted to tell you something big. Remember how you wanted a job?" He waited for another answering flutter. "Well, I picked out a special one for you. You'll get to be with dogs and cats—you'll like that, huh?" He didn't mention the Squawks part of the services.

Slowly John's eyelids opened to half-mast. His gold-flecked eyes appeared glassy with fever, but a small smile showed behind the mask.

"Yeah, I thought you'd like that." Philip squeezed John's hand, feeling a weak, answering squeeze. "But you've got to get better, okay? The dogs and cats are waiting."

John looked at Philip for another long moment, and then his eyes slid shut. Philip stepped back, turning to Marin. "Poor guy. He's really wiped out."

Marin nodded, her gaze on John. "I know. He needs lots of prayers."

Philip guided her to the other side of the curtain. "I called the prayer chain at church before I came over, so prayers are being delivered right now. Eileen said she would pray, too. I was awake around three, and I prayed for both of you before going back to sleep." Philip didn't bother to explain that part of his prayer was she would find the ability to forgive him.

Marin's eyes widened. "You did? I was awake then, and I wondered if—" She broke off, her face flooding with color.

"You wondered if...," he prompted.

But at that moment, the door flew open, and an older woman burst through, her face set in a frown of worry. She descended on Marin, bestowed a short hug, then demanded, "How is he?"

Philip recognized the woman from church—Marin's aunt, Lenore. He listened as Marin answered.

"He's sleeping right now. He seems to be breathing easier, thanks to the oxygen." She shook her head, tears threatening again. "Aunt Lenore, I feel so guilty. He's been rather lethargic and snuffly the past couple of days, but I just thought he had a summer cold. I never imagined—"

Lenore shook her head firmly. "You stop that. Things sneak up on John—always have. Why, your mother would put him to bed at night, thinking he was fine, and come morning he'd be in a terrible state."

"Really?" Marin's tone sounded dubious.

But Lenore nodded firmly. "Really. No sense in crying over spilled milk. He's where he needs to be to get better." She spun and stomped to the curtain. She peeked behind it, gave a brusque nod, then returned to Marin.

"I came over before I had my coffee, and I could sure use a cup." Lenore peered into Marin's face. "It looks as if you need one, too." She reached with a wrinkled hand to caress Marin's cheek. "Now you stop that worrying. God took my sister, but He's not going to take John—not just yet. Not until I've had the chance to really love him." Tears appeared in the woman's eyes, but she thrust out her chin and blinked, eliminating the moisture. Whirling on Philip, she asked, "Who are you?"

Philip held out his hand. "Philip Wilder. I'm—"

"You're the friend John talks about—the one who sat with him in church a couple of weeks ago," she inserted, nodding. "It was good of you to come. Maybe you can talk this girl into leaving for that coffee." When Marin opened her mouth to protest, Lenore cut in, "Now I can sit and watch him sleep just as well as you can. And I'll send out a cry if something changes. Go on—the cafeteria is in the basement. Drink your coffee slow, let it put some life back into you, and bring me a cup when you return."

Marin turned a tired smile on Philip. "We might as well. Aunt Lenore usually gets her way."

"And don't you forget it," Lenore agreed. "Go." She grabbed the chair on which Marin had been sitting and scooted it next to John's bed. She plunked herself into it, her back straight as a poker, and took John's hand. Without turning her gaze away from John's face, she ordered, "Didn't I tell you to go?"

Philip put a hand on Marin's back and guided her into the hallway. He released a chuckle. "She's something else."

Marin nodded. "Yes, she is. As gruff as Mother was gentle. And I never thought I'd have her as an ally. God can do amazing things."

Philip thought about what he needed to tell Marin. Considering the harm he'd done, it might take one of God's amazing miracles for her to forgive him. "Let's go get that coffee," he said. "There's something I'd like to talk to you about."

In the cafeteria, Philip led Marin to a private corner and pulled out her chair. He seated himself across from her and watched as she doctored her coffee with generous portions of cream and sugar. She looked up and found him watching, and a light blush stole across her cheeks. The blush gave her an innocent look that was nearly irresistible. Her hazel eyes were soft, warm, full of appreciation, and for a moment, he faltered in his resolve to confess. He didn't want her expression to change to one of harsh anger.

She took a careful sip and murmured, "Mm, that's good. Aunt Lenore was right—this should put some life back into me." She then tipped her head; concern colored her tone. "Philip, you look so serious. Is it worry for John making you seem so—austere?" Her fine brows came down. "Actually you've not been yourself with me since last Saturday. Did I do or say something to upset you?"

Philip took a draw of his own coffee, giving himself time to collect his thoughts. Although he'd thought of little else since Saturday than telling her, now that the opportunity had presented itself, he couldn't find the right words.

"Philip, please talk to me." Marin reached across the table to take his hand. "I hope you know how much John and I have come to...care...about you. If I've done something, then—"

He pulled his hand away. "It isn't something you've done, Marin. It's something—" He stopped, took a deep breath, and began again. "Marin, I'm not going to be able to accept any more money from you—not unless you know the whole truth and can make a decision with all the facts in place."

She scowled, clearly puzzled. "Well, Philip, if John stays with Aunt Lenore or starts working, then I won't be—"

He held up his hand. "Not *that* money. Of course you won't pay me anymore for letting John come to New Beginnings. I'm talking about the other money. The donation."

Marin shook her head, the scowl deepening. "Philip, what are you talking about?"

Impatient, he admitted, "I know, okay? I know you wanted it to be anonymous, but when my lawyer told me the original donor had died in an accident and his beneficiary was continuing with the donations, I figured it out. I'm sorry if my knowing ruins your pleasure in giving it."

Marin slumped back in the chair, her face turning white. "You mean—it was to you? To New Beginnings? That's where Dad sent—?" She stopped, shaking her head in disbelief. "I didn't know."

Philip found this hard to believe. "How could you not know who you were giving money to? That isn't possible."

Marin frowned at him. "It *is* possible. Dad's lawyer told me Dad wanted the donations to be secret from everyone—including you and including his family. When I found he had been transferring funds, I told the lawyer to continue it, but Mr. Whitehead never told me where the money was going. Dad didn't want his left hand to know what his right hand was doing, and I honored that." She shook her head again, her gaze drifting off somewhere behind him. "So all along, Dad was supporting New Beginnings. . . ."

Philip could see this knowledge had significant meaning to her, but he didn't have time to pursue it right now. He had something else he needed to tell her. "Marin, look at me, please." He waited until he had her full attention. "Since last Saturday, when you told me about the boys who hurt John, I haven't been able to rest."

Her expression softened. "I know. I could tell you were bothered."

"But you don't know why," he insisted, not allowing her to sidetrack him again. He linked his fingers together and pressed his clenched fists to the tabletop. "Marin, even before you told me, I knew about that day. I can even tell you what you were wearing—green plaid shorts and a sleeveless white shirt with a frog embroidered on the right shoulder. And John had red high-top sneakers with white stripes. Am I right?"

Marin's eyes widened. "How did you know that?"

"I know, because I was there."

Her jaw dropped. "You—you were—?"

He nodded miserably. "I stood on the sidewalk and watched it happen. And I kept willing my brother to *just come on*. But he didn't." He swallowed, unable to meet Marin's gaze. "Not until he had finished his fun would he come on." He heard the bitterness in his own tone. With an effort, he faced her again. "Rocky was a bully, Marin. And I was afraid of him. That's why I didn't interfere."

"It was you. . . ." Marin spoke in a barely discernible whisper.

His fingers twitched with the desire to reach out to her. "I am so sorry. I know how much that day cost you. And if there were any way I could do it all over again, I'd help. I'd pull Rocky away. I'd climb the tree for John and put the little bird in its nest. I'd walk you home to make sure you weren't bothered again. I'd—" He broke off, shrugging helplessly. "But I can't do any of those things because it's past. All I can do is tell you how very, very sorry I am for my part in what happened to John and ask you to forgive me." He paused, seeking some sign of what she was thinking. She seemed dead inside—no response at all in her azel eyes. He lowered his gaze. "I know it's a lot to ask."

They sat in silence for several minutes. Finally he heard her swallow, and he ooked at her, hoping for absolution. But instead she pushed back her chair and aid in an emotionless tone, "I'm going to get a cup of coffee for Aunt Lenore nd go back to John's room. Thank you for coming, Philip." Then she walked way without a backward glance.

Philip watched her go. Had he really thought he would feel better once she knew? He closed his eyes, fighting tears. *Oh, Lord, how could I expect her to forgive ne when I can't forgive myself?*

# Chapter 15

John spent five days in the hospital before being released with the instructions to take it easy for another two weeks. Marin, concerned about staying away from the office for that length of time, had nearly wilted with relief when Aunt Lenore stepped in and took over. To Marin's astonishment, their aunt cared for John as if she'd done it for years. The bond between the two of them blossomed quickly, and it was a beautiful thing for Marin to watch.

This afternoon, Marin returned to find the two of them giggling together over a game of checkers. Once again her heart filled with gratefulness to God for working this miracle in her aunt's heart. It reminded her of Philip's statement: "When people like John spend time with people like you and me, they discover just how much alike they are."

As had been the case for the past two weeks, each thought of Philip brought a stab of pain. Although she knew he'd been by the house—John always told her when he had a visitor—he had only come when she was at work. He'd made no effort to contact her. And she had made no effort to contact him. She didn't know what to say to him.

With a sigh, she laid her purse on the counter by the door and crossed to the table, placing her hands on John's shoulders. "Who's winning?" she asked, forcing a cheerful tone.

John twisted around. "I am winning. Aunt Lenore says I am a checker whiz."

Lenore sent a smile and wink in Marin's direction. "He's beaten me three games in a row. I think that's enough for me." She rose, pointing a finger at John. "You just wait, young man. I'm going to practice and come back; then I'll beat you next time!"

John laughed. "Oh, you cannot beat a checker whiz like me." His chest puffed up.

Lenore leaned down to place a kiss on his cheek then hugged Marin. "There's cold chicken and a tub of my potato salad in the refrigerator," she said, heading for the door. Just before stepping out, she added as an afterthought, "Oh—and that Philip Wilder from New Beginnings needs you to call him. Something about John's placement."

"My job!" John exulted.

Marin's heart began thumping a rapid tattoo. So she wouldn't be able to avoid him any longer. "Thanks, Aunt Lenore. I'll give him a call." Her aunt waved and left.

John stood, wringing his hands with excitement. "I will start my job, Marin! I will take care of dogs and cats. I will be kind to them."

Marin listened with half an ear as John bubbled, her thoughts racing ahead to what she would say to Philip. She felt torn in two. Part of her wanted nothing more than to forget what he'd said so they could go back to the easy friendship they'd developed, and part of her wanted to forget he existed. But she knew neither desire was possible. How could she ever forget Philip—his warm smile, his giving heart? And how could she ever forget that day—that hurtful, hateful day? She sighed. She couldn't.

"Marin!" John's fretful voice broke through her thoughts. "I am talking to you!"

Marin gave a start. "Oh, I'm sorry, John. I was lost in thought."

He frowned. "You are not lost. You are in the kitchen."

She laughed, her gloomy feelings washing away. "Oh, John!" She wrapped him in a hug.

He allowed it for a moment then wriggled free. "Marin, you call Philip so I can start my job with the dogs and cats." Taking her hand, he led her to the living room and pointed to the telephone. "Call right now."

Marin's palms began to sweat. "Don't you want to eat first?" she hedged.

He shook his head, his blond hair falling across his high forehead. "No. I want my job first. Call."

She didn't have much choice. She sat down and picked up the phone. The number of New Beginnings was in her telephone's memory bank, so a push on number 3 sent the call through. John stood nearby, his stubby fingers working against each other in happy anticipation. Marin wished he'd go sit down somewhere.

"Hello, New Beginnings," greeted the voice Marin knew well.

"Hi...it's Marin." Her voice came out in a breathy whisper.

There was a long pause and then, equally soft, "Hi, Marin."

She cleared her throat while her heart pounded out a Sousa march. "Aunt Lenore said you called."

"Yes, I did. I have some paperwork that needs to be completed to finalize John's job placement." He sounded businesslike, but not brusque. "Would it be possible to bring it by the house? The sooner it's done, the sooner John can start."

"That—that would be fine," Marin stammered, wondering how she would face him when it was this difficult just to talk to him over the phone.

"Okay. Six or so?"

"Yes—that'll work."

"All right. Thanks, Marin. I know John will enjoy this position." A pause and then: "Good-bye." *Click.* The line went dead.

Marin sat with the phone in her hand, feeling as if something had clicked off inside herself, too.

———⟨⟩———

The doorbell rang at five after six. "That is Philip about my job!" John crowed and started to get up from the kitchen table.

But Marin held up her hand to stop him. "No, John, finish your dinner. I have to fill out the paperwork, but when it's finished, you can visit with Philip, okay?"

John sat back down. It was clear he was disappointed, but he didn't argue. Marin crossed to the door, her stomach in knots, and swung it open. But instead of Philip, she found Eileen on the porch. "Eileen—come on in." She couldn't decide if she felt disappointed or relieved by this surprise.

John was far from disappointed. He joined them at once. "Eileen! Did you bring Roscoe the Wonder Cat?"

Eileen gave John a hug, laughing. "No, no, Roscoe is at home, probably snoozing on the back of the couch. I only brought some papers."

Marin frowned. "I thought Philip was bringing them by."

Eileen pulled away from John, her expression grim. "He should have. But that fool man sent me instead." She waved the packet. "I'll take care of this for him, but what I'd really like to do is thump him upside the head a time or two for his stubbornness."

Marin could tell Eileen was gearing up. She touched John's back. "John, finish your supper and then clear the table for me, would you? Eileen and I need to talk."

John gave Eileen another hug before returning to the kitchen. Marin turned to Eileen, gesturing toward the hall. "Should we go to my office?" It amazed her how easily the words "my office" had slipped from her lips—when had it stopped being Dad's office?

Marin sat behind the desk. Eileen plopped the papers in front of her then sat on the small settee against the wall. The older woman crossed her arms and fixed her with a stern stare. Marin braced herself.

"Marin, I've never been one to mince words, and I'm too old to start now, so I'm just going to tell you like I see it."

Marin shrugged. "Go ahead—although I warn you, I can't guarantee anything you say will make a difference."

Eileen huffed. "That's the problem with the *two* of you. You're both as stubborn as mules." A small smile tugged at her lips as she added, "But God planned you that way. Philip needed the stubbornness to be able to break free of the hold of his dysfunctional family and make something of himself. Which he's done, and I'm as proud as if he were my own. You needed the stubbornness to rise above living in John's shadow."

Eileen cocked her eyebrow, peering at Marin with her chin tucked low. "Do you know how many people try to hide the fact they have a family member with a disability? More than you can count, I'd wager. But not you, Marin—and I'm proud of you, too." She crossed her arms. "Stubbornness has served you well, but this time—this time it's hurting you."

Marin frowned. How much did Eileen know? Cautiously she asked, "What has Philip told you?"

"Not much. He did tell me you're our mystery donor. And he said he can't take the money anymore because he doesn't deserve it." Eileen threw her hands outward in disgust. "Doesn't deserve it? That doesn't make sense to me. Philip has done more for the disabled in this community than everyone else combined! New Beginnings is the biggest project, but he organizes Special Olympics events for both summer and winter.

"Somehow he arranged bus service from the Elmwood Towers even though the city council said they couldn't do it because of insurance issues. He runs all over town setting up job placements for people who most wouldn't give the time of day. Doesn't deserve it?" she repeated, losing her crusty edge and finishing on a note of praise. "Philip deserves a lot more than a monthly donation, I can tell you that. Why, he deserves a gold crown!"

Marin sat back, stunned. She had no idea Philip was involved in all of these things. One of his involvements didn't seem to fit, however. "Elmwood Towers?" she asked. "Isn't that a retirement center? Why Elmwood Towers?"

Eileen looked at Marin in surprise. "Didn't you know? One quad in each section has been designated as assisted living for people with disabilities. Philip talked the directors of the complex into making the change about three months ago. Three apartments of each of those designated quads will be rented by a person with a disability, and the fourth will be for the caretaker." Light seemed to dawn in the woman's face. "Marin, that would be perfect for John. He'd have some independence, with someone close by to help as needed, and it would give you your independence at the same time."

Marin held up her hand. "Wait a minute. I'm not ready to—"

Eileen cut her off with a shake of her head. "I know, I know—you're not ready to let the birdling out of the nest. Stubbornness again. But you just watch John as he starts this job—he'll let you know when *he's* ready to be more independent." She laughed softly, her eyes twinkling. "Dear John—he's something else. If ever there was a young man designed to spread good cheer, it's John." She leaned forward and encouraged, "Marin, you should look into it. At least fill out the application."

Marin had to admit the situation seemed ideal—his own apartment, a resident caretaker. She argued weakly, "But we've never wanted to put John away."

Eileen's eyebrows flew high. "Put John away? My dear, you wouldn't be putting him away—you'd be setting him free!"

Marin digested this. It was definitely something to think about and pray about. She brought Eileen back to a previous topic. "Eileen, I want you to know that I'm not going to stop making the donations to New Beginnings, no matter how Philip feels. My father believed it was a worthy cause, and now that I've seen what you do, I believe it, too."

Eileen nodded slowly, peering at Marin with lowered lids. "Mm-hmm. Your father started donating—do you have any idea why?"

Marin felt heat build in her cheeks. She'd been considering that question ever since Philip had told her he was the recipient of those funds. She had a good idea why. Aunt Chris was right—Dad had obviously wanted something more for John. Marin believed he made those donations to ensure the service would be available when Mother finally allowed John to spread his wings. She was so thankful she'd stumbled upon the telephone number for New Beginnings and allowed John this opportunity to grow. *Dad would be thankful, too*, she thought.

Eileen cut into her thoughts. "Marin, I have to tell you something."

Marin raised her gaze. Eileen's serious expression captured her full attention. She nodded silently in response.

"I don't know what happened between you and Philip, and I don't need to know—that's best left between the two of you. I admit I tried to force it out of Philip—got tired of his moping around, and I figured if he'd spill it he'd feel better. But all he said was 'We've got irreconcilable differences.'" She snorted. "If two people love God and love each other, there is no such thing. You just talk and pray and talk and pray until you've reached a compromise you both can live with, that's all."

Marin burst out, "You make it sound so easy! But some problems. . ." She floundered. "Well, some problems are just too deeply embedded."

"Bosh!" Eileen flapped her hand in dismissal. "There's nothing buried so deep the good Lord can't unbury it and make it right again." She leaned forward to place her hands on the desk and look directly into Marin's eyes. "That man is hurting, but he's too stubborn to come over here, face you, and make it right. So I'm just going to say it straight out. It's up to you. Philip is a man worth fighting for. Don't let him slip away. I believe with everything I've got that God brought you to New Beginnings. God brought you to find help for John, and He brought you to help mend whatever's eaten away at Philip for as long as I've known him. But if you don't do it. . ." She leaned back, sighing sadly. "Well, there will be two hearts that never get to see God's good plan carried out. And that's pretty sad."

Marin lowered her gaze, her mind replaying Eileen's words. *When two people love God and love each other*. Did she love Philip? Is that why her heart ached so badly? But how could she love the man who had been so unspeakably heartless to John?

And it struck her. The man she loved hadn't been unspeakably heartless. The man she loved had been warm and accepting and indescribably kind to John. He had reached out with both arms and brought John into his friendship. He had nurtured and cared for John with Christ's love.

Tears filled her eyes. How foolish she had been. The Philip who had stood silently by and allowed John to be taunted no longer existed. Somehow the experience had transformed him into a man whose heart was big enough to love the ones often despised and rejected by society. God had used that awful experience to turn Philip into the man he was designed to be.

She whispered, " 'The old has gone, the new has come!' " She saw it so clearly now. And, she realized, all it would take was her forgiveness to help Philip see it, too. She looked up to find Eileen still seated, patiently waiting. An idea immediately formed in her head.

"Eileen, thank you for bringing these papers over." She allowed a smile to creep up one cheek, sending Eileen a secretive look. "But they don't make a lot of sense to me. And I'm pretty sure you won't be able to answer my questions. So I think I'd better give Philip a visit."

Eileen hooted with laughter. "Ah, Marin, you are wily." She slapped her thighs and rose, her eyes twinkling. "When I left, he was poring over the books. I'm sure he's still there."

Marin rounded the desk, picking up the packet. "Could you stay with John? It might take awhile to get everything straightened out."

Eileen wrapped Marin in a hug. "Take as long as you need. I'll be praying for you, Marin."

"Thanks, Eileen."

Marin told John she'd be back in a bit, got into her car, and headed for New Beginnings.

—ⸯⸯ—

Philip sat at his desk, holding a half-eaten sandwich and staring at his dog-eared ledger. *God, I have to give that money back, but I can't see how I'll make it financially without it. Help me out here—open my eyes so I can find a solution.*

Someone banged on the front door. He nearly jumped out of his seat. He glanced at his wristwatch. Almost seven. Who would be here now? The banging came again. Whoever he was, he was persistent. With a sigh, he dropped the sandwich onto a crumpled napkin and strode to the door. His heart leaped into his throat when he found Marin Brooks waiting outside. "Marin?" He took a step backward as she charged in. She looked incredibly beautiful with her hair twisted into a loose knot on the crown of her head. Dressed in a kelly green knee-length dress and high-heeled white sandals, with a soft scarf of green, yellow, and orange looped around her slender neck, she gave off an aura of sophistication without seeming snobbish. Even though her hazel eyes snapped and her chin was set at a determined angle, it was all he could do to keep from reaching out for her. He shoved his hands in his pockets. "What are you doing here?"

She closed the door and wheeled on him, holding up a stack of papers. "I had the impression you were going to help me with these," she said, her tone accusing. "But to my surprise, Eileen brought them over." She dropped them on the small table near the door and pursed her lips. "I never figured you for a coward, Philip Wilder, but that's what you are. A coward."

Philip felt his temper building. How dare she stomp in here uninvited and hurl insults at him? Didn't she have any idea how he'd lain awake nights, worrying about how he'd impacted her life? He'd sent Eileen so she wouldn't have to be reminded again of the hurt he'd caused her. He opened his mouth to tell her as much, but she pointed to the chair and gave a quiet order:

"Sit down, Philip. We need to talk."

# Chapter 16

"Now just a minute," Philip blustered, bringing his hands out of his pockets. "You're being awfully pushy here."

"Yes, I am," Marin acknowledged. "I just spent a good half hour with Eileen, and she had a magical effect on me."

"I'm not so sure I like the changes." Philip frowned, examining her from head to toe. Why did she have to be so pretty? Even with that scowl on her face, her attractiveness drew him like a magnet. His feet itched to move forward, his hands twitched to reach for her, and his arms ached to hold her—maybe he *should* sit down, he decided. He lowered himself into a chair without taking his gaze off her.

Marin seated herself next to him, crossed her legs, then fixed him with a firm look. "We need to get something straight. And I would really appreciate it if you would just sit there and listen." She paused, waiting for his agreement.

Although he found it difficult to hide a smile—she was too little to pack all this gumption—he managed to nod seriously.

"Thank you," she said primly and lifted her pert chin. "First of all, I *will* continue contributing to New Beginnings, just as my father did. Dad knew a worthy cause when he saw one. I've had some time to consider why he wanted it kept secret, and I think it's because he didn't want Mom to feel as if he were forcing her to do something she didn't want to do. Dad always let Mom have the lead with John. But I think, deep down, he hoped the program would be around long enough to be of benefit to his son." She paused for a moment, her hazel eyes shining brighter with the tears that suddenly appeared in their corners. "And it has been."

She sniffed, shifted the knot of her scarf higher on her shoulder, and went on. "Second, if John is going to take this position with"—she consulted the paper—"Barks, Squawks, and Meows, he's going to be under your jurisdiction, which means we'll be running into each other from time to time. And this—evasion—just won't work."

Philip couldn't let that go. "Now, Marin, I'm not the only one who's been practicing evasion."

She had the good grace to blush. For a moment, she dipped her head, her bluster fading, but then she popped back up and came at him again. "I know, but you've been by the house three times since John got out of the hospital, and every time, you chose an hour of day when you knew I wouldn't be there. I haven't had any reason to come to you till now, so you're the *bigger* evader."

"In more ways than one," he quipped.

A smile flashed through her eyes, but she pointed at him and admonished, "Don't try to be cute. And I told you not to talk."

"Yes, ma'am." He saluted her, biting down on the insides of his mouth to keep from laughing.

She frowned severely then went on. "Last, but certainly not least, is the issue of—" Suddenly her expression changed from sternness to great remorse. The tears that had made an earlier appearance recurred to spill down her cheeks in a silvery trail. Her fingers trembled as she swept them away, but her gaze never left Philip's face.

He held his breath, wanting to take her in his arms but fearful of how she'd react. So he pressed his palms against his thighs and waited for her to gain control.

Finally she spoke in a tremulous tone. "Last is the issue of your apology. And how wrong I was not to accept it the moment it was offered."

Philip's heart pounded in double-time. "Marin—"

"No, let me finish." She swallowed and leaned forward slightly. "I realized something. I've always seen that day as the day everything changed, and I always saw it as a negative. But it wasn't all a negative change, Philip. Look at everything you've done because you saw the suffering of one boy and his little sister! Look at all the good that has come out of it."

She gestured to indicate their setting, a single strand of hair slipping free to frame her cheek. "Philip, I could hardly believe it when Eileen told me everything you've done for the disabled in this community. Your whole adult life, you've been giving so people with disabilities can lead more productive, happier lives. Would you have chosen that route had it not been for an April day and a baby bird and a brother and sister who felt helpless against a bully? Answer me—would you?"

Philip sat thinking about the question. In all honesty, he realized, probably not. The event had been the impetus that drove him away from Rocky's influence and straight into the friendship with David, whose influence had been so much more positive. In all likelihood, he would have continued trailing after Rocky, living in his shadow, never discovering the joy of knowing God and giving back to Him. Slowly he shook his head.

She beamed through her tears. "So don't you see? As hard as it was, God has used it to bring you toward your perfect plan." She pointed to the verse displayed above their heads. "You have become God's workmanship, performing the good work He planned for you."

"But what about you and John?" Philip demanded. "How has any of this been for your good?" The guilt stabbed again, the memory of John's cries and

Marin's grief-stricken face surfacing once more to haunt him.

"I don't know." Her honesty surprised him. Then she flipped her palms outward. "But who am I to question? Maybe there was a good, but we missed it. Maybe Dad was remembering that day when he decided to help get your business up and running. Maybe it was Dad's contribution that kept your business running long enough for me to find you when I needed you. Maybe. . ." Her voice drifted off, and she gave a delicate shrug. "Maybe I won't know until I get to heaven. Some things are like that—mysteries until we're at His side, and then we'll know."

Philip felt tears sting behind his nose as Marin continued softly.

"But I do know this. You've made a difference in John's life and in mine. And I can never regret making the phone call that connected me with you." Her chin quivered. "Philip, whatever happened that day twelve years ago has been more than made up for with what you've given to John and me. You've given me the confidence to allow John to step out and become his own person. You've given John the opportunity to reach. And I'm sorry I didn't say so at the hospital. I know I hurt you with my silence. I was just so confused and worried."

He finally gave in to his feelings and leaned forward, taking her hands. "I know. I understand. When I think about what I did—what I didn't do—I was so wrong."

Marin's eyes shone as she tugged on his hands. "But don't you see, Philip? You aren't the same person who stood there and did nothing. The old Philip has passed away; the new Philip is a man determined to do good. You've made so many things new for so many people. I admire you for that."

"Then"—he hardly dared to ask—"does this mean you've forgiven me?"

Her response came so quickly it left no doubt in Philip's mind of her sincerity. "A million times over."

His heart lifted. The burden of guilt seemed to leap from his shoulders. A smile burst on his face as if of its own volition. "Thank you."

"No," Marin corrected, turning her hands to link fingers with him. "Thank *you*. Thank you for becoming who you are. And thank you for helping me become who I needed to be for John."

They sat in silence, hands linked, while the clock on the wall counted off the seconds and their hearts pattered in offbeats with the intruding *tick-tick*. At long last, Philip released a sigh and asked, "May I speak now?"

Marin giggled, dropping her gaze. When she raised her head again, her expression appeared self-conscious. "I must have sounded like a real harpy, ordering you around like I did. But it was the only way I could find the courage to get it all out."

Warmth flooded Philip's chest. "Don't ever be afraid to tell me what you think, Marin. I. . .care about you. . .and your feelings. You don't ever have to be afraid with me."

She nodded, her gaze locked with his. "I know. And I'm not afraid."

"Good." He squeezed her hands before releasing them and rose. Amazing how good it felt to know he'd been forgiven. The knot of sorrow that had filled his belly for the past two weeks fled. And suddenly he wanted something more than the cold sandwich turning crusty on his desk. He slapped his tummy. "I'm hungry. Have you had supper?"

She stood up, laughing. "That was an abrupt change in subject."

"Sorry, but my stomach growled. So—have you?"

"Yes, actually Aunt Lenore had supper ready when I came home tonight."

Philip grinned at her. "You know, I've gotten to where I like that lady. Spunky. Tells it like it is."

Marin gave him a sidelong look. "And what exactly has she told you?"

He threw back his head and laughed, delighted to be teasing with her. "Oh no, that's none of your concern." He ignored her hands-on-trim-hips pose and interjected, "So do you want to go get an ice cream or something and watch me eat?"

Marin hesitated, and for a moment, Philip's chest felt tight. She finally answered. "I left John with Eileen, but I didn't plan to be gone so long."

Philip shrugged. "Then let's get John. He likes ice cream, too."

Marin looked at him uncertainly. "Are you sure?"

Philip reached out to touch her soft cheek with his knuckles. "Marin, I like John. Spending time with him is not a trial." He dropped his hand. "So—what are we doing?"

Marin smiled. "We're going for ice cream."

Philip snatched up the papers she'd dropped earlier. "Afterward I'll come in, and we'll fill these things out, okay? I think John's ready for his job."

"I think John's ready for *life*."

⸺⸺

Philip insisted that Eileen join them for ice cream, too, rounding out the group. John licked his cone happily while the other three adults visited. Midway through her sundae, Eileen fixed Philip with a guarded look and announced, "I'm going to tell you something while I have protection."

"Protection?" he queried, leery of the expression in her eyes.

"Yep." Eileen pointed her thumbs at John and Marin. "These two. You like them too much to cause a scene in front of them."

Philip suspected he wasn't going to like what he was about to hear. "Well, as you're so fond of saying, spill it."

Eileen pushed her plastic spoon into the mound of ice cream and followed his directive. "Philip, I've worked for you since New Beginnings opened, and I've loved it—most every minute of it. But I have to be honest—lately I've wondered if I need to make a change."

The unease in Philip's belly grew. "What do you mean, a change?"

Eileen frowned at the interruption. "I grow attached to the clients, and then they march out the door, and it's hard on my old heart to say good-bye over and over again. Maybe I need a place to work where I won't have to go through that constant letting go process." Her expression softened. "I said good-bye to my husband ten years ago, Lord bless him. All my kids trooped off to other states to start their own lives, and I only see them on holidays. I need connections with people—connections that aren't always going to be leaving me behind."

"Are you quitting?" Marin asked the question.

"Yes, I think I am."

Philip shook his head. "But, Eileen, what will I do without you? You're my right-hand man."

John looked up, his eyes wide. "Philip, you have made a mistake. Eileen is a lady."

Eileen patted John's arm, chuckling indulgently. "It's just an expression, John—he knows I'm a lady." Then she turned back to Philip. "A lonely lady, Philip. I want to find—well, a surrogate family that isn't going to outgrow me every six to ten weeks." She took in a deep breath. "So—I've applied at Elmwood Towers to be an assisted living caretaker. That should meet my desire to be needed and give me somebody to fuss over. But"—she gave him a pleading look—"I'll need a good recommendation from my former boss."

Although it pained Philip to think of Eileen leaving, he loved her too much to hold her back if this was what she wanted. He reached across the table and placed his hand over hers. "You'll get it. I'll miss you, but I understand. I can't think of anyone better for the job."

John crunched the last of his cone and spoke around the remnants. "I will have a job now, too. And I will be the most better at my job. Right, Eileen?"

Eileen put her arm around John's shoulders and gave a squeeze. "That's right, John. You will be terrific with the cats and dogs at Barks, Squawks, and Meows."

John beamed.

Eileen lowered her eyelids and looked at Marin, although Philip believed her words addressed John. "And maybe, just maybe, we'll see each other again."

"Maybe, Eileen," Marin responded in a thoughtful tone.

Philip glanced back and forth between the two women, taking in their expressions. Obviously secret messages were being exchanged.

"Oh, I will see Eileen," John inserted confidently. "You will bring Roscoe the Wonder Cat to Barking Squawking Meows, and I will take care of him."

Eileen laughed. "That sounds good to me." She looked at Philip again, and her faded blue eyes softened. "I hope to stay in touch with you, too, Philip. You're a connection I don't want to lose."

Philip realized in that moment how much Eileen meant to him. She'd become more than a friend—he'd come to depend on her in the absence of his mother, who had died more than ten years ago. In many ways, Eileen had been more available and loving than his mother had been. "You can count on that," he assured her. "You're my sounding board and advice-giver. Won't last long without you."

She gave him a smile then yawned. Glancing at her wristwatch, she exclaimed, "Is it after nine already? Poor Roscoe—I've got to get home." She rose, sent a hurried good-bye around the table, then rushed out.

Philip turned to Marin and sighed. "Well—I guess we should head out, too. We still have that paperwork to complete."

Marin nodded, scooping up her purse. "Yes. If John's going to be the 'most better,' we need to let him get started."

"Hurray!" yelled John.

And Philip noticed that Marin didn't even cringe when people turned to stare.

## Chapter 17

The third Monday of September, Philip stepped into the cool interior of Barks, Squawks, and Meows. A whirring fan overhead stirred the scent of cinnamon—a scent chosen, no doubt, to mask the odors of animals and antiseptic. He smiled, taking in the wallpaper that showed cartoon cats and dogs raining from the heavens. Black paw prints were painted on the floor, guiding him to the receptionist counter, which was constructed to resemble a pile of dog biscuits. He chuckled to himself, thinking how the fun-spirited décor matched the whimsical title of the veterinarian's office.

He passed rows of benches where customers waited their turn with the doctor, each person holding a small cage or a leash. Offering a nod of hello to the clients, he crossed to the counter and greeted the receptionist. "Hi, Nancy."

Nancy looked up from the computer and offered a bright smile. "Philip! Here to check on John?"

Philip nodded. He leaned on the counter. "Yep. How's he working out?"

Nancy laughed. "He's a character, that's for sure. Just settled in and made himself at home. He never complains about anything we give him to do, he's great at following directions, and he loves the animals. I'd say you found a perfect match for us."

Philip wasn't surprised by this news. He'd had a feeling John would fit in here. Dr. Powers and his wife, Nancy, were the kind of sponsors Philip preferred—kind, Christian, patient people who offered a warm, accepting working environment. "I'm glad to hear that."

"Larry has the evaluation all filled out for you," she added, flipping through a stack of papers next to the computer keyboard. She frowned. "I had it a minute ago." She looked at another stack then sighed. "It's been a zoo this morning. It might take me awhile to locate it. Why don't you go back and say hi to John? Larry's got him cleaning kennels—just follow the barks."

Philip laughed and pushed off from the counter. "Thanks—I'll be back in a bit." He headed out the side door and followed the sidewalk around the back of the office where a long row of fenced kennels stood. As he passed the tall cages, the dogs barked their greetings, jumping against the chain link to welcome him with lolling tongues and wagging tails. He reached through the openings in the fence to scratch a few ears as he made his way to the farthest kennel, where he finally located John.

"Hey, buddy!" he hollered over the sound of the barks.

John held a water hose, spraying the concrete floor of the kennel. At Philip's greeting, he turned his head, and his whole face lit up with happiness. He dropped the hose, splattering his shoes, and rushed to the end of the kennel to wrap his fingers around the chain link. "Philip! What are you doing at Barking Squawking Meows?"

Philip hid a smile. John would never get the name right. "Came to see you," he answered, "to make sure you're okay. How's it going?"

"It is going good." John's almond-shaped eyes shone. "I like this job. I like Dr. Larry. I like Nancy. I like the dogs and the cats. They like me, too."

Philip nodded. "I'll bet they do."

John's face clouded for a moment. "Sometimes the dogs and cats have to get shots, and that makes them sad. But then Dr. Larry lets me pet them. That makes them feel better again."

"I'm sure they appreciate your petting them, John," Philip assured him.

"Are you coming for supper tonight? Marin is cooking hamburgers on the grill." In his excitement, John signed the words as he spoke. "And we baked a chocolate cake, too. Are you coming?"

Philip smiled. He'd been eating more meals with John and Marin than he ate at his own place lately. But he couldn't decline the invitation. "I'd like to. Are you sure it's okay with Marin?"

"Marin said the way to a man's heart is through his stomach and she will bake cakes every day for you."

Philip laughed. There were no secrets with John. He wondered how Marin would like it if she knew what John had just shared. "Then I'll be there," he said. "I have to go now. Have fun."

"Okay. 'Bye, Philip." John turned and retrieved the hose. He went back to spraying, a look of concentration on his face.

Philip headed back to the office, chuckling to himself. He knew that the first few days here had been unpleasant for John. A couple of high school boys who came in after school had given him a hard time, convincing him to do their jobs and teasing him. But Dr. Larry had made it clear that type of behavior was unacceptable and then gave the boys the option to straighten up or find another place to work. One of the boys had immediately quit, but the other—Andy— had promised to change his attitude. Since then, Andy and John had formed a friendship. John had invited him to church, and Andy was attending regularly. It gave Philip's heart a lift to see the positive influence John had made on that young man.

Nancy had uncovered the evaluation, which she handed to Philip, and he left with a reminder to call if any problems arose. As he drove through town toward New Beginnings, his thoughts drifted across all of the changes that had occurred in John's life—and consequently Marin's—over the past several weeks.

Four weeks earlier, he had used Dixie to help Marin move John into an apartment at Elmwood Towers, right across the hall from Eileen's. While he and Marin arranged the furniture taken from John's bedroom and the Brookses' basement rec room, John had wandered the halls, greeting his new neighbors and letting them know they were welcome to visit anytime.

Her first night without her brother at home, Marin had called Philip and mourned for nearly an hour, certain she had done the wrong thing—John would never survive, he would feel abandoned, he would resent being forced from his home. The second night, she had called to confess John was fine with the new arrangement, but she missed him terribly and wished Eileen had never mentioned the idea, and how would she bring him home without making him feel as if he had failed? But the third night's call had been full of cheerful self-deprecation—"I'm the most overprotective, self-centered sister in the world. John *loves* his apartment and his freedom. How could I even *think* of telling him to come home again?"

Letting go of John had helped Marin trust that no matter where John was, God was with him, and she could let him go without fear. Philip knew how difficult the letting-go process had been, and he admired her for putting John's needs ahead of her own.

Those three nights of calls had started a habit of daily communication, which Philip eagerly anticipated. His friendship with her had blossomed until he couldn't imagine what he would do without it. Increasingly his thoughts turned toward the future and making Marin a permanent part of his life. But as yet, he hadn't found the courage to tell her.

John still ate all of his evening meals with Marin, at her insistence. She picked him up from work each afternoon and took him to his apartment mid-evening. She had confided to Philip it would be hard when the time change and weather conditions forced her to end the ritual. But if Philip were honest with himself, he looked forward to it. Perhaps he'd have an evening completely alone with Marin. Maybe then he'd find the ability to speak the words that hovered on his heart: *I love you, Marin. Marry me.*

—

As Marin drove toward the veterinarian's office to retrieve John, she looked ahead to the evening's cookout—probably the last one of the year since fall was nearly upon them. She'd confirmed Aunt Lenore and Eileen were coming, but she hadn't reached Philip. When she'd called New Beginnings, he had been out, and apparently the person who took the call hadn't given him the message because she hadn't heard from him. She sighed. Although there would be plenty of company, she knew she would miss Philip's presence. She admitted things felt lonely unless Philip was there, too.

When, she wondered, had her relationship with him taken on such meaning?

It had crept up on her, much like the sunrise—starting soft and pink and dreamy, then growing to beam bright yellow and strong. Her heart filled as she thought of everything he had done for her and John. Philip was such a special man—a special, loving, giving, tender man, and she wished she could find a way to tell him without making a fool of herself. For wasn't it the man's responsibility to make the first move? But what if he never did? What if the guilt he carried from the past—the remembrance of that day—forever kept him from proclaiming his feelings for her? What then?

She pulled into the parking area of Barks, Squawks, and Meows and waited. After only a minute or two, John ambled out and climbed in, his face glowing. He leaned across the seat to give Marin a kiss then fastened his seat belt.

"Phew, John. You smell like a wet dog." Marin softened the complaint with a smile as she turned the car toward home.

John grinned, not at all insulted. "I have been with a wet dog. He was scared after I accidentally watered him with the hose. So I held him and let him know I was sorry."

Marin's heart expanded at John's tender concern for all creatures. "I'm sure he appreciated it."

"Oh yes. He licked my hand." John signed, "All is forgiven." Then he turned to Marin, his eyes wide. "Oh! Philip came today"—Marin's heart leaped at the mention of that name—"and I told him come eat a hamburger and cake so you could get to his heart through his stomach."

Marin nearly drove the car onto the sidewalk. "You told him *what*?"

John scratched his head. "I said what you said. You said the chocolate cake was because the way to a man's heart is through his stomach."

"You *told* him that?" Marin clutched the steering wheel with both hands. She couldn't decide whether to laugh or cry. "Oh, John!"

"What?" John's tone showed his puzzlement.

"I didn't mean for you to repeat that." Her face felt hot. She turned up the air conditioning even though the car was comfortably cool. "John, you can't go around repeating everything I say."

"I do not repeat everything you say," he said defensively. "I cannot remember everything you say."

Despite her embarrassment, Marin couldn't hold back a hoot of laughter. "Oh, John," she repeated, but her tone bubbled with humor.

They visited cheerfully the rest of the way home; then Marin put John to work cutting up celery and carrots for a relish tray. By six, her guests began to arrive—Eileen first, carrying a platter of aromatic, homemade onion rings, then Aunt Lenore with her famous potato salad. Philip came last—with a bouquet of yellow roses and daisies and a smile that went straight to Marin's heart.

The evening passed in a pleasant time of camaraderie, and although Marin enjoyed each minute, she could hardly wait for everyone to leave so she could give Philip a private thank-you for the flowers. Philip came along when she drove John to his apartment, and of course they had to walk up with him and visit for a few minutes. Impatience tugged at Marin's chest—when would she and Philip be alone? Finally John yawned and indicated a readiness for sleep.

"Lock your door," Marin admonished as she kissed him good night. "And I'll see you tomorrow. Call me if you need anything."

"I know, I know," John grumbled, pushing her out the door. "You are a worry-wart." He shut the door in her face.

Marin waited until the lock clicked before she turned to Philip with a shrug. "I guess John's doing okay on his own."

Philip smiled. "I guess John's doing *great* on his own." They started toward the elevator. "And so are you."

"Yes," she mused, "I suppose so." But did she always want to be on her own? Of course not. She wanted her own family—a husband, children, maybe a dog. But she kept silent.

⁓⌒

They crossed the parking lot beneath a star-studded sky. Philip stretched out his hand to capture hers. When she looked up at him, he explained lamely, "It's dark—I don't want you to stumble."

She smiled and gave his hand a squeeze that sent a jolt of reaction clear to his midsection. They reached the car, and he opened her door for her then climbed in on the opposite side. His knees nearly touched his chin, his lanky frame much too long for the seating area of the compact car.

Marin laughed at him as she started the engine. "You really don't fit in here, do you?"

He gave her a sidelong glance. In the muted light from the dashboard, her eyes took on a deeper hue, her blond hair turning honey brown. He found himself saying, "I don't fit too well in your car—but how about in your life?"

He watched as her hand froze on the gearshift and her face flooded with color. "M—my life?"

He nodded. Reaching across the console, he took her hand. "Marin, I've been trying to tell you something for weeks, but I can't ever seem to find the right words. I tried to tell you tonight with the flowers." He paused. "Do you know the meanings behind yellow roses and daisies?"

She pushed silken strands of hair behind her left ear. "No one's ever given me flowers before."

Philip raised his eyebrows. "A pretty girl like you? You've never gotten flowers?"

Marin shook her head. "Most boys. . .well, once they met John. . ." Her voice trailed off as she gave a slight shrug. "I never dated much—too many other things to take care of."

He made a mental note to bring her flowers once a week, at least. Rubbing his thumb over her knuckles, he explained, "The yellow roses stand for friendship. Our friendship is so important to me, Marin. I've learned to trust you, confide in you, and rely on you. You're my best friend."

Her hazel eyes took on a softness. She whispered, "I feel that way about you, too."

He smiled, his heart swelling. He went on. "And the daisies have several meanings—innocence, purity, and loyal love. I believe all three of those fit you perfectly. I especially admire the loyal love you bestow on John. The relationship you two share is unique and special, Marin. I envy it."

She tipped her head, her expression pensive. "Philip, do you ever see your brother?"

Philip lowered his gaze. The thought of Rocky brought a rush of unhappy remembrances. He shook his head, his heart heavy.

"Don't you think you should?" she prodded. "Family is so important—and he's all you have. You're all he has. You should try to build a relationship with him."

Philip knew Marin didn't understand all the idiosyncrasies of his disjointed family. He suspected that even if she did know, she'd still encourage him to try to be Rocky's brother in the true sense of the word. Apparently he remained silent too long, because she pulled her hand free to shut off the ignition and open the glove compartment. She removed a small New Testament and snapped on the overhead light.

Flipping pages, she asked, "Philip, remember when I told you the old Philip was gone and you had become new?"

He nodded.

She held the open testament to him. "I didn't come up with it myself. Read verses 17 and 18 of 2 Corinthians 5."

Obediently he took the book and held it up to the light. It wasn't an unfamiliar text, but he was curious why she'd chosen it. When he'd finished, he looked at her.

Intently she met his gaze. "I wanted you to read verse 18, too, because it speaks of reconciliation. Awhile back, Eileen told me you'd said irreconcilable differences had come between us, but she said God could fix anything if you pray and talk and pray and talk."

She reached for his hand, and he linked fingers with her, her palm warm against his. "Philip, God took the old thing from our past and created something new and beautiful out of it. He can do the same thing for you and Rocky, if you'll pray about it and give Him a chance."

Philip considered her words. She was right that he'd believed the event from their past would forever hold them apart. Yet forgiveness had let them bridge the gap, reconciling their friendship. Maybe there was hope for building a relationship with Rocky. He closed the New Testament, returned it to the glove box, then turned to Marin once more.

"Would you be willing to go with me when I talk to my brother? I've met most of your family—maybe it's time you met what's left of mine."

Marin didn't hesitate, which proved the changes that had taken place in her heart. "Of course I'll go. And I'll pray for a reconciliation and a brand-new start for the two of you."

Philip had never loved her more.

⸺◌⸺

Nearly a month passed before Philip was able to arrange a get-together with Rocky. Rocky had insisted they meet at a restaurant on the outskirts of town—he didn't want Philip in his neighborhood. So Philip picked up Marin in his beloved, battered Dixie truck, and together they joined his brother at Pete's BBQ, a dim, smoky hangout with which Rocky seemed quite familiar. Although the meeting wasn't a loving reunion, the two brothers managed to relax enough to have a decent conversation, and when they parted, Rocky gave Philip a light punch on the shoulder and said, "Now keep in touch, huh?"

Philip walked Marin to Dixie and helped her in. Once he was behind the steering wheel, he turned to her and said, "So—what do you think?"

Her eyes shone with tenderness as she replied, "I think we need to have Rocky to my place one day soon for a home-cooked meal. He's too skinny."

Philip shook his head, his chest expanding with love for this beautiful, God-fearing woman. She'd seen the worst of his life, and she was ready to welcome it into her home. "Marin," he said, his voice husky from emotion, "you're willing to accept my brother?"

"You accepted mine," she pointed out. "How could I do any less for you?"

And Philip knew without a doubt she loved him. If she could look at Rocky—see the background from which he'd come—and still care for him, her love was of the daisies: loyal and pure. *Lord*, he breathed, *You've given me Your perfect gift for a wife. Thank You.*

He just needed to choose the perfect time to let her know.

# Chapter 18

John sat on the floor in front of the Christmas tree, a fuzzy Santa hat on his head and a pile of gaily wrapped gifts at his side. It tickled Philip to watch John open the boxes. He was so meticulous in removing the paper—first loosen the ends, then slide his finger below the edge along the bottom and finally peel the paper back away from the box. Then he would fold the paper into a neat square before looking at the contents of the box. If Philip had been an impatient man, it might have been irritating, waiting for John. But Philip didn't care if this day never ended. John could take all the time he wanted.

While John worked on one of his presents, Philip reached into his jacket pocket and removed a tiny velvet box, which he hadn't placed beneath the tree. His heart pounded, a brief concern rising as to whether Marin would accept this gift; then he recalled every precious moment of time with her over the past months, and he knew what he was doing was right. Marin would see it, too. They'd been designed for one another.

She sat perched on the edge of the sofa, her gaze on John, a soft smile lighting her face. The twinkling red lights from the Christmas tree gave her profile a rosy glow. It took great control not to lean forward, take her face in his hands, and place a kiss on her sweetly upturned lips.

His fingers closed around the box. He held both fists outward, palms down, and nudged her lightly with his elbow. "Pick one."

She turned to look at him, her smile growing. "Does your left hand know what your right hand is doing?" she teased.

He laughed appreciatively. Bobbing both hands, he said again, "Go ahead—pick one."

With a giggle of delight, she tapped the back of his right hand. He turned it over and opened his fingers, revealing the box. Her eyes grew wide, and her gaze bounced up to meet his. Her expression said clearly, *For me?*

He nodded, his heart pounding. She reached with both hands and lifted the box with her fingertips. Cradling it in her palm, she opened the lid with slow, deliberate movements, as though prolonging the pleasure. The moment the lid was fully up, she gasped and looked at him again, her eyes flooding with tears. "Oh, I'm so glad I picked that hand."

"Me, too." Philip plucked out the gold band with its single marquise diamond and slipped it onto Marin's finger, his own hands trembling. To his relief, it fit perfectly. He watched as she examined it for a moment with an expression of awe; then she lifted her face to Philip. The emotion that shone from her sparkling hazel eyes took Philip's breath away. But she didn't speak to him—instead she leaned forward to gain John's attention.

John looked up, a half-unwrapped present in his lap. "Yes?"

Marin fluttered her fingers. "Look what Philip gave me."

John held Marin's hand and admired the ring. "Ooh, it is pretty." He gave Philip a knowing look. "That must have cost a pretty penny."

Both Marin and Philip laughed.

Philip explained, "It's an engagement ring, buddy. You know what that means, don't you?"

John's face lit up. "That means you will marry Marin!"

Marin held her arm straight and admired the sparkle of the stone. Philip felt it couldn't compete with the sparkle in her eyes.

"That's right, John. I will be marrying Philip."

John gave a cheerful nod and turned his attention back to the box in his lap.

With a slight frown, Marin turned to face Philip. "Philip, you do realize that I come as"—she glanced at John—"a package deal."

He shook his head, a smile tugging at his cheeks. Following his earlier impulse, he cupped her cheeks with both hands and whispered, "Ah, Marin—when will you realize I see the package as a gift?"

Marin's eyes flooded and overflowed. "Oh, Philip, I do love you."

Their kiss was salty from tears, but it took nothing from the sweetness of the moment. When they separated, Marin turned to John again. "John, when I get married, I would like very much for you to give me away."

John swung to face them, his eyes wide. "For good?" he exclaimed, obviously abashed by the thought.

Marin burst into laughter. "No, of course not. I'll always be your sister. I'll always be here for you." Briefly she explained the tradition of giving away the bride. When she finished, John nodded, a somber look on his face.

"I will do that, Marin. I will give you to Philip to be his wife." He pointed at her. "And you will be happy."

Marin leaned into Philip's embrace, and he encircled her with his arms. "Yes," she said with a contented sigh, "I will be happy."

Philip, smiling into the hazel eyes he loved, added, "God wouldn't have designed it any other way."

—⁂—

Two months later, Marin stood before a cheval mirror in a small room at the back of the church while Aunt Lenore and Aunt Chris fussed around her, straightening her veil, tightening bobby pins that held her hair in a sleek French twist, and adjusting the miniature yellow rosebuds that nestled behind her left ear. Marin stood still, aware of their busyness but somehow above it as her mind relived moments from the past weeks.

There had been times when Marin had missed her mother with an ache that was nearly unbearable, but each time, she had reminded herself of how God had given her surrogate mothers—Aunt Chris, as well as Aunt Lenore and Eileen. Neither Lenore nor Eileen had her mother's meek disposition; yet their love was as evident, and Marin's heart swelled with appreciation for their steadfast presence.

Marin smoothed her hands over the sleek skirt of the trim-fitting satin gown, which her mother had worn thirty-five years earlier. Her stomach fluttered with eagerness for Philip to see her in her wedding finery. Outside the door, John waited—no doubt pacing—in his black tuxedo, crisp white shirt, and black bow tie. If her father were here, he would be the one waiting and pacing, but how proud John was of his role! She smiled, remembering the rehearsal and John's stiff, formal bearing. Although Marin missed her father, she was grateful to know he had met Philip and obviously approved of him. Dad would be pleased with her choice for a life mate.

"Well, Marin, I don't know that I've ever seen a more lovely bride." Aunt Lenore stepped back and swept her gaze from Marin's head to her toes. She turned to Chris. "Did we cover everything? Something old, something new. . .?"

Chris touched the frothy veil that lay in beguiling layers across Marin's shoulders. "The veil is new, but the dress was Mary's, remade, so we've covered the old, too."

Marin added, "And the dress covers 'borrowed' since it was originally Mother's."

"Something blue. . ." Aunt Lenore tapped her finger against her lower lip. Then she burst out, "Oh! I brought something!" She rummaged through her purse. "I must be getting old. I meant to give this to you earlier, but we've been so busy." She turned with a small, weathered jewelry box in her wrinkled hand. Tears brightened her eyes as she pushed it into Marin's hands. "Here, Marin. Your uncle gave this to me for my eighteenth birthday. You know I didn't have daughters, and this isn't something you'd give a son, so. . ." She flapped her hands, her cheeks flooding with pink. "Oh, just open it!"

Marin popped the lid to discover a sapphire and diamond pendant suspended on a dainty gold chain. "Oh, Aunt Lenore. . ." Marin raised it from the box and held it out to Aunt Chris. "Aunt Chris, look at it—it's just beautiful."

"And it isn't borrowed," Aunt Lenore inserted firmly. "It's your wedding gift from me." She paused, cupping Marin's cheeks with her hands. "You know, the sapphire is my birthstone—and your mother's. Maybe having that hang around your neck will be a remembrance of her."

Marin felt tears build. "Aunt Lenore, having you here is a remembrance of

Mother—but thank you so much for this beautiful necklace. When I wear it, I'll think of both of you."

The two women exchanged an emotional hug. How Marin had come to appreciate her mother's twin!

"Here—let's put it on," Aunt Chris suggested. She fastened the tiny clasp, and then all three women looked into the mirror, admiring the bride's image conveyed there.

Marin sighed, touching the pendant where it rested in the V-neck of the lace bodice. "It's perfect. This day is perfect." Then she stomped one slipper-covered foot in impatience. "But isn't it time to go?"

As if on cue, a knock sounded on the door. Aunt Chris opened it. John stood in the doorway. He pointed at his watch, a stern look on his face. "Are you not paying attention? It is time."

Marin laughed and skipped to his side. "I'm ready, big brother. Let's go." Aunt Chris and Aunt Lenore hurried past them. The ushers would escort them to their seats as part of the wedding party. Marin slipped her hand through John's arm, and they walked together to the double doors of the sanctuary, listening for the bridge in the music that would signal her moment to enter.

Pachelbel's "Canon in D" reached their ears. *It's time!* her heart rejoiced. The ushers opened the doors, and suddenly Marin wished to prolong this moment—this sweet moment of anticipation.

But John gave her arm a little tug. "It is time," he reminded her in a raspy whisper.

She nodded, and their feet moved in one accord as they began their progress toward Marin's future.

Wedding guests rose as she and John appeared at the head of the aisle. Hurricane lanterns glowed from windowsills. White bows holding clusters of yellow roses and daisies adorned the ends of pews, the scent from the flowers mixing with those in her bouquet and creating a heady perfume that filled Marin's senses.

At the end of the aisle, Philip waited, so formal looking in his tuxedo. He'd had his hair trimmed for the occasion, giving him a dignified bearing that set Marin's heart a-pattering. How she loved this man—the man chosen for her by God. His handsome face wore an expression of joy that surely matched her own. She tried to hurry, eager to reach her groom, but John followed cues perfectly and refused to move faster than the gentle tone of the music dictated.

It seemed as though years passed before they reached Rev. Lowe and Philip stepped near, offering his hand. But John held tight to his sister, his gaze on the minister, waiting for the precise moment to place Marin's hand in Philip's.

Rev. Lowe asked, "Who gives this woman?"

John straightened his shoulders, cleared his throat, and answered with all due solemnity: "I do." Then he pointed at Philip and added, "But not for good."

A light titter of laughter sounded from the gathered guests, but Marin knew it wasn't malicious. Marin kissed John's cheek, whispering her promise, "Forever and always, John, I'm here for you." Her heart swelled with appreciation for the man who would allow her to be there for her brother.

John kissed her back, making his own promise. "I am here for you, Marin. I love you."

John pressed her forward, into Philip's waiting embrace, then crossed to sit between Aunt Lenore and Aunt Chris. She raised her smiling gaze to Philip—her groom, her God-chosen love—and his brown eyes crinkled into an answering smile. His hand pressed warmly against the base of her spine as they turned to face the minister.

The service flowed smoothly, perfectly, and finally came the moment Marin had longed for. She and Philip faced the congregation as the minister announced, "What God has brought together, let no man put asunder."

From his spot in the front pew, John asked, "What is *asunder*?"

Aunt Lenore sighed, fondness underscoring her tone. "Dear John. . ."

And Marin lifted her face to receive Philip's kiss.

# THAT WILDER BOY

# Dedication

For Kristian, who believes the most "tarnished" life
can be made shiny and new.

# Chapter 1

Carrie Mays hung the little cardboard Out to Lunch sign on the door handle of the manager's office and stepped into the bright August sunshine. Her lunch bag in one hand and a romance novel in the other, she moved briskly around Tower One, which housed the office, and made her way to the grassy courtyard.

For a moment she stood and perused the area surrounded by the six apartment towers then chose a bench directly in the center where an ornamental flowering tree provided an umbrella of dappled shade. Settling on the bench, she crossed her legs, opened her paper lunch bag, and withdrew her sandwich. She hummed as she unzipped the plastic bag and removed the tuna salad sandwich. Lowering her head, she offered a brief prayer then raised the sandwich to her lips.

Just as she took the first bite, a strange rattle sounded from somewhere behind her. Puzzled, she peeked over her shoulder. Unable to determine the source of the sound, she shrugged and turned her attention back to her sandwich.

The rattle became a *rat-tat-tat,* and then something cold slapped her across the back. With a startled shriek, she leaped from the bench, knocking her lunch bag to the ground. She spun around in time for a second slap of water to catch her in the front, right across her knees, soaking the hem of her capris.

"W–what?" For a moment, she remained rooted in place, unable to process what was happening. But as the arc of water came at her again, she realized the watering system on the north half of the courtyard had come to life. At noon? She jumped backward, avoiding another blast of water, but to her chagrin, her book, which still lay on the bench, took a solid hit.

"Oh no!" She waited for the arc to move on, snatched up her book and lunch bag, then dashed for safety on the sidewalk next to Tower Two. She stood, dripping, holding her sodden sandwich and book away from her body and shaking her head in disbelief at this disruption of her peaceful lunch.

A man trotted around from behind Tower Three and stopped at the edge of the sidewalk. Carrie watched him shield his eyes as he surveyed the area. A smile grew on his face, and he socked the air, releasing an exultant "Yes!" The word carried clearly across the expanse of grass to her ears.

*"Yes"?* She felt her fury mounting. Had *he* turned on the system at noon? Her notes said watering was to be done from five to six-thirty in the morning,

*not* at noon. So what was that "yes!" all about? She started to call to him, but he turned and jogged behind the building.

In a few moments, a stuttering *chop-chop-chop* then *hiss* signaled the shutdown of the sprinklers. Water droplets glistened on blades of grass like tiny diamonds. Carrie stared for a moment at the grass, waiting to see if the system would spring to life again. When it didn't, she stomped down the sidewalk, her anger increasing with every step in her squishy sandals, to the place where the man had disappeared. She rounded the corner of Tower Three at a good clip and collided full force with a solid chest.

"Ack!" The force knocked the book from her hand and bounced her backward two feet.

Dirty hands caught her upper arms, keeping her from falling on her seat. The moment she had her footing, she jerked loose and opened her mouth to let loose a tirade.

"What're you doing, running down the sidewalk like that?" The man's scolding voice cut off Carrie's words. "You could get hurt, especially when the sidewalk's wet. That makes it slippery."

Carrie's jaw dropped. *He* was chastising *her?* Without answering his question, she posed one of her own. "And just why *is* the sidewalk wet?" She swung her soggy lunch bag in the direction of the courtyard. "Since when do we run the watering system in the middle of the day?"

The man took one step backward and crossed his arms. Muscular arms, Carrie noted, tanned from the shoulders of his sleeveless T-shirt to his knobby knuckles. She swallowed and drew herself to her full height—which was minimal compared to his; he was so tall!—then threw back her head in a pretense of haughtiness to disguise the sudden quivering in her belly. "I asked you a question. Why was the watering system turned on at noon? It's clearly against policy."

A muscle in the man's jaw twitched as his gaze roved from the waterlogged bag in her hand to her dripping capris. In a low drawl, he answered, "This morning at five o'clock, according to policy"—he had the audacity to offer a teasing smirk—"when I ran the system, I noticed one of the sprinklers wasn't working. So. . .I replaced the head. I had to turn things on to make sure that's what the problem was. I was hoping it wasn't underground, in the line. Pretty big relief to me to see it working."

So he was the groundskeeper, Carrie realized. He had a valid reason for running the system, but still. . . "But still, couldn't you look before you turn things on? I was right out there on that bench, and getting wet was a rather unpleasant surprise." She gestured toward her capris. The linen was beginning to dry, turning into a crunch of wrinkles around her knees.

He glanced at her clothes then stooped over and picked up her book. He examined it for a moment, his lips tucking in as he ran his thumb across the damp, curling pages. Holding out the book on his broad hand, he met her gaze squarely. She noticed his eyes were a deep brown with very thick, curling lashes. Lashes most women would love to have. But they did nothing to downplay his rugged masculinity. She felt a blush building.

"I did look, but you weren't there at the time. You must've come out when I was behind the building. I'm really sorry." He raised his wide shoulders in a boyish shrug. "Maybe I didn't look closely enough. Rarely are any of the residents in the courtyard at noon—they're all inside eating."

His calm, penitent reply deflated Carrie's anger. She snatched the book from his hand and hugged it against her chest. "It's okay. I'll dry. It just surprised me is all."

A low chuckle emitted from his throat. "Yeah, I imagine." His gaze dropped to her soggy sandwich. "Can I replace your lunch?" He jerked his thumb toward Tower One. "There are some snack machines in the lobby—nothing fancy, but you won't go hungry."

Carrie backed up two slow steps. "No. No, thank you. I—I'm going to need to run home and change my clothes."

He followed, advancing the same two steps, a lazy smile on his handsome face. "So you'll be back?"

Carrie nodded, the movement rapid and jerky. Why was she feeling so. . . discombobulated? "Yes. I'm filling in as office manager while Jim's on vacation." She reversed another slow step.

He advanced another slow step. "Ah. So I'll see you around?" The idea seemed to please him.

It pleased her, too. "I suppose so, if you're here every day." She stopped moving backward.

He stopped, too, and stuck his hands into the pockets of his well-worn jeans. "I'm here every day. I'm Rocky."

She shook her head. "You're—what?"

He laughed softly, a pleasant sound. "Rocky. That's my name. Robert Jr., really, but I've always been called Rocky." He paused, tipping his head, the sun bringing out glints of yellow in his tousled brown locks. "And you are—?"

"Carrie." She allowed a grin to tip up her lips. "Caroline, really, but I've always been called Carrie."

A full smile grew on his face, exposing white teeth, the front two slightly overlapped. Dimples appeared in his honed cheeks, causing Carrie's heart to skip a beat. "Carrie. It's nice to meet you."

"You, too, Rocky." They stood for a silent minute, smiling at one another. Then Carrie jerked to attention. "I—I've got to go. I'll need to open the office again by one."

He nodded. "Better scoot then. Take care, Carrie. I'll see you around."

"Yes. . ." Why was her breathing so erratic? Blowing out a big breath, she said, "Good-bye, Rocky." She spun and trotted to the office where she retrieved her purse, climbed in her car, and headed for home. She resisted the urge to look back and see if Rocky was watching.

—

Rocky watched Carrie slide gracefully behind the wheel of a compact sports car, the layers of her long blond hair swinging forward to hide her profile from view. He swallowed as she tucked the hair behind her ear, revealing the sweet curve of her jaw. Pretty girl. Really pretty girl.

And very nice car. . .

He watched until the car left the grounds then turned back toward the tool shack. The car settled it. Carrie was out of his league. He'd thought as much when he'd seen the outfit she was wearing. All the beadwork on the top and around the cuffs of the pants gave her away. She didn't shop discount stores. Still, he hadn't been able to resist flirting a little bit.

Flirting came naturally. He admitted it without a hint of bigheadedness as he placed the tools in their spots on the peg board. Girls usually thought he was good-looking. There'd been a time when he used that to his advantage, but—and a rush of pleasure washed over him—he'd learned not to use people like that anymore.

Six months ago, he'd given his heart to Jesus. And ever since, he'd been working at replacing the bad habits with things from the Bible. He didn't use girls anymore. But he did enjoy a little healthy flirting. He hoped Jesus didn't mind.

The tool shack back in order, he grabbed his lunch box and headed for the courtyard, to the bench where Carrie'd been sitting. The concrete bench was dry to the touch, but darker gray showed where the spatter of water had struck.

He couldn't help smiling, thinking about how that cold water must have shocked the wind out of Carrie's lungs. Then he stifled his amusement, remembering the ruined book. He sure would like to replace it. He wracked his brain. What was the title? *Loyal. . .Something*. And the author? Marie. . .Somebody. He released a huff of aggravation. He'd seen similar books somewhere recently.

Ah! He slapped his thigh as remembrance dawned. In Eileen Cassidy's apartment. She had a whole shelf full of romance books. He looked toward Tower Three's fifth floor. He knew she'd welcome his company, and she probably had a full cookie jar. Decision made, he jumped up and headed for Tower Three.

Eileen answered his knock on the third tap. As he suspected, she offered a huge smile and waved him in. "Just in time for lunch! I've got some corned beef and Swiss on rye and some store-bought potato salad. Help yourself." She settled herself at the kitchen bar and pointed to the stool beside her. "Climb up."

"Are you sure?" Rocky stood beside the bar, the sight of the towering sandwich inviting him to dive in.

Eileen nodded. "I made an extra one for John, but he said he'd be going for hamburger for lunch. So I've got a spare."

That was all the prompting Rocky needed. He sat. "Thanks." He offered a brief prayer then lifted the hefty sandwich. "Corned beef and Swiss sounds a lot better than my bologna."

"Bologna. Phooey. Give it to Roscoe." Eileen laughed as her huge yellow and white cat, who lazed in a spot of sunshine in the middle of the living room, lifted his head and chirped a *"Brow?"* in response to her suggestion.

Rocky liked Eileen. She was really more his brother Philip's friend. She had worked at Philip's job-placement service for disabled adults before becoming a resident caretaker here at Elmwood Towers. But in the past months, she had adopted him, as well. Eileen adopted everybody, Rocky thought as he bit into the thick sandwich. He still had a little trouble relating to her boys, as she called the three adults with developmental delays who were in her charge, but his Bible said he was to treat people the way he wanted to be treated. All people. And he was trying.

"So what're you up to today?" Eileen asked, working her words around a bite.

Rocky propped his elbows on the edge of the bar, wiping away a bit of mustard with his knuckle. "Fixed the watering system this morning—bad sprinkler head. This afternoon, I've got to mow the north yard and the courtyard and do some weeding around your flower beds."

Eileen grinned. "Flowers are blooming like crazy, aren't they?"

"Yeah. But they sure create extra work for me." He grinned to let her know he wasn't complaining.

She laughed and nudged him with her elbow. "Aw, they're worth it. The boys and I are scoping out the grounds, looking for new places to plant. We want to add a garden or two every year. Might even try to bury some daffodil or tulip bulbs yet for a nice surprise next spring."

"Well, let me clear the spots for you when you find them, okay? Digging up that sod is too hard for you." The protectiveness caught Rocky by surprise. He remembered a time when he wouldn't have cared if an old lady worked too hard.

"I'll do that. But you will let the boys and me plant the flowers, won't you?"

Rocky nodded. "Sure." He finished his sandwich.

Eileen pointed into the kitchen. "Cookie jar's full."

He grinned. "Thanks." He ambled around the corner, pulled out two good-sized chocolate chip cookies, then headed back toward the bar. His gaze lit on the bookshelf that stood on the north wall of Eileen's living room. A row of short paperback novels drew him like a magnet. In four steps, he was in front of the shelf.

A chuckle sounded from beside him. Eileen stood at his elbow. "What are you looking at?"

He tapped one book with his finger. "These. You sure have a bunch of them."

Eileen nodded. "Yes. Ro-omances." She sighed the word, clasping her wrinkled hands beneath her chin and fluttering her eyelashes.

Rocky laughed, shaking his head. Who'd have thought romance still bloomed in the hearts of old ladies?

Eileen quirked a brow. "*You* don't read romances, do you?"

"No." He scanned the titles. "But I need one." Briefly he explained the morning's catastrophe and shared what he could remember of the book's title.

Eileen's eyebrows shot up. "Oh! One of my favorites—*Loyal Traitor*. I think Marie Harrison wrote that one." Eileen trailed her finger along the spines then crowed, "Yep! Right here." She pulled the book from its spot and held it out. "Is this it?"

"Yeah!" Rocky licked a bit of chocolate from his finger and took the book. "Can I buy this from you?"

Eileen shrugged, crossing to the sofa and sinking into the cushions. Roscoe immediately jumped in her lap. She petted the cat with one hand and flapped the other hand in his direction. "Take it."

Rocky hesitated. "But you said it's one of your favorites."

Eileen chuckled. "As you can see, I have a shelf full. I'll survive. Besides, if you're going to dig up a spot of sod for me, you'll earn the price of that book."

Rocky shook the book at her. "Thanks. Appreciate it." He glanced at his wristwatch and sighed. "I gotta get back to work."

Eileen pushed the purring cat from her lap and rose to walk him to the door. She gave him a quick hug before opening the door for him. "Enjoy your afternoon. And I hope the book does the trick."

Rocky turned back. "The trick?"

Eileen smirked. "Uh-huh. I saw the light in your eyes when you mentioned the girl on the bench."

Rocky felt heat climb his neck. "Oh, but—"

Eileen shook her finger at him. "Don't start that with me. I'm old, but I'm not stupid."

Rocky ducked his head, fighting the urge to smile. "Come on, Eileen. . . ."

She laughed and gave him another impulsive hug. "She could do worse! Now go get that book delivered and get your mowing done." She shooed him out the door.

*"She could do worse. . . ."* Eileen's words replayed themselves in Rocky's head as he stepped into the elevator. Who would have imagined someone saying that about Rocky Wilder, the troublemaker from the wrong side of the tracks? He punched the lobby button and felt the car begin its descent. As much as Eileen's

words touched him, he knew his limitations. Carrie was obviously not within his reach. He tapped his leg with the book. He'd make amends for ruining her novel; then he'd forget about her. She was only filling in for two weeks. It would be easy to forget her.

The elevator came to a stop, and he headed back to the courtyard. As he crossed the grass toward Tower One, a splash of pink and white caught his eye. Eileen's impatiens. Impulsively he veered to the right and pinched off a few blooms. The flowers would make up for her ruined lunch.

He'd make amends and then forget her. Easy.

*Yeah, right.*

# Chapter 2

Her wristwatch showed a quarter after one when Carrie zipped into the reserved parking space at Elmwood Towers. Stepping from the air-conditioned interior of the car into the August heat was a shock, but within minutes, she entered the manager's office and drew in a breath of cool air—apple-scented, thanks to the little plug-in air freshener she'd brought yesterday. Her sundress swirled around her ankles as she moved to the desk and set down her purse next to a wilting cluster of pink and white blossoms that rested on top of—

She straightened in surprise and looked around. Someone had been in here! And the only "someones" who had a key for this office, other than her, were the owners, the maintenance manager, and the groundskeeper.

The groundskeeper. Rocky. Of course.

Her heart turned a little somersault as she envisioned his tan, long-fingered hands plucking those delicate blossoms and arranging them into a little bouquet. Turning to the desk, she lifted the flowers to her nose, then picked up the book. The flowers were obviously from the courtyard, but where could he have gotten the book? She had no idea, but she couldn't believe how special it made her feel to think he had gone to that trouble. How long had it been since someone had done something so unexpectedly sweet for her? Not since Carl.

The happy lift in her heart plummeted as she thought of Carl. Even after two years, it stung to remember how hopelessly in love she'd fallen only to discover Carl's kindness was meant to win her trust fund, not her heart. With a sigh, she pushed aside thoughts of Carl and focused on the pink and white bouquet.

The poor little petals drooped. Maybe a drink would refresh them. She hoped so. She walked to the kitchenette and scrounged around for a plastic cup which she filled with water. Then she arranged the flowers in the cup. They spilled over the cup's brim in a haphazard manner, but she didn't care. Returning to the office area, she cleared the corner of the desk and placed the flowers where they'd receive a splash of afternoon sun.

Funny how cheerful the whole room seemed with the addition of the flower bouquet. As she worked, her gaze often drifted to the flowers, and each time, her heart gave that same happy lift. Around two thirty, she heard the rev of a lawn mower starting up—*Rocky*—and she nearly jumped out of her seat to race to the window. But just as her palms pressed the desktop, ready to push herself from the chair, good sense took over.

How ridiculous would she look, running to the window for a peek at the gardener? The man accidentally ruined her lunch and her book—and he made a simple gesture of apology. She shouldn't read any more into it than that. The last thing she needed was for him to get the wrong idea.

She kept herself in her seat, but as the mower's motor volume increased, indicating the mower was moving closer, she couldn't help straining upward to peer out for a glimpse of him as the machine went by. And as it passed the window, he turned his head and caught her looking.

She jerked her gaze back to the desktop where it collided with the romance novel. Her heart rate increased to double-time. *RRRRRRRrrrrrrrr.* . . . The mower moved on. But her pulse didn't slow. She pressed her hand to her chest and said, "Stop it! Just get busy here."

She tried. But when she heard the mower's approach—*rrrrrrRRRRRR*—she couldn't resist another peek. Sure enough—he looked, too. And this time, he smiled.

She smiled back. She couldn't stop herself. Then she looked away, certain her face flamed red even through her tanning booth bronze. *RRRRRRRrrrrrr.* The mower and its rider moved beyond her sight. She stuck out her lower lip and blew, ruffling her bangs. Enough of this now! Determinedly she set her attention on the rent receipts. But the mower's coming and going continued to disrupt her focus.

—❦—

Rocky couldn't hold back his grin. He'd seen Carrie's big blue eyes peeking through that window as he went by on the mower. And he'd seen her face break into a smile.

She'd found the book and flowers. And she appreciated them.

Felt really good to do something nice like that. When he looked back on his life, he couldn't find too many instances of doing good. He'd terrorized smaller kids in grade school, hungry for the power bullying brought. In junior high and early high school, he'd run with a rough crowd and had gotten into more than his fair share of trouble from vandalism to breaking curfew. But not until he got caught stealing did he figure out the consequences weren't worth the risk. He'd quit breaking the law, but he'd never really grasped the idea of doing good deeds. Instead he'd remained a bully. Made his heart ache now, thinking of how many people he had hurt with his actions.

He sure wished it hadn't taken him twenty-nine years to figure out doing good brought more pleasure than causing trouble, but at least he was finally there. Now he had a lot of making up to do. Funny how God had plunked him here at Elmwood Towers, right where one of the people he'd wronged was living.

In his mind, he could still see the teenaged John's trusting face, expecting

Rocky to offer assistance when he needed it, but instead Rocky had played a dirty trick. At the time, he'd thought it was funny, causing the disabled boy to look like a fool, but now? His grip tightened on the steering wheel. As uncomfortable as it made him to be around John and the reminder of how mean he'd been, he was glad for the opportunity to set things right. He whispered a prayer for John right then, that the man would have a good day at work and no one would do anything unkind to him. It felt good to talk to God so easily, too.

Rocky slowed the mower to maneuver around the rock border of one of Eileen's garden plots, and the sight of those flowers reminded him of his promise to dig up another garden spot for her. A grin tugged at his cheeks. That Eileen—she sure was something, friends with everybody. He could learn some lessons from her on being Christlike, that was for sure.

He straightened the mower again, aiming it past the office's window. His attention immediately reverted to the girl in the office. Would Carrie step out, flag him down, thank him for the book and flowers? His hopeful gaze drifted to the window, but this time, Carrie didn't even look up as he went by.

He blew out a breath of discouragement and thumped the steering wheel with the heel of his hand. That was the problem with a mindless task like mowing—it let a person's mind wander too much. What was he doing thinking about Carrie anyway? He had no business sneaking glances at someone like her. She was obviously quality. Quality wasn't a word anyone would attach to Rocky. Not even Eileen in her kindest moment.

The mower made a final swing through the center of the courtyard. Out of the corner of his eye, he caught a glimpse of a floral sundress. Against his will, his head swiveled in that direction. Sure enough, it was Carrie. His heart pounded hard under his sweaty T-shirt. Was she waiting to talk to him? But no, she was moving—heading down the sidewalk toward the parking lot.

He swallowed the lump of disappointment that filled his throat as she climbed into her little car and pulled away without a backward glance. Defeated, Rocky turned his gaze straight ahead. Sure, he was making changes on the inside, but on the outside? He was still rough ol' Rocky Wilder. Nothing but a glorified gardener. His pop had told him he'd never amount to a hill of beans, and in all likelihood Pop was right. His brother, Philip, had been the smart one. Rocky barely squeaked by in high school. Manual labor was all he was good for. Carrie must have seen the truth, too. Why would a girl like that bother with a rough laborer like him?

*Just focus on your work,* he told himself firmly, wiping sweat that trickled from his forehead. *Remember that verse. . . Whatever you do, do it as for the Lord, not for men. Even if it's just gardening, do your best. But quit thinking about impressing some girl who's out of your league. It's a waste of time.*

⟋⟍

Carrie sat at the stop sign, letting several opportunities to pull into the flow of traffic escape, while she fingered the copy of *Loyal Traitor*, which rested on the console. Guilt pinched her conscience. She should have thanked him. It was rude not to acknowledge a kind gesture. Her mother had certainly taught her manners! Why hadn't she said anything to Rocky?

She knew why. Fear, plain and simple. Rocky was a gardener. Probably didn't make much more than minimum wage. The minute he found out she had money, he'd be after her at full throttle, but not because he liked her. Because he liked her wealth. Maybe he'd already figured it out. After all, everyone in town knew of the Steinwoods. Even though she insisted on using her deceased father's name rather than her stepfather's, it was common knowledge that Carrie Mays was Mac Steinwood's stepdaughter. Between her father's millions and Mac's millions, men looked at Carrie and saw dollar signs. It had happened before. She wouldn't let it happen again.

It didn't matter at all that Rocky set her heart to fluttering as it hadn't fluttered in more than two years. What mattered was that her heart would only be broken if she allowed him in. And Carrie wouldn't suffer through another broken heart.

She removed her foot from the brake and eased into traffic, aiming her car toward home. She drove automatically, her mind refusing to let go of Rocky. What was it about him? He was undeniably handsome with his thick, unruly hair and chiseled features. His boyish smile, with the overlapping front teeth, had a charm that was nearly irresistible. His muscular arms, wide shoulders, and narrow hips spoke of a man who knew how to work hard. That strength appealed to her, she realized. So many of the men her stepfather encouraged her to date used their minds rather than their muscles at their jobs, and most had gotten soft. She couldn't call Rocky soft. The name *Rocky* fit him well—he seemed as solid as a rock.

Yet there must be a tenderness underneath. Concern had made him scold when she'd run down the wet sidewalk. His penitent expression when he realized he'd ruined her book and her lunch also showcased kindness. He'd offered to replace her lunch, had managed to replace her book, and had even taken the time to pick her some flowers as an apology. Sweet. . . Despite his rough appearance, Rocky was very, very sweet.

Her fingers found the book again, and she caressed the smooth cover, wishing she were running her fingers across the back of Rocky's hand instead.

*Stop it!* This was ridiculous. She was fantasizing like some lovesick high school girl. How silly to fixate on a man she would likely never see again. Her time at Elmwood Towers would last as long as Jim's vacation—another nine days. Obviously she and Rocky moved in different social circles. She'd be back in graduate school soon, finishing her second degree. Why spend time mooning over someone who would be in and out of her life in a matter of days?

Ridiculous. Absolutely ridiculous.

She pulled up to the gates of the Steinwood estate, pushed the button to lower the car's window, and punched in the security code on the button pad. The gates obediently swung wide, and she pulled through, following the curving bricked driveway to the four-car garage behind the house. She pushed the remote to open her port in the garage, guided the car into its spot, then pushed the remote again to seal herself inside. Opening the car door, she reached for her purse and the book.

The moment her hand closed over the novel, guilt slapped her again. She owed Rocky a thank-you. Not only was it bad manners to ignore his gesture, but it was unchristian, as well. She knew the Bible verse about whatever a person did for the least of these was like doing it for God. She had failed her Savior by ignoring Rocky this afternoon.

She lowered her head and offered a brief prayer of apology to God. She then asked Him to help her find a way to apologize to Rocky. "But don't let me lead him on, Lord," she added fervently. "He's too. . .appealing. I don't want to give him the wrong impression. I just want to say I'm sorry. Help him see only an apology in my words, not an invitation to pursue me. I don't want that, Lord!"

Her prayer finished, she left the garage and entered the house through the service porch and into the kitchen. Her favorite scent—cinnamon and apples—greeted her nostrils the moment she stepped through the door, and she sniffed appreciatively, shooting a wide smile at Myrna, the cook.

"Mm, something smells great!" Her gaze located a dozen muffins cooling on a rack on the marble-topped counter. "Are they for anything special? Mom having her book club ladies over or something?"

Myrna returned Carrie's smile, her full cheeks dimpling. "No, Miss Carrie. I bought a bushel of apples this morning, and I've been making pies all afternoon to put in the freezer. I had some leftover slices, so I grated them for muffins. They're still warm. Would you like one now?"

Carrie eagerly reached for a muffin. The crumbly topping of brown sugar and cinnamon melted in her mouth with the first bite. She rolled her eyes and released a groan of pleasure. "Oh, Myrna, these are wonderful!" She licked the cinnamon from her fingers and winked. "And I bet you left out the calories, too, right?"

Myrna laughed, and Carrie joined in. But both women kept their voices quiet. Carrie's parents didn't approve of her carrying on with the staff. She finished her muffin while Myrna began stacking dirty mixing bowls in the dishwasher.

"Thanks so much," Carrie said after finishing the last bite. "That was scrumptious."

"You're welcome, Miss Carrie," Myrna said with a warm smile.

Carrie started to leave the kitchen, but then an idea struck. She spun back o face the cook. "Myrna, if those muffins aren't for anything special, could I possibly have some of them? Maybe a half dozen—or even just four—to take to work tomorrow?"

Myrna shrugged. "Certainly. When they're cool, I'll put them in a container for you. They'll be in the butler's pantry."

Carrie dashed back and gave the sturdy cook a quick hug. "Thanks, Myrna! You're a doll!"

Myrna blushed with pleasure, but she didn't say anything.

Carrie headed for her bedroom, a smile on her lips. Her thank-you would be made in a way sure to please Rocky. And then she could set aside her guilt and forget all about him. But when she placed *Loyal Traitor* on her bedside table, the title suddenly mocked her. Would Rocky prove to be loyal or a traitor if she gave him a chance?

She shook her head, irritated with herself. It seemed apparent her heart would prove to be traitorous when it came to forgetting Rocky.

# Chapter 3

Rocky trooped across the still-dewy grass, a spade over one shoulder and length of garden hose looped through his elbow. He hoped Eileen wou' be pleased with the area he'd cleared for her tulips and daffodils. H research indicated a sunny area was preferable, so he'd chosen a spot along th walking path behind the Towers, the one that led to the recreation areas.

Instead of clearing a rectangle, he'd laid the hose in a shape that resembled th top of a grand piano, its straight base against the concrete walkway. He'd do son checking and see if he could locate another concrete bench in the storage barn. he bought a flowering bush and some perennials, the garden would make a pleasar spot for residents to sit and relax from spring through fall. Maybe he could even r up one of those solar lamps to provide light in the area at night and add a touch elegance.

Whistling, he rounded the corner toward the toolshed, and something caug his eye. His steps slowed. A little wicker basket with a napkin draped across it hur from a nail in the doorjamb. Where'd that come from? He swung the spade fro his shoulder, leaned it against the shed wall, and unhooked the basket. Pinchir the napkin between his thumb and first finger—his hands were filthy—he lifte the edge of the blue-and-white-checkered cloth and peeked inside.

Muffins, shaped like oversized toadstools, with some sort of crumbly stu across their tops. He stuck his nose over the basket and sniffed, and the scer of cinnamon tickled his nostrils. Licking his lips in anticipation, he carried th basket into the shed and set it down on a shelf. He hung up the hose and put th spade away then smiled at the basket as he passed it on the way back outside the hydrant where he washed his hands.

He knew who left them. He'd seen Eileen troop off about an hour ago wit her boys, obviously taking them to work. She must have seen him, too, and fig ured out he was clearing her garden spot. The muffins were her thank-you. We as soon as he was cleaned up, he'd head to her apartment and give her a big hu of thanks.

He dried his hands on the seat of his pants, tucked the basket under his arr and headed to Tower Three. He hummed as he rode the elevator to the fift floor. A knock on Eileen's door brought an immediate response.

"Rocky!" Eileen greeted him. Her cat, Roscoe, hung from her arm. Sh waved a hand, inviting him in. "Taking a break?"

"I just came to say thanks." He tipped the basket in her direction. "These look great."

Eileen lifted the edge of the napkin and peeked inside. Her eyebrows shot upward. "They do look great." Roscoe tipped his nose toward them, too, so she put the cat down. "But why are you telling me thanks?"

He frowned. "Didn't you leave them for me?"

She shrugged. "Can't blame me. I bake cookies, not muffins." She ran her pudgy finger along the edge of the woven basket. "Besides, I wouldn't package something up that fancy. Baggies or recycled margarine tubs are my containers of choice."

"Oh." He looked into the basket. "I just figured you'd seen me clearing your new garden spot and left me these as a reward."

Eileen put her hands on her hips. "Now wait a minute. That's what the book was for, right?"

Rocky grinned.

"But where'd you put my new spot?"

The eagerness in her voice increased Rocky's eagerness to share it with her. He guided her to the kitchen where he could point out the window. Roscoe followed and rubbed against his leg.

"See along the walking path? I cleared an area big enough to hold a bench as well as a nice flowering shrub—maybe a hydrangea or butterfly bush." He gestured as he spoke, envisioning the finished garden. "I could plant some ground cover, something your tulips and daffodils can pop through, and then after they've bloomed and died out, we could put in some annuals so the garden will keep blooming all through the summer and into fall."

Eileen stared at him in amazement. "Rocky, that sounds wonderful! All I wanted was a few holes to drop bulbs in. I didn't expect a whole landscaped garden."

Rocky shrugged. "Once I got started, the ideas kept growing. I hope that's okay."

"It's more than okay," she said. She crossed her arms, leaned against the counter, and smirked at him. "You've got a knack, young man. You're going to have this place looking so spiffy they'll raise the rent."

He laughed. "Not likely."

"I'm serious, Rocky. You should consider hiring yourself out as a landscaper."

Rocky felt his chest puff with pleasure at her praise. Still, he countered, "You have to go to school if anybody's gonna take you seriously as a landscaper. I couldn't do that."

"Why not?"

He shrugged. There were a number of reasons, funding being a major part of it. But he said, "Too dumb, I guess."

"Nonsense. You should think about it. And *pray* about it. God gives gifts, and He expects us to use 'em." Then she pulled her mouth sideways and added, " 'Course, we didn't solve the mystery of the muffins, did we?"

Rocky looked into the basket again. "No, I guess we didn't."

"Well, I think I can solve it." Eileen crossed to the refrigerator and pulled out a jug of milk. She poured two glasses as she continued. "This morning, when I took the boys to work, we passed the manager's office and waved at that cute little substitute. She was eating a muffin that looked an awful lot like those in the basket."

Rocky felt his ears go hot. "She—she was?"

"Yep." Eileen plunked the two glasses of milk on the kitchen bar and gestured for Rocky to sit. "So my guess is those muffins are a thank-you—but not from me. They're a thank-you from the girl you gave *Loyal Traitor* to yesterday."

Rocky sat down and took a sip of cold milk. Carrie, huh? He felt a smile growing, but he tugged it down with his finger. *Can't read too much into it*, he told himself. Just a you-scratched-my back I'll-scratch-yours sort of thing. Still, imagining her sneaking over to the toolshed and leaving that little basket made his chest feel tight.

"So can I have one?"

Eileen's voice brought Rocky back to the present. "Huh? Oh. . .sure." He flipped the napkin off the basket. "Go ahead." They each took a muffin and munched in companionable silence while Roscoe moved back and forth between their feet, his gold eyes turned upward in hopefulness.

When Eileen had wiped her hands clean on a paper towel, she turned to Rocky and asked brightly, "So what's your next move?"

Rocky jerked his gaze in her direction. "What?"

She shook her head. "Your next move. It's your turn, you know. You gave her a book; she gave you muffins. Now it's back to you."

"Oh." Rocky rubbed the back of his neck. "I—I guess maybe I should at least say thanks, huh?"

Eileen nodded. "Yep. You should."

Then something occurred to him. "But what if it wasn't Carrie? I thought it was you, and I was wrong. What if you're wrong? What if whoever gave me the muffins also gave some to Carrie? That could be why you saw her eating one."

Eileen scratched her chin. "I suppose that's a possibility. . . ."

The more he thought about it, the more certain he became. Carrie had just taken off yesterday without so much as a good-bye. Was it likely she'd bake him muffins after ignoring him? But then again, maybe the muffins were an "I'm-sorry" message. Maybe she felt bad about not acknowledging the book. Maybe this was her way of apologizing. . . .

"What're you thinking?" Eileen cut into his thoughts again.

He offered a sheepish grin. "I was just trying to figure out why Carrie might've left them. Assuming she's the one who did."

"Seems obvious to me," Eileen said as she got up and swept the crumbs from the counter into her palm. She headed for the kitchen wastebasket with Roscoe on her heels. "It's a thank-you gesture, pure and simple. 'Course"—she fixed him with a firm look—"there's only one surefire way to find out."

He sucked in his breath.

"You just gotta go ask."

—◦◦—

Carrie rustled through the file of applications, searching for a blank document. She heard the office door open and felt a brief rush of warm air that activated the apple scent from the air freshener. Without turning around, she said, "I'll be with you in just a moment."

"No hurry."

The deep, masculine voice fired her heart into her throat as if from a slingshot. She spun around, slamming the drawer shut with her elbow. The *crack!* made her jump, and she felt a blush climbing her cheeks. She twisted her hands together behind her back to keep from covering her face.

"G—good morning." Her voice sounded unnaturally high, unnaturally bright. The heat in her face increased. *Just knock it off, Carrie!*

"Good morning." A lazy smile—the same one that had set her heart to beating like the bass drum in a marching band yesterday—tipped up his lips. His brown eyes sparkled warmly. He wore another T-shirt with the sleeves cut off, and on the right side, a string dangled, calling attention to his clearly defined bicep.

She forced her gaze downward to his hand and encountered the wicker basket she'd left outside the toolshed, its napkin crumpled in the bottom. So he'd found the muffins. She swallowed hard and raised her gaze to meet his.

"I—I wondered. . ." Rocky lifted the basket and waved it up and down. "Someone left me a little surprise this morning. Was it you?"

For a split second, Carrie considered denying it just to avoid having to explain why she'd done it. But she couldn't make herself lie. She also couldn't find her voice. What was it about this man that made her tongue-tied? She'd never suffered such an intense reaction to anyone. Silently she offered a quick nod. Scurrying across the floor to the desk, she began shifting things, creating stacks, knowing she was only going to have to unstack everything again later.

His smile widened, bringing out crinkly lines around his eyes. The effect was devastating. Her hands stilled as she found an answering smile building on her face.

"Thank you," he said. "They were really good. I shared them with my friend Eileen. She said they were good, too."

Eileen? Carrie's heart skipped a beat. So he had a girlfriend. Well, that settled that. Then she mentally kicked herself. What on earth was she thinking? "Oh? Well, good." She finally found her voice. It snapped out tartly. "I'm glad you and *Eileen* enjoyed them."

He seemed to falter for a moment, his smile fading. Then he reached out—she held her breath as his hand neared—and placed the basket on the edge of the desk.

"You'll want your basket back. Thanks again, Carrie." He turned to leave.

He'd pushed the door open, had his foot raised to step out when she called, "Wait!"

He turned back slowly, allowing the door to shut. "Yeah?"

"I—I need to say"—she pulled at the collar of her blouse with one finger—"that is, I thank you for the book. And the flowers yesterday." Curiosity got the best of her, and she blurted out, "Where did you find a replacement for *Loyal Traitor?*"

Rocky's grin returned. "Eileen. She has a whole slew of those romance books, so she was willing to part with one. I'm glad I could replace it."

Eileen again. Carrie turned back to the desk. "Yes, well, tell her thank you for me, will you? It was kind of her to give it up."

Rocky nodded slowly. The smile slipped away again at her sharp tone. "I'll do that. See you around, Carrie." He left.

Carrie sank into the chair and covered her face with her hands. She'd been rude. Again. An attack of jealousy had done it. And she had no reason to be jealous—none whatsoever. With a sigh, she shook her head, unstacked all the papers she had slung together and tried to put them in order. But she couldn't concentrate.

Releasing a huff of aggravation, she pushed herself from the desk and stomped toward the door. Her conscience pricked sorely, and she wouldn't be able to work until she'd set things straight. She'd have to find Rocky and apologize. Where would he be in the middle of the morning? Then she heard something fire up—a weed trimmer, maybe? She followed the sound and located Rocky slicing down the growth next to the foundation of Tower Four.

She waited on the sidewalk until he paused, shutting off the machine to lean over and pick up something. As he bent forward, his T-shirt slid up in the back, and a small book in the rear pocket of his jeans caught her attention. A little testament with a green cover, like the ones the Gideons used to hand out in elementary schools.

Rocky read the Bible? He carried it to work with him? Her heart began to thrum as happiness filled her chest. That must mean he was a Christian.

He turned then and found her watching. He ran his fingers through his hair, leaving it in sweat-stiffened spikes. "Hey. Did you need something?" He seemed wary. She couldn't blame him, after the way she'd just acted in the office.

She took two steps forward, nodding. "Yes. To apologize. I'm sorry I got snappy." She didn't offer an explanation.

He didn't ask for one. Just raised one shoulder in a shrug. "It's okay. Apology accepted." His gaze shot past her shoulder, and he raised his hand to wave.

Carrie looked behind her to see an older lady—midsixties probably—on the sidewalk across the courtyard. She recognized her as the resident caretaker for a group of men with handicaps.

The lady held up a plastic grocery sack and hollered, "Martin forgot his lunch! I'm taking it to him. Want to meet at noon at my place for some tuna casserole? Pay you back for that muffin."

"Sure!" Rocky called. "See you then!"

Carrie spun back to face Rocky. So that was who he'd shared the muffins with. Then that meant. . . She fought the urge to giggle as she realized how misplaced her jealousy had been. Eileen was obviously not Rocky's girlfriend. Rocky's attractiveness, the gift of the book and flowers, and the little testament in his back pocket all combined to create a picture Carrie wanted to explore more thoroughly.

"Rocky," she heard herself say, "what are you doing after work?"

He shielded his eyes with his broad hand. "Nothing. Why?"

Surprised by her own audacity, Carrie asked, "I thought maybe we could take a walk around the grounds. Get. . .acquainted."

He seemed to study her for a few silent minutes, and she held her breath, certain he would refuse. But finally he nodded. "Yeah. Okay. That sounds good. Want me to come by the office around four?"

"How about I come looking for you when I'm finished?" She thought of the mess she'd made of the stacks of paperwork on the desk. "I have some catching up to do in the office."

"Okay then."

Her heart tripped happily at the prospect.

He stepped forward, swinging his hand toward her. "Here you go. It's just a weed, but I hated to whack it off when it's so pretty."

Between his fingers, he held a fragile green stem with a cup-shaped white flower on its end. Carrie thought her heart might melt. She took the tiny blossom, pressed it to her bodice, and gave Rocky the biggest smile she knew how to give. Then she dashed down the sidewalk.

# Chapter 4

Rocky lifted the handle on the hydrant behind the toolshed. The pipe jerked for a few seconds; then water spurted out in a solid flow. He pushed his forearms under the rush and used his hands to scrub away the bits of grass, dust, and sweat all the way from his wrists to his shoulders. The water was ice-cold. It made him shiver, but it felt good. Cupping his hands, he trapped water and splashed it over his face once, twice, then again. Finally he ran his wet hands over his hair, smoothing the wild strands into place.

He slammed down the hydrant's handle, stopping the flow, and glanced at his clothes. Too bad he couldn't pop his whole self under that water and really get clean. His jeans showed signs of his labors—dirt smudges, grass stains, and even a blotch of oil from refilling the mower's oil pan. Nothing he could do about that, though. Maybe he should start carting a clean pair of jeans and a shirt to work every day, just in case. . . .

Aw, what was he thinking now? He stomped away from the hydrant and entered the shed to lean against the workbench. It was stuffy in the shed, but he stayed put anyway, out of sight. He felt a strange tremble in his belly that had nothing to do with the shock of cold water after being in the sun all day. The tremble was nervous excitement.

*Carrie.*

Just her name was enough to make his gut clench. He couldn't quite figure out what made her so special. He'd been around pretty girls before. Been around girls who dressed nice and smelled good, too. But somehow when Carrie dressed nice, it looked natural, not made up. And instead of perfumey, she smelled—he crunched his forehead, trying to identify the scent—like apples. That was it. She always smelled like apples—a clean, fresh scent that suited her clean, fresh appearance.

He chipped at some loose paint on the workbench with his thumbnail as he considered the next hour or so in her company. He pictured them side by side—him in his grubby work clothes, smelling of earth and sweat, her in her green blouse and flowered skirt, smelling of fresh fruit. What a pair they made. Why would she want to spend time with him? He couldn't imagine.

But one thing he knew—he'd enjoy every minute of it. It was doubtful Carrie would ever ask to go for a walk with him again. When would they have the chance? So he'd enjoy today. He sure wished his stomach would settle down, though. To calm himself, he slipped his New Testament from his back pocket and hunted for words of encouragement.

He felt inept as he flipped random pages, scanning text that was still pretty unfamiliar. But then in the fifteenth chapter of John, he latched onto verse sixteen. He read the words aloud. " 'Ye have not chosen me, but I have chosen you, and ordained you, that ye should go and bring forth fruit, and that your fruit should remain: that whatsoever ye shall ask of the Father in my name, he may give it you.' "

Rocky chuckled. "Well, God, that sounds pretty good, considering how Carrie smells like apples and I spent some time transplanting a crab apple tree by the swimming pool this afternoon. And I like the idea of asking for something in Your name and actually getting it. So, if You don't mind, could You give me a calm stomach? Get rid of the nervousness. I'd like to enjoy my time with Carrie, not be afraid of it."

Funny. The prayer did make his stomach feel better. He smiled toward the ceiling. "Thanks a lot, God." As he slipped the Bible back into his pocket, he heard a scuffle. His gaze landed on the doorway, and he found Carrie waiting, a timid smile on her face. He pushed off from the workbench. Had she heard him praying?

He shot past her into the sunshine, a cold sweat breaking out across his shoulders and back. "Hey, Carrie. Ready for that walk?"

She stepped aside as he closed the shed doors and slipped a padlock into place. "Yes. But you'll have to choose where we go. I'm not all that familiar with the grounds. It's been awhile since I was out here on a regular basis."

Rocky heard the quaver in her voice. She must be nervous, too. He found that comforting. Offering a smile, he said, "We've got a nice walking path that leads to the pool, along the golf course and back. It's about a two-mile hike. Are you up to that?"

"Sure."

"Then let's go."

They walked in silence for several minutes, taking slow, relaxed steps. Carrie had some sort of high-heeled sandals with a strap across her toes but no other way to hold the shoe on her foot, and Rocky worried she might fall out of the things. He noticed she moved gracefully, though, despite the dangerous-looking footwear. He swallowed and turned his gaze across the grounds. Pride filled him as he took in the neatly manicured lawns, trimmed shrubs, and garden plots. All the fruits of his labor.

The verse from John—the part about being ordained to bring forth fruit—mingled with Eileen's words "You've got a knack," and he found himself admitting a real interest in doing this kind of work on his own. Could it be God had that in mind for him, too?

"Things look so nice and neat." Carrie's soft voice intruded into Rocky's thoughts.

"Thanks." He glanced at her, giving her an appreciative smile. "I work pretty hard at it."

"I can tell." She paused beside the spot of ground he'd dug that morning for Eileen's tulips. "I mean, just the shape of this area. It mimics the curve of the sidewalk yet is different enough that it's eye-catching, something an artist would do. Did you get the idea from a gardening book?"

Rocky shoved his hands into his pockets. "No. I just laid out a garden hose and played with it until I found a shape I liked."

She looked at him, her blue eyes wide. "A garden hose? What an ingenious idea."

Ingenious. She'd said he was ingenious. Rocky thought his chest might explode. He shrugged and forced a calm tone. "Whatever works."

They started walking again, following the concrete path. The sun felt hot on Rocky's head, and though he noticed little beads of sweat on Carrie's nose, she didn't complain. He didn't either. Usually by this time, he was plunked in his recliner in front of the little window air-conditioning unit in his trailer. But walking in the sunshine with Carrie was even better than sitting under that cold blast of air.

"So. . .all of these garden areas. . ." She tucked her hair behind her ear and peeked up at him. "Did you design all of them?"

Rocky shook his head. "No, not quite. Eileen and her boys—that's what she calls John, Tim, and Martin, the three men in her quad—started planting flowers last spring. Eileen likes color, and the grounds had bushes but not many flowers. She was spending her own money, buying flowers; then she and her boys would plant them."

He scratched his head, chuckling. That Eileen was something else. "I told her I'd help, so I started looking for places where the residents might enjoy seeing some flowering plants and also tried to think of the overall appearance of the grounds, giving it a balance of grassy and flowered areas."

"Well, you've done a commendable job. I would imagine the owners are pleased."

"I hope so. They haven't fussed about it, anyway."

They passed the swimming pool where two women in one-piece suits and bathing caps stood in waist-deep water and visited. Carrie waved when the women did; then she turned back to Rocky. "How long have you worked here?"

"About eight months. I like it, but—" He stopped his flow of words, aware he nearly let something slip that was a barely formed idea in his mind.

Carrie came to a halt and looked up at him, squinting against the sun. "But?"

Rocky chewed his upper lip. His hand found the testament in his back pocket, and he ran his thumb along the top edge of the book. Carrie's compliments, Eileen's comment, and the verse from John seemed to point him toward accepting the idea as one he should pursue. Yet there were stumbling blocks. Big ones.

Instead of addressing Carrie's question, he asked bluntly, "Are you a Christian?"

Those blue eyes snapped open. She tucked her hair behind her ears and nodded. "Yes. I accepted Christ about a year and a half ago, at a college crusade meeting."

College. Rocky swallowed hard. "Then can I ask you to do something?"

She waited, her expression expectant.

"Would you pray for something? I—I have this idea. A dream, I guess, of what I'd like to do. But it'll be tough. It'll take some minor miracles, I think, to make it happen."

Her soft laughter made him want to smile, too. She held her hands outward in a gesture of inquiry. "Well, what is it?"

Rocky pointed to a bench along the pathway and guided her there. They sat, and eagerness built in his chest as he finally gave voice to his thoughts. "I really like landscaping. Eileen says I have a knack, and—well, I've never been quite sure what I wanted to do with myself." He scratched his head again, somewhat embarrassed. "I guess it's not too good to finally be deciding that when I left high school behind eleven years ago, but. . ."

Carrie's gaze never wavered from his face. Her genuine interest gave him the confidence to continue.

"But I've been thinking maybe I could open my own landscaping business. Contract myself out to plan the grounds for homes and businesses."

Carrie tipped her head. "Why do you think that will take a minor miracle to make happen?"

Rocky stretched his legs out straight and crossed his ankles. "Well, I'm sure not rolling in dough, if you know what I mean. Schooling takes money."

Carrie seemed to stiffen suddenly, her gaze narrowing.

Rocky went on. "And I'm sure not smart enough to get those scholarships and things some people do—besides that, I'm probably too old to apply. It also takes money to get a business up and running. Advertising, tools, employees. So somehow God's gonna have to come up with the funds. So there's my prayer request. Would you mind praying with me—that if this is what I'm supposed to do God will make the money available?"

⟶ᴄ͜⟵

Carrie stared hard into Rocky's face. She felt as though a boulder had dropped into her stomach when he'd said he wasn't "rolling in dough." Did he know she was? Did he expect her to offer him the money? She didn't want to think ill of Rocky—his simple prayer in the toolshed had touched her. He'd admitted to being afraid of spending time with her. She had assumed it was nervousness, but now she wondered. Did his fear stem from knowing she had the financial backing to make his dream a reality?

Oh, how she wished she could escape the Steinwood legacy of wealth! She was so tired of second-guessing people's motives. Just once, she'd like to relax, to know without any doubt the person wanted to be with her for herself, not for what she could give them.

Rocky sat silently, waiting for her response. She had to say something. "How—how much have you researched this idea?"

He grimaced. "Not a lot, I admit. It's really a new idea. In fact, you're the first person I've even talked to about it."

"Oh, really?" Her heart constricted. Why would he choose her?

"Yeah. Maybe you can help me out some. You must be friends with the owners of Elmwood Towers since you're filling in for the manager. Do you know whether they'd recommend me for other jobs if I started a landscaping business?"

Friends with the owner? Didn't he know she was the owner's stepdaughter? Or was he playing dumb, hoping to convince her to use some of Mac's money to give him what he wanted? Confusion raced through Carrie's head. She didn't want to play games with Rocky. She wanted him to be honest with her. And she needed to be honest with him, so she took a big breath and confessed, "I guess you could say I'm friends with the owners. Mac Steinwood is my stepfather."

He jerked backward so sharply he nearly fell off the bench. "You're Caroline Steinwood?"

His shock did not seem contrived, but a part of Carrie still wondered. "You honestly didn't know that?"

"No. I mean. . ." He shook his head then ran his hand through his hair. "We never gave our last names. Caroline Steinwood."

"Actually Mays," she corrected. "I go by my father's name. Mac never adopted me." His genuine surprise convinced her he hadn't deliberately set out to use her influence. A sense of relief came with the realization.

"Still. . ." Rocky scooted over a few inches, putting some space between them. His breath huffed out. "Wow, I would've never imagined spending time with Caroline Steinwood."

He sounded impressed. Carrie lowered her head. Now things wouldn't be the same. Dollar signs. All he'd see would be dollar signs from here on out. She stood. "I'd probably better head for home. My folks will be expecting me."

Rocky stood, too. He pushed his hands into his pockets. "Okay. Let's go back to the office then." They continued along the walking path, neither speaking, until they were nearly to the Towers. Suddenly Rocky touched her arm, bringing her to a halt. "Carrie, I really would appreciate it if you'd pray for God to make my idea happen. If it's meant to be, I mean."

She looked into his brown eyes, searching for any sign of insincerity. Maybe it was wishful thinking, but she could see none. She licked her lips and nodded. "I will pray for you, Rocky."

The smile that broke across his face set her heart to thumpity-thumping. "Thank you."

"You're welcome." She stepped away from his warm hand. "Maybe we could meet for lunch tomorrow. I could give you some ideas on classes that would be helpful to a landscaper."

"I *knew* you were the one to ask!" He socked the air, the same way he had the day he'd sprayed her with water. "Sure. Let's have lunch in the courtyard. It's shady there."

Oh, how she hoped she wasn't making a mistake. Before retrieving her purse from the office, she asked, "Rocky, what's your last name?"

"It's Wilder. Rocky Wilder."

Did she imagine it, or did he hesitate? She forced a smile. "Rocky Wilder." She'd heard that name somewhere before. "Okay. Lunch in the courtyard tomorrow. But leave the watering system off, okay?"

He laughed, showing his white teeth. "You got it, Carrie. See you tomorrow." He turned and trotted in the opposite direction across the neatly trimmed grass.

She stood for long moments, watching him, conflicting emotions at war. How her heart wanted to trust him. But her head maintained some doubt. "Lord, don't let me be used again, please," she begged as she finally moved toward the office. "I don't think I could handle it this time."

# Chapter 5

Rocky stopped beside a camellia bush and used his pocketknife to slice through a stem, releasing one red bloom. He'd gotten a glimpse of Carrie through the window this morning, so he knew the flower would match the red and white pantsuit she was wearing.

He whistled as he headed for the office. Each day for the past eight days, he'd delivered some sort of flowers to Carrie to put in the little vase she'd brought from home; then they had eaten lunch together in the courtyard. After today, Jim would be back, which would bring an end to his daily contact with Carrie. He would miss her. His whistle faded, and he released a sad huff of breath, his shoulders slumping. He would miss her a lot.

But, he reminded himself, picking up his pace, there was still today. One more lunch. One more conversation. That was something to enjoy. He opened the door to the office and stepped through. "Hey, ready for lunch?"

Carrie rose from the desk with a smile, holding out her hand to take the blossom he offered. "Yes, I am. And thank you for the flower. It's lovely." She rolled the stem of the camellia between her fingers while she talked. "I brought some brownies today. They have white chocolate chunks and macadamia nuts in them, and Myrna says they're famous at her son's school."

"That sounds great," he said.

She leaned toward the vase, ready to place the camellia with yesterday's Michaelmas daisies.

"Wait!" He took the bloom back and stepped beside her. "Here." She'd pulled her hair into a sleek ponytail, held with a silver barrette at the base of her skull. He carefully slipped the stem of the flower into the hair behind her left ear, then moved back and smiled. "Yes, that's perfect." The flower sat directly above her ear, bringing out the sparkle of her blue eyes. "Although I have to say, as pretty as that flower is, it pales when compared to you."

To his delight, a blush stole across her cheeks. "Rocky, really, you are such a flatterer."

"Hey, whatever works," he quipped with a grin. Then he shrugged. "I heard some movie hero say that to his girl, and I've waited for the right girl to repeat it to."

Her blush deepened, and she pointed to the door. "Let's go get started on lunch, huh?" She gave his shoulder a playful push, and they headed for their bench.

Once settled, Rocky said grace, feeling a little nervous about praying out loud in front of Carrie, yet good, too. They ate their sandwiches—Carrie had her favorite, tuna salad with raw spinach, and Rocky had his typical bologna and American cheese—and they shared the brownies, all the while chatting easily about anything that came to mind.

When Rocky finished the last bite of brownie, he let out a sigh of pleasure and admitted, "I'm gonna miss seeing you every day, you know? You've become a pretty good friend, for a girl."

Carrie laughed. "Well, I'm not sure whether I should be insulted by that or not."

He grinned. "You know what I mean. Doesn't happen too often that guys and girls become friends. Usually you start talking to a girl, and she either decides she doesn't like you and runs in the opposite direction, or she decides she likes you too much and runs after you. It's kind of nice just to ease into things, you know? Comfortable."

Carrie nodded, her expression thoughtful. "I suppose I hadn't thought of it that way, but you're right. It has been comfortable. I've enjoyed getting to know you, too."

"So." His lips suddenly felt dry, and he rubbed them together as he gathered his courage. "What do we do now? I mean, obviously you won't be back since Jim's vacation is over. But—can we maybe still continue the friendship? See each other away from Elmwood Towers?" He thought his heart might pound right out of his chest while he waited for her to answer.

"Well. . ." She looked across the courtyard, as if deep in thought. "I'll be back in school again in another few days. My course schedule is pretty taxing, Rocky, and my days are full."

She was letting him down. His chest felt tight. She'd had her summer fling, but now it was over. He steeled himself for the rejection.

"But weekends? I work hard during the week to keep my weekends free. Maybe we could get together on a Friday or Saturday evening sometime."

He tried not to sound too eager. "That would be great."

She turned a smile in his direction. "I think so, too. How about a week from today? That will be my first Friday evening after starting classes. I'll be ready for a break."

He supposed he could last a week without seeing her. "Okay, sure." Suddenly he scowled. "By the way, Carrie, what are you working toward—in college, I mean? You don't talk much about yourself."

"I have a degree in business administration and am working toward one in computer programming." Her nonchalant tone nearly cut Rocky to the quick. "It will take me another year, probably, to finish everything up, but it will qualify me for many executive positions. My parents strongly encouraged me to be marketable."

Did he hear some resentment in her tone? He couldn't be sure. But he knew this—her words made him feel inadequate. Business administration. Computer programming. Executive position. Marketable. And here he sat, with his biggest dream being able to plunk plants in the ground for the rest of his life. He shouldn't even be sitting on this bench with her, let alone pursuing a relationship beyond the confines of Elmwood Towers. Who did he think he was?

Carrie watched Rocky's demeanor change. He'd been attentive and open only a moment ago, but now he closed off. She saw his withdrawal in the way he pulled his arms inward, pressing his palms together and forcing them between his knees. She hoped he wasn't upset that she wouldn't be available every day. As much as she had enjoyed meeting him for lunch and chatting each day, she had to be honest with him—her college course work took up most of her week. Spending time with him on weekends seemed ideal to her, but it didn't seem to please him. How she hoped he wouldn't turn possessive now. She simply did not have the energy to deal with that and concentrate on her studies.

She glanced at her wristwatch. "I guess it's almost one, isn't it? I'd better get back to the office. I want to make sure everything is well organized so Jim won't have any question about what I did in his absence."

Rocky stood, crumpling his lunch sack. "I've got things to do, too. Eileen and I are going to bury her tulip bulbs this afternoon when the boys return." But his voice lacked the usual enthusiasm.

Carrie swallowed hard. "Well, then—will I see you next Friday?"

"You really want to?"

She shook her head, smiling. "Rocky, I wouldn't ask if I didn't want to." The safest course, to stave off any possessiveness, would be to keep things casual. Before he could ask if he should pick her up, she suggested, "There's a pizza place—the Ironstone—on the corner of Main and Baker Avenue. Should we meet there at seven? We can share a stone-baked pizza and a pitcher of pop."

He offered a slow nod, and although his lips tugged into a smile, his eyes remained dim. "Sure, Carrie. That sounds good."

What should they do now? Shake hands? Hug? Carrie found herself floundering. The one thing she hadn't felt around Rocky was awkward; yet the moment was rife with discomfort as they tried to say good-bye. Finally, in Rocky's silence, Carrie just blurted out, "Well, I'll see you in a week then. 'Bye, Rocky."

His good-bye came out softly, tinged with a regret she didn't understand. It echoed in her mind the remainder of the afternoon and tormented her on the drive home. Men! Would she ever understand them? Once home, she headed to her bedroom and removed the camellia from her hair. She laid the flower on her bedside table, changed into a pair of khaki shorts and a silk tank top, then flopped across her bed with her telephone in her hand. If anyone could help her make sense of Rocky's behavior, it would be Angela Fischer.

Angela was the most well-dated friend in Carrie's circle. She openly admitted she enjoyed the company of men, and she flitted from one to another without ever making a serious commitment. Sometimes Carrie thought Angela was an airhead, and while she certainly disapproved of some of her choices, in this case perhaps, Angela could offer some advice on how to proceed with Rocky.

Angela answered her phone on the second ring with a chirpy "Hello!"

"Hi, Angela. This is Carrie."

"Carrie!" The word nearly squealed out. "Does this mean you're done with that job? Are you free tonight? We're having a major gathering at my pool house—an end-of-summer bash. Want to join us?"

Carrie rolled to her back. "Probably not, although I appreciate the invitation. I've got some things to catch up on here at home since school is just around the corner."

"Oh, girl, you're too serious." Angela's chiding voice carried clearly through the lines. Carrie could picture the other girl's face pinched in displeasure.

"Besides," Carrie inserted gently, "your parties always seem to include alcohol, and I'm not comfortable with that."

"As I said, *too* serious." Angela never took anything seriously. "Okay. Don't come. There will be plenty of action without you. So. . .what did you need?"

"Actually, some advice." Carrie suddenly wondered at the sense of asking advice from Angela. Her opinion would surely be tainted by her own lack of Christian morals. Yet she wasn't sure who else would have the experience Angela did when it came to dating. She proceeded cautiously. "You see, I've gotten acquainted with someone the past couple of weeks."

"Ooh, do tell!"

Carrie cringed at the undertone. "It's nothing like that." She stroked the petals of the camellia with her finger. "Just a friendship, really, but I'm not sure whether I should continue it."

"So what does he do for a living?"

Of course. The roundabout way of finding out if he was rich. Carrie sucked in her breath. "He's a gardener." The laughter at the other end of the phone made Carrie mad. "Quit it, Angela. He's a really nice guy."

"Okay, okay, sorry." The laughter stopped, but humor was still evident in her voice. "Does this *gardener* have a name?"

Carrie considered hanging up, but she forged onward. "Yes, he does. It's Rocky Wilder."

There was a shocked silence, followed by an explosion. "Rocky Wilder! Carrie, you have got to be kidding!"

Carrie frowned. What was that all about? "No, I'm not kidding. Why do you say it like that?"

"Carrie, Rocky Wilder was in my sister Audrey's class in school." Angela babbled so fast Carrie had a hard time catching all the words. "He was a *mess* with a capital *M*! Always creating a ruckus, picking on people, stealing things, arguing with teachers. He set the record for in-school suspensions. Honestly, Audrey was scared to death of him! He got into some real serious trouble when he was, like, thirteen or fourteen and even got sent to reform school for a while.

"Rocky Wilder is *trouble,* Carrie. Don't even think about a friendship with him! He'll rob you blind, and I'm not just talkin' money. I'm talking about your heart, honey. He'll use it, abuse it, and leave you high and dry. Run—don't walk—run away as fast and as far as you can from that man! You'll be much better off, believe me."

Carrie sat in stunned silence. The person Angela just described couldn't possibly be the same man with whom she'd spent the last two weeks. She managed a weak thank-you then hung up, reeling. Staring at the ceiling, she envisioned Rocky as she'd seen him once earlier this week. He hadn't even been aware of her presence, because he'd been reading the New Testament he carried in his pocket. The look on his face as he'd read the Bible—he'd been so engrossed that it almost seemed as though he were absorbing the words. She hadn't had the heart to bother him, so she'd crept away.

The man she'd seen soaking up God's Word couldn't be anything like the one Angela had depicted. . .could he? If Angela was right, if Rocky truly was someone who'd been consistently in trouble, then he certainly had learned how to play games. He could deceive her. Suddenly she felt queasy. She really didn't want to believe it, but doubts pressed in.

How many other men had duped her in the past, complimenting her, pursuing her. . .and doing it only because she had money. Rocky didn't have money—he'd openly admitted that. Did he see her as his opportunity for wealth? Would he use her and abuse her, as Angela had said? Or could she trust him?

She groaned, pressing her face against her pillow shams. "Dear Lord, please help me sort this out. What is the truth?" She prayed for several minutes, pouring out her frustration and worries to her heavenly Father. The prayer finished, she had no clear answers, but she felt calmer.

Slipping from the bed, she crossed to the window and looked down at her mother's rose garden in the backyard. Their gardener took as much pride in his work as Rocky did in his. How fortunate both men were, Carrie decided, to be able to see so clearly the results of their labor. How wonderful to create something of such beauty. She propped her chin on her hand, catching her elbow with her other hand, and stared pensively down at the profusion of color.

The man Angela described would not be capable of creating beauty. Angela had spoken of a man who created chaos. She supposed Rocky was creating chaos in her heart, but she wasn't quite ready to believe he would create chaos in every other aspect of her life. She needed to explore his person more deeply—develop their friendship and allow it to bloom as fully as one of the prize roses in Mother's garden. Once the bloom was open, she'd be able to see Rocky for who he truly was.

But to see that open bloom, she would need time with him. She turned from the window and picked up the camellia blossom again. It was wilted and sad-looking now, but the color was still deep and rich. She cradled the flower gently in her palm as she made her decision.

She would meet Rocky next Friday. And she would ask the kinds of questions that would help her see his true character. In the meantime, she'd pray for God to open her eyes to the truth, whatever that might be.

# Chapter 6

The Monday following the manager's return, Rocky went to the familiar bench in the center of the courtyard to eat his lunch, but it didn't feel right without Carrie. His sandwich tasted like cardboard. Dissatisfaction filled his middle, making it hard to swallow. Plunking the sandwich back into its bag, he blew out a frustrated breath. Who would have thought Rocky Wilder, toughest kid on the block, would be struck down by puppy love?

Yet it was true. He couldn't get Carrie off his mind. And he needed to. The relationship couldn't go anywhere. He'd suspected they were different when he'd first seen her in her cute little beaded outfit with a soggy sandwich in her manicured hand. But when she'd said she was a Steinwood—that pretty much settled it. They were worlds apart.

He recalled his embarrassment when she'd told him about the degree she was working toward in college. Carrie had to be smart to handle all that. One degree in business administration and another in computer programming. He shook his head, trying to comprehend all that would entail.

Rocky had used computers in high school, but he didn't own one—he couldn't afford it. And business administration—his brother, Philip, ran his own business, but Philip had the brains in the Wilder family. He was fooling himself, thinking he could handle running his own landscaping business. He wasn't smart like Philip and Carrie. He didn't have money like Carrie, to hire someone to help him. If, as he suspected, he was falling in love with Carrie, he'd want to take care of her and the children they might have together. How would he be able to do that on a gardener's salary? He couldn't. It wasn't possible.

He groaned, leaning forward and resting his elbows on his knees, dejection striking. A part of him could hardly wait until Friday arrived, when he'd be able to see her again, and a part of him dreaded Friday, when he'd have to see her again and be reminded of just how impossible continuing a friendship would be.

He felt so lonely out there on the bench by himself.

"Rocky!"

The voice jerked him out of his reverie. He looked over his shoulder and spotted Eileen standing in the open doorway of Tower Three.

She waved her arm at him. "Come upstairs and have lunch with me! And you can call Philip on my phone."

Rocky balled up what was left of his lunch as he trotted to Eileen. Pitching his lunch in the trash can next to the entrance to Tower Three, he said, "Sounds great! But call Philip? Why?"

Eileen shook her gray head as she led him to the elevator. "No emergency. He just said he needed to talk to you about something going on at church, and he couldn't reach you at home. Says you need to get a cell phone."

Rocky nearly laughed out loud at that. A cell phone? Those things were for preppy teenagers or business execs, not a man a gardener's salary. Carrie probably had one, though. He pushed that thought away as he followed Eileen out of the elevator to her apartment. A tantalizing smell greeted his nostrils as she opened the door, and his stomach rolled over in eagerness. He stepped past a sleeping Roscoe, who lay on his back in the middle of the walkway with his front paws curled beneath his furry chin.

"Boy, I sure appreciate this invitation." Rocky sat at the bar and let Eileen serve him a steaming bowl of noodles swimming in a thick broth with chunks of chicken and topped by two plump dumplings.

"I appreciate the company," she told him. "Pray and eat."

He followed her direction, and when he'd finished, he used Eileen's telephone to give his brother a quick call. "Hey, Philip, what's going on?"

"Oh, good, Eileen found you. Listen—there's a Bible study starting at church this Wednesday I think you would enjoy. I took the class a year or so ago, and I really gained a lot from it."

Rocky twisted his face into an uncertain scowl. "Bible study? I don't know." He thought about Sunday mornings and the length of time it took him to find references as the preacher spoke. He felt stupid when he couldn't locate things quickly. And a Bible study would be held in a smaller group. His groping would be more noticeable.

"It's a good one," Philip's voice went on, "on the Fatherhood of God. It helped me come to terms with my earthly father. Our dad wasn't all bad, but he wasn't the best influence. This study helped me settle into my place in God's family. I think you'd get a lot out of it, Rocky."

Rocky scratched his head. "Well. . .Wednesday, you said?"

"Yes. In the church basement." A light chuckle came through the line. "They serve refreshments with it, if that sweetens the pot."

Rocky laughed. "Great motivator. I'll think about it, okay?" He hung up and joined Eileen at the kitchen sink where she washed their few dishes.

"Philip told me about a Bible study he thinks would be good for me," he told her as he picked up a dish towel and dried a bowl. "Something about the Fatherhood of God."

Eileen swished her hand through the water then rubbed the soapy rag over the spoon she located. "Bible study's always good for people."

"Yeah, but"—he opened a cupboard to put away the dry bowl—"I always feel lost scrambling around for verses. Maybe I should wait until I know my way around the Bible better."

Eileen gave him one of her famous eyebrows-high-chin-tucked-low looks. "That's just silly. How do you get familiar with something? You use it regularly. How'd you get so good at that landscaping out there? By standing on the sidelines? Nope, had to dive in and do it. Same thing applies to that Bible of yours. Might as well be practicing getting around while you're learning something at the same time, right? Go to the study, Rocky."

Rocky shook his head, chuckling. "You never mince words, do you?"

She shrugged and handed him the last of the silverware. "Too old to be mincing words. So are you going or not?"

"We'll see," he said, unwilling to commit just yet. The dishes done, he thanked Eileen for the lunch and the use of her phone, took a few moments to scratch Roscoe's neck, then headed back to work.

The Bible study and the idea of looking at God as his Father teased Rocky's thoughts for the next two days. His earthly father hadn't been the easiest man to live with, and, truthfully, Rocky wasn't sure he liked the idea of applying the term "Father" to God. He'd rather keep his ideas of father and God separate. Yet when Wednesday rolled around, the opportunity to gain a better understanding of his relationship with God found him climbing into his old clunker and driving to church.

Roughly twenty people were already in the basement when Rocky arrived, and relief washed over him when he saw they were casually dressed. He wouldn't stick out in his clean dungarees and snap-up Western-style shirt. He helped himself to three vanilla cream-filled cookies and a cup of tea then sat on the outside aisle of the second row. He ate his snack while waiting for things to get started.

At seven o'clock on the dot, the teacher—a midthirties man with a receding hairline and thick glasses—stepped behind the podium and had them go around the room and introduce themselves. Rocky's hand trembled as he stated his name. He never knew whether someone would recognize him as that messed-up Wilder boy, and he was relieved when the attention moved on to the person seated behind him.

Once the introductions were over, the teacher instructed everyone to open their Bibles to the book of Galatians, chapter four, starting with verse six. Rocky found the reference in time to hear the last few words of verse seven: "God has made you also an heir." He slipped a pen from his pocket and made a note in the margin to remind him to go back and read the section again later.

As the evening wore on, he forgot his discomfort about not being able to locate things quickly and got caught up in the lesson. His heart pounded with eagerness to accept not only that Jesus was his Savior but that God was his Father.

He, Rocky Wilder, could take his place as one of God's heirs. To think God loved him enough to adopt him into His family.

A feeling of acceptance, the likes of which Rocky had never before experienced, filled him and brought tears to his eyes. He swallowed hard to bring himself under control, then fixed his gaze on the teacher and listened with his whole heart.

—⌒

Carrie was disappointed she'd missed the first part of the Bible study. Frustration with her stepfather still sat like a weight on her chest as she slipped in quietly and took the least obtrusive open seat, in the middle of the last row.

She settled in the chair and peeked at the Bible in the lap of the person on her left. Flipping open her own Bible to the same place, her thoughts raged on. Why couldn't Mac just let her go to church without creating a scene? Her church attendance took nothing away from him; yet he opposed it as adamantly as if she were attending a meeting to overthrow the government. Right now she needed to lean into the idea that God was her Father. How she hoped her Father in heaven would help her deal patiently and kindly with the father she had on earth!

She tried to focus on what the teacher was saying, but her thoughts were still too jumbled from the confrontation at home. Mac insisted she needed to give her whole attention to college and job-seeking, that anything outside of that created a diversion which might ruin any future opportunity for success. Church attendance ruin her opportunity for success? That made no sense to Carrie. Mac was completely unreasonable.

Mac's ranting had certainly created a diversion from gaining anything from this study! She had to get focused here. To settle herself in, she allowed her gaze to drift across the rows one by one, seeing how many people she knew. After attending this church for a little over a year, she'd gotten acquainted with a handful of college-age students, but most of these people weren't from her Sunday school class.

Her gaze reached the second row from the front, and she had to tip her head slightly to see all the way to the end. When she found the familiar thick head of sun-bleached dark hair belonging to Rocky Wilder, her heart jumped into her throat and lodged.

Angela's words echoed in her mind: *Run—don't walk—run away as fast and as far as you can from that man!* Almost of its own volition, her body recoiled, pressing against the cold back of the metal folding chair in an attempt to shield herself from his view. Her pulse raced—how did he know she would be here this evening? Then she made herself calm down. She hadn't even known she would be here until earlier in the day when one of her Sunday school classmates had called. There was no way Rocky could have known. It was a coincidence. Angela's ominous words were making her paranoid.

*Get a grip, Carrie,* she told herself firmly. *Rocky's no stalker.* In fact, as she watched him, it became clear he was unaware of anything in the room except what the speaker was saying. His gaze bounced from the teacher to his Bible—a full-size one, not the little testament he carried to work. His fingers raced to find the scriptures mentioned. A napkin holding a half-eaten cookie rested on his knee, but he ignored it, his attention obviously on gaining spiritual food.

Something warm and soothing spiraled through Carrie's middle. She relaxed in the chair, a smile found itself forming on her lips, and a silent prayer went up from her heart. *Thank You, God, for giving me this glimpse of Rocky. He's no longer that man Angela described; he is a new creature in You. I can see it.*

She turned her attention to the teacher. It was nearly seven thirty, the class half over. She'd better pay attention to what remained. At the close of class, the teacher asked for prayer requests. Several people voiced concerns, which the teacher wrote on a white board behind his podium. Carrie waited for Rocky to ask for prayer for his new business venture, but he remained silent. She considered asking for him, but she decided that would be breaking a confidence. Instead, as the teacher prayed, she prayed, too, asking that if Rocky's dream was God's will, it might become a reality.

People rose to leave, and Carrie slipped her purse over her shoulder, intending to catch Rocky and talk to him. But someone grasped her arm and turned her around.

"Carl!" What was he doing here? Although it had been months since she'd seen him, the reaction to his presence was intense. Her heart picked up its tempo, she felt a prickle of awareness tingle down her spine, and she fought an urge to dash away.

"Hi, Carrie." His thumb caressed the bare skin of her upper arm. "Mac told me I'd find you here. I've been waiting outside the door for class to finish."

She pulled her arm free. "Why?" She tried not to sound snappish, but her jangled nerves made the word come out more harshly than she intended.

He ducked his head, bringing professionally added blond highlights to view. "I hoped we could talk."

"What about?"

He glanced around, his expression solemn. "It's kind of personal, Carrie."

She hesitated. As much as she hated to admit it, his grave countenance stirred her sympathy.

"Please?"

The sincerity in his tone did her in. "All right. But give me a minute, will you?" She glanced around, seeking Rocky. She finally located him, but before she could call out, he moved through the doorway leading to the stairs. She sighed.

"Everything okay?" Carl asked.

"I wanted to talk to someone, but it's too late now." She turned toward the doors. "Come on then."

He put his hand on the small of her back and escorted her to the stairway. She bounced up the steps, managing to elude his touch until they reached the foyer, but then his hand was back, warm and firm and possessive. She didn't like it.

He guided her to her car then braced his hand on the roof, leaning in too close for comfort. "I appreciate your doing this for me, Carrie. You're a real doll, you know that?"

Oh yes, she was a real doll, she thought disparagingly, taking a step back to put some distance between the two of them. More likely she was just a sucker who would later regret this time with Carl. She didn't respond.

"Where can we go?"

Carrie considered his question. She didn't want to be seen in public with him. If any of their mutual friends saw them together, tongues would start wagging. She didn't want to go to his townhouse—that would give him the wrong ideas. There was only one alternative.

"Why don't you just follow me to the house? It's a pleasant evening. We can sit on the porch and talk there." She waited for him to move aside so she could get in her car. To her chagrin, when he removed his hand from the roof, he reached out and cupped her cheek, his fingers gracing the line of her jaw.

"Thank you, sweet thing. I really appreciate it."

The nickname he'd given her struck like a blow. Instead of bringing a rush of affection, it brought a jolt of revulsion. She turned her face from his touch. Swallowing the nausea that threatened, she said in a tight voice, "Let's just get going, huh, Carl?"

He smiled, his teeth even and white in the dusky evening light. He opened the door for her. "Okay. I'll follow you to your place. Thanks again."

She nodded. To her relief, he pushed off from the car and strode away, his shoulders back and chin high in the familiar pose she'd once thought spoke of confident strength. Now its arrogance turned her stomach. With a sigh, she slipped behind the wheel of her car and started the engine. "Let's just get this over with."

# Chapter 7

Rocky drove toward home, his right arm stretched straight out with his hand gripping the top of the steering wheel, the other arm propped on the window frame—a pose he'd perfected in high school to look cool. But right now he wasn't thinking about looking cool. He was lost in thought.

Wind rushed past his ear, tossing his hair and making his eyes water. He squinted, battling mixed emotions. Part of him celebrated the knowledge he'd gained this evening—God saw him as His adopted son. That realization made his heart sing. Then there was the other part—the heart-crushing part.

Seeing Carrie with that other man.

His fingers tightened on the steering wheel, the image taunting him. The man's thumb slipping up and down on Carrie's skin, the gesture familiar, intimate. Carrie's face turned up to his. Both of them in their designer clothes and styled hair and unscuffed shoes. They fit together. His heart clenched. They matched.

Once again, the differences between Carrie's world and his own struck hard. Just who did he think he was? Maybe he needed a reminder. He glanced at street signs and realized he wasn't too far from his old neighborhood. Slapping the directional signal, he made a left-hand turn and wove his way to Avenue D.

Familiar landmarks—the Tasti-Freeze, a weed-infested ball diamond, and a boarded-up warehouse—brought a rush of childhood memories. Turning north on Avenue D, he slowed to a crawl and stared through the gloomy dusk at sad-looking houses, their unkempt lawns littered with bicycles, broken toys, and empty beer cans. Pulling to the curb in front of 1713 Avenue D, he popped the gear shift into NEUTRAL and sat, his fingers cupping his chin, and let his gaze slowly sweep across the house where he'd grown up.

Nothing fancy, that was for sure. A post-WWII bungalow—square, the front door centered between two windows. The window on the left was the living room, the window on the right his parents' bedroom. He and Philip had shared the second bedroom which was behind his parents'. He wondered if the same faded cowboys and Indians wallpaper hung on the walls of that room. No way to tell without going in, and he wouldn't ask to do that. He had no desire to go inside that house again.

He took in the sagging shutters, torn window screens, and peeling paint. It didn't look as if anyone had tried to make improvements since his parents' deaths. Of course, there wasn't much to improve on, Rocky acknowledged. No porch softened the appearance of the house, only a cracked concrete slab with one sloping concrete step. Not even a railing. His mother had tried to plant flowers around the base of the porch, but he and Philip always jumped off the sides and trampled any living thing, preventing the plants from blooming. How Mom hollered at them for that.

And Dad did more than holler. . . .

Rocky sighed. Not many happy memories in that house. He glanced up and down the block, which was nearly hidden in shadow already. A few lights glowed behind window shades. He wondered if any happy childhoods were being played out in other houses around him. He hoped so.

It had seemed to him, as a child and rebellious teen, that happiness only existed in the homes six blocks over—in the neighborhoods with names like Morning Glory Circle and East Briar Estates. Homes with neat lawns and swimming pools and spindled porches where swings or wicker furniture invited a person to sit, relax, and bask in all he owned. On impulse, Rocky shifted to DRIVE and made a U-turn, angling his vehicle toward the "rich district."

He crept out of the neighborhood as slowly as he had entered, almost with reverence, offering a prayer for the occupants of each house as he passed by. The houses slowly changed shape and appearance as he rolled along, from small disheveled dwellings to small neater dwellings then to large neater dwellings until he reached the large, ostentatious neighborhood of East Briar Estates.

He felt like an interloper as he guided his old car between the brick pillars standing sentry on either side of the opening to the elite housing district. Homes protected by iron fences, many of them with gates blocking the curving driveways, stood in stark contrast to the neighborhood he'd left behind.

Making a right-hand turn at the first opportunity, he drove slowly past the stately Tudor home where Mac Steinwood and his family lived. How many times, as a boy, had he driven over here on his bicycle and stood outside the iron fence, peering in, wondering what was inside that house? The Steinwood mansion had been his dream house—tall, rambling, surely full of all the things his own family couldn't afford.

If Rocky closed his eyes, he could imagine the shining chandeliers and polished woodwork and—he allowed himself to release a rueful chuckle—a wood-paneled den with a pool table bigger than a king-size bed. Funny the things that had seemed important back then. . .

He passed the Steinwood house and cruised around the block, aware of bright lights not only inside but outside each house, like hundreds of eyes watching, protecting. The feeling of being an intruder increased with every change of his odometer. His gaze drifted from the homes themselves to the beautifully landscaped yards. Probably the owners of those houses each had a crew to keep their yards nice—gardeners, like him, paid to bring beauty to the owners' surroundings.

He bet those gardeners never got inside the house, though. Someone who dug in the dirt sure wouldn't be good enough to step through the front door. He clenched his jaw and swallowed. He didn't belong here, and he'd better leave before someone called the cops on him.

One more swing past the Steinwood estate for old-times' sake; then he'd go home. He paused at the intersection, prepared to turn toward the Steinwoods' when headlights appeared on his right. He waited, and when the car passed him, he realized it was Carrie's sports car. She was home from church. His heart pounded as he watched her go by, and it was all he could do to keep from blaring his horn to let her know he was there. But the sight of a second car—a fairly new sport utility vehicle—right behind hers stopped him. The driver was the man he'd seen with Carrie at church.

He held his breath, watching Carrie stop outside the gates for a moment to punch buttons in the box beside the drive. The gates opened, she drove through, and the utility vehicle followed.

Rocky felt sick. The man obviously meant something to Carrie. The man obviously matched Carrie in wealth and education. As it had before, the realization at how well they matched struck like a blow. It was just as well he'd seen them together. It made things clear. He did not belong with Carrie. He did not belong in her world.

Turning his car in the opposite direction, he gunned his motor and raced out of the neighborhood. "So long, Carrie," he shouted out the open window. From here on out, he'd leave her alone.

⎯⎯☙⎯⎯

Carrie stepped out of the garage and met Carl in the driveway. She didn't want to take him in the house where Mac would see them together and make assumptions, so she pointed to the gazebo in the backyard. It was well lit, thanks to the solar lanterns that hung in evenly spaced intervals around the cedar-shingled roof. "Let's sit out here."

Carl followed her without a word across softly illuminated stepping-stones, and he waited until she seated herself in one of the cushioned bamboo-framed chairs before choosing the chair directly opposite her. He shot her a practiced smile and said, "This is perfect. You're absolutely breathtaking in the moonlight."

"Stop it, Carl." She frowned to let him know she meant it. "Flattery won't work anymore. You said you needed to talk, so go ahead. I'm listening."

He leaned back, crossed his leg, and let out a huff of laughter. "You're in a sour mood."

His cajoling tone did nothing to soften her. "I'm not in a sour mood. I just don't have time for your insincere compliments."

His posture didn't change an inch nor did his tone. "Insincere compliments? You think I'm insincere?"

"I think you say what you believe will benefit you the most." She pressed into the cushioned back of the chair, bracing her hands on the armrests. "And I'm not the same naive girl you duped two years ago. So let's just skip the flattery and get to the point."

A night bird sang a lonesome chorus while Carl sat in silence and examined Carrie. She kept a stern pose, her face turned in his direction, and offered no more encouragement. At long last, he blew out his breath, raised his hands in a gesture of defeat, and said, "Okay. I'll lay it out. I've missed you desperately. I realize I love you." He leaned forward, his voice dropping to a sultry whisper. "I want you back."

Carrie gave an unladylike *hmph*. "Yes, I'll bet you do." She shook her head, the slight breeze tossing one strand of hair across her cheek. She anchored it behind her ear. "But it isn't me you really want, is it, Carl?"

He scowled. "Of course it is. What are you talking about?"

"Come off it. I know you investigated my trust fund. I know you know, to the penny, exactly what I'm worth. And I know you know I'll be given control of that money in another month, when I turn twenty-five."

His eyebrows shot upward in well-feigned surprise. "Really?" He settled himself back into the chair. "Your birthday is around the corner? Oh, it is! I'd forgotten."

Carrie rolled her eyes. "Please, don't patronize me. I haven't seen or heard from you in almost two years, you show up conveniently just before I'm ready to have a large sum of money at my disposal, and you want me to believe you love me and want me back." She shook her head, her gaze never wavering from his. "What you love is the idea of gaining access to my father's wealth. It's not me. It never was."

Carl stroked his lower lip with his finger while he stared at her, unblinking. "You underestimate yourself, Carrie. Don't you see yourself as lovable without your money?"

She refused to be sidetracked by his glib tongue. "It's not a matter of what *I* see; it's a matter of what *you* see. And when you look at me, you see dollar signs."

He laughed out loud at her, stirring her ire. "Sweet thing, you really are too cute for words. Dollar signs." He continued to chuckle.

"Cute, ugly, it wouldn't matter, as long as I come with the fortune." Carrie ignored his amusement. "And I want something more than a relationship built on a pile of banknotes."

Carl stopped chuckling and leaned forward, his expression fervent. "Tell me what you want, Carrie. Whatever it is, I'll give it to you. Tell me how to prove that I love you."

How could she have ever seen him as handsome? His perfectly placed features were physically appealing, but the hunger in his eyes for material things made him seem so shallow. She berated herself for having given him a piece of her heart. She whispered a silent prayer of thanks for learning the truth before she'd accepted his marriage proposal.

"Carl, there's no way you can prove that to me. And I don't want you to try. It would be demeaning."

"I'd demean myself for you, Carrie. Just say the word."

"Stop it!" He was embarrassing her, and he was embarrassing himself. All for money. It was all so pointless and. . .*sad*. She took a deep breath. "This whole conversation is ridiculous. We have nothing in common, except the fact we both happened to be born to wealthy families. Beyond that"—she lifted her shoulders in a shrug—"there's nothing."

"Define nothing," he shot back.

She had no difficulty with that. "First, and most important, there's faith. I believe Jesus Christ is the Son of God, sent to the world to save us from our sins. I've accepted His gift of salvation. You haven't."

"Tell me how. If that's what you want, I'll do it right now."

His flippant reply made her heart ache for his lack of understanding. "That isn't something you do for someone else. It's something you do for yourself. And it's a commitment, Carl, not a statement you make to impress someone."

He nodded his head slowly. "Okay. Then go on. What else do we not have in common?"

Now she floundered. On many levels, she and Carl were compatible, which was why he'd managed to win her before. They had similar backgrounds, similar interests, similar tastes. But she'd found a personal relationship with Jesus since she and Carl had broken up, and she knew none of their similarities would be enough without the common foundation of faith in Christ. Uncertain how to explain herself, she remained silent.

Carl took her silence as an opportunity. Reaching out, he caught her hand, his thumb painting lazy circles on the back of her wrist. "See? There's only that one thing. It could work, Carrie. Give me a chance."

She snatched her hand free and rose. "No, it wouldn't work. That 'one thing,' as you put it, is everything. Without that, we have nothing. So there's no point in continuing this discussion. If that's all you wanted, then—"

"Please, Carrie. Don't turn me away." He stood and captured her shoulders with his smooth, tapered fingers. "You still care for me. You aren't dating anyone else."

"Yes, I am." Her adamant contradiction surprised Carl no more than it surprised her. Was she dating Rocky? Not really, yet she knew she wanted to. She stepped backward, freeing herself from his grasp, and darted behind her chair.

Feeling safe with the barrier between them, she said boldly, "So this conversation needs to end immediately."

Carl's gaze narrowed as he examined her. "Are you lying to me to get me to back off?"

"I'm not lying. I met someone recently, and we are seeing each other." A picture of Rocky, his head bent over his Bible, his forehead creased in concentration, brought a smile to her lips.

Carl must have seen it, because his expression hardened. "Okay. Fine. I concede defeat." He started for the opening of the gazebo then stopped and turned back, his hand braced on a spindled beam. "But what makes you so sure this guy is any different from how you see me? What makes you so sure he's not after your money, too?"

Carrie felt heat fill her face. She found no words.

He gave a knowing nod. "That's what I thought. Well—be careful, Carrie. You can't separate the girl from the money, you know." He turned and strode away. In moments, the engine to his vehicle revved, and he backed out of the drive.

Carrie sank back into the chair, staring into the dark. As much as she hated to admit it, Carl's words had found their mark. Once again the old doubts surfaced. Rocky wasn't wealthy. What if he truly did see her as an end to his financial needs?

"Carrie?"

She glanced up. Her mother stood on the walkway. How long had she been out here? "Hi, Mom."

Her mother entered the gazebo and sat down where Carl had been. "Carl left in a hurry. Is everything okay?"

Briefly Carrie recounted their conversation. She ended with, "Mom, I don't trust Carl, but I do trust Rocky. I know you and Mac think Carl and I would be ideal together, but—" She shook her head, unable to proceed.

"Honey, I know Mac can be pushy, but underneath, he only wants what's best for you, as do I." Her mother tipped her head, her silver earrings glinting in the soft light cast by the lanterns. "How well do you know this. . .Rocky?"

Carrie grimaced at the way her mother said Rocky's name. "Not all that well, yet. But I want to get to know him better. He has a gentle strength that I admire, and even though he's a new Christian, he's growing. I can see it."

A soft smile graced her mother's face. "You're smitten."

Carrie released a light laugh. "Yes, I suppose I am."

"Well, honey, I suppose you've heard that old adage that opposites attract. But the adage doesn't guarantee the attraction has lasting value. This Rocky of yours isn't a part of our social circle, so I won't lie and say I don't have my concerns. A common background is very important in building a relationship."

Carrie lowered her gaze.

Her mother reached out to grip Carrie's chin and raise her face. "Promise me you'll go slowly. Think things through before you make a commitment to this man."

Carrie met her mother's gaze squarely. "I'm doing more than thinking, Mom. I'm praying. If Rocky is the right person for me, then I trust God to help us work out all the differences we might encounter."

Lynette Steinwood drew back, her expression closed. "Just be careful."

Carrie nodded. "I will." But inwardly she rebelled—just once she wished she could simply trust and move forward without worrying about hidden motives. Would God grant her that peace?

# Chapter 8

Carrie spritzed apple-scented body spray into the air, then stepped into the mist, giving herself a subtle essence of the fragrance. One last glance in the full-length mirror, and she decided she was suitably attired for an evening at the Ironstone. It wasn't a fancy place, so her denim capris, saucy pink T-shirt with lime green rhinestones imbedded around the V-neck, and rhinestone-studded pink flip-flops would be appropriate. She'd pulled her hair back into a ponytail and tied it with a pink and lime green scarf. The thick ponytail swished back and forth across her shoulders as she bounced down the stairs.

Rounding the corner from the hallway to the kitchen, she heard her step-father call her name. She turned back, resisting a glance at her wristwatch. She didn't want to be late.

"Yes, Mac? I'm on my way out." She offered a quick smile and remained poised to leave, one hand on the kitchen's swinging door, hoping he'd take the hint.

"I can see that." His gaze roved from her head to her toes, then back again. "But not to anything formal, I assume."

Carrie felt a blush building, but she forced another smile. "No. Nothing formal. Just pizza with a friend."

Mac crossed his arms and peered down his nose at her. His pale green eyes narrowed into probing slits, making Carrie feel much younger than her twenty-four years. She fought the urge to squirm.

"This friend—would it happen to be the gentleman in whom your mother said you've expressed an interest?"

Carrie pressed her memory—what all had she said to Mom? Very little, truthfully. Mac was obviously digging for more information. She chose a casual tack. "Yes, as a matter of fact, it is, and I hate to keep him waiting, so if you don't mind—"

"Tell me about him."

Carrie drew in a breath, silently praying for patience. She knew her step-father well enough to know he would keep her there until his curiosity had been satisfied. She might as well tell him what he wanted to know. Still, she'd give him the *Reader's Digest* condensed version. "His name is Rocky Wilder, he's the groundskeeper for Elmwood Towers, and we've developed a friendship."

Mac stood for several long seconds, just looking into Carrie's eyes, his expression unreadable.

Carrie stood, looking back, waiting for Mac to make a disparaging remark or to suggest she change her plans. But his reply, when it came, surprised her.

"Well, if this is someone with whom you're taken, perhaps it's time for your mother and me to meet him."

Carrie's jaw dropped. Was he being serious? She looked at him carefully to determine whether he was teasing her. "You really want to meet him?"

Mac shrugged, a slow smile creeping up his cheek. It didn't light his eyes, but it did soften his austere appearance. "If you're going to be spending time with him, I think it's only proper that we become familiar with one another." He slid one hand into the pocket of his tailored navy dress slacks. "Would tomorrow night for dinner be too soon?"

"N–no. Tomorrow would be fine." Carrie's heart beat a hopeful double beat. If Mac approved the relationship, it would eliminate one major worry. "I'll ask him and see if he's free."

"Fine." Mac's smile widened; yet there seemed to be a cunning undertone in his expression. "Let's say dinner at seven, and that will give us time to visit a bit afterward. We can all become better acquainted."

Carrie nodded eagerly. "Yes. Thank you, Mac."

She smiled all the way to the Ironstone. The smile remained as she chose a corner booth, where she could watch the door for Rocky's arrival. She ordered a soft drink from the teenage waitress, then settled back to wait. A jukebox played country tunes, and she hummed and sipped, waiting.

"Carrie!"

The enthusiastic greeting pulled Carrie's attention away from the door. She shifted her gaze to the left and found Angela's grinning face peering down at her from over the top of the partition which separated the booths. Carrie swallowed her groan of displeasure and pushed a smile into place.

"Well, hello, Angela. Are you here alone?" In a way, Carrie hoped Angela wasn't alone—she didn't want to be obligated to ask Angela to join her. The girl's flushed face indicated she had been imbibing something.

"Me? Alone?" Angela pretended great shock then laughed raucously. "No, I'm here with Janine, Todd, and Alex." Alex's head popped up next to Angela's. Angela gave him a kiss on the cheek, giggled when he tried to return the kiss, then pushed him away. Alex sank out of sight as Angela said, "But you seem to be alone. Come join us, girl!"

Carrie shook her head as a burst of laughter sounded from the other side of the partition. They must have already consumed a pitcher of beer; they were all so obnoxiously jolly. She had no desire to be a part of that, not even as a witness. So she shook her head. "No, thanks. You all enjoy yourselves. I'll just wait for my d—." She managed to stop herself from saying *date* and ended lamely, "Friend."

"The gardener you told me about?"

Carrie cringed at Angela's strident tone. She gave a quick nod in reply, praying Angela would drop the subject.

"Suit yourself." Angela shrugged and disappeared, leaving Carrie alone.

Carrie whispered a thank-you for the answer to her prayer, but the laughter and loud conversation continued, making Carrie feel more and more alone as time slipped by and Rocky still didn't appear.

Where could he be? Each time the sleigh bells hanging above the door jingled the arrival of someone new, her heart leaped with eagerness. And each time someone other than Rocky entered the restaurant, her heart plummeted with disappointment and worry. She certainly hoped nothing had happened to him.

She finished her first soft drink, ordered a refill, ignored the raised eyebrows of the waitress when she repeated she wouldn't order food until her friend arrived, and waited some more.

Angela, hanging on Alex's arm, came around the partition. She stopped beside Carrie's booth and tossed her head, swinging her auburn hair back over her shoulder. In a voice loud enough for the entire place to hear, she said, "Well, good-bye, Carrie. I sure hope your gardener shows up. Otherwise, won't you look silly?" She released a shrill, brittle laugh.

Alex sent Carrie an apologetic look. "She's had one too many, kiddo. Ignore her." He gave Angela a tug that nearly sent her nose first to the floor. "Come on. You're making a fool of yourself."

"Me?" Angela's voice pierced an octave higher than usual. "I'm not the one who's sitting alone. I have a date!" She poked Alex in the chest with her long fingernail. "That's you, remember?" She squinted at Alex and said, "You aren't a gardener, are you?" She giggled again, peeking back at Carrie. Leaning in close, she lowered her voice to a raspy whisper. "This is what happens when you date gardeners, Carrie, dear. They aren't dependable. Remember that."

Alex jerked Angela away from Carrie. "Come on. I'm taking you home. 'Bye, Carrie." He led her out of the restaurant, with Janine and Todd following.

Carrie watched them go, her face burning as she realized how many people had turned to stare at Angela's display. She tried to pretend she didn't notice, just sipped her pop and drummed her fingernails on the checkered tablecloth, but eventually embarrassment got the best of her.

She waved the waitress over and said with a tight smile, "Something must have come up with my friend." She dropped a five-dollar bill on the table and rose. "Keep the change." Lifting her head high to retain what was left of her dignity, she strode out of the restaurant. Outside, she wilted against the brick exterior and allowed tears of mortification to fill her eyes. But she didn't let them fall. She blinked them away.

Surely Rocky didn't stand her up on purpose. Surely something happened. But why hadn't he called the restaurant and let her know? Sniffing, she pushed off from the building and headed to her car. She'd make a few phone calls, check to make sure he was okay. And if he was—well, she'd decide how to handle that after she'd figured out what kept him away.

⎯◌⎯

Rocky marked another passage with a yellow highlighting pen, rubbed his eyes, and looked up at the clock. Again. Eight fifteen. By now Carrie had probably given up and gone home. Regret twisted his stomach. It had been cruel not showing up, but sometimes you had to be cruel to be kind. Wasn't that what the old song said, anyway?

With a sigh, he reread the passage he had been studying. One tiny phrase in Psalm 49 stood out—"rich and poor, together." He leaned back in his secondhand recliner, closed the Bible, and released a sigh. Rich and poor together wasn't a concept he could grasp. Maybe in God's eyes, he conceded, the rich and the poor were equal and therefore could be together, but in man's eyes? Rocky couldn't imagine it happening.

Last Wednesday, seeing Carrie's friend behind the wheel of an SUV that probably cost more than a year's income as groundskeeper had been enough to convince him he had to back off. Caroline Mays Steinwood belonged with somebody who could buy SUVs and wear designer clothes and keep his fingernails clean.

He lifted a piece of paper on which he'd scribbled Carrie's name then his own below it. The pairing looked odd on paper. It was beyond odd in person. He dropped the paper and pressed his palms to his Bible. At least he had acceptance with God. He belonged to God's family. God called him a son.

Despite his despondency over Carrie, joy pressed upward as he considered being an adopted son in God's own family. And Carrie was a daughter. That made them brother and sister in Christ. He toyed with the idea. Could they be friends as brothers and sisters in Christ? Could they have a relationship that was strictly friendship? He'd told Carrie how special it was to be friends with her, and he'd meant it. He'd never eased into a relationship the way he had with Carrie. Their time together had been unique, special, and after only a few days of separation, he missed it. He missed *her.* . . .

He set the Bible on the end table and rose, crossing to the window to peer out at the darkening landscape. The closest neighbor was more than a mile down the road, and the lights in their windows looked like wavering dots from this distance. That was okay, though. He didn't mind being alone. At least he hadn't minded until lately. Until Carrie.

Pushing off from the window frame, he stomped to the television and snapped it on. But after scrolling through the few channels that came through, he found nothing of worth to watch. He jammed his thumb on the OFF button, dropped the remote, and sat back in his chair.

The moment his backside connected with the chair seat, the phone rang.

And Rocky knew without a doubt it was Carrie.

He sat, frozen, holding his breath, as the telephone blared. *Ri-i-ing...* *ri-i-ing...ri-i-ing...* But he didn't answer it. After ten rings, it stopped, and he blew out the air he'd been holding. He sat in tense silence, his shoulder muscles aching, while he waited to see if it would start again.

Nothing.

His throat felt dry, so he pushed himself out of the chair and headed to the kitchen. While he held a glass under the water spigot, the phone began blaring again. *Ri-i-ing...ri-i-ing...ri-i-ing...*

Water splashed over the rim of the glass and across his hand. He smacked the handle down and raised the glass to his lips, gulping water as if he hadn't had his thirst quenched in years. At the last swallow, the phone stopped.

"Whew." He put the glass in the sink and hung his head low, his hands braced on the edge of the counter. Before it could start again, he'd have to get out of here. Go see Eileen? No, it was Friday—she and several residents got together for a Red Hat tea every Friday evening. Philip and his wife, Marin, might be home, but they were still pretty much newlyweds. He hated to intrude uninvited. He'd given up most of his other friendships when he'd accepted Christ. Where could he go?

Loneliness struck hard, and he wished he'd just gone to the pizza place to see Carrie one more time before deciding he couldn't do it anymore. He stomped again to the window and peered across the acreage he'd purchased. In his mind's eye, he envisioned rows of hybrid irises and roses and shrubs—his own plantings, which could be transplanted into other people's yards. He had the space. He just needed the know-how.

Suddenly he knew how to fill the remainder of his evening. The public library was open until ten on weekday nights. He'd go in, do some research on the Internet, find out if any correspondence courses were available in landscaping, and check out some books on starting a business. He'd engross himself in his future plans. That should help him forget his past, brief relationship with Carrie Mays.

Just as he snatched his keys off the end of the kitchen counter, the phone started to ring again. His hand hovered over the receiver, the temptation to answer nearly overwhelming. *Please, God, give me the strength to let her go. She's too good for a no-good wild boy like me.* He balled his hand into a fist, ordered himself to ignore the sound, and headed out the door.

⟿

Carrie slammed her telephone onto her mattress. Why didn't he answer? When, out of concern, she had called his brother, Philip had assured her nothing was wrong. As Rocky's next of kin, he'd have been notified if there had been an accident. As far as Philip knew, Rocky was spending his evening at home.

But Rocky was supposed to have spent his evening with her!

Fury filled her as she remembered sitting in that booth, straining toward the door at every jingle of those bells. Angela had said she looked ridiculous, and Angela was right. She had been ridiculous to wait that long for Rocky to show up.

She yanked the scarf from her ponytail, and her hair fell in an unruly tumble across her shoulders. Impatiently she shoved the strands behind her ears. She yanked drawers open, pulling out clean pajama pants and a T-shirt for bed. Changing with jerky motions, she deposited her clothes into the hamper the way a basketball star deposits a slam dunk. Then she flumped across the bed, crossed her ankles, folded her arms, and glared across the room for several minutes, letting the anger keep the hurt at bay.

But it couldn't last. In time, the fury faded, and all that was left was a feeling of intense betrayal. Another man had let her down. And she suspected that, once again, it had to do with her money. But this time, instead of the man trying to find a way to get to it, she was pretty sure Rocky was trying to get away from it.

When she'd told him her full name, his reaction spoke of intense discomfort. It didn't take a rocket scientist to figure out Rocky felt inferior to her. Although she'd feared that he, like so many others, might chase her for her money, it now appeared her money was chasing him off.

"Why, God? Why can't I find a man who looks at me and only sees me, not the money I have? I just want to be loved for *me*. . . ."

She rolled onto her side and cuddled a plump pillow, hugging it against her chest as she tried to overcome the pressing desire to cry. But despite her best effort, she didn't succeed.

# Chapter 9

Carrie lifted a bite of Myrna's succulent beef roast to her mouth, chewed, and swallowed. But she might as well have been eating shredded paper for the enjoyment she found in the meal. Her parents sat at opposite ends of the dining table, candlelight flickering across their faces, as they exchanged occasional glances. Conversation lagged, and Carrie knew why. The empty seat across the table from her—the seat in which Rocky would be sitting had she been able to invite him—provided a tremendous distraction.

Although neither Mac nor her mother had quizzed her when she said he wouldn't be joining them, Carrie knew the question was rife in both their minds. She had no desire to address the issue because she'd have to admit she'd been stood up. The humiliation still stung. She'd tried calling Rocky off and on all day, still with no answer, and the acute sadness that had brought on her tears last night had changed once more to anger. At least the anger was easier to carry than the sadness had been.

Myrna came in quietly to clear away the plates then served dessert—apple pie with scoops of vanilla ice cream sprinkled with cinnamon. The cook looked into Carrie's eyes when she placed the warmed dessert dish on the table, and Carrie rewarded her with a smile. She appreciated Myrna's attempt to cheer her up. Even if this pie was flavorless, she would consume every bite, for Myrna's sake.

When Myrna returned to the kitchen, Mac leaned his elbows on the table and fixed Carrie with a dour look. "Well, I'd say it's time to talk."

Lynette raised her gaze and suggested, "Should it wait until after dessert?"

But Mac shook his head. "I've waited long enough. She needs to know."

Carrie's heart leaped into her throat. Fear assaulted her so fiercely she dropped her fork. "What?" She looked frantically back and forth at her parents. "What do I need to know? Is it about Rocky?" Oh, something was wrong! Something had happened to Rocky! She clasped her trembling hands together and pressed them into her lap, the dessert forgotten. "Tell me, Mac, please."

Mac pursed his lips for a moment, his eyes turning steely. He took in a deep breath. "I've done some checking on this groundskeeper from Elmwood Towers. When you mentioned his name last night, I was certain I'd heard it somewhere before. I was right."

Carrie processed Mac's remarks. From what he had just said, she gathered nothing had happened to Rocky. A feeling of relief washed over her, followed by a wave of anger. If nothing was wrong, he should be here! She nearly missed Mac's next comment.

"Are you aware that when Rocky Wilder was a young man he stole several hundred dollars' worth of lumber from one of the Steinwood building sites?"

Carrie blinked, staring at her stepfather. That explained why his name had seemed familiar when he'd told her. Now she remembered how Mac had raved about some juvenile delinquent who dared to walk off with his property. Still, she couldn't see Rocky doing that. "Stole? From you?"

Mac nodded grimly. "That's correct. He was caught red-handed, taken into custody, and spent six weeks in a juvenile detention center." Mac leaned back, propping one elbow on the high back of his chair. "It would have been more had the lumber not been recovered, completely undamaged."

"Carrie, darling, I know you're taken with this man"—Carrie's mother spoke softly—"but perhaps you should give this relationship some serious thought. My main concern when we spoke was the differences in your backgrounds, but now, with what Mac has uncovered. . ." Lynette pursed her mouth in sympathy. "It doesn't seem wise, to me, to pursue someone who so clearly lacks scruples."

Carrie spun back to Mac. "How old was Rocky when this happened?"

Mac waved his hand as if it didn't matter, but Carrie leaned forward, intent on having her question answered. Finally Mac huffed. "Junior high age, I believe—thirteen or fourteen." Then he pointed at her. "But that's beside the point. The point is the man is a thief. To be honest, I'm not sure I want him to continue as an employee at Elmwood Towers. What's to keep him from pilfering things from the residents there?"

Carrie's hackles rose. Her stepfather was being unfairly judgmental, and she couldn't let his comments pass. "Rocky does an excellent job as groundskeeper. The landscaping is beautifully done, and the residents adore him. He's friends with them. Please don't interfere in his job there."

Mac shook his head. "Carrie, you are hopelessly naive. I might admire your desire to look for the good in people, but good simply does not exist in some people. That Wilder boy is one of those people. He's rotten to the core." His imperious finger aimed in her direction again. "He's after your money, Carrie, plain and simple. He smelled it the minute he spotted you, and he plotted from the beginning how to win you so he could get at your wealth."

Carrie rose from the table, heat filling her face. She prayed for control as she forced a quiet tone. "You're wrong, Mac. If Rocky were after my money, he'd be sitting in that chair right now, doing his best to impress you and win you over. But he isn't there, is he? He didn't show. He didn't show because he's scared to death of my money. He knows he doesn't have any, and he thinks that makes him unworthy. *You* think that makes him unworthy. But I don't. In God's eyes, we're all equal, and—"

Mac waved his hand, rolling his eyes. "Don't bring God into it, Carrie."

"I have to bring God into it," she insisted, surprising herself with her boldness. "I can't set Him aside. He's a part of me." She took a step toward her stepfather and touched his arm. "Mac, I know you're only acting out of concern for me, and I want you to know I appreciate it. But you've got to understand—you're wrong about Rocky."

Mac jerked his arm away and thrust out his jaw. "I don't believe I am."

"Think about it." Carrie used her best persuasive tone, swinging her gaze back and forth to include both of her parents. "If he wanted something from me, wouldn't he be pursuing me? Instead he's running away. Doesn't that prove anything to you?"

Mac stood and tossed his napkin on the table. He towered over Carrie with flashing eyes. "It proves to me he's wily enough to have found a way to hoodwink you. And you're foolish enough to fall for it." He raised both hands in defeat. "Fine, Carrie. Believe what you want to believe. But when he's absconded with your trust fund and left you crying in a gutter, don't come creeping to me for a handout. The agreement your mother and I reached was that when your inheritance from your father became available, you would no longer be my concern. My responsibility toward you ends on your twenty-fifth birthday, young woman, so don't anticipate receiving a penny of Steinwood assets. And you'd better carefully consider how much you trust that Wilder boy."

Without giving Carrie a chance to reply, he turned and stomped from the room. His final words had struck like blows, leaving Carrie feeling as though her heart was bruised. She turned to her mother, and her voice quivered as she asked, "Is what he just said true? You discussed my no longer being a part of the Steinwood family after I turn twenty-five?"

"Now, Carrie, there is enough money in the trust fund set up with your father's assets to—"

"It isn't the money I'm worried about, Mother!" Carrie could hardly believe what she was hearing. Couldn't anyone see beyond the money to the relationship? "I've spent the last twenty years in this house. I know Mac and I have had our differences, but he's the only father I know. He plans to simply cut me loose when I no longer need his financial support?"

Her mother lowered her gaze, refusing to answer. That gave Carrie all the answer she needed. Rejected. Again. Her heart ached with the implication. She muttered, "I've got to get out of here." She headed for the door. She heard her mother call her name—she heard the apology in her tone—but she ignored it and kept going. Obviously she could not depend on her mother and stepfather. She had to find out whether she could depend on Rocky.

—⌒—

Rocky gave an all-body stretch that lifted his feet from the footrest of the recliner.

He set the gardening book he'd been reading aside and padded to the kitchen. Removing a bottle of pop from his fridge, he unscrewed the top and drank directly from the bottle. Just as he placed the bottle back on the shelf, someone knocked on his front door.

Frowning, he glanced at the clock. Who would be out here now? A couple of years ago, his friends dropped by at all hours, cases of beer in hand, ready to party. But visitors were few and far between now that he'd given up those wild habits. He crossed to the door and swung it wide then nearly fell backward when he saw who stood on the metal steps that served as his porch.

"Carrie?"

She didn't wait for an invitation, just opened the screen door and stepped in as if she'd been there a dozen times before. Embarrassment washed over him as he took in her neat appearance. Her pale orange pants, just high enough to show off her shapely ankles, and the sleeveless top sporting pastel-colored squares on a white background made him think of a garden styled by Van Gogh. Standing there in his cutoff jeans shorts and missing-sleeves T-shirt, he wished he could dive behind the recliner and hide.

"Hi, Rocky. I'm sorry to intrude on you this way, but I couldn't reach you by telephone."

Her sweet voice held none of the loathing he deserved for his despicable treatment. The desire to hide increased. "Yeah. . ." He scratched his head. "I've been—" But he had no excuse, and he wouldn't lie to her. He blew out a lengthy breath and admitted, "I haven't been answering my phone." He frowned. "How did you know where to find me?"

She raised one eyebrow. "Your brother, Philip, gave me directions. He's a nice guy."

He wondered if that last comment was meant to be a barb. If so, he deserved it. He let it pass. "Well, come on in and sit down. It's nothing fancy." What an understatement. How could his used trailer, although he kept it clean, hope to compare to the mansion in which she lived? Still, she showed no disdain as she crossed to the afghan-draped sofa and seated herself.

Rocky perched in his recliner, but he left it upright. He found himself blurting out, "I'm sorry I don't have a nicer house. I thought maybe one day I'd build one out here, but in the meantime. . ."

Carrie shook her head, a soft smile on her face. "Rocky, quit apologizing. I don't care what kind of house you live in. All I care about is you. And I have to tell you, you had me worried when you didn't show up last night as we'd planned. I was afraid something had happened to you."

Rocky hung his head, guilt striking hard. He should have considered that. He hadn't meant to worry her. "I'm sorry about that." He hoped she knew he meant it.

"What happened?"

He brought his head up to meet her gaze. She looked so sweet and concerned, no hint of the anger she should be feeling evident in her eyes. He couldn't answer her, though. He needed to know something. "Carrie, why do you care at all about me?"

The question seemed to startle her. She straightened, her eyes widening, her lips parting as if searching for words. After a moment she asked, her voice filled with confusion, "Is there some reason why I shouldn't?"

Rocky stood and threw his arms outward. "There're at least a dozen reasons why you shouldn't! Look at me. Look at this place. Then look at yourself. What do you want with me?"

"Your friendship." The answer came quickly.

"Why?" He fired the word.

She offered a soft laugh, lifting her shoulders in a graceful shrug. "I don't know. I just know I do. I like you, Rocky."

Her words took the bones out of his legs. At least that's how he felt. Suddenly they couldn't hold him up anymore. He sat back in his chair and shook his head, amazed. He admitted, "I like you, too, Carrie."

"Then why'd you let me down?"

For the first time, he heard genuine pain in her voice. Without conscious thought, he reached for her. Her hand met his and clung hard. In her grasp, he sensed the hurt he'd caused her, and his chest tightened in remorse.

"I'm so sorry, Carrie. I shouldn't have left you sitting there alone last night. It was cowardly of me. But when I saw you with that man Wednesday night—"

"Man? You mean Carl?"

Rocky shrugged. "I don't know his name. He showed up at the end of the Bible study and followed you home. When I saw you with him, I just thought you two. . .I don't know. . .*fit*. And I knew I didn't. Not with you. Not like he does. So. . .I backed off."

She gave his hand a tug. "Rocky, whatever you thought you saw, Carl and I most certainly do *not* fit. He has no use for God, and that's reason enough for me to keep my distance. But there's more. Carl wants me to believe he's interested in me, but I happen to know he's most interested in my money." She lowered her gaze, her forehead creasing. But when she lifted her head again, her expression had cleared. "I can't be with someone who only wants what I can give, monetarily. Does that make sense?"

Rocky thought about what she'd said. He had to admit, the idea of all that wealth was appealing. He wouldn't be honest if he said otherwise. Yet there was so much more to Carrie than her wealth. The fact that she'd come looking for him, was worried about him, told him a great deal about her heart. He nodded. "Yes. It makes sense."

"Good." She withdrew her hand and tipped her head, fixing him with a steady gaze. "I forgive you for standing me up last night, but you do owe me."

He felt a grin tug at his cheek. "Oh yeah?"

"Yes. I got no supper last night because of you."

"I'm really sorry about that, Carrie."

"Prove it."

He raised one brow. "How?"

"Buy me lunch. Tomorrow. I want sandwiches and fruit at the park. You know where the duck pond is?"

He nodded.

"One o'clock at the duck pond. Tuna salad with raw spinach. Golden Delicious apples with caramel dip. And lemonade to drink."

He couldn't help himself. A chuckle rumbled from his chest. She didn't pull any punches, and he liked it. "And that'll serve as a proper apology?"

"As long as the apples are crisp, not mealy," she retorted with a grin.

He laughed out loud. "Okay, Carrie, you've got it. I'll be there."

She looked at him, her expression suddenly wary. "Really? You'll be there?"

He saw the insecurity lurking beneath the surface. It pained him how much his failure to show up last night had cost her. He took her hand and said earnestly, "I'll be there."

She smiled and rose. "Good. See you tomorrow, Rocky." She slipped out the door.

He sure hoped the grocery store had some fresh, crisp Golden Delicious apples in their produce department.

# Chapter 10

Rocky didn't bother to change out of his church clothes before meeting Carrie. She'd said be there by one o'clock, and he was determined to be early so there'd be no question in her mind as to whether he was coming. The grocery store not only had crisp Golden Delicious apples, but it also had a deli with tuna salad, so he had the sandwiches made there. On impulse, he grabbed a loaf of white bread from the day-old case. Carrie could feed it to the ducks.

He found half-liter bottles of lemonade in the cooler beside the checkout counter, paid for his purchases, and piled everything in a plastic grocery sack. Nothing fancy, but he knew Carrie wouldn't mind. It was one of the things he admired about her—she didn't put on airs.

When he arrived at the park, several other people were already gathered in small clusters or pairs, but he didn't see Carrie. He walked to the duck pond and sat gingerly on the grass. He didn't want grass stains on his good pants. He heard a burst of laughter from one of the groups, and it made him feel lonely as he sat by himself. Suddenly insecurity hit. Would Carrie come? Not showing up would be a good payback for what he'd done to her last Friday night. But as quickly as the fear stabbed, he pushed it aside. Carrie wasn't vindictive. She'd be here.

He was right. He'd no more than had the thought when he heard her sweet voice from behind him.

"You're right on time."

Peeking over his shoulder, he watched her approach, graceful in a pair of strappy sandals and flowing sundress. Her hair lay loose across her shoulders, the sun catching the shimmering strands of blond. It struck him again how beautiful she was. And she wanted to be with him. He didn't deserve her at all.

He rose and greeted her with a quick, impersonal hug, wishing he had the courage to give her a kiss. "You look so pretty—too fancy for a picnic."

She smiled and flipped his tie with the ends of her fingers. "What about you? You look like an executive in your tie."

He felt a blush building, but it was strictly due to pleasure, not embarrassment. Who else would tell Rocky Wilder he looked like an executive? Uncertain how to reply, he changed the subject. "I'm sorry I didn't bring a blanket or anything. I'm afraid you'll get your dress dirty."

"Did you bring the food?"

"Oh yeah. Just what you asked for."

"Then I'm satisfied," she said, and her smile proved it.

"Well, then, here." He removed the items from the bag then pressed the square of plastic flat against the grass. "You sit on this. At least it'll protect your skirt."

"Thanks." She flashed him another smile and seated herself. Her movements were so graceful that Rocky felt like a clod plunking down beside her.

He handed her a sandwich and bottle of lemonade, leaving the bag of apples and tub of caramel dip in his lap. "These can be dessert," he said, indicating the apples.

"Perfect." She tipped her head. "Do you want to say grace?"

He nodded and bowed his head. "Dear Lord, thank You for the beautiful day, the beautiful companion, and this picnic lunch. Bless the food so it may nourish us to do Your service. Amen." Although praying in front of others usually made him self-conscious, it seemed natural with Carrie. When he opened his eyes, he found Carrie's gaze fixed on him.

"That was perfect, Rocky. Thank you."

"You're welcome." He swallowed, forcing his focus away from her beguiling blue eyes and to his sandwich. "Better eat. The breeze'll dry out your bread."

Two ducks waddled in their direction, and Rocky handed Carrie the loaf of day-old bread. "I think your friends are hungry. They'll take your sandwich if you aren't careful. Throw them some of that bread."

She laughed. "What a wonderful idea!" She opened the loaf, tore one piece in half and tossed it to the ducks. Their happy clamor immediately drew a crowd. Carrie had the bag empty in no time, but the ducks quacked for more. She looked at Rocky with raised brows. "Now what?"

"Greedy quackers," he muttered. "Well, I'm not giving them my lunch. Come on. Maybe if we move off a bit, they'll get the hint and go bother someone else."

Fortunately his suggestion proved true. When they moved to a picnic table in the shade, the ducks waddled off toward another group of picnickers. Carrie watched them go, a soft smile curving her lips.

"I haven't fed the ducks in years. Not since I was a very little girl. My dad brought me to the park to feed the ducks." She turned to look at Rocky, and he saw a hint of sadness in the depth of her eyes. "He's been gone for twenty years, but sometimes I still think about him."

"Yeah. Mine died four years ago. I think of him sometimes, too." He didn't add that the memories weren't pleasant ones.

"Mom married Mac less than a year after Dad's death. He and my dad had been friends. Mac isn't nearly as warm and loving as my dad was, but at least I've had someone in that role." Carrie took a bite of her sandwich and chewed, her expression thoughtful. "Dads are pretty important people, you know? I've been thinking about the Bible study at church. I didn't realize how much a dad can influence how you see God."

Rocky frowned, not sure he understood what she meant. "How so?"

She pursed her lips for a moment. "Well, for instance, if you grew up with a very loving, protective dad, you'd see God as loving and protective. But if you grew up with a distant dad, one who only talked to you when you did something wrong, then you'd see God as a punitive figure, only there to make you feel shamed."

Rocky considered this. His dad had been hard, unyielding in his expectations, rarely affectionate. When he'd first heard about God, he couldn't imagine that God would care about him. Now he wondered how much of that idea came from his relationship with his father. He remembered how he'd resisted even thinking of God as Father. Carrie must be right.

She went on. "Mac hasn't been all that loving, but I do have my memories of my real dad, and all of those are good. That must be where I based my ideas of God, because as soon as someone told me about God, I was ready to embrace Him." She flashed him a smile. "Being a Christian, being part of God's family, is the best thing I can think of."

"Even better than being rich," Rocky remarked, recalling how all his life he'd simply wanted wealth. Now it didn't seem to matter so much. But his words made Carrie flinch. He touched her arm. "What's wrong?"

She put her sandwich down, her head low. "It's always about money. . . ."

Rocky regretted his impulsive words, but he hadn't meant them the way she took them. He tugged her arm, encouraging her to look up. "Carrie, I'm sorry I said that. It had more to do with me, and the way I used to be, than you."

She looked at him with pain in her eyes. "You mean you can honestly look at me and not see my money?"

He pulled his hand back, searching for a truthful reply. His voice faltered as he answered. "Carrie, I like you. I really do. You're sweet and pretty and fun. And when I just think of you as Carrie, I'm okay. It's when the other intrudes—the realization that Carrie is also Caroline Steinwood—that's when I have trouble."

⌒⌒

Carrie nodded miserably. She suspected as much. It was unfair that Mac looked at Rocky and only saw the bad things Rocky had done. It was just as unfair that people looked at her and only saw her money. How to overcome those preconceived notions? She didn't know. The happy feeling of picnicking with Rocky drifted away, replaced by regret. Maybe they'd never be able to overcome the issue of her money.

Well, if they were to try, Rocky would need to know the whole truth. She raised her gaze to look directly into his eyes. Their warm, velvety depths, open and attentive, gave her the courage she needed.

"Rocky, in less than a month, I'll turn twenty-five." He opened his mouth to say something, but she held up her hand. "And you need to know what happens then. My father was a very wealthy man. When he died, he left nearly everything in a trust fund for me. Sometimes I think that's why my mom married Mac—Daddy provided for my future, but it was my distant future, and he left very little to Mom for the present. She needed Mac's money to survive. So did I.

"But on my twenty-fifth birthday, the trust fund becomes truly mine to do with as I please. I won't be dependent on Mac anymore, and I won't need to be. I'll be very wealthy in my own right." She searched Rocky's face. He didn't so much as blink. She continued. "I need to know if this causes a problem for you."

He drew in a long breath, his gaze drifting to the side for a moment as he appeared to gather his thoughts. When he turned back to face her, she was frightened by what she saw in his eyes. She was certain it was remorse.

"Carrie, I have to be honest. When I was growing up, I had very little. I guess that's why I stole—I wanted what other people had. I thought those things would make me happy. Of course they didn't. I didn't recognize it at the time, but I think my own guilt made me unable to enjoy the things I took. The best thing that happened to me was getting caught stealing and being forced to face the consequences of my actions. I never stole again, but I still wanted things."

He shook his head, a lopsided smile appearing. "Do you know I used to stand outside the fence of your house, wishing I lived in the Steinwood mansion?"

"You did?" She wondered why she'd never seen him.

A quick nod made his hair slip across his forehead. He ran his fingers through the strands, smoothing them back in place. "Yes. I wanted your house. I wanted your money. I wanted. . .everything you had. I thought I'd surely be happy if all those things were mine. For years that's all I thought about—becoming wealthy. Becoming happy."

He shrugged. "Obviously I haven't become wealthy. I work as a gardener and live in a trailer house. About as unwealthy as a person can be." He chuckled a bit at his own expense. "And for the most part, I think I managed to get past that dream of being rich. Until I met you." He shook his head, whistling through his teeth. "Boy, I don't know how to explain this."

Although Carrie's heart beat in trepidation, she said, "Try. I'm listening."

"I think I managed to find contentment in just being Rocky Wilder, grounds-keeper, but then you came along in your fancy clothes and your fancy car, and suddenly being groundskeeper wasn't enough again. I wanted more. But not for *me* this time, for you. I like you, and I want to give you things. Things like you're used to having. And I can't do that. So. . ."

"So that's why you avoided me Friday night? Because you can't give me things?" She wanted to make sure she understood.

He nodded. The strand of hair slipped again, and it was all Carrie could do to keep from guiding it into place for him. "Yeah. I can't compete with all you have, Carrie. And it hurts my pride, you know? Even if I get my business up and running, it'll only be a landscaping business. Nothing like what you want to do with your life—executive position, using computers and all that." He huffed in aggravation, his forehead creased. "I'm nobody compared to you."

His last statement made her mad. "You aren't *nobody*, Rocky. Not compared to me or anyone else. Do you think God sees you as a nobody? No. He sees you as His creation, and He loves you just the way you are. You've got to stop putting yourself down because you don't have money. It isn't right."

"It also isn't easy," he shot back.

She nodded, acknowledging his words. "I know. But you have to *try*, Rocky. Because if you don't, we. . ." She turned her gaze away. Was there a "we" where she and Rocky were concerned?

After several quiet minutes, she turned back. "I don't want my money to come between us. Is it going to?"

He rested his chin in his hand, his gaze pinned on hers, while he seemed to struggle with forming an answer. Finally an answer came, but it wasn't the one Carrie hoped for. "I don't know. I want to see just you—Carrie, my friend—but Caroline Mays Steinwood keeps getting in the way."

"So think about something else!" She threw her hands outward, disgusted with his shortsightedness. "Think about. . .your own landscaping business and what it will take to get it running. Don't even think about me and my goals. Focus on your own."

"But don't you see I can't? They're all intermingling!" He appeared as frustrated as she felt. He rammed his hand through his hair. "When I think of me landscaping, the picture ends up side by side with you in a business suit in a meeting with multimillionaires. I think of my trailer house, and your family's mansion looms over it. I think of my past, all the wrong things I did, and when I compare that to your sweetness. . . The two don't fit together, Carrie—don't you see?"

"All I see," she said, blinking to hold back tears, "is that you're going to ruin something good if you don't let go of my money. The money doesn't mean that much to me, Rocky. But if it means that much to you, it's always going to be in the way. And we don't stand a chance of making this relationship work."

"I know." The simple answer came out in a groan.

Although Carrie recognized how deeply Rocky wanted to make things work, she also knew it was not going to happen easily. She took his hand. The calluses on his palm and the ends of each finger felt scratchy against her flesh. She squeezed hard to let him know they didn't bother her.

"Rocky, please. I need someone who will see me for who I am. Not Caroline Mays, recipient of a massive trust fund. Not Caroline Steinwood, stepdaughter of Mac Steinwood. Not rich-girl Carrie. Just. . .*Carrie*. Can you do that?"

He met her gaze, his fingers tightening on hers. "I can try." His voice sounded raspy. He cleared his throat and added, "I'll do my best."

Carrie wasn't sure that was good enough, but for now it would have to do. She turned to watch a pair of ducks glide across the pond toward one another. They touched beaks then continued side by side. She sighed. All the people in the world who thought money was the answer to their problems—if they only knew the problem money could be. . . Her mouth felt dry, and she licked her lips.

Rocky bumped her arm with a bottle of lemonade. "It won't stay cold much longer. Better drink it."

She took it, but it was slippery from condensation and she nearly dropped it. Rocky recovered it by grasping both the bottle and her hand. Their gazes collided for a moment, and she allowed him a glimpse of her agony. She saw a matching sadness in his eyes, too.

"Do you have it?" he asked, his voice barely above a whisper.

"Yes." She pulled her hand away, the bottle secure. She unscrewed the cap and lifted the bottle to her lips for a sip of the sweet, cool liquid. It soothed her throat, but her heart remained burdened.

She had prayed for God to bring a man into her life who wouldn't pursue her for her money. She never dreamed she'd need to pray for one to accept it.

# Chapter 11

Carrie slipped in the back door and headed directly to her bedroom. No servants were around—Sunday was their day off. Her mother's suite door was closed, indicating she was taking her Sunday afternoon nap, and Mac was nowhere in sight. That suited Carrie. She wanted some time alone.

She changed out of her dress and put it in with the clothes going to the dry cleaners. For a moment, she stood in her walk-in closet and let her gaze rove across the variety of clothing items available to her. So many fancy, unnecessary things. Her mother loved to dress her up—she always had. Mother glowed with pride when someone said, "What a pretty girl your Carrie is."

Carrie frowned. Would Mother have loved her as much had she been a plain-looking girl? She pushed that thought away and moved to her dresser, where she pulled out a pair of pajama pants and a T-shirt. Nothing fancy, but merely comfortable. In the privacy of her bedroom, she could get by with that.

Climbing into the four-poster bed, she stacked up the plump pillows and leaned into the comforting softness. How different Rocky had looked today. He had a rugged appeal in his work clothes that showed his developed biceps, wide shoulders, and narrow hips. But today, in a pair of pleated trousers, button-down oxford shirt, and tie of muted blues and greens, she'd been given a different glimpse of Rocky. Her heart thumped as she remembered the jolt of reaction that had attacked her middle when he'd turned and flashed his welcoming smile. Rocky in dress-up clothes was an arresting sight.

She sighed, shifting into a more reclined position, as she allowed her thoughts to drift, dissecting all the reasons she found Rocky desirable. His height and strong arms gave her a feeling of protection. She knew she was safe with him. Those moments when he'd hugged her—just one brief, almost impersonal embrace—had turned her insides to mush. If a hug did all that, what might a kiss do? She felt an embarrassed flush fill her face as she considered it. Would she ever find out?

Grabbing one of the pillows, she hugged it to her chest, an attempt to calm her accelerated heartbeat. She suspected he wouldn't be the aggressor. Angela had said he was a player in high school, but she saw none of that in his behavior. He was always a gentleman—flirtatious but respectful.

What would he do if she kissed him? She considered it, wondering if she could find the courage to be bold enough to kiss him. Always the men had pursued her, never the other way around. They'd pursued her because she was pretty, but also because she was rich.

Rocky wouldn't pursue her because she was rich. Her wealth left him feeling inadequate. She remembered the look in his eyes as he'd admitted he had a hard time separating Carrie his friend from Caroline Steinwood. She huffed in aggravation, throwing the pillow aside. Why couldn't he see her for herself? Just once, why couldn't someone see her for herself?

"It's always been this way." The words came out in a harsh whisper. She believed her mother loved her because she was attractive and intelligent—the perfect trophy child to put on exhibit for her friends. Mac provided for her to please her mother, not because of any real affection for her. The friends she'd had while growing up had spent time with her because it was prestigious to be invited to the Steinwood mansion. Carl had ardently pursued her because of the magnitude of her trust fund. Carrie's heart ached as she realized how many people cared for her to suit their own needs, not to meet her needs for love and affection.

Raising her gaze to the coffered ceiling, she spoke aloud. "Thank You, God, for loving me for me. Thank You for not loving me for what I could give You, but loving me just because. There isn't anyone else in my life who's done that. . . ."

Not even Rocky. Not honestly. It hurt her to acknowledge it. She believed Rocky was trying, but even with him, the money created a diversion. Closing her eyes and lowering her head, she continued talking to her heavenly Father. But this prayer was one of desire. "Please, God, I'm falling in love with Rocky, and I believe he's falling in love with me. Let him look past the dollar signs to my heart. Let him see me—just me. . . ."

⁓

"Hand me another one of those mums." Eileen reached her gloved hand toward Rocky.

Rocky had promised to help her get a variety of mums planted before she needed to pick up the boys from work Monday afternoon. They'd spent nearly an hour together, with him pausing in the distribution of fertilizer to offer a hand when needed, and half the mums were already in the ground. He looked where she had the trowel poised now. "You gonna put it there?"

Eileen blinked at him, her lips pursed. "That was my intention. Why?"

He rose, his knees popping, and crossed to her in three long strides. He pointed. "If you put it that close to the rhododendron, it'll get the afternoon shade. Besides that, from this angle, it'll be nearly hidden. Since this garden will be mostly enjoyed from the bench on the other side of the walking path, I'd say shift it forward and to the left about twelve inches."

Eileen pushed to her feet and waddled to where he stood on the grass. Hands on hips, she looked at the garden area from his viewpoint. Then with a rueful chuckle, she shook her head. "Okay, I concede. You're right." Squinting up at him, she gave him a playful poke on the shoulder. "You do know what you're doing, don't you?"

She bent over, snatched up one of the potted mums, and returned to the garden spot to begin digging a hole to receive the plant. While she dug, she asked, "So have you done any more checking on the classes you need to become a landscaper?"

Rocky pushed the fertilizer spreader back and forth, its gentle hum competing with the scratch of Eileen's trowel in the dirt. Good sounds. "I've checked. But. . ."

She sat back on her haunches, fixing him with a stern look. "But?"

He stopped, blew out a breath, and shook his head. "But I don't know if it's worth it."

Eileen scowled, the lines around her mouth becoming pronounced. "What is *that* supposed to mean?"

"Aw, don't look at me like that," he protested, getting the spreader going again. "Think about it. There're all kinds of reasons to forget about that stupid dream. For one, I'm gonna be thirty years old in another year. I'm too old to be going to college—I'd look silly with all those young kids. Besides that, I'm too stupid. Barely made it through high school. How would I survive college classes on botany and biology and business? I'm just kidding myself."

"Rocky Wilder, you stop pushing that machine and come here."

The stern tone brought him to a halt. He looked at her and swallowed a grin. She was doing her best to appear fierce, but her fiercest was pretty tame compared to what Rocky grew up with. Still, he followed her direction just because he liked her so much.

She had to tip her head back to look him in the face. "It isn't the college that's got you running scared. You could handle the classes. You know you aren't stupid." Waving her arm to indicate the grounds, she said, "All the signs of your handiwork indicate you aren't stupid. You have the ability. So what's the problem?"

"It's just a silly dream!" The words burst out more forcefully than he intended.

"Why is it silly?" She matched his tone.

"Because it is."

"Well, that's a silly answer." She glared up at him, daring him to contradict her. "Do you think God gives silly talents? No! He plants in each of His children the ability to do *something*, and the 'something' is for good. Nothing silly about that. You bring beauty to our corner of the world, and I won't let you call it silly."

"But anybody could—"

"No, they couldn't! Look at what I nearly did with that mum. Would've hidden it in the shade. But not you—you could see the big picture. You're a natural, Rocky, and you need to use that talent."

Rocky dropped his chin, shaking his head. "Look, Eileen—it was fun to think about, but it just isn't realistic."

She waved her hand in dismissal. "You're too hard on yourself. You could handle those classes if you wanted to. It isn't unrealistic to expect yourself to succeed in school."

"It's not just that," he blurted out, surprising himself.

"Then what is it? Spill it."

He swallowed. "I—I want a family, Eileen. I want a family I can take care of. *Really* take care of. Not just give 'em the basics, but give 'em the extras; you know what I mean? Vacations and braces"—he ran his tongue over his crooked teeth—"and a nice house. Even if I get a business started, even if I do landscaping for other people as my job, I'm still nothing more than a glorified gardener. I'll never be rich, not rich enough to do all those things for my family."

Eileen listened intently, her brow creased. "That's really important to you?"

"Yes!" He flung his arms outward. "I spent all my growing-up years feeling envious of the kids who had nice clothes and new bicycles every year for Christmas and silver braces making their teeth straight. I don't want my own kids feeling that way."

"Oh, Rocky. . ." Eileen shook her head, a sad smile softening the lines around her mouth. "Sit down here with me for a minute, huh?"

They sat side by side in the grass, while the early fall sun heated their heads. Eileen plucked one strand of grass and used it to point at him.

"I understand why you feel the way you do, but I think you're selling yourself and your future family short. Happiness isn't something you get because you've got things. Happiness comes from. . .well, from loving each other." She worked her jaw back and forth for a moment, as if gathering her thoughts, then continued. "I've known your brother, Philip, a long time—five years now—and he's been pretty open with me. So I'm going to make an observation based on what Philip's shared. Hold onto your hat."

Teasingly, Rocky put his hands on his head.

Eileen grinned and went on. "That desire of yours to give all kinds of extras, as you put it, comes from your misguided perception that *things* were what you lacked as a child. Rocky, it wasn't things; it was a feeling of belonging and affection. Your parents, for whatever reason, didn't know how to give that to you. But I know if they'd really made you feel loved, not getting a new bicycle or braces wouldn't have mattered a bit. I know, because that was my childhood. Never had more than two sets of clothes to my name, sure never got new toys, but I was never unhappy—because my house burst at the seams with loving each other. I was so happy I never knew I was poor."

Rocky raised his eyebrows. He had a hard time believing her.

"Stop looking at me like that." She shook the blade of grass. "It's absolutely true. I had the love of my mama and daddy, and they taught me about the love of God, and that same God made sure every last one of my needs was met. I never once hungered for anything more than what I had. I was happy. Because I was loved."

"But times have changed," he argued.

Eileen sputtered, "Don't try telling me old values are outdated! They aren't! It's people that've changed, not the times. People have become dissatisfied with having their needs met and get all caught up in wants." She glowered at him. "You really think those rich people who live in East Briar are happy all the time? Bah! They're still people, Rocky, and people all need the same thing to make them happy—love. Love of God first, and love of family second."

She rolled to her feet and peered down at him for a moment, her expression thoughtful. "Maybe you need to spend some time in prayer, young man. Ask God to get your priorities in alignment. And while you're at it, you might let God know you trust Him to meet your needs. He can do it. And while He's at it, He can give you the desires of your heart. But what you've got to remember is the biggest desire should always be to grow in your relationship with Him. That's where true happiness resides—in recognizing just how much He loves you."

She turned her back and returned to her digging. Rocky watched her for a few minutes, his thoughts tumbling haphazardly, sorting out what she'd said. He got to his feet and emptied the rest of the fertilizer in the spreader, but his mind wasn't on the task. He kept replaying what Eileen had said about God meeting his needs, God being the source of his happiness. He wanted to accept her words as fact, to set aside all the ideas of providing his family with the extras he'd mentioned, but a bit of doubt held him back.

What if Carrie's needs were different from most people's? After all, having grown up in a mansion, given all the extras money could buy, wouldn't those things that were wants to him have become needs to her? And how could he hope to provide those things for her with a simple landscaping business?

"Eileen?" He waited until she raised her head. "I'm going to put the spreader away; then I'll be back to help you put the rest of those mums in the ground. You okay out here by yourself?"

She waved a dirty glove in his direction. "Go on. I'm old, not helpless." As he started to walk away, she called, "And think about what I said! I'm not stupid, either."

He gave a nod in reply and rolled the spreader to the storage shed, cleaned it, and put it away before heading back to assist Eileen in placing the remainder of the mums he had purchased. *Let God know you trust Him to meet your needs. . . .* Eileen's words repeated themselves in his memory. His heart pounded as fear struck. Maybe his faith wasn't strong enough for that yet. He had a lot of serious thinking nd praying to do.

# Chapter 12

Carrie awakened before her alarm clock sounded, jolted from sleep by a troubling dream. She scowled into the dusky room, trying to pinpoint what had bothered her, but as was so often the case with dreams, she was unable to recall the details that would bring understanding. With a sigh, she rolled sideways and blinked the sleep from her eyes. A glance at the calendar hanging above her desk reminded her that in only six more days she would be twenty-five. And she would be independently wealthy.

She rolled the other way to avoid thinking about it.

Her contact with Rocky for the past three weeks had been nonexistent. Frustration built in her chest as she thought about it. She had known school would occupy her time during the week, but she had intended to see Rocky each weekend. Between her stepfather's interference and Rocky's commitment to help his brother do some renovating at his job placement service, she hadn't seen him since their dissatisfying picnic at the duck pond.

A sigh escaped. It hadn't seemed to matter much that she hadn't spent time with Rocky in person. He was constantly present in her thoughts. And her prayers. Despite spending a portion of each day in prayer concerning the roadblock that stood between her and Rocky, she hadn't found a solution. No matter how she looked at it, the trust fund would always be there.

She groaned and buried her face in her pillows, petitioning heaven once more. "How can You make this work, Lord? I love Rocky, and I believe he loves me. Money should never stand in the way of how people feel about each other." She threw back the covers and rose, padding to her desk and tapping her finger thoughtfully on the date that would change her life irrevocably.

Not only would she become responsible for a large sum of money, Mac had informed her she needed to find her own place to live. "You've got the means to purchase a house. I'll put you in touch with a Realtor who can assist you in making a wise choice," Mac had said two nights ago at supper. At the time, Carrie had nearly fallen out of her seat in surprise. She hadn't suspected Mac would throw her out of the only home she'd known since she was a very small girl. But now, thinking about it, it seemed like a good idea to go.

Purchasing a house and getting it ready for her habitation was a challenge in itself. Doing that while facing the starting rush of a taxing, final school year seemed daunting. But it also seemed exciting. She could make her own choices, decorate as she pleased—and she certainly had ideas for decor! Nothing flashy. She wanted homey, warm, and welcoming. Soft colors, durable furniture, and lots of flowers.

The thought of flowers brought her back to Rocky, and suddenly the dream that had awakened her drifted through her memory. Only a whisper of it, but enough to grasp the meaning. She'd dreamed she stood in the middle of a huge flower garden, with Rocky darting from cluster to cluster, his hands reaching, as if trying to decide which bloom to pick. She waited, holding her breath, for him to finally choose one, knowing it would be a flower with special significance; finally he turned to her with great sorrow in his eyes. Holding out his hands in defeat, he said, "I'm sorry. I can't afford any of them." And instantly she'd awakened.

Now she jerked upright, an idea striking like a lightning bolt from the sky. So Rocky couldn't afford those flowers—*she* could! With her trust fund, she could buy a field of flowers. But she didn't want a field of flowers already blooming; she wanted to buy the field in which to plant flowers, and a greenhouse, and tools and equipment needed to get a landscaping business on its feet. Remembering the sadness in the dream—Rocky's eyes when he was unable to gift her—was all the motivation she needed to start her plan in motion.

So Rocky couldn't afford to start his own business. All he needed was the capital. He'd asked her to pray for the means to make his dream a reality, and she'd overlooked the most obvious answer to the prayer—her very own trust fund. She wouldn't use it for herself; she'd use it for the good of others, starting with Rocky.

She dashed through a shower, dressed in a soft linen suit of beige, and pulled sling-back pumps onto her feet. Back in the bathroom, she twisted her still-damp hair into a coil on the back of her head and secured it well with pins then applied makeup with a careful hand. Just enough to bring out her cheekbones and enhance her already thick, full eyelashes. Taking a step back, she surveyed her reflection in the mirror. Satisfied, she marched out of the bathroom, snatched up her purse and keys, and headed for her car.

It was Saturday; people would be busy, but they'd make time for Mac Steinwood's stepdaughter. A twinge of guilt struck as she realized she was doing exactly what she'd always disdained—using money to gain favors—but this favor wasn't for her. This was for the man she loved. It would be worth it.

⁓

Rocky rolled over in bed and stretched, yawning widely, as he forced his body to awaken. Normally on Saturdays, he let himself sleep in since during the week he was at work by 5:00 a.m. But today, as he had the past two Saturdays, he would be meeting Philip at New Beginnings to work on updating the training center.

He sat on the edge of the bed and rubbed his eyes. They should finish today—just touch-up painting and putting everything back where it belonged.

It had been a challenge for Philip to operate with things in a mess—many of his clients didn't adjust well to change, and the odd placement of partitions and furnishings had made things rather tense—but all would be in order by the end of this weekend.

And maybe, after this weekend, he could get his own life in order. While he'd worked with Philip, his thoughts often drifted to Carrie. It had been hard on his heart, not seeing her at all for twenty straight days. He hadn't called her, either. It didn't feel right to call the Steinwood mansion, so he'd waited for her to call him. But she hadn't. That bothered him. Maybe she'd decided a relationship with him wasn't a good idea after all.

He shook his head. He didn't want to think about that. What an unpleasant way to start a day. But he knew how to turn it around. Eyes still open, he prayed, "Dear God, thank You for this day and the chance to do some good work. Be with me as I help Philip finish up at New Beginnings. Be with Carrie, whatever she's doing. Bless her time and protect her. Let us both bring glory to You today. Amen."

The prayer made his heart feel light. Rising, he entered the bathroom and ran a washcloth over his face, scrubbing away the remainder of sleepiness. He gave his whiskery chin a quick shave, pulled on a clean pair of jeans and a T-shirt, then locked up the house and headed to New Beginnings.

Philip was already there, as was his wife, Marin, and Marin's brother, John. He greeted Philip with a clap on the back, gave Marin a hug and a kiss on the cheek, then turned to John.

"Good morning, John." Rocky kept his hands at his sides. Even though a dozen years had passed since his youth, when he had tormented John and others like him, the guilt of his former behavior still plagued him when he saw John.

John's almond eyes crinkled into a smile as he replied, "Good morning, Rocky. Today we are finishing so things will be neat and tidy." His stubby hands signed the words as he spoke.

"Neat and tidy sounds good to me," Rocky agreed then hesitantly gave John a light pat on the shoulder.

John didn't shrink away, just slung his arm around Rocky's back and patted, too. How forgiving John was. Rocky wished he could be as accepting as John was of others.

"Well, let's get going," Philip said. "Paint cans and brushes are over there. Be sure to lay out the plastic sheet before you get started. I don't want paint spatters on my new floor."

"Okay, okay, tyrant." Rocky forced a grumbling tone as he grinned at his brother and headed toward the paint.

John shook his head. "Rocky, this is not tyrant. This is Philip. You do not remember your brother?"

Philip laughed lightly. "He remembers, John. He's just teasing me."

John laughed, too. "Oh, he is teasing. Okay." Then he shook his finger at Rocky. "But no more teasing. Teasing is not nice."

Another pang of guilt struck. John was right—often teasing hurt. John would know. He saluted. "No more teasing."

They all got busy. Philip cranked up his radio on a Christian music station, and the soul-stirring songs inspired Rocky as he worked. He hummed along with the tunes, mouthing the words occasionally, while his paintbrush swished in beat with the music. He heard the phrase "Jesus makes all things new" come through the speaker, and it reminded him of the verse in Second Corinthians that had captured his attention a few nights ago during his reading.

He paused, the paintbrush still, as he tried to recapture the exact wording from his Bible. In a whisper, he recited, " 'Therefore if any man be in Christ, he is a new creature: old things are passed away; behold, all things are become new.' " He was pretty sure he got it word for word. He said it to himself again, absorbing the meaning of the words.

Dipping the brush once more, he reflected on old things passing away. He glanced over his shoulder to spot John with his shoulder against a partition, pushing while Philip guided it into place. John's face creased in concentration, his tongue showing in the corner of his mouth, made Rocky smile.

Who would have thought Rocky Wilder would spend time with a man with Down syndrome? The old Rocky wouldn't have, except to torment him, but the new Rocky was finding an admiration for people with disabilities. Despite any shortcomings perceived by society, John continued to do his best with what he'd been given. Everyone should be as friendly, accepting, and diligent as John.

" 'All things are become new.' " Rocky whispered the words as he stroked paint onto the wall. New. Shiny. Rocky hadn't owned very many new, shiny things in his lifetime. His folks had shopped garage sales and donation sites for clothes and toys. His first car had been fifteen years old when he'd bought it, all the new worn off. Hard to take something like that, buff it up, and make it appear new.

Not so with a man's heart, though, he thought with a rush of joy. When God got hold of a person, He didn't just blow off the dust, sandblast the rust, then polish it to hide the old worn-out parts. God replaced the old parts with brand-new, shiny parts. He made things *new*.

Rocky glanced once more at John. "God, I sure wish I could go back and change the mean things I did," he whispered, his heart aching as he thought of the pain he'd caused. "But thank You for the opportunity to be John's friend now. I hope I can keep things shiny in my relationship with him."

He turned back to the wall, examined his handiwork then stooped to touch up a scuff mark near the baseboard. The swish of paint eradicated the mar, giving the entire wall a new appearance. He smiled, satisfied with his work. Suddenly, against the backdrop of pale beige, Carrie's image appeared. Fresh, clean, honest.

How did that verse in Second Corinthians apply to people like Carrie, whose lives had been lived with everything shiny and new?

The telephone jangled. Philip answered it and then called, "Hey, Rocky! It's for you."

*For me?* Rocky trotted to the phone, took the receiver with two fingers, and pressed it to his ear. "This is Rocky."

"Hi, Rocky, it's Carrie."

*Carrie!* His knees turned to jelly. Bracing himself on the edge of Philip's desk, he squeaked out, "Hi. How'd you find me here?"

A soft laugh came through the line, causing Rocky's heart to double its tempo. "I've called all over Petersburg, it seems. You weren't home, your brother wasn't home, so I finally called Eileen, and she told me where you were. Oh—she said to tell you she'll bring lunch over for all of you."

"Thanks," he said. "But—"

"And speaking of food. . ." Did he hear hesitance in her voice? "You know I've got a birthday around the corner. I'd like you to have dinner with my parents and me to celebrate. Can you come?"

A lump formed in his throat. Dinner in the Steinwood mansion? There wasn't enough polish in the world to shine him up enough to match that place. But how could he refuse? "I'd enjoy that. Thanks for asking."

"Good." She told him the day and time then added, her voice tender, "And don't be nervous. Just be yourself. That's good enough."

The lump nearly strangled him. How he loved this woman. He swallowed hard. "Thanks, Carrie. I'll see you then."

⁓

Carrie hung up the phone then leaned back in her desk chair, satisfied. She'd had a productive morning. In front of her were the forms used in filing for a new business, a list of probable expenses related to starting said business, paperwork from the bank to transfer funds from her account to Rocky's as it was needed to cover start-up expenses, and donation forms from the college to establish a scholarship for his use.

Her fingers trembled as she stacked the papers and slid them into a folder marked simply "for Rocky." It pleased her that the money left by her father could be put to use for good. She suspected Rocky's pride might make him balk at first, but she hoped she could persuade him to accept this gift in the manner intended. She wanted it to convey her belief in his abilities. Everything had fallen so neatly into place this morning that she couldn't help but believe it was God's will for Rocky to start his business, and it gave her great joy to be part of the answer to his prayer.

While out, she had also stopped by a Realtor's office and requested a listing of all available single-dwelling houses in town. The agent who greeted her had been only too eager to show her the most ostentatious, costliest houses on the market. He'd looked at her as if she'd lost her mind when she indicated she wanted a modest home, but he had given her the information she wanted. She knew she needed to look right away—Mac seemed eager to have her out on her own—yet she felt uneasy choosing a house by herself.

It wasn't as if she didn't know what to look for. Mac was in the business of constructing quality houses and businesses. She'd grown up watching, listening, learning. So she could choose a house that was structurally sound. What she wanted was someone at her side who would see the house from the viewpoint of its becoming a home.

She wanted Rocky to help her. But would he? She thought of his trailer house—its lack of pretension. He'd seemed embarrassed by its simplicity, and her heart had ached when he'd apologized for it. If she asked him to help her choose a home for herself, would he be able to do so without feeling second-best? She wanted to build Rocky up, not intimidate him.

Sighing, she tucked the folder into a drawer in her desk, out of the sight of prying eyes. She'd just have to do some more praying, ask God to open Rocky's heart to understand her intentions. Because, if she had her way, Rocky would be a permanent fixture in her life from here on out.

# Chapter 13

Rocky pulled up to the curb outside the Steinwood mansion and turned off the ignition. He sat for a minute, his heart thudding painfully, as he gathered the courage needed to get out of the car. He looked up and down the street—no other vehicles in sight. Had the other guests pulled into the drive and parked behind the house? A large garage and expanse of concrete provided a parking area back there. Should he do the same? Then he shook his head—no, his older-model car would look ridiculous next to the cars driven by the no-doubt wealthy guests waiting inside.

Carrie waited inside, too.

He drew in a great breath then released it slowly, an attempt to calm his ragged nerves. "Get out and go into the house," he mumbled. With a trembling hand, he pulled the door release and stepped onto the street. Standing beside his car, he took a moment to tighten the knot on his tie and straighten the lapels of his new jacket. He resisted the urge to run his hand through his hair. The new, shorter cut, styled only that morning, felt alien to his fingers.

Pushing his keys into his pocket, he forced his feet to move to the iron gates that had intrigued him as a child. He paused beside the keyboard, wondering what to do; then he saw a button marked INTERCOM. With one finger he pressed it then leaned forward to listen.

"Yes?" came a voice—female and formal.

He straightened. "Yes, I—" His dry throat made his voice sound croaky, so he swallowed and tried again. "I'm here for Carrie's birthday dinner."

"Name, please?"

Rocky shoved his hands into his pockets. "Rocky Wilder."

Not even a pause before the instruction came. "You will hear a buzz; then the gates will open. You will have fifteen seconds to proceed through before the gates begin to close."

"Thank you."

The words were barely out of his mouth when the buzzer sounded. Rocky didn't waste any time stepping through. He was halfway up the brick driveway before the gates reversed themselves and sealed him inside. As the gates clicked, he stopped and turned back to look. As a kid, how often had he imagined what it would feel like to be on the inside looking out?

The gates were the same from both directions—scrolled, black iron with a solid oval in the center bearing the gold letter *S* for Steinwood. When he was young, he thought he'd feel different, special, to be allowed inside the sacred grounds of the Steinwood mansion. But for some reason now, realizing he was stuck in here until someone let him out, he only felt trapped. A chill crept up his spine.

Giving himself a shake, he turned and went the remainder of the way to the porch. He stepped past deeply cushioned white wicker furniture and potted plants and crossed to the double doors that would allow him access to his childhood dream house. As he raised his hand to press the brass doorbell, the door swung open and Carrie caught him with his finger pointed in midair.

Her smile made his insides spin like the blade on a power mower. "Hi, Rocky. I'm so glad you made it. Come on in."

She moved aside, allowing him entry, and he stepped over the threshold to root himself on the marble floor of a two-story foyer. Although curiosity made him want to gawk at everything, see if it was all the way he'd imagined, he kept his gaze on her. It wasn't too difficult to focus on her, though—she was beautiful in a flowing dress of white scattered all over with roses. He allowed his gaze to rove from her tumbling blond curls to the bright pink sandals on her feet, and he whistled softly.

"Wow, Carrie, you look. . .wonderful." He couldn't find a word good enough to describe her.

She laughed, touching one curl that fell across her shoulder. "Thank you. So do you." Her slender hand took hold of the tip of his tie, lifted it, and let it fall, much the way she had at the park. "I like this—is it new?"

Rocky cupped his fingers around the tie and ran them down its length. "Tie's not, but the jacket is." He leaned forward and whispered, "Am I dressed okay? I didn't want to—you know—stick out."

Her tender smile touched him deeply. "You're perfect, Rocky. Quit worrying."

"And I didn't bring you a present. I. . ." He faltered. To be honest, he hadn't known what he could buy that she didn't already have. He should have picked up some flowers—maybe a bouquet of pink roses. Those would coordinate perfectly with her appearance this evening.

"Just coming this evening is present enough," she assured him. Then she put her hands on her hips and gave a mock scowl. "But what did you do to your hair?"

He chuckled ruefully as he touched the cropped strands above his left ear. "Got it all styled for you. Some lady named Diana did it. What do you think?"

Carrie leaned sideways, a teasing grin on her face, and thoroughly examined his new haircut. Finally she shook her head. "It looks nice, Rocky, but it'll take some getting used to. I sure liked those curls along your collar. I've always been tempted to give one a tweak."

His brows shot upward. She had wanted to tweak the curls at his collar? Her words must have surprised her as much as they had him because her face suddenly flooded with pink that matched the roses on her dress. His own grin grew broad as he teased, "So now the truth comes out."

Assuming a stern expression, she pointed a finger at him. "Yes, well, don't let it go to your head. Especially now that it's impossible—no curls in sight."

He nodded, his grin still stretching his cheeks.

"Carrie? Are you going to introduce your guest?"

The deep voice from behind them startled their gazes apart. Carrie took him by the elbow and turned him toward a man Rocky immediately recognized— Mackenzie Steinwood. The last time he'd seen Steinwood was in juvenile court, when the man had testified against him. Back then, although tall for his age, Rocky had been the shorter of the pair. Now he towered over Steinwood by at least three inches.

The man had aged—graying hair was combed straight back from his high forehead, and lines around his jowls gave him a stern appearance. But he twisted his face into the semblance of a smile as Carrie made the introductions.

"Mac, this is Rocky Wilder. Rocky, this is my stepfather, Mac Steinwood."

Rocky held out his hand, and Steinwood took it, the man's palm soft against Rocky's calluses. "It's nice to meet you, sir."

"Well, it's hardly a first meeting, is it?" The man's sardonic voice let Rocky know exactly where he stood. "We have met before, although these circumstances are certainly more pleasant."

Rocky wasn't sure how to respond. Before he could form an answer, Carrie gave his elbow a tug.

"I know Myrna has things ready for us. Let's go to the dining room, shall we?" She guided him past Steinwood, through a wide doorway, and across highly polished floors scattered with thick, patterned rugs to what was clearly the formal dining room. Rocky kept his gaze straight ahead, aware of Steinwood behind him. He felt certain the man watched his every move.

An older version of Carrie stepped into the room from a door on the opposite wall just as they entered the dining room. Although Rocky could see beauty in the woman's delicate features, a hardness in her eyes distracted him. She crossed immediately to Rocky and offered her hand. It was so thin Rocky was afraid to touch it.

"Good evening. Mr. Wilder, is that correct? Carrie has spoken so highly of you. I'm her mother, Lynette. I'm pleased to make your acquaintance."

"Thank you, ma'am." Rocky gingerly clasped the woman's hand, considering her words. Though welcoming in content, the lack of warmth in the delivery gave him a chill. He glanced over his shoulder to find Steinwood fixing him with a distrusting glare. There was no question—Rocky did not belong here. He had a sudden desire to excuse himself, head right back to the double doors, and go home.

"Rocky?" Carrie sensed the tension in Rocky's frame. She wished she could give both of her parents a good tongue-lashing for making him feel so uncomfortable. It certainly wasn't hospitable! But it would have to wait until later. The important thing to do now was make Rocky feel at home.

She waited until he glanced down at her—even in her three-inch heels, he still stood inches taller than her. She loved the feeling of protection his height offered. "Let me show you to your seat." She guided him to the table which was set for four.

His gaze bounced from the table to her face. "Just the four of us?" His voice rasped out in a whisper meant only for her ears.

"Yes." She leaned closer, her shoulder against the firm muscle of his upper arm. "That's what I wanted. You'll be fine." She gave his arm a reassuring squeeze as she smiled into his face. Then, raising her voice, she said, "You sit here, next to me."

He pleased her by pulling out her chair before seating himself. By the time they were settled, Mac had seated Lynette, and she rang a little bell to signal Myrna to bring in the first course.

Stilted conversation carried them through the appetizer of french onion soup and the main course of chicken breasts smothered in grilled mushrooms, onions, and peppers, served with wild rice and steamed baby carrots. As the birthday girl, Carrie had been allowed to choose the menu. She'd selected her favorites, but she hardly tasted the food, keenly aware of Rocky's discomfort. And Mac wasn't helping that one bit! Her anger stirred as Mac set his fork aside and pinned Rocky with a look that could only be described as challenging.

"So, Mr. Wilder"—the disdainful tone set Carrie's teeth on edge—"tell me how you've occupied your time since last we talked."

Carrie watched Rocky fold his hands together, his fingers so tightly linked his knuckles looked white. He cleared his throat, his Adam's apple bobbing. She longed to put her hand on his knee, offer some support, but she was afraid to move.

"Well, sir, as you know, after our last meeting, I spent some time in a detention center. It wasn't exactly summer camp." He managed a light, self-deprecating chuckle. "But it served its purpose—made me determined to straighten myself out."

"So can I assume you did straighten yourself out?"

Carrie wanted to give her stepfather a kick under the table. Since when were guests treated so rudely? But Mac was sending her a clear message—Rocky wasn't considered a guest but an intrusion in his home.

"Yes, for the most part. I never stole anything again." Rocky offered a shrug, the navy blue jacket pulling tight across his broad shoulders with the movement. "Doesn't mean I was perfect, but I was better."

"So you finished school?"

"Yes, sir. Graduated from high school."

"And what college curriculum did you choose?"

Carrie bit down on the end of her tongue. Mac was being deliberately cruel!

Rocky had every reason to rail at the man, but his mild answer made her chest expand in pride. "I haven't had the privilege of college. . .yet."

Mac perked up at the subtly dangled bait. "Yet?"

At that moment, Myrna bustled in to remove dinner plates and ask Carrie if she was ready for her cake. Carrie nodded, relieved by the distraction the dessert would provide. She went through the formality of blowing out the candles, although the birthday song went unsung. Myrna cut and served huge squares of the decorated confection then disappeared back into the kitchen.

The moment the door swung shut behind the cook, Mac picked up the dropped topic. "Can I presume you intend to begin a study at college?"

Rocky put down his fork, swallowed the bite in his mouth, and swiped his napkin across his lips before answering. "Yes, sir. I do hope to attend college. I plan on opening a landscaping business."

Mac leaned back, raising his eyebrows high in a look of feigned interest. "Landscaping? Well, I believe Petersburg has one landscaper at work now. Have you investigated the need for a second?"

Carrie's gaze flitted back and forth between the two men as the conversation moved quickly.

"Yes, sir. I believe there's enough work, with all the new construction going on right now, to support two landscaping businesses in town."

"And our local university provides the necessary course work?"

"Courses in both science and business. I could get everything I need right here."

"You would continue working at Elmwood Towers while attending school? Or do you plan to quit work altogether and focus on college?"

"Frankly, I can't afford to quit. I'll have to take as many evening classes as possible so I can keep my job."

"Mm-hm. . ." Mac crossed his hands over his chest and fixed Rocky with a penetrating look. "Evening classes. It will probably take twice as long to finish that way. That would mean you'd be—what? Thirty-five? Thirty-six years old when you finish?"

Mac's cruelty made Carrie's heart ache. Must Rocky be knocked down at every turn? She opened her mouth to defend her friend, but Rocky spoke first.

"I realize it'll take me longer. I realize I'm late getting started." His quiet, respectful tone pleased Carrie. "But God planted this dream, He gave me the ability to do the job well, and I trust I'm doing what He's planned for me. I trust Him to help me make it all happen."

Mac waved his hand, his expression contemptuous. "God is fine for old women and children, but men—"

"Men are wise to recognize their need for their Creator," Rocky interrupted softly. Although tension showed in the lines around his eyes, he faced Mac without rancor and continued. "I thought it would be a sign of weakness, too, to give myself over to God, but when I accepted the gift of salvation through His Son's sacrifice at Calvary, I suddenly realized how wrong I was. My own strength was nothing compared to God's strength in me. I don't know how I made it as long as I did without Him."

Carrie felt tears behind her lids. Nothing proved God's presence in Rocky's heart more than his calm rebuttal to Mac's intentional goading. Love and admiration welled up within her, and she looked Rocky full in the face, praying he'd recognize the light of approval in her eyes.

He met her gaze, and the soft smile he offered let her know he appreciated her silent support. Suddenly he rose. "Thank you for inviting me here this evening. I've enjoyed myself. And, Mrs. Steinwood"—he swung his gaze toward Carrie's mother—"please tell your cook everything was delicious. But"—he turned back to Carrie—"it's getting late, and I don't want to wear out my welcome."

Although Carrie was disappointed he wanted to leave so soon, she understood. Why would he want to spend any more time visiting with Mac? She rose, too, taking hold of his elbow. "I'll walk you out."

They walked without speaking until they reached the gates, which Carrie opened. Then they paused on the drive with the gates spread around them like a giant pair of wings.

"I'm sorry Mac was rude." Her heart ached at the way Rocky had been treated.

He offered a shrug. "I don't blame him. His memories of me aren't too great."

Carrie would have admired him less had he spoken disparagingly. His refusal to berate Mac spoke clearly of God's influence. She wrapped her arms around his neck and gave him a hug. "Thank you for coming, Rocky."

His firm arms came around her briefly; then he stepped back, pushing his hands into his pockets. "Thank you for inviting me. I–I'd better go."

She watched him drive away, waving until his car turned the corner; then she looked back toward the house. Squaring her shoulders, she prepared for a storm. She marched to the house, stomped directly to the dining room and wheeled on her stepfather.

"Of all the rude, uncivilized ways to treat someone." It gave her satisfaction to see Mac pull the coffee cup away from his lips and lift his startled gaze to her. "Rocky was a guest in your home, but you treated him like an intruder. What were you doing?"

"Carrie, darling," her mother said, lifting her hand toward Carrie.

Carrie shook her head. "It's too late, Mother. You said nothing the whole time he was here, which was just as reprehensible as Mac's attempts at intimidation. Neither of you treated him well. He was my guest—my only guest. Was it too much to ask you to be polite?"

Mac rose to his feet, glowering. "Yes, as a matter of fact, it was. He doesn't belong in this house. That Wilder boy is a common thief and a delinquent. He'll never amount to anything, and I hope this evening proved to you just how ridiculous your association with him is."

Carrie met her stepfather's angry gaze without flinching. "All this evening proved was how much Rocky has changed since he was a boy. The old Rocky would have risen to your bait, gotten angry, said things that were unkind. But he didn't, did he? He was respectful even when you weren't. 'That Wilder boy,' as you call him, no longer exists, Mac. He's a new creation with Christ in his heart, and I love him."

"Love." Mac released a snort of derision. "You're insane."

"No, I don't believe so. But I won't spend time debating that with you. I will tell you this, however—I intend to support Rocky in his business venture. I believe in his talent and ability, and I am going to do whatever I can to make his dream a reality."

"Well, that explains why he would spend time with you—for what he can get," Mac said in a derogatory tone. He thrust out his chin. "But what can he possibly give in return?"

Mac's question, though thrown out in anger, made Carrie take a step back. She offered an honest reply. "All I want from him is his love and respect. That's the greatest thing one human being can give another."

"Bah!" Mac spun toward the door. His back toward her, he grated out, "You're a fool, Carrie. Love and respect won't pay bills. You'll waste your money on that piece of trash, and he'll leave you high and dry. I just hope that God of yours will be able to pick up the pieces." He stormed out of the room.

Carrie turned to her mother. "Is that how you feel, too?"

Lynette dropped her gaze to the tabletop. "Mac is rarely wrong, Carrie."

Carrie could have argued that, but she knew it was pointless. It saddened her that her parents were so close minded. The acquisition of money and prestige had become their god. Their hearts were hardened to anything else. She released a sigh. "I'm sorry you feel that way, Mom, because what I told Mac is true. I love Rocky, and I will help him, even if you disapprove."

Her mother stood slowly, as if very tired, and crossed to Carrie. She touched Carrie's cheek and offered a weary smile. "You're an adult, darling, and you don't need our approval to spend the money your father left you. But—" She bit down on her lip, and whatever she'd intended to say went unsaid. She gave her head a little shake. "I must go see to Mac now." She walked out, leaving Carrie alone.

Carrie closed her eyes and whispered a prayer. "I'm so sorry I've upset them, God, but they're wrong. What I'm doing for Rocky is the right thing to do. Please help them see that, and let them somehow find their way to You."

# Chapter 14

A sense of relief washed over Rocky as he drove away from the Steinwood mansion. Who would have guessed that spending time in that house—that beautiful, flashy, made-of-dreams house—would leave him feeling so cold? Now, remembering how he had fantasized about the house as a child, he felt foolish. He turned his vehicle toward his own humble home, realizing the people living in the Steinwood mansion were no happier than the ones who had lived in his old neighborhood. In fact, they might even be less happy.

Mrs. Steinwood had sat silent through the entire dinner, picking at the delicious foods on her plate rather than eating. In her silk pantsuit and tastefully chosen jewelry, she was stunningly attired, but she had reminded him of a decorated skeleton—there seemed to be no life inside the shell of her body.

And then there was Mr. Steinwood. He clearly didn't trust Rocky. While Rocky understood that, he suspected Steinwood didn't trust anybody. He lived in fear of someone taking away the things he owned. Instead of finding pleasure in his wealth, the wealth had made him bitter, jealous, and suspicious. Rocky shook his head. He sure didn't ever want to be like that. Maybe being wealthy wasn't such a great thing after all.

Eileen had told him having his needs met was enough. At the time, he'd wondered if she could possibly be right. Now he understood what she meant. Having too much changed a person, and from what he'd just seen of the Steinwoods, it didn't change someone for the better.

He paused at a traffic light, a sudden thought striking him. What of Carrie? Would her sudden acquisition of the trust fund change her, too? *Lord, don't let it spoil her,* he prayed inwardly. *Don't let it make her bitter and distrustful, the way it has Steinwood. . . .*

He turned onto the final stretch that would lead him home. If he were going to have his needs met with his own business, he'd better get things going. He'd made some preliminary inquiries already, but he hadn't done anything official to make the business happen. Monday, he'd see if he could take the afternoon off. That would free him to go to the licensing bureau and start paperwork. He'd also visit his sister-in-law, Marin, at Brooks Advertising, find out what she could do for him, then stop by the college and pick up an application.

There was much to do, and Rocky was eager to get it going.

⎯ↂ⎯

"I'd love to work with you on this, Rocky." Marin's enthusiastic tone made Rocky even more excited about his new business venture. "You know Philip and I will do anything we can to help you get this started."

"Thanks." He hadn't expected anything less from Marin, but he wanted to be sure he wasn't putting her in an awkward position. "I know Jefferson Landscaping is already one of your clients. It's okay to take care of my business, too, though we're both landscapers?"

She smiled, her eyes crinkling slightly. "Not to worry. We design the advertising campaign; we don't personally endorse our clients, so there's no breach of confidence here." She leaned back in her chair and winked. "Since you're family, though, it might be tempting to endorse you."

Rocky laughed. "Don't get yourself in trouble." Cupping his chin, he posed a hesitant question. "If I get this going. . .do you think. . .John might be interested in working with me?"

Marin's eyebrows shot upward. "John?"

Rocky nodded. "Yes. He's helped Eileen with several garden plots at Elmwood Towers and seems to enjoy working in the soil."

"And you'd really consider hiring him?"

Rocky understood the surprise in Marin's voice. "I know how I used to be about people who are different, but as I've gotten to know John. . ." He shrugged. "I like him. He's a neat guy."

She smiled. "I think so, too." She paused for a moment, nibbling her lower lip. "I would have no problem with him working with you, but he really likes his job at the veterinary clinic." Marin's tone sounded thoughtful. "I suppose, once you have things started, we could ask him if he'd like to change jobs. And if not John, perhaps another of Philip's clients?"

Rocky nodded. "Sure. That'd be fine. I'll mention it to Philip." He stood up. "Thanks, Marin. When I get everything going, I'll be back and we can talk about how I'll pay for your services."

Marin rose, too, and walked him out of the office. "Let's worry about that later. You're family—I have special rates for family."

Rocky gave Marin a quick hug and headed back to his car. College applications for admission and financial assistance waited on the passenger side of the seat. He fingered the papers as he drove to the licensing bureau. He felt a little overwhelmed by all the paperwork—the lady in the financial aid office had said things must be filled out accurately in order to be processed. What if he made mistakes? Maybe he'd ask Philip to help him with that. After all, Philip had already gone through college.

Rocky felt a pang of regret. His little brother was miles ahead of him when it came to establishing his future—he had a college degree, owned his own business, which offered help to people with handicaps, and was married. Rocky, the older brother, was only getting started. Was it too late, like Mac Steinwood had said? Then he shook his head. No, it was never too late to do the right thing. Determination straightened his spine. He'd see this through.

He parked in front of the licensing bureau then headed inside. A middle-aged receptionist greeted him. "Hello," he responded. "I'd like to find out what I need to do to get a new business started in town."

She flashed a smile. "Certainly! You've got to get city approval, fill out tax documents, and file an application with the business bureau." She turned toward a file and began removing forms, making a stack on the corner of the counter. "What kind of business are you planning to start?"

Rocky leaned his elbows on the counter. "Landscaping."

"Landscaping, hm?" The woman paused, releasing a light chuckle. "There seems to be a lot of that going around lately."

Foreboding made the hair on Rocky's neck prickle. "Oh yeah?"

"Yes. Someone was in here a few days ago talking about starting a new landscaping business."

Rocky stood up straight. "Who was it?"

The woman shrugged. "I'm not at liberty to say. She just mentioned the paperwork was for a landscaping venture."

She? Rocky's heart pounded. A sick feeling struck his stomach.

The receptionist took one more form from the drawer, added it to the stack, then placed everything in a large manila envelope bearing the business bureau's mailing address. "You can send everything back in this same envelope," she said.

"Thank you." Rocky pursed his lips for a moment. "You're sure this other person was interested in a landscaping business?"

"Oh yes, I'm sure." With another bright smile, she said, "Now don't let that bother you. Competition is good for businesses." She handed him the envelope. "Good luck with yours."

"Thank you." He stepped out of the office into the afternoon sunshine. He stood for a moment outside the door, tapping his leg with the envelope, his thoughts racing. Could it have been Carrie getting information about a landscaping business? Rocky had heard of Mac Steinwood undercutting others to get the best profit. If he had his own landscaping company, he wouldn't need to rely on someone else to landscape the grounds of the businesses and houses he built. Maybe, now that Steinwood knew Rocky's plans, he had convinced Carrie to get a family landscaping business going first. After all, Carrie had her business administration degree, so she had the training, not to mention the financial means, to get a business started.

But surely Carrie wouldn't. . . He shook his head. No, Carrie wouldn't do that to him. She knew how much this business meant to him. But, his thoughts countered, she'd grown up with Mac Steinwood. He was the only father she'd had for most of her life. Her loyalty to Steinwood would certainly be deeper than any loyalty to Rocky.

He slapped his leg with the envelope and charged to his car. He didn't want to think ill of Carrie. He'd go see her, talk to her, and let her laugh and tell him how silly he was for even thinking such a thing. It would be okay, he told himself as he drove once more to the Steinwood mansion. Everything would be okay.

⸻

Carrie turned the corner, and her heart skipped a beat when she saw Rocky's car parked along the curb. Getting to see him twice in three days after their lengthy separation was almost too good to be true. She pulled into the driveway but didn't open the gates—instead she popped the car into PARK, bounced out, leaving the door hanging open, and crossed to meet him as he stepped onto the asphalt road.

"Hi!" She felt lighter just seeing him. It had been a stressful day of labs and exams, and time with Rocky seemed the perfect antidote to stress. "What are you doing here?"

He didn't smile in return. "I came to see you."

She rested her weight on one foot and tipped her head, offering a smirk. "Well, from the look on your face, your day hasn't been much better than mine. How long have you been waiting?"

He glanced at his watch. "Since around four."

"Four!" She couldn't believe he'd been sitting out there for more than two hours. "Why didn't you just call?"

His shoulders lifted in a shrug. She waited for him to make a teasing remark about her being worth the wait. When none came, trepidation struck. "It must be important then. Do you want to go inside?"

Rocky shook his head, his gaze flitting toward the closed gates. "No. Not really. Can—can we just sit in my car and talk?"

"Sure." She backed toward her own vehicle. "Let me shut off my engine. I'll be back." She trotted to her car, her heart pounding. Something was wrong. Dreadfully wrong. She prayed for God's strength as she twisted the key in the ignition, closed her door, then joined Rocky.

He had to shift aside an envelope as she slid in. She recognized the address on the label—the business bureau. She hoped he hadn't gotten bad news about using the land he'd purchased to start a landscaping business.

Forcing a cheerful tone, she asked, "So what's up?"

Rocky rested his elbow on the steering wheel, his finger across his lips. He stared out the window for a few seconds before turning to face her. "I just wondered if you might know something about another landscape business starting up in town."

Carrie processed her best response to his question. If she told him what she was up to, it would spoil the surprise. Also, based on his mood, he might reject her assistance outright. She didn't want to face either prospect. Yet she couldn't lie to him. So she asked carefully, "Do you mean one other than the one you're planning to start?"

"That's right."

She could reply honestly to that. "No, I don't. Why do you ask?"

Rocky drew in a big breath. He tapped the envelope on the seat between them. "I went in today to get information about how to apply to start a new business, and I was told a woman was in a few days ago, asking about the same type of business. It. . .worried me, I guess."

"Afraid of a little healthy competition?" she teased, praying he wouldn't out-and-out ask if she were the woman.

"Not at all," Rocky replied, his expression serious. "Competition is fine. I just want to be sure I stand a chance of making the business work. After all, Petersburg isn't exactly a metropolis. It can certainly support two landscaping businesses with all the new construction going on here and in surrounding communities, but three? It would be pretty foolhardy to think that many would stand a chance of succeeding."

Carrie gave a slow nod. "You might be right."

He twisted his face into a scowl. "With Jefferson Landscaping already well established, I'm taking a risk, coming in new. I sure hope there isn't another one." He gave her a sharp look. "You're sure you don't know of a third one?"

Carrie laughed. "Rocky!" She hoped she sounded convincing. "I told you I don't know about a third one." She needed to get this conversation turned. Although she had intended to wait until he started college to tell him about a computer program she'd found, she decided this might be a good way to get him focused on something else.

"But I do know something that might be of use to you."

"Oh yeah?" He didn't sound terribly interested, but at least he asked. "What's that?"

"A landscaping program for the computer." She shifted in the seat, angling herself toward him. "It's amazing. You can put in the geographic location of the area being landscaped, and the computer makes suggestions for types of plants that grow well in that area. It even breaks it down between leafy versus flowering plants, and shade lovers versus sun lovers, and everything in between. Then, if you put in the dimensions of the garden area—four feet by ten feet, for instance—it offers some blueprints of plots you can follow."

Rocky gave her a funny look. "I don't know how to use the computer, Carrie."

He certainly was a Gloomy Gus today! She patted his knee. "You'll learn. It really isn't that hard. And this program—"

"I like planning it myself."

She frowned at his argumentative tone. "Well, you still could do the planning if you wanted to and just use the program to determine what kinds of plants to use."

He looked at her for several long seconds, his expression unreadable. Finally he said, "I suppose you're right." His gaze drifted out the window again.

She huffed in annoyance. "Rocky, couldn't you at least be a little enthusiastic? I mean, here you are, preparing to open your very own business, and this program could be a great help. Why not at least consider using it?"

He turned to face her, his brows pulled down into a worried look. "How do you know about this program, Carrie? Why were you even looking for programs related to landscaping?"

His apprehensive tone bothered her. She flipped her hands outward in a gesture of inquiry. "Didn't you ask me to pray for your business and to help? I look at different programs for one of my classes. I found this one, and I thought of you."

He nodded, his gaze never wavering from hers. "Oh. Well...thanks. But...as I said before, I don't know how to use computers."

She shook her head. He had no idea how easy it would be to use these computer programs. She gave his knee another encouraging pat and said, "It's okay, Rocky. I know how."

Now she was sure he looked worried. And shamed. She reached to touch his arm, but he twisted to face forward, reaching for the ignition. "Thanks, Carrie. I'll—I'll look into that program, okay? I'll bet you've got studying to do, right? I won't keep you from it." He glanced briefly in her direction, his eyes tired. "Will you be at Bible study Wednesday?"

For some reason, she fought tears. "Yes. Shall we sit together?"

"That would be fine." His voice sounded tight, controlled.

She put her hand on the door handle, ready to leave, then spun toward him. "Rocky?"

"Yeah?"

"I—" But then she clamped her jaw shut. If she told him now about filing the application and setting up a scholarship, she would be ruining a wonderful surprise. She didn't want to do that. Although he was worried now, he'd understand everything later. She shook her head. "Nothing. Never mind. I'll see you Wednesday."

She stepped out of the vehicle, leaned forward to wave good-bye, then closed the door. Watching him drive away, she felt a little twinge of anxiety. But she pushed it aside. When Rocky learned the truth, he'd be too excited to care about her evasiveness. A smile grew on her face—besides that, she'd have another way to distract him by Wednesday. She'd know by then whether the house she bid on would be hers.

Hopping back in her car, she punched in the code for the gates, started the engine, and headed for the garage. She couldn't wait to tell Myrna about her new soon-to-be home.

# Chapter 15

Rocky slammed through his front door, giving it a kick with his heel to bang it closed. He threw himself onto the couch, his head back and eyes closed, hurt pressing so hard he feared his heart might stop beating.

He didn't like to think of it, but Carrie had lied to him. He'd been around enough liars in his lifetime to recognize untruths when they were spoken. She hadn't been able to meet his eyes, her laugh had been too high-pitched to be real and her tone too cheery. It all pointed to one thing—she wasn't being honest.

She was hiding something, and since all the issue-skirting pertained to the information about another landscaping business, he knew it had to do with that. She was in up to her eyeballs. But why shouldn't she be? She had the know-how to start a business, she had the finances to get it going, she had the connections through her stepfather—everything for success was already in her hand. Born with a silver spoon in her mouth, the old saying went. And now she was waving it, ready to use it to her advantage.

*The wealthy just get wealthier,* he thought, a bitter taste on his tongue, *while the rest of us get shoved aside.* It burned like a fire in his gut to have Carrie be the one to do the shoving, but he really couldn't blame her. She had witnessed her stepfather shoving people aside for years—it must be second nature to her by now.

His nose stung, a sure sign he wanted to cry. But what would that help? His father had told him tears were a waste of energy, and for once, Pop had been right—tears accomplished nothing. *Focus on something else,* he told himself. Supper. Get something to eat. Fill up the emptiness in his belly.

Bolting to his feet, he stomped to the kitchen and flung the refrigerator door open. Not much in there—he needed to go grocery shopping. He whacked the door shut and started swinging cupboard doors open and closed. With a huff, he considered his choices for supper—cold cereal or canned ravioli. Yuk on both counts.

Leaning against the counter, he shook his head, his shoulders slumped. Why had he set himself up this way? Hadn't he told himself from the beginning that being with Carrie was a mistake? They were from two different worlds. She had tried—she had honestly tried—but the tug of the Steinwoods was too strong. They'd reeled her back. He'd hoped. . . His nose stung again. But, no, it was foolhardy to hope for a relationship with someone like Carrie.

"Oh, Lord, I just wish it didn't hurt so much."

At least he had his relationship with his Father God. The Bible study lessons came back to him—how God was always there, would never forsake him. An old-fashioned word, *forsake*, but Rocky liked it. It meant God was totally dependable—he didn't have to worry that God would abandon him. God would never let the search for money or prestige get in the way of His relationship with His child Rocky. A feeling of comfort wrapped around Rocky's aching heart.

He dropped to his knees in the kitchen and poured out his hurt to God. Then he prayed for Carrie, for her happiness. "Let her discover the key to happiness isn't in gaining more money, God. Don't let her turn out like her parents—she's just too good for a life like that." It helped to pray for her, and he remembered the biblical advice to pray for those who persecuted you. He'd always thought that odd—why pray for someone who wanted to harm you? Yet praying for Carrie brought a great sense of peace.

He got to his feet, remembering the picnic lunch he'd shared with her. That day she had nearly convinced him her money didn't mean anything to her—that it shouldn't come between them. She had listened so intently to his dreams, had told him God loved him the way he was, and had encouraged him to pursue opening his landscaping business. He pushed his hands deep into his pockets, his shoulders stiff, as confusion struck. Why would she do all that if she was just going to turn around and undermine him? It didn't make sense.

And standing there, staring off into space, didn't make sense either. Carrie had made her choice. He'd have to accept it. Reaching for his phone, he made his plans for the evening. He'd order a pizza, watch some TV, then fill out all that paperwork so he could get it in the mail. Just once, the Steinwoods were going to come in second. Rocky would play their game of hardball, and he would win.

─◌─

Wednesday evening, Carrie sat on a metal folding chair in the church basement and fumed. Rocky had done it again. The last time he'd left her sitting alone was in the pizza parlor, and she'd wondered what happened to him. This time she knew what happened—he was running scared. Again.

There'd been something in his eyes Monday when he'd stopped by the house. The old worry was back about how he could compete with the Steinwood money. How she wished he'd set that silliness aside and just accept her for who she was! She was willing to accept him, warts and all. Couldn't he do the same for her?

She got very little out of the Bible study with thoughts of Rocky distracting her, and her college classes Thursday weren't much better. On Thursday evening, when the Realtor called to tell her she could stop by and sign paperwork for her new home on Friday, she hung up in excitement and immediately began to dial Rocky's number. Then remembrance struck again, and she slammed down the phone in frustration. By Friday morning, when she still felt tense and annoyed, she knew she'd have to hash things out with him.

She got out of class a little after one and, instead of going to the Realtor's office, headed for Elmwood Towers. Walking toward the courtyard, she encountered Rocky's friend, Eileen, who greeted her with a huge smile.

"Why, hello! I bet you're here to see Rocky."

Carrie forced her lips into a smile. "Yes, I am. Do you know where I might find him?"

Eileen nodded, her eyes crinkling. "Oh yes, I do. He's placing some rocks in the flower garden we started a few weeks ago—he decided it needed some texture." She winked. "And *you* might be just what *he* needs. He's been a real grumble-bear this week." Eileen pointed. "Just follow the footpath. You'll see him."

Carrie thanked Eileen and headed down the footpath she and Rocky had taken on that afternoon when she had boldly asked him to spend some time with her. She spotted him, in his ratty sleeveless T-shirt and worn denims, and the sight of his flexing biceps and tanned skin immediately made her stomach turn a flip-flop. The effect this man had on her senses. . .

"Rocky." She called his name when she was still several yards away.

He turned, a sizable rock in his hand, and his gaze narrowed. He waited until she stood in front of him before asking, "What are you doing here? Don't you have class?"

"I get out early on Fridays. And speaking of class. . .where were you Wednesday night?"

He turned back to the garden, bending over to place the rock between a middle-sized bush and a cluster of something that must have bloomed at one time but now was flowerless. He took his time, shifting the rock just so, then straightened and brushed his gloved palms against each other to dispel dirt.

"I was busy."

She tipped her head, frowning. "Well, you might have let me know. I held a seat for you, and you didn't show up."

"I'm sorry." But his tone didn't sound sorry.

Carrie's ire raised. "Listen, Rocky—after you stood me up at the Ironstone, you said you wouldn't do that again. And then you did do it again. Is this going to be a habit?"

He jerked off his gloves, throwing them into the wheelbarrow. Then he stuck his fingertips into his pockets and looked at her. His brown eyes, normally warm and welcoming toward her, seemed cold and distant. She felt a chill.

He drawled, "I guess. . .habits. . .are hard for all of us to break."

Her scowl deepened, and she put her hand on her hip. "What is that supposed to mean?"

"Nothing." He turned back to the wheelbarrow, reaching for his gloves.

She grabbed his arm and tugged, forcing him to look at her. "Rocky, we're beyond this. Don't shut me out. I had some news I wanted to share with you Wednesday, and when you weren't there, it really disappointed me. The least you can do is tell me why you didn't come."

He looked into her eyes for a long moment, his face puckered up in—what? Frustration? Confusion? She wasn't sure. Finally he gave a shrug and said, "Okay, I'll tell you why I didn't come. I couldn't stop thinking about that woman who got information about starting a landscaping business. I couldn't stop thinking that, even though you tried to hide it, it was you. You're not a very good liar, Carrie."

She felt a blush climbing her cheeks.

"See—you're getting all pink. You lied to me Monday. Are you going to lie to me now and say it wasn't you who picked up those applications?"

He had her trapped. She couldn't look him in the face and tell an outright fabrication. She shook her head miserably. "No. It was me."

"That's what I thought." He snatched up his gloves and jammed his hands in, adjusting the fingers, his lips set in a grim line. Then he lifted a rock, grunting with the effort of clearing the side of the wheelbarrow. He took two stumbling steps forward and thumped the rock down. Still leaning forward, hands on knees, he added in a tired voice, "And I just couldn't sit there next to you, knowing what you'd done."

Carrie felt her heart plummet. He'd known all along. There never was a surprise. Disappointment hit hard—she had so wanted to surprise him. "You mean you *know* what I was doing?"

He pushed himself upright and faced her, his expression hard. "Of course I do. It's clear. Your stepfather builds things. All of those buildings are on un-landscaped ground. It only makes sense that having a landscaper in the family would be to his benefit." He rubbed the back of his neck, grimacing. "Of course it smarted to think you'd be the one to start it, since you knew how much I wanted to get my own business going, but from a business standpoint, I—"

"Wait a minute." Carrie took a step forward, one ear turned toward him in an effort to hear more clearly. "You think I picked up that paperwork so I could start my own landscaping business—one that would be in direct competition with yours?"

He threw his arms outward. "What else was I to think? I'm not stupid, even if I don't have a college degree. You've got everything it takes—knowledge in business administration, the skills to get whatever you need right off the computer, the money to hire workers and make it all happen." He snorted. "Your whole life you've watched Mac Steinwood find ways to add to his bank account."

Suddenly he seemed to deflate, shaking his head and looking toward the ground. "Look, Carrie—I understand. Sure, it hurt, but. . .I do understand. It's the way you were raised. I don't blame you."

She stood, staring in disbelief, the ache so intense it nearly doubled her over. He thought she was working against him instead of for him. He thought her upbringing as Mac Steinwood's stepdaughter would make her stoop low enough to pull the rug out from under the feet of someone she genuinely cared about. Tears clouded her vision, and she took a step backward. He was like everyone else, only seeing her money, not seeing her heart. She had thought Rocky was different, but he wasn't. She choked back a sob.

His head came up, his gaze locking on hers. "Carrie, don't cry. I told you it didn't matter."

"Oh, but it does." Her voice quavered with the effort of maintaining control of her emotions. "It matters a great deal. And if that's what you really think of me, then—" She shook her head, another sob nearly strangling her. Should she tell him why she picked up that paperwork? No—he wouldn't believe her. And she couldn't face more of his rejection.

"I–I've got to go. Good-bye, Rocky." The last two words nearly broke her heart. She spun on her heel and clattered down the sidewalk, determined to escape. But how would she escape this pain in her heart?

Rocky sat on the metal step in front of his trailer, a bottle of pop in his hand and a heavy weight in his heart. He'd made Carrie cry today. As upset and hurt as he'd been, he hadn't wanted to do that. Seeing her distress had created a whole new hurt inside of him. Why should he care if he'd upset her after what she'd done? He knew why. Because he loved her.

He rubbed the sweaty bottle across his forehead, trying to cool his thoughts. Yep, he loved her all right. But what good did that do him? She'd come right out and admitted the truth—that she had picked up the paperwork for a landscaping business. But her parting comment—something about if that's what he thought of her—kept plaguing him. If she were guilty of plotting against him, why would she assume he'd feel anything but bitterness? It didn't make sense.

He released a breath, his cheeks puffed out, then looked across his acre of ground. In his mind, he could still see the little green stems pushing their way through the soil, the seedlings stretching toward the sky. It was a good dream. One he wasn't willing to relinquish. Eileen had told him God planted the talent in him and he needed to let that talent bloom. How ugly would a rosebush be without the blooms? That's how he felt now, having someone try to steal his dream away—like a prickly rosebush stem with no blossoms.

Carrie's stricken face appeared again in his memory. He heard her words again—"If that's what you think of me"—and he scowled. He wished he could set that memory aside. He didn't want to think of her right now. It hurt too much.

Swallowing the last of the carbonated beverage, he gave the bottle a toss to the Dumpster at the edge of the yard. It smacked the rim and bounced out. Immediately he got to his feet, strode across the ground, snatched up the bottle, and dropped it in. As the bottle thudded in the bottom of the barrel, he couldn't help chuckling. Who would have imagined it—Rocky Wilder, worrying about trash on the ground? God sure had worked a change in him.

So why couldn't God work a change in Carrie, too?

The thought struck hard. His heart pounded. He'd broken his habits of apathy and intimidation. If God could help him set aside those lifelong traits, couldn't He also help Carrie set aside her lifelong lessons of putting money first?

A Bible verse about it being harder for a wealthy man to enter the kingdom of heaven than it was for a camel to pass through the eye of a needle flitted through his mind. He raised his eyes to the sky, now tinged with pink, and asked aloud, "You said it was hard, God. But is it impossible?"

He didn't receive an answer. He didn't even feel any peace. With a sinking heart, he turned toward the trailer door. His feet scuffed through the dirt as he crossed the yard. Maybe he'd better focus on something else. All this nervous energy should be put to good use, and he'd use it all right. He'd use it getting his landscaping business going. Now. His brother would be able to help. First thing tomorrow, he'd see Philip, get his advice.

"And I won't even think about Carrie," he told himself firmly.

But his thoughts added disparagingly, *Yeah, right.*

# Chapter 16

O kay, I think that's a pretty comprehensive list." Philip tapped his pencil against the yellow writing pad on the kitchen table.

Rocky glanced at the pad, his resolve faltering as he took in the lengthy list of things to do. Then he straightened his spine and said, "It's a lot, but I'll do it. I'll leave Steinwood in the dust."

Philip's forehead creased into a scowl. "Rocky, I think it's great that you want to open your own business. And you know Marin and I will do anything we can to help."

Rocky met Philip's gaze, his lips twisting into a wry grin. "I hear a 'but' coming on."

Philip shrugged, grimacing. "But. . .I'm worried about the hostility I hear in your voice. You seem more interested in outdoing Steinwood than anything else. That doesn't seem healthy to me."

Rocky shifted his gaze to the kitchen window. The morning sun backlit the yellow gingham curtains, making them glow with cheeriness. The curtains reminded Rocky of daffodils nodding their heads on a spring morning. Everything reminded him of flowers—landscaping seemed to be in his blood. He wanted this business so badly he could taste it.

"Is it wrong to want to be successful?" he asked, his gaze still on the window.

"Of course not." Philip's firm tone brought Rocky's gaze around. "But at the expense of someone else's failure?"

Rocky gritted his teeth. "Look—you and I both know Steinwood won't be a failure. He'll get business—his own. But I'm determined to get everyone else's, whatever that might take." He leaned back and folded his arms across his chest, his throat constricting. "He has this coming. He and Carrie cooked up this scheme to start their own business just so I wouldn't stand a chance. Steinwood hates me—I stole from him. He doesn't want me to be successful. So he used a weapon I couldn't fight against—Carrie—to bring me to my knees. Well, it isn't going to work. I'm going to be successful, and they're going to have to swallow their pride and acknowledge that they lost."

Philip shook his head. "Listen to yourself, Rocky. Now you're even turning on Carrie."

Rocky felt pressure build in his chest. He clenched his fists. "I don't have a choice! She turned on me first!"

"Are you sure?"

Philip's calm question stirred Rocky's anger. "Of course I'm sure. She admitted it."

"She admitted picking up paperwork for a landscaping business. She didn't admit to trying to put you out of business."

Rocky snorted in disgust. "They're one and the same."

"Are they? How can you be sure?"

Rocky pushed his chair backward, lurching to his feet and stomping across the linoleum floor to lean against the kitchen counter and peer out the window. Philip's questions had brought a niggle of doubt to Rocky's mind. He didn't want to believe ill of Carrie—he really wanted to believe she hadn't intended him harm. But he didn't know how to balance her confession of guilt against what he felt in his heart.

"I'm just a sucker for a pretty face." His quiet admission was tinged with self-deprecation.

Philip rose and stood beside him, resting his hand on Rocky's shoulder. "I can't tell you what to do—never could—you were always so stubborn."

Rocky managed a slight smile at those words.

"But I'd like to give you a word of advice."

Rocky turned his head to look at his brother.

"If you care about this girl as much as I think you do, don't let it go like this. The bitterness will eat you alive. Talk it out. *Work* it out."

"I don't think we can," Rocky said, shaking his head. "We're so different."

"I thought the same thing about Marin and me," Philip pointed out. "We had a huge stumbling block to overcome—a seemingly insurmountable issue that had to be forgiven. I didn't think it was possible either, but look at us now. With God, all things are possible. Don't underestimate Him, Rocky."

Rocky considered Philip's words. Was it possible for him to forgive Carrie for this act of sabotage? Would they be able to bridge the differences in their upbringings and find a common ground? It seemed overwhelming. He blew out a breath of frustration. "I don't know. . . ."

"You don't have to know," Philip said, giving Rocky a firm clap on the shoulder. "You just have to trust. But I hope you'll make the effort, because if you don't, you'll always wonder what could have been. And that's a regret I can't imagine you'd want to carry for the rest of your life."

—◌—

"Put it right over there against the north wall."

Carrie directed the movers in the placement of her couch. The plastic covering crinkled as the two men pushed the overstuffed couch into place. She smiled her thanks, but before she could voice the words, a ringing intruded. Her cell phone, which was in her purse. But where was her purse?

She dashed around the room, peeking behind boxes and stubbing her toe before she located the leather bag squashed between two boxes on the kitchen counter. Standing on one foot, she flipped the phone open and panted, "Hello?"

"Miss Mays?"

"Yes."

"This is Vicki at the university financial-aid office. I was calling to let you know the scholarship fund you requested is available now. We'll hold the paperwork for Mr. Wilder. Do you want to notify him, or would you prefer we sent him a letter?"

Carrie's heart began to pound at the mention of Rocky's name. She hadn't spoken to Rocky in two weeks—not since that day when he'd accused her of intending to put him out of business.

"Um," she hedged, rubbing her throbbing toe. "I guess send him a letter."

"That's fine," the woman chirped. "We can give him all the instructions for enrollment at the same time."

"Yes, that would be good." Carrie wouldn't have to do anything—just slink away and let Rocky take care of himself. Her heart ached more than her toe.

"Do you have his mailing address?"

Carrie dug through her purse for the little address book she kept with her calendar and recited Rocky's address. Then she disconnected the call, her duty done. She plopped the phone back into her purse, leaning her head on her hand for a moment as regret washed over her.

How differently she'd envisioned all this when she planned it. Taking Rocky to the college, seeing his face light up when he realized schooling was paid for, telling him how God had prompted her to use her money to answer his prayers.

But the misunderstanding had changed all that. His accusations still stung, and she didn't know if she could ever face him again. Surely when he got the letter, he'd understand what she had tried to do, but even if he apologized, would she be able to forget the hurtful things he'd said about her?

With a sigh, she limped through the kitchen doorway back to the living room where the movers deposited the country-style hutch for her dining room. She glanced around. That was the last of the furniture she'd purchased—their job was done. Retrieving her purse, she tipped them generously for their help and saw them out.

She stood in the doorway of her new home, watching through the full-length glass storm door as the moving truck pulled away from the curb and growled down the street. The silence of the house pressed around her. Loneliness struck. She whispered, "God, I feel very alone right now. Remind me of Your presence, please?"

Turning from the window, she searched for the box which contained her stereo and CDs. She finally located it, shoved some things aside on the floor to uncover an outlet, and soon the room shook with music from a Christian male band. Carrie sang along, her doldrums lifting as the music reminded her she was never alone.

An hour later, she had her kitchen cupboards in order and a pile of empty boxes to carry out. She stacked the boxes together and placed them in the garage out of sight. As she stepped back inside, the words "Jesus only speaks the truth" rang out on the CD. Carrie paused, listening as the song ran its course.

She wished Rocky would listen to the truth instead of believing she had lied to him. It hurt so much, having him turn on her that way. Stepping out of comfort zones was something both she and Rocky would have to do if they were to make their relationship work. They'd have to meet somewhere in the middle. She'd already taken the first step, moving out of the Steinwood mansion to live on her own. But Rocky would have to make the bigger step—accepting her money without allowing it to trample his pride.

She imagined him receiving the letter from the college, reading the invitation to enroll, seeing the financial sheet marked "paid in full." In her mind's eye, she envisioned two scenarios—the first, him socking the air in joy and shouting a thank-you for the opportunity; the second, him wadding up the letter and throwing it away, angry that someone had interfered.

She sighed, defeated. The second scenario seemed much more realistic based on her last encounter with him. Rocky wouldn't accept it. His pride wouldn't allow him to accept it. What had she been thinking? She should never have forged forward with this ridiculous scheme. Her heart had been in the right place, but she should have thought it through.

She reached for her purse and removed her phone. A quick call to the college could divert that scholarship to some other needy student. Then she wouldn't have to worry about Rocky Wilder and his oversized sense of pride.

But she stood, finger poised over the keypad, while something held her back. Even as much as he had hurt her with his misplaced accusation, she wanted him to have this advantage. He'd had few advantages growing up. Surely he deserved this one. She closed the phone and pushed it slowly back into her purse, her thoughts tumbling.

She would leave the decision in his hands. If he rejected it, then she would ask the college to give it to someone else. But before he could reject it, he'd have to know the motivation behind the gift. She needed to talk to him just once more. The thought of him believing she would deliberately sabotage him was a thought with which she could no longer live. He'd face the truth no matter what it took.

Should she invite him here? She considered that. She wanted him to see her house, to show him she had moved out of the Steinwood mansion and was no longer a part of that world. Yet she sensed she needed to meet him on his court.

No, she wouldn't invite him here. He might not come. But she could go to him, and she would. One more surprise for Rocky—a surprise visit—and she'd at least have the opportunity to defend herself. If he still chose to believe the worst, then she would accept it. But she had to try just once more. She cared too much to let it go.

⌒

Rocky closed his Bible and leaned back. Guilt pressed at him. The last verse of the fourth chapter of James weighed heavily on his heart. If a person knew to do good and didn't do it, it was sin. And sin, Rocky knew, grieved his Father.

He'd been wrong to accuse Carrie, to hold himself aloof. She was his Christian sister, and even if she had behaved inappropriately, he'd been wrong, too, to harbor anger against her. One sin was as bad as another in God's eyes—Rocky knew that.

"What do I do, God? How do I make it right?" He spoke the words aloud. The first time he'd wronged Carrie, it had been a simple matter to fix it—flowers and a book. But this wrong was far different from accidentally spraying her with water. This wrong had been deliberate. He'd purposely avoided her, purposely accused her, purposely hurt her. This couldn't be fixed with a handful of impatiens and a used romance novel.

Drawing in a deep breath, he considered his options. He could ignore the situation and hope it would stop bothering him. He shook his head—the guilty feelings wouldn't go away. Philip had even said he might regret it for the rest of his life, always wondering what might have been. Ignoring it wasn't an option.

He tapped his lower lip with one finger. Well, then, he could write her a letter, apologize in writing, and hope she accepted it. But that didn't seem right, either. Besides, his writing wasn't all that great. It would be embarrassing to have someone as smart as Carrie trying to figure out his chicken scratchings and misspelled words.

He ran his fingers through his hair, releasing a huff of breath. The only other thing he could think of was to talk to her. By telephone? He snorted and berated himself. "Quit trying to take the coward's way out." No, he'd have to talk to her in person. He broke out in a cold sweat as he thought about pushing that intercom button at the Steinwood mansion's gates and asking to speak to Carrie. But there was no other way. And the sooner he got it done, the better it would be.

He slammed the footrest down on the recliner and stomped, barefooted, to his bedroom. He changed into a clean pair of jeans and a shirt that had sleeves, making sure he tucked in the tails neatly. He dug under his bed for a pair of socks that weren't too dirty and his tennis shoes. He tied the laces extra tight, frustrated by the quiver in his hands. After running a comb through his hair and splashing on some aftershave, he felt ready to face Carrie.

The drive to the Steinwood mansion took a little over fifteen minutes.

Fifteen minutes of battling his nerves. By the time he reached the gates, his hand trembled like a leaf in a hurricane. But he managed to get his finger to connect with the intercom button.

"Yes?" A female voice. He surmised by the warm tone it did not belong to Mrs. Steinwood. It must be Myrna.

"Yes. . .um, I'd like to speak to Carrie?"

"I'm sorry, sir," the voice came, "but Miss Carrie no longer resides here."

Rocky drew back, stunned. "She doesn't?"

"No, sir. She's—"

"Who is this?" A new voice intruded, masculine and demanding. Mac Steinwood.

Rocky swallowed hard. "This is Rocky Wilder, Mr. Steinwood. I'm looking for Carrie."

"She moved out. And I assured her I would allow *her* the privilege of sharing her new address with others. Have a good day, Mr. Wilder." A click indicated the intercom had been disconnected.

Rocky leaned back and ran his hand through his hair. Now what? How would he find her? If she'd requested her new address be kept private, then she didn't want to see or hear from him. Regret struck. Philip was right—he should have taken care of this days ago.

With his shoulders slumped in defeat, Rocky shifted his car into reverse, backed out of the driveway, and turned toward home. The drive seemed to stretch forever as the weight of guilt pressed on him. "Help me, Lord. I don't know what to do. Please—somehow bring Carrie to me."

A quarter mile from his house, the sight of a car waiting in his yard set his heart to pounding so hard he feared it might break free of his chest. A little red sports car. "Heavenly Father, is it—?" It was. It was Carrie's car. And Carrie waited in the driver's seat.

# Chapter 17

Even as she stepped out of her car and watched him pull into the drive, Rocky still had a hard time believing she was really there. He'd just prayed for her to come to him, and—*boom!*—there she was. He didn't know prayers could be answered so quickly.

He shut off his ignition and shot out of his vehicle, closing the distance between them in less than a half-dozen long strides. "Carrie?" He heard the disbelief in his own voice. "What are you doing here?"

"I came to see you." She sounded subdued, hesitant. Not that he could blame her. "Can we talk?"

"Yeah. Sure. Let's—let's go inside, huh?" He gestured toward the door, and she followed him up the metal steps and through his front door. Inside, she hovered on the square of linoleum that served as his foyer area, her hands clasped in front of her. How uncomfortable she appeared.

"Go ahead and sit down," he encouraged. "Can I get you something to drink? I've got a cola in the fridge, or some ice water."

"No, nothing, thanks." She seated herself on the edge of the couch, resting her hands in her lap.

Her blue-eyed gaze followed him as he moved to his recliner and sat. He wrapped his fingers around the armrest of the chair and met her gaze. Neither spoke for several long, tense seconds. Then he heard a chuckle rumble from his own chest. "This is so...weird."

She tipped her head, her blond hair spilling across her shoulder. "What is?"

"I just came from the Steinwood mansion. I went to talk to you, but your stepfather said you'd moved out."

"Yes. Once I got my trust fund, Mac said I should be on my own."

Trust fund. Rocky's gut clenched with those words. A reminder of their vast differences. "He wouldn't tell me where you live now." There was a hint of accusation in his tone. He hadn't intended it, but it was there—leftover resentment.

Her chin shot up, a stubborn thrust to the line of her jaw. "I planned to tell you about my new house that night at church, but you didn't come." Her tone matched his in accusation.

He cleared his throat and made the apology he had planned. "That was wrong of me, Carrie. Will you forgive me?"

Her gaze lowered for a moment. "Actually, Rocky, your not showing up hurt

228

a lot less than the reason you didn't come."

Hurt welled up in Rocky's chest. Hurt for her duplicity. Hurt for the discomfort he had caused her. One hurt was for himself, the other for her, and he couldn't decide which one took precedence. "I'm sorry about that, but I couldn't face you. Not knowing. . .what I knew."

She met his gaze squarely. "But that's just it. You didn't know. You made an assumption, but it was incorrect. That's why I came here tonight. You need to know the truth."

Rocky pushed himself firmly against the backrest of the recliner. The chair squeaked. "What is the truth, Carrie?"

She leaned forward, resting her elbows on her knees and fixing him with a fervent look. "The truth is, I picked up that paperwork for you. I wanted to help you. I knew how to get things rolling, and I thought that if I could start it all, it would simplify things for you."

He shook his head, unsure he understood. "You were trying to get *my* business started?"

She grimaced. "You sound as if I were trying to take it over."

"I didn't mean it that way." But, he wondered, what did he mean? If Carrie had done all that for him, was it because she didn't think he was capable of handling it on his own, or was she really trying to be supportive? Old insecurities made him want to believe the former. "I'm curious why you'd do that."

She sat up, raising her shoulders in a graceful shrug. "I care about you, Rocky. You wanted it so badly. You'd asked me to pray about your landscaping business. When I prayed, it occurred to me that I could be a real help. So I pressed forward, thinking I would surprise you by getting some of the paperwork out of the way. But"—her gaze dropped to her hands where she fit her fingertips together, forming a steeple—"you found out and jumped to a conclusion, and. . ."

When she didn't finish her thought, Rocky completed it for her. "And you couldn't tell me because you were afraid I wouldn't listen." Philip had been right. Regret was hard to carry.

A slight nod confirmed his guess. "You were so cold that day. I didn't know how to fix things. So I left." Cupping her hands over her knees, she said, "But I couldn't leave that disagreement between us. I wanted you at least to know the truth. So I had to come."

He leaned forward and captured one of her hands. "I'm glad you came, Carrie. And I'm so sorry I hurt you that way." He shook his head. "I should have known." Swallowing the lump of regret, he confided, "Growing up, I didn't find many people I could trust. I guess, as much as I'm trying not to be that Wilder boy who carries a chip on his shoulder, sometimes he still makes an appearance. I shouldn't have jumped to conclusions."

"I can see why you thought what you did," she said, surprising him with her understanding. She pursed her lips for a moment, a hesitance coming across her expression. "And actually I haven't told you everything yet."

He held his breath, waiting.

"In addition to picking up paperwork at the business bureau, I also set up a fund for you at the college. All you have to do is go in and enroll. Your expenses are covered."

He leaned back, releasing her hand. A pressure built in his chest, and words burst out. "I can't let you do that."

"Why not?"

"It–it's too much. College is expensive."

"I can afford it."

"That's not the point!" He shot out of his seat and paced across the room. Desire and defiance mingled in his chest. How he wanted this degree. He'd prayed for it, asked for God to provide the funds, but how could he take Carrie's money? There would be no way he could repay her. "I can't—I can't take something I didn't earn."

A soft laugh escaped her lips. "Really? Then why did you accept salvation? Or are you telling me you earned that?"

He spun around. "That's not the same thing."

She rose and crossed to him. "I know. Salvation is a much bigger gift than anything I could offer." She took his hand. "Rocky, what I'm offering comes with no strings attached. You asked me to pray for you, and God laid it on my heart to help you. If you truly don't want to use the fund I set up for you, then I'll give it to someone else. But I'd prefer you used it."

He stood in silence, her slender fingers cool against his palm, while he battled mixed emotions. A part of him wanted this opportunity. A part of him balked at the idea of taking money from her. Despite himself, he released a throaty chuckle. Rocky Wilder was trying to avoid taking something from someone? Who would have guessed it?

"Look, Rocky—all you have to do is swallow your pride and the money is yours. You have a gift—you can bring beauty to the world. Accept the fund, get your degree, start your business, and use that gift for others. It's only as difficult as you choose to make it."

He drew in a deep breath then released it slowly. He reached out, pulling her into his arms. The scent of apples filled his nostrils as he rested his chin on her hair. "This is tough, you know? I'm not used to people being so nice to me."

She laughed and pulled free. "Well, get used to it. Because I can see me being even nicer."

He raised his eyebrows. "Oh yeah? How so?"

"Well. . ." She moved a few feet away, her hair swaying across her back. "I've got my business degree, too, you know. And I've always liked the idea of starting my own business rather than working for someone else. What's to say we couldn't combine forces? With your talent and my business acumen, it would surely be a raving success."

He couldn't stop the grin that grew on his cheek. Combining forces with Carrie sounded better than anything he could have imagined. "That sounds pretty good." He crossed his arms and smirked at her. "I like the idea of Wilder and Mays Landscaping."

"Wilder and Mays?" She quirked her brow, her expression teasing. "Haven't you ever heard of alphabetical order?"

He laughed.

"Or that a lady precedes a gentleman?"

He laughed louder. How had he managed to get along for even so brief a time without her? "You're too much, Carrie."

"I hope not." All teasing was set aside. "I hope. . .nothing about me is too much."

He knew she referred to her wealth. He closed the gap between them, taking hold of her hands. "I'm sorry I've let your money come between us. It's awkward, you know? As the man, I feel like I need to be the stronger one in all areas, including financial."

She lifted her gaze, tears twinkling in the corners of her eyes. "I know, Rocky, but I can't make it go away. I come as a package—me. . .and my money. I can't tell you how hard I've prayed for someone to be able to accept me for myself and not want me because I'm wealthy. You're the first person who has rejected me because I was wealthy. That didn't hurt any less."

Rocky wished he could kiss her pain away. But he remained still, her hands in his, as she continued.

"I know when you look at me, there's a part of you that sees my stepfather. But, Rocky, I don't want to be like Mac. I don't want to hoard this money. I don't want to use it to control people or impress people. I've got it, and I can't change that, but I can choose to use it for good."

Rocky, looking into her shimmering eyes, saw how much his false accusation had cost her. Before he could apologize again, she went on.

"I bought a house, and I bought some things to go in it. I think my father would approve of that. But for the most part, I want to give the money away. Your college fund is the first of many scholarships I want to give to people who might otherwise not be able to get an education. I'm setting up an account with the college for that.

"I also want to donate a sum to your brother's business—I really admire what he does in the community for our members with handicaps. And I know there will be other charity organizations that can benefit."

"You—you're going to give it away?"

Carrie heard the astonishment in Rocky's tone, and for a moment, she faltered. Was he disappointed? Had he finally decided having her *and* her money would be a good thing? Her heart pounded as she answered, "Yes. I have no desire to live the lifestyle of my parents. I want simplicity, Rocky. Does—does that make a difference?"

He released her hands and took a step back, his eyes wide. Running his hand through his hair, he shook his head. "I'm just amazed, that's all. I mean, you could do anything you wanted to with your money. Travel, buy a house on the beach, send your kids to the best private schools. Why not do that?"

"Because I've seen how money changes people. It makes them greedy and suspicious, and they start thinking they're worth more because their bank account is bigger. Oh, I'm sure not all wealthy people are like that, but the ones I've grown up around?" She shook her head. "I don't want to be like that. I don't want the money to turn me into someone unlikable."

Rocky grinned. "Like that could happen."

She refused to find humor in the situation. "It could, Rocky. I saw it happen with my own mother. I believe she loved Daddy, but after he died, she didn't go looking for love—she went looking for money. She'd become so accustomed to moving in the highest social circle that she couldn't accept anything less. She married Mac, and I'm not sure she's ever been happy." She sighed, her heart aching. "That old saying about money can't buy happiness is sure true—I've seen the evidence in my own household."

Rocky didn't say anything, just stood with his gaze angled toward the picture window.

"Are—are you disappointed?"

Suddenly he seemed to come to life. Turning toward her, he shook his head, a smile lighting his face. "You are amazing, Carrie. The most unselfish person I've ever. . ." He dropped his gaze for a moment, as if gathering his thoughts. Finally he raised his chin, meeting her gaze. "I don't want your money, Carrie. I never did. It. . .unsettled me. I knew I couldn't compete with it." Taking a step closer, his expression turned serious. "You aren't giving it away to satisfy me, are you? You're doing this because you really want to, not because you feel pressured?"

Warmth flooded Carrie's middle. As much as her money intimidated him, he didn't want her to part with it to satisfy him. He cared for her—her, Carrie—so much that he was willing to accept the money if it was what she wanted. The knowledge made her feel as light as air.

"I don't feel pressured. I want to use it for others' good."

He nodded, approval shining in his eyes. "Good. That's really good."

"And you'll accept the college fund?" She held her breath, hoping.

Although he hesitated, at last he gave a slight nod. "Yes. I'll accept it." His voice turned husky as he added, "Thank you, Carrie."

"You're welcome."

They stood without speaking, gazes locked, while Carrie wished he would lean forward and kiss her. But instead of leaning toward her, he suddenly rocked back on his heels and clapped his palms together.

"So. . .you bought a house, huh?"

She blinked twice in surprise at this sudden change in topics. "Yes. Yes, I did." She took two hesitant steps in his direction. "Would you like to see it?"

"Sure!"

His enthusiasm brought a smile to her face. "It's still pretty messy—boxes everywhere. I haven't had time to put everything away yet."

"I could help with that, if you like."

She gave a nod. "I'd like that."

He crossed his arms and frowned down at her. "How's the yard landscaped?"

She sighed. "It's nothing to brag about. One big maple in the front yard, and another in the back, as well as what I think is a Russian thistle—at least it's covered with seedpods that look like little Christmas ornaments. But shrubs and flowers? Nothing. It's almost a clean slate."

He grinned. "Betcha I can help with that, too."

She laughed. "I just bet you can." Smirking, she added, "The first project for Mays and Wilder."

He pointed his finger at her. "That's Wilder and Mays, young lady."

She raised one eyebrow and didn't respond.

"Or perhaps we could try something else."

Carrie tipped her head. "Like?"

"Like. . .Wilder and Wilder."

# Chapter 18

Carrie angled her gaze to observe Rocky as they headed toward the college. How at ease he appeared, leaning back in the driver's seat, his wrist slung over the steering wheel, the other arm propped on the window opening. He had a cat-who-swallowed-the-canary look about him, and his handsomeness, as always, made her heart thrum in her chest.

He whisked a glance in her direction, his face breaking into a smile. "Whatcha looking at over there?"

"You."

"Oh yeah?" He chuckled, his gaze on the road. "Can't imagine that would hold your attention for too long."

She resisted giving him a bop on the arm. "Don't underestimate yourself, Rocky. You have to remember you're no longer *just* Rocky Wilder—you're a child of the King. Tell yourself that each time you look in the mirror."

He gave her a smile that sent her heart ka-wumping. Taking hold of the steering wheel with his left hand, he reached across the seat with his right and clasped her fingers. "Thanks, Carrie. Sometimes I'm just. . .overwhelmed, I guess. . .that you see me that way. You're so good and so—"

She squeezed his fingers. "Hold it right there. I'm not any better than you, so don't go in that direction. We're all sinners saved by grace, Rocky. I'm no better and no worse than you. We're both new creatures in Christ. That makes us even, okay?"

Another smile thanked her for her words. He released her to put both hands on the steering wheel and guide the car into a parking space. But as they headed across the sidewalk toward the administration building, he took hold of her hand again, and this time, he held tight until they reached the financial-aid office.

Carrie reluctantly released his hand—it felt so good, so secure to have her hand within his broad, strong fingers—so he could pick up a pen and sign the paperwork that would officially enroll him for the spring semester.

As he filled in boxes with black ink, she raised on tiptoes and whispered, "I can help you with your homework, if you'd like."

His lips twitched into a grin. "You sayin' I won't be able to handle myself in these classes?"

A shake of her head denied his statement. "Not at all. Just making myself available."

The grin deepened, bringing out the dimples she loved. "Hmm. . .might need you *every* evening. Sure you're up to that?"

She saw the teasing glint in his eye, but something else lingered there, too. She'd seen it the night at his house when he'd dropped the idea of calling their business Wilder and Wilder. A longing, perhaps, coupled with a hesitance.

She pressed her shoulder to his upper arm. Using a deliberately light tone, she said, "For you, I could make the sacrifice of every evening." Her heart thudded—what might he say next?

But he didn't reply, just gave her a wink and returned to his paperwork. Carrie remained silent, too, allowing him to concentrate, but underneath her calm exterior, her thoughts tumbled. Was he trying to gather his courage and ask her something important? Or was he merely teasing? How she wished he would get to the point!

Finally Rocky signed the last document and handed it to the secretary.

"Welcome to Petersburg University," the woman said.

Rocky nodded in the woman's direction, but when he said, "Thank you," he looked at Carrie.

―❦―

"So. . ." Rocky stuck his hands in his pockets. His fingers found the little tissue-wrapped package he'd tucked away that morning. A tremble filled his middle, and he had to force a smile. "Do you have anything special to do right now?"

Carrie lifted her wrist and checked her watch. "Hmm. . .no pressing engagements I can think of." She lifted her head and peeked up at him. "Why? Did you have something in mind?"

Oh yes, he had something in mind all right. He licked his lips. "Thought maybe we'd swing by Elmwood Towers." His pounding heart made him seek a temporary diversion. "Maybe see how Eileen is doing."

She offered a quick nod. "That sounds fine. I haven't talked to her in several weeks."

They headed out of the building together, and Rocky kept his hands in his pockets. He wanted to hold her hand again, but his palms felt all sweaty, and he was afraid they'd give him away. But he did allow his elbow to brush her arm occasionally, and each time he did it, she glanced up at him. The smiles that flew between them increased the tempo of his heartbeats with each connection.

Carrie leaned back on the headrest and closed her eyes as he drove to Elmwood Towers. He knew she wasn't asleep—her eyelids twitched—but he decided not to disturb her. She looked so peaceful, so content. Gratitude hit like an ocean wave. How readily she trusted him—her relaxed pose told him that more clearly than words could have. *Thank You, God, for the changes You've created in me. Thank You for helping me feel worthy of this woman.*

The moment he shut off the ignition, Carrie opened her eyes and smiled in his direction. "Ready?"

"Yep. Let's go." This time he took her hand. He couldn't help it—she rounded the car and held her hand toward him, an expression of expectation on her face. Before he took it, however, he swiped his own palm down his pant leg to remove any moisture.

Swinging their hands between them, he guided her to Tower Three, and they rode the elevator to the fifth floor. Their knock on Eileen's door went unanswered. Rocky consulted his wristwatch. "Hmm. . .I wonder if she met some friends for lunch and is chatting."

Carrie released a light laugh. "If so, it may be awhile before she returns. Eileen does enjoy visiting."

Rocky's heart pounded. Carrie was right—it could be an hour or more before Eileen returned. Well, no time with Eileen meant no more delays. He might as well get to it. He raised his shoulders in a shrug. "Well, we're here. Want to. . . go sit on our bench?"

"Sure." Carrie slipped her hand into the bend of his elbow. On the elevator, she leaned her forehead against his shoulder for a moment, her eyes closed in contentment. Again Rocky was struck with the trust she placed in him. He vowed from that moment forward never to do anything that would make her regret giving him her trust.

Carrie seated herself on the bench and lifted her face to him. The sun above the flowering pear tree crept between leaves and created dappled shadows across her cheeks. Rocky longed to kiss each splash of shade. He swallowed hard.

"Are you going to sit down?"

He gave a start, realizing he still stood beside the bench. "Oh! Yeah, sure, I'll sit." Stiffly he bent his knees and perched beside her. He wished his heart would settle down. Any minute it might boom right out of his chest. Maybe he should get this over with; yet he wanted to do things right. Carrie deserved things done right.

"Rocky, are you okay?"

The concern in her tone made him reach for her hand. "I'm fine. I'm just. . ." He chuckled, rubbing his finger beneath his nose in an attempt to stop the quiver in his upper lip. "I just want to tell you something, and I'm looking for the right words."

"Do you need me to sit quietly and not bother you?"

He looked into her sweet face, saw the love and acceptance shining in her eyes, and suddenly he knew exactly what to do. Cupping her cheeks with both hands, he leaned forward and placed a tender kiss on her soft lips.

She released a little gasp, but then her hands came up to clasp his wrists. Tears appeared, trembling on her thick lower lashes, reminding Rocky of dewdrops on rose petals. He brushed the droplets away with his thumbs.

"Carrie, I love you. You already knew that, didn't you?" He heard his husky tone, felt the emotion rumble beneath the words.

She drew in her breath, her face still held within his palms. Although she didn't speak, he saw the answer in her eyes. She knew.

Slowly he released her face. Slipping from the bench, he knelt in front of her and reached into his pocket. His gaze never wavered from her eyes as he removed the little package and began peeling back the paper.

The slight crackle of tissue paper underscored his words. "Carrie Mays, I believe God has grown a love in my heart for you that will endure throughout eternity. You would make me the happiest man on the planet if you would do me the honor of becoming my wife."

From the wad of paper, he lifted the slim gold band he'd chosen. Sun filtered through the tree branches overhead, lighting the diamond set within a circle of prongs. Carrie gasped as he took her left hand and slid the ring onto her finger. She stared at the ring, and tears splashed down her cheeks past the curve of her smile.

Finally she met his gaze, her blue eyes bright with more unshed tears. "I love you, too, Rocky. I would be honored to become your wife." She slipped from the bench to melt into his arms. They clung, hearts pounding in unison, for long seconds, each absorbing the moment, memorizing it, celebrating it.

Finally Rocky pulled back to lift her onto the bench once more. He settled himself beside her then lifted her hand to kiss the knuckle of the finger that wore the ring. He held her hand out in front of them and drew in a deep breath. "It looks perfect there."

"It is perfect there," she agreed on a breathy sigh.

A hint of regret wiggled down his spine as he looked at the simple ring. "Stone's not as big as I wanted, but—"

"Don't ever apologize, Rocky." She tugged at his hand until he met her gaze. "You chose this for me, and it's perfect for me. Just as you are perfect for me."

He shook his head, the wonder striking again. Carrie. . .Carrie loved him. It was as hard to fathom as God loving him. Yet he accepted it. He drew her into his arms once more. "I love you, Carrie."

"I know."

She rested her chin on his shoulder, and although she embraced him, he knew only one arm was wrapped around his back. He chuckled. "Are you peeking at that ring?"

Pulling free, she laughed. "How did you know?"

He imitated her position, hugging her while extending one arm straight out from her back, which showed her how he'd known. She laughed again, the joy in the laughter making Rocky's heart skip a beat. He planted another quick kiss on her laughing lips. Taking her hands, he captured her attention.

"Carrie, I can't guarantee we'll live like kings, but I do promise you your needs will always be met."

"Oh, I know." She sighed, her soft smile lighting her eyes. "Rocky, I've told you again and again that I have no desire to live like kings. Having my needs met is all I could ask for." Her smile turned coquettish. "And right now, all I need is another kiss."

He obliged her willingly, and suddenly the sound of applause intruded. They pulled apart and looked over their shoulders then burst into laughter.

Lined up on the sidewalk stood Eileen and her boys—John, Martin, and Tim—each smacking their palms together with enthusiasm and smiling brightly enough to rival the sun.

"Rocky, we saw you kissing!" John covered his mouth with his hands, his shoulders shaking with laughter.

Rocky gave Carrie a sheepish look, but she merely shrugged and grinned.

"Do I hear wedding bells?" Eileen called.

John looked at her in surprise. "There are no bells, Eileen. That is clapping you hear. Right, Martin and Tim?"

The other two men nodded solemnly, and Eileen's laughter joined that of Rocky and Carrie. Taking Carrie by the hand, Rocky jogged across the grass. He wrapped Eileen in a bear hug while Carrie looked on and Eileen's boys snickered.

Rocky whispered in Eileen's ear, "She said yes."

And Eileen whispered back, "I'm not surprised. She's a smart girl—knows a good catch when she sees one."

Rocky gave Eileen's wrinkled cheek a kiss then pulled away to wrap an arm around Carrie's waist. "Yes, you definitely heard wedding bells," he announced, "and all of you will be invited to the wedding. Which will be. . . ?" He looked at Carrie.

She smiled up at him. "In the early spring, when the tulips you are going to plant in our backyard are in full bloom. I want tulips in every color of the rainbow. And we'll recite our vows in the yard, with our friends"—her gaze swept over Eileen and the boys—"and family close by." Leaning her head against his shoulder, she sighed. "And then we'll show everyone the meaning of living happily ever after."

# Epilogue

Carrie peeked out the kitchen to the backyard, where guests mingled on the grassy carpet. Some stood in small groups along the walking path that gently curved through the garden area, which showcased hundreds of plump tulips at full bloom. Her eyes feasted on the splashes of bright color—every color of the rainbow, just as she'd asked.

The yard would be Rocky's best advertisement for his landscaping business. The arrangement of tulips was perfectly balanced, undeniably eye-catching. He'd created a walking path of concrete stepping-stones, each of which bore a different insect—from butterflies to bumblebees—formed with broken pottery, glass chips, and marbles. She could see guests pointing, nodding, admiring.

She winged a quick prayer of thankfulness heavenward for this perfect spring day. Kansas could be unpredictable in the spring so, just in case, they had decorated the living room in preparation for an indoor wedding. But the weather was ideal—warm but not hot, breezy but not windy. A beautiful, sunshiny Kansas day. Being outside on the manicured lawn with its profusion of color was exactly what Carrie had envisioned, and she rejoiced at the culmination of her dream-come-true wedding.

Her eyes sought and found Rocky, and she stifled a giggle. There he was, on his wedding day, plucking something that didn't belong from between the leafy tulips. She shook her head—gardening was most certainly in his blood. He would be successful in his business venture. She had no doubt.

Pride welled in her chest as she thought about everything he had accomplished in the past several months. In addition to completing his first semester of college and making the dean's honor roll, he had tilled the ground around his trailer and planted seedlings of various flowering trees. Although nothing else was growing out there, he had a blueprint of plans for the remainder of the ground.

After today, he would no longer live in his trailer house—her heart caromed at that thought—and he had plans to turn the trailer into his office. She smiled as she remembered him saying, "A man needs a place to call his own. I won't clutter up our yard and house here with all my stuff—it can stay out there, and that will be my playground." She knew he would keep his playground neat and orderly. He took such pride in everything he did.

With a sigh, Carrie turned from the window to find Eileen in the kitchen doorway, watching her with a smile on her wrinkled face. Carrie laughed self-consciously.

"You caught me peeking."

Eileen crossed the floor to join Carrie. "Yes, I did, but I don't believe in that bad-luck-to-see-the-groom-before-the-wedding nonsense." She rose up on tip-toe to peek outside. "He looks awfully handsome, doesn't he?"

Carrie looked again, her heart rising into her throat at the sight of Rocky with his brother, Philip, talking with the minister. "Oh yes," she released on a breathy sigh. "He's very handsome."

Rocky had said, somewhat apologetically, that a formal wedding wasn't his comfort zone. Could they do something simple? And Carrie had cheerfully agreed. Instead of a tuxedo, Rocky wore a neatly pressed pair of pleated navy trousers with a crisp white button-down shirt—she chuckled to herself—with sleeves intact. His tie lifted in the breeze, and he caught it, smoothing it down across his taut stomach. The muted colors of the tie included all the colors of the tulips, and he blended in perfectly with his surroundings.

Her eyes drifted to his hair, which he had insisted on having trimmed for this day, but to her relief, he hadn't cropped the waves that touched the top edge of his collar. She loved those sun-kissed curls.

"It's nearly time," Eileen said softly. "Are you ready?"

For a moment, Carrie's chest pinched. Among the guests were her mother and Myrna, but Mac hadn't come. He remained adamantly opposed to Carrie taking up with "that Wilder boy" and refused to witness the union. His stubbornness put a tinge of sadness on an otherwise perfect day, but she wouldn't allow Mac to be a rain cloud on her wedding.

She pressed her hands to her tummy for a moment as nervous excitement roused a flurry of butterflies. "Yes, I'm ready. At least I think I am. Do I look okay?"

Eileen's gaze traveled from Carrie's tumbling blond curls down the length of her pink lace dress, ending with her white high-heeled sandals. The woman's smile grew as her gaze returned to Carrie's eyes. "Honey, you're perfect. You'll take Rocky's breath away."

"That's good," Carrie quipped, "because I seem to have none of my own!" Her heart beat at twice its normal rhythm, and her words came out in breathless gasps.

Eileen's forehead creased. "Scared?"

Carrie processed what she was feeling. She shook her head. "No, I'm not afraid. I'm eager."

Eileen nodded in approval. "That's just what you're supposed to feel. C'mon, Carrie—let's go."

Through the open sliding door, piano music gently wafted from the CD player. Eileen handed Carrie her bouquet of tulips, their stems bound with an abundance of curling pink ribbon, then slipped out the garage door to join the others in the yard.

Carrie stepped through the sliding door. Guests, standing on the grass, turned to watch her progress. But Carrie was barely aware of their presence—her focus was on Rocky who waited beside the minister at the edge of the tulip garden. His brown-eyed gaze pinned to hers, a smile grew on his face. The joy in his expression brought a great rush of eagerness to Carrie's heart, and it was all she could do to keep from running across the yard and catapulting into his arms.

But Carrie forced her feet to move evenly, steadily, toward her groom, matching the relaxed beat of the music. Her heart celebrated. *Lord, thank You for answering my prayer for a man who would love me for myself. Your gifts are perfect.*

When she was within two yards of Rocky, she could no longer maintain the slow progress, and she skipped the final few feet, her face upturned, her smile so wide she could feel the rounding of her cheeks.

They had written their own vows—simple, straightforward promises from the heart. The minister read a brief passage of scripture—First Corinthians 13— and advised the couple to make the words a part of their lives. Less than fifteen minutes from the time Carrie stepped through the sliding door, the minister presented them to their waiting guests as man and wife.

Rocky's arms wrapped around Carrie's waist, lifting her off the ground, and his lips found hers. Her own arms looped around his neck, holding him tight. When the kiss ended, they laughed into each other's face while applause broke around them.

Rocky let her feet slip to the ground, but he still held her close as he whispered, "Today is the bud, Carrie. We have the rest of our lives to make the bloom. We are going to create the most beautiful blossom the world has ever seen."

She shook her head, laughing softly. "You just can't leave gardening for one moment, can you?"

"I can't leave God's plan for me," he corrected her, tapping the end of her nose with his finger. "And I'm so happy you're a part of it."

She nestled into his arms. "Oh, me, too, Rocky. Me, too."

They released one another to receive the congratulations and hugs of their guests. When everyone had partaken of the cake and punch and left for home, Rocky and Carrie walked arm in arm along the path. Dusk was falling, throwing rosy shadows across the lawn and deepening the colors of the tulips. Rocky sat on the bench in the back corner of the yard, Carrie curled beside him, her head cradled against his shoulder.

"So, Mrs. Wilder. . ." Rocky's arm was tucked snug around her waist, his thumb tracing a lazy circle on her hip. "How does it feel to be Mrs. Wilder instead of Miss Mays?"

"Wonderful." Carrie twisted her head to deliver a kiss on the underside of his jaw. His hand tightened on her waist.

"I'm still in awe." His low-voiced comment captured Carrie's attention. "It all seems kind of like someone else's life, you know?"

Carrie understood what he meant. "I know. Who would have thought someone would love Carrie enough to look past the money to the person?"

"Who would have thought someone would love Rocky enough to look past 'that Wilder boy' to the man he's become?"

Relishing the feel of her husband's arms wrapped securely around her, Carrie released a contented sigh. "That's the wonder of God, isn't it? He makes all things new."

Rocky didn't reply, but she felt his kiss on the top of her head. Then he rose, tugging her to her feet. His brown eyes crinkled into a warm smile as he took her hand. "C'mon, Mrs. Wilder. Let's go get started on that happily ever after."

# PROMISING ANGELA

# Dedication

For my critique partners, past (Beverly, Jill, and Darlene)
and present (Eileen, Margie, Ramona, Staci, Crystal, and Donna).
Thank you for your consistent mentoring.
And with a special hug to Eileen. You know why.

# Chapter 1

Angela Fischer hugged her counselor, waved good-bye to the receptionist, wrapped her fingers around the handle on her suitcase, and walked out the door to freedom. When she'd entered the South Central Drug Rehabilitation Center eight weeks ago, she had a chip on her shoulder the size of Mount Gibraltar and an attitude to match. Today the only weight she carried was that of her well-filled suitcase. She smiled. It felt good to have those burdens lifted.

Squinting against the mid-July sun, she turned toward the bus station. When she'd called her parents to let them know she'd be free to come home, she'd hoped Mom or Dad would volunteer to drive over and get her. But Dad had a charity golf game, and Mom gave the excuse of a meeting with the library board about hosting a multicultural exhibit.

"Can't you take a bus home, darling? I know you have money for a ticket," her mother had purred. And Angela had consented. Angela didn't fault her parents for their community involvement, but it had rankled a bit that a golf game to raise money for a piece of sculpture to stand in the center of the city's newest roundabout and a planning meeting took precedence over their daughter's release from an intensive drug-abuse rehabilitation program.

Of course, Angela acknowledged as she waited at the curb for the WALK sign, seeing the center would be a reminder to her parents that she hadn't been away at summer camp or something equally innocuous. Their embarrassment at her being ordered to go through the rehabilitation program was beyond description.

Angela stepped off the curb and followed the crosswalk, the leather soles of her sandals slapping the asphalt a little harder than was necessary as she contemplated the real reason for her parents' shame. She suspected it had more to do with her getting caught, and the subsequent publicity, than it did with her need for the program.

But more than one good thing had come as a result of her time at the center. Not only had Angela confronted the reason why she'd chosen to use drugs and made the decision to avoid them in the future, she'd also discovered a relationship with Jesus. A friend from back in Petersburg, Carrie Wilder, had visited. She'd brought Angela a Bible and shared the message of salvation. Maybe it was loneliness that first made Angela listen to Carrie, but recognition of her need for a Savior brought about the decision to accept Jesus into her heart.

Her steps lightened. She was going home a new person—drug free and

Spirit-filled. That thought brought a lift to her heart, and she almost skipped as she made her way down the sunny sidewalk.

Weaving between other Saturday-morning pedestrians, she flashed a smile and offered an "Excuse me" when her suitcase bumped the leg of a middle-aged woman. Despite her effort to be polite, the woman snapped, "Watch what you're doing!"

Angela spun around, a sharp retort forming on her tongue. Before she could spout the words, lessons from the Bible Carrie had given her winged through her mind, dispelling the unpleasant rejoinder. With a meek smile, Angela said, "I'm terribly sorry," turned, and hurried on.

She sucked in a big breath of the dry summer air and offered a silent *Thank You* to the Holy Spirit for controlling her errant tongue. Angela knew she would need the help of the Holy Spirit in the next weeks—and not just in keeping her tongue under control. In her final one-on-one session, her counselor had cautioned her the first weeks back "in the world" would be the most challenging.

"Habits are hard to break," the woman had warned, her expression serious. "Here, in a safe environment, it's easy to stay drug free. But back in your community, back with your old friends, the desire to be a part of that lifestyle will be a fierce pull. It will take a great deal of strength to resist the temptation."

At the time, Angela had released a laugh and said blithely, "Oh, don't worry about me! I'm as headstrong as they come. Nobody can make me do something I don't want to do." And then she'd added, "Besides, I have Someone helping me stay clean. I won't go back to those habits."

The near argument with the grumpy lady on the sidewalk had seemed to be a small test of the Holy Spirit's hold on her heart, and it pleased Angela that she'd passed with flying colors. Now if she could continue doing the right thing when it was bigger than making a cutting retort. . .

"Angela!"

The call pulled Angela from her introspection. She swung around, her hand shielding her eyes from the glaring sun, and sought the source of the voice. She broke into a smile when she saw Carrie Wilder trotting down the sidewalk. The moment Carrie caught up, she wrapped Angela in a huge hug.

Angela laughed in Carrie's ear, releasing her suitcase to return the hug. "Carrie! What are you doing here? Did you come to visit? I got out today."

"I know." Carrie slipped her sunglasses to the top of her head, the earpieces acting as a headband for her long blond waves. "I wanted to give you a ride home."

"Oh, Carrie!" Angela grabbed her friend in another hug. "That's so sweet of you! You drove three hours over here just for me?"

Carrie's light laugh brushed aside Angela's concern. "Well, why not? It's a great day for a drive."

"Oh, this is wonderful. Thank you!" Angela picked up her suitcase and admitted, "I was dreading that bus ride."

"Well, I parked at the center, so now we have to walk back there. I've been chasing you for two blocks—you walk fast!"

Angela laughed and looped her elbow through Carrie's. "Yes, I suppose I'm eager to get home."

"I don't blame you," Carrie said. They ambled easily down the sidewalk, no longer in a need to rush since they didn't have to follow the bus schedule. "I imagine it's been a long eight weeks."

Angela puckered her lips into a brief, thoughtful pout. "Yes, it has, but it's been a good eight weeks. I learned a lot—about myself and about why I felt the need to use drugs in the first place. And I hope I've learned how to keep from giving in to that need in the future. I don't want to have to come back."

Carrie sent her a worried look. "Do you really think that might happen?"

Angela shrugged. "My counselor told me it isn't uncommon. But I'm determined to beat the odds. Besides"—she smiled, giving Carrie's elbow a squeeze—"thanks to you, I'm not fighting this battle alone. One of the verses you underlined in the Bible you gave me says, 'I can do everything through him who gives me strength.' I'm going to bank on that."

Carrie slung an arm around Angela's shoulders and gave her a one-armed hug. "Good for you!" Releasing Angela, she stepped off the curb and popped the trunk on her sports sedan. "Let's get you home and put those words into action."

They pulled through a fast-food place and ordered burgers, fries, and shakes before catching Highway 54 East and heading for Petersburg. Angela took a long pull on the straw, savoring the sweet chocolate flavor of her milk shake. The food at the center had been filling but bland. She sighed, tipping her face to smile at Carrie's profile.

"I'm going to have to be careful. Food tastes so good right now. I'm afraid I'll overindulge and outgrow my wardrobe."

Carrie laughed and popped a crispy french fry into her mouth. "I wouldn't worry too much about that. You'll be too busy to be snacking."

Angela put her shake in the cup holder as worry struck. "Do you know what I'll be doing?" When she'd been arrested for drug use, the judge had handed down a one-year sentence, starting with the eight-week rehabilitation program. There were still ten months to be served somewhere. It was at least a small comfort to know someone who worked in the county clerk's office. Hearing the details of her sentencing might be less painful coming from a friend.

One hand on the wheel and her gaze on the road, Carrie reached into the backseat and groped around. It took a minute before she brought her hand forward and dropped a large manila envelope in Angela's lap. "The judge's recommendation is in there."

Angela peeled the envelope open and pulled out a sheaf of stapled pages while Carrie continued.

"Basically, it says since this is a first offense, you will serve your term with community service. He's assigned you to work at New Beginnings, starting this coming Monday."

"Monday already. . ." Right around the corner. Then Angela's hands froze on the papers as a wave of fear rose up inside her. "New Beginnings? You mean the place Rocky's brother runs, where they train handicapped people for jobs in the community?"

Carrie nodded, a soft smile appearing on her face with the mention of her husband's name. "The very same. I suggested it to Philip, he thought it was a great idea, and the judge approved it."

"But—but—" Angela shook her head. "I don't know anything about working with people with disabilities!"

"You'll learn."

Carrie's nonchalant comment set Angela's teeth on edge. "You don't understand, Carrie. I wish you'd asked me before you talked to Philip." Angela shifted sideways in the seat to face her friend. Her mouth felt dry, and she took another quick slurp of melting milk shake to moisten her tongue. "People with handicaps. . .they make me nervous."

Carrie flicked a brief glance in Angela's direction. "How so?"

Angela thumped the shake back into the cup holder. "I don't know. They just do! I've hardly visited my aunt Eileen since she took that job as resident caretaker for those three men at Elmwood Towers. Every time I'm around them, I get. . .nervous. I don't know how to talk to them, how to be around them. . . ."

"You'll learn."

Angela clutched the hair at her temples. "Stop saying that!"

"Why? It's true." Carrie munched another fry, unconcerned. "The more you're with them, the easier it will get."

Angela flopped back in the seat, her eyes closed. "I'm not so sure about that. . . ." Her stomach churned. New Beginnings! She would never have imagined being sent there. . . .

"Well, it's either community service at New Beginnings or a women's detention facility. I was pretty certain you'd prefer New Beginnings."

Angela opened her eyes. She drew in a big breath and then released it slowly, forcing her tense shoulders to relax. When it came to choosing between glorified jail or working with adults with disabilities, it was pretty much a no-brainer. Of course she preferred the latter. It was just. . .awkward.

"Listen"—Carrie's soft voice held a hint of sympathy—"what was that verse you were telling me about before we got in the car? 'I can do everything. . .'"

" 'Through him who gives me strength.' " Angela sighed, shaking her head.

"Okay, okay, Carrie, you got me. New Beginnings it is." Shooting her friend a sharp look, she added, "But don't expect me to be good at it. I know nothing about working with people with disabilities."

Carrie chuckled. "You'll learn."

⟶⌒⟶

Ben Atchison placed the clipboard on his desk, crossed his arms, and scowled across the room. That new hire, Angela Fischer, was backing off from Doris when she should be moving closer. He shook his head. What had Philip Wilder been thinking when he brought that girl on staff?

If Philip weren't happily married, Ben would have suspected the boss just intended to add to the decor. That little turquoise and black number she had on today fit her to perfection, showcasing every trim curve. How she managed to stay upright—not to mention look graceful—in those skinny-toed, back-half-missing, toothpick-heeled shoes was nothing short of miraculous.

And her hair! Ben had never seen anything like it—reddish brown spirals that bounced across her shoulders and caught the light with every movement. The first time he'd seen those curls, he'd been tempted to catch one and pull it to see how far it would stretch. But of course he had kept his hands to himself. She also had the most unique eyes—pale blue with a deep gray-blue rim around the irises. A man could get caught up staring into those eyes and lose track of time without any effort at all.

He drummed his fingers on the clipboard, the *thp-thp-thp* underscoring his thoughts. Yep, that Angela was one gorgeous woman. But she obviously had no desire to work here. The tight smile, wringing hands, and stiff posture gave her away. So why was she here? He snorted. It sure wasn't for the paycheck. He didn't think she needed it, based on the high-class outfits she'd worn each day this week. Plus, he'd seen what she drove to work—the sleek silver rocket had brought a neck-popping double take and an appreciative whistle from his lips. She obviously had a source of income from somewhere that exceeded anyone's salary here at New Beginnings.

So again. . .why was a woman like that working here?

Across the room, Doris, her round face shining, opened her arms for a hug. Ben watched, holding his breath, waiting for Angela's response. Although they worked with the clients to teach them the appropriate time and place for hugs, affirmation was needed and freely given in appropriate ways. If Angela rebuffed Doris, refusing to acknowledge the other woman's silent plea for approval, he'd have some choice words to share at the end of the day.

Angela tipped her body backward away from Doris, extended her arm, and patted the other woman's back in a stiff, impersonal manner. Her face twisted in a grimace. Ben frowned, wondering if that grimace was an expression of dislike or discomfort. He did understand that sometimes people had difficulty relating to those with handicaps, and the discomfort could display itself in dislike when it was truly just insecurity.

Doris giggled, covering her mouth with both hands and hunching up in pleasure. She patted Angela's shoulder, then reached once more for the broom and dustpan. The two women went to another area of the work floor to practice more. *Thp-thp*. . . Ben's fingers drummed. Dislike or discomfort? He couldn't be sure when it came to Angela.

But it was his job to make sure the clients were treated with respect and dignity. No hired worker—not even one with such a pleasing appearance—would be allowed to destroy the fragile confidence of his clients. He'd keep an eye on this new hire—Angela Fischer. A few more days—just a few more days to give her a chance to settle in. If he didn't see improvement, he'd visit with Philip, and his recommendation would be to let Angela Fischer go.

# Chapter 2

Angela uncapped her pen and drew a big *X* over the last Friday square on the calendar that hung inside her work locker. Two weeks down... How many to go? With a rueful chuckle, she decided not to count.

She closed her locker, leaned her forehead against the cold metal, and sighed. Tiredness smacked her, but it was a good kind of tired, she realized. The tired that comes from working hard and giving of yourself. In spite of the tight knot between her shoulder blades, satisfaction filled her. All that praying to get through the days must be helping.

Pushing off from the locker, she turned and gave a start. Ben Atchison, seated at his desk, had his gaze aimed right at her. Without conscious thought, she flipped her head to tousle her curls then ran her fingers from forehead to crown, teasing the curls into an uneven side part. It was a gesture she'd used to good effect many times in the past when she'd wanted to capture a man's attention.

She'd noticed Ben watching her quite a lot since she started at New Beginnings. And to be honest, she didn't mind. Ben was a hunk deluxe. Broad-shouldered. Trim-hipped. With bulging biceps that told of time in a gym.

He could let his hair grow, though. It was short enough to qualify for the military. So short it was hard to determine its true color—maybe blond, maybe brown, maybe brownish blond. But she didn't have to guess at his eye color. Those piercing eyes of deep blue, hooded by thick, arched brows, were like beacons in his square, chiseled face.

Oh yes, Ben Atchison was a very pleasant package. She allowed a smile to curve her lips, tipping her head and meeting his gaze directly so he'd know the smile was meant for him. Then, realizing what she was doing, she spun to face her locker, her cheeks blazing with heat. She shouldn't be flirting. It was a habit she struggled to break, along with so many other habits she knew didn't please her Savior. And flirting with one of the bosses was certainly a huge mistake. Opening her locker, she hid behind the door to get a grip on her embarrassment.

Her gaze fell on the Bible resting on the top shelf. She lifted it out. She had formed the routine of reading during her afternoon break, and she wanted to continue the schedule at home over the weekend. Bible in hand, she closed the locker with a snap and turned to leave. And she yelped in surprise. Ben Atchison stood beside the lockers, his blue-eyed gaze pinned on her face. They hadn't been in such close proximity since her first day when he'd shown her the time log and assigned her a locker. Up close, those eyes were like magnets, drawing her in. She gulped.

He didn't smile, and his deep voice sounded very formal. "Angela."

Clutching her Bible to her chest, she croaked, "Yes?"

Ben folded his arms, his weight on one hip. "I just wanted to let you know I have your two-week evaluation completed. I plan to show it to Philip this evening, and then you'll receive a copy on Monday. If you agree with my assessment of your performance, you'll simply sign off, and we'll have a second evaluation at six weeks. If you have any areas of disagreement, you, Philip, and I will schedule a conference to discuss it."

Angela managed a nod. So that's why he'd been watching. She suddenly felt very foolish. "I–I'm sure your assessment will be fair." Dropping her gaze to the floor, she confessed, "I know I'm not very good at this, but I am trying."

"I know. I can tell."

Her chin shot up, her startled gaze bouncing to meet his once more. He'd sounded. . .nice.

He pointed to the Bible she continued to hug like a lifeline. "I noticed you reading during breaks. What book are you studying?"

Angela glanced at the Bible in her arms. A light, self-conscious laugh escaped. "I'm not sure you'd call what I'm doing studying. The Bible is kind of new to me, so I've just been skipping around, reading here and there." Realizing how flighty that sounded, she hastened to add, "But I'm enjoying it, and a lot of it is really making sense."

Ben tipped his head, his brows coming down. "Are you a Christian?"

"Yes, I am," Angela said. "But I'm afraid I'm as new to Christianity as I am to New Beginnings. I have a lot to learn in both areas."

His nod seemed to hold approval. "What church do you attend?"

Angela blinked. "Church? Well, I don't—I just got back from"—she swallowed, seeking words that would be honest yet would protect her—"a training program, and I became a Christian while I was away. I haven't found a church yet."

"Your family doesn't attend?"

Angela stifled the laugh that threatened. Her parents? In church? Her mother gave up that "gobbledygook," as she called it, when she graduated from high school, and her father had never been interested. They did attend the big church downtown for Easter and Christmas services, but that was more for public appearances than anything else. If Petersburg didn't have a huge, statued, bricked, bell-towered church, her parents probably wouldn't bother at all, but Dad felt walking into that ostentatious building gave him some prestige.

She realized Ben still waited for an answer. She shook her head. "Uh-uh. My parents aren't churchgoers."

"Well, I attend a small church out on the highway. It's called Grace Fellowship. The building used to be a restaurant, but it closed years ago. I know it isn't fancy"—his gaze swept up and down her outfit, creating a rush of embarrassment—"but we have a growing young adult group, with services on Sunday morning and evening, as well as a Wednesday night Bible study. Would you be interested in attending?"

Her heart skipped a beat at the thought of being in a formal study group. Carrie had encouraged her to join a church where she could grow. "Oh yes, I'd like that a lot!"

His warm smile made her tummy tremble. "Good. Would you like to attend this coming Sunday morning? I'd be glad to give you a ride."

Fluttering her lashes, Angela quipped, "It's a date."

Immediately she regretted her action. How easily she'd slipped into flirtation. Again. But it wasn't appropriate—not for this setting and with this situation. The warmth in Ben's eyes disappeared, to be replaced with a guarded look that was like a splash of cold water over Angela.

"I—I mean I would very much appreciate a ride. Thank you." Her stuttered words did little to ease the tense moment.

Ben gave a brusque nod. "What's your address?"

At least he was still willing to take her. Her hands shook as she penned her address on a scrap of paper and handed it over. She offered a meek smile. "Thank you again, Ben. I do appreciate the ride."

He looked at the address, and his eyebrows shot upward. She knew what he was thinking—everyone in town was familiar with the Eastbrook Estates. She waited for him to change his mind and tell her she wouldn't fit in at his simple, used-to-be-a-restaurant church, but he slipped the paper into his breast pocket and said, "I'll be by around nine fifteen. Sunday school starts at nine thirty, and the worship service at ten forty-five."

"That's fine. I'll be ready. Well. . ." She waved a hand toward the door, inching in the direction of the exit. "I told my aunt I'd stop by after work and have some milk and cookies with her." A nervous giggle erupted. Had she really just told Ben she'd be having milk and cookies?

But he didn't make any snide remarks. He didn't even smirk. With a quick upturning of lips, he turned toward his desk. "I'll see you Sunday morning. Have a good weekend."

"Yes. . .Sunday. And thank you." Before she could say or do anything else to embarrass herself, she escaped.

⁓

Ben curled the fingers of one hand around the steering wheel as he maneuvered through the late-afternoon traffic toward Elmwood Towers. His other hand tapped restlessly on the fold-down console. A pepperoni pizza sat in the passenger seat, its aroma teasing Ben's senses. He tried to focus on his upcoming dinner with his cousin Kent to get his mind off the mouthwatering spicy smell—and off Angela Fischer.

Why had he invited her to church? Or more specifically, why had he offered to take her? She had transportation—he whistled—boy, did she have transportation! Yet he'd opened his mouth and offered her a ride in his six-year-old mid-size truck that didn't even have a backseat to put some distance between them. He gave the console a pat. At least the twelve-inch barrier would be in place.

If he didn't want to get close to her, why had he issued the invite? He knew why. There had been something in her unusual light blue eyes. . . . When she'd admitted she had a lot to learn both as a New Beginnings employee and as a Christian, a little something inside him had melted. The insecurity lurking in her eyes had been all too familiar. He understood the feeling. Empathized with it. A dozen years ago, he had felt lost and uncertain, and a schoolmate had reached out to him. What a difference it had made!

He didn't know how he would have managed the past few years without the strength of Christ bolstering him. The loss of his father and uncle in a boating accident, followed by Kent's spiral into drug addiction, were burdens that would have overwhelmed him had it not been for his reliance on Jesus. Ben's heart ached at the route Kent had taken to find comfort. He sensed in Angela the same longing for acceptance and peace.

As Angela's direct supervisor, it was his responsibility to mentor her at work. As a Christian, it was his responsibility to be a good example. Inviting her to church was one way of mentoring.

Mentoring. . . That was it. Just mentoring. . .

A red light brought him to a halt. His thoughts skipped backward, replaying the flutter of her eyelashes and the flirtatious, "It's a date." His fingers curled over the edge of the console. He hoped he'd managed to squelch that idea. In his observations over the past two weeks, he'd surmised Angela had lived a rather self-serving lifestyle. She was entirely too flippant, too self-absorbed. If he were going to date, he'd want someone warm and soft, with an aura of holiness brought through a relationship with Jesus.

Not to mention someone who didn't shy away from the disabled. Shaking his head, he replayed several recent scenes. Yes, as he'd told her, he knew she was making an effort, but she had a long way to go to be completely accepting and supportive of the clients at New Beginnings. Anyone he dated would eventually be around Kent, and he wouldn't risk having Kent hurt by someone's withdrawal.

The light changed, and he pulled forward, a small niggle of guilt striking at his thoughts. He hoped he wasn't being judgmental. But Angela, despite her physical beauty, didn't possess the qualities he wanted in a life mate. It would be unkind and dishonest to lead her to believe he had any interest in her beyond employer to employee, Christian mentor to mentee. He'd have to watch himself, not give her the wrong idea.

He turned onto Elmwood Avenue, the last stretch. The six high-rise apartments of Elmwood Towers loomed ahead. Kent waited in Tower Four. Ben whispered a quick prayer of gratitude for the assisted-living apartments in each of those towers. It had taken some fancy footwork by New Beginnings' owner Philip Wilder to get one quad in each of the retirement village's apartment buildings designated for adults with handicaps, but what a service it was to those in the community who faced challenges.

Getting Kent into one of those apartments had done him so much good. The small measure of independence had boosted Kent's confidence, built his self-esteem, and put him more on a level with his peers. What single man in his late twenties wanted to live at home with his mother?

Ben pulled into a visitor's space, shut off the ignition, and picked up the pizza box. Hitting the automatic lock on his key chain, he turned toward Tower Four, but a glint of silver caught his eye. He stopped, turned, and stared.

Sure enough. The silver rocket—Angela's car—sat six stalls over.

# Chapter 3

Angela popped the last bite of her fourth chocolate chip cookie into her mouth, swigged the final gulp from her half-pint carton of milk, and released a satisfied sigh. "Oh, Aunt Eileen, that was wonderful." She patted her stomach, laughing. "But I think I'd better skip supper tonight! I'm going to waddle out of here!"

Eileen and her friend Alma, on the couch facing Angela across the low walnut table scattered with magazines, empty milk cartons, and cookie crumbs, both laughed. The older women exchanged winks.

"Now, Angela, when you look like me"—Eileen gave her own bulky midsection a two-handed squeeze—"you can worry about waddling. Until then, neither of us wants to hear about it!"

All three women laughed. When Angela arrived at her aunt's apartment after work, Eileen had suggested taking the cookies to the foyer of Tower Four and sharing with a friend of hers who'd been down in the dumps since a hospital stay. At first Angela had balked, not willing to share Aunt Eileen with anyone else. But seeing Alma's enjoyment of the cookies and conversation made her regret her selfishness. She had a lot to learn about reaching out to others, she realized.

Aunt Eileen would be a great teacher in that regard. Her mother's older sister was unpretentious, warmhearted, and open, unlike the rest of Angela's family. Eileen and Angela's mother had grown up dirt-poor, but while Mother had sought riches in married life, Eileen had married a salesman who made little more than enough to pay the necessary bills. Uncle Stan had passed away years ago, leaving Eileen alone, yet she had never wallowed in self-pity. Angela held great admiration for her aunt, even though her parents often commented with a hint of disdain that their lifestyles didn't "mesh."

The smell of pizza wafted through the foyer, and Angela looked over her shoulder toward the double doors. She did a double take when she saw who carried the pizza. She leaped to her feet. "Ben?"

"Ben?" Eileen repeated, shooting Angela a smirky grin.

Angela felt her face flood with heat. How disconcerting to have him walk in after having spent a good fifteen minutes entertaining the two older ladies by describing his physical attributes and being teased about his Sunday invitation.

He glanced in her direction and imitated her double take, coming to an abrupt halt that nearly sent the pizza flying from his palm. Grabbing the box with both hands, he took two steps in her direction. A wary smile creased his face. "Angela. . .hi. I didn't expect to see you here."

Angela brushed cookie crumbs from her lap. She hoped she didn't have any crumbs on her face. "Ben, I'd like you to meet my aunt, Eileen Cassidy, and her friend Alma. . . ?" To her embarrassment, she couldn't remember Alma's last name.

But Ben smiled. "Hello again, Mrs. Andrews. It's good to see you home and looking well. Kent told me you had quite a time. And, Mrs. Cassidy, nice to see you, too. Philip was just mentioning he needed to come by here and see what you're up to."

Angela swung her gaze back and forth, listening, her jaw hanging open. Eileen knew Ben?

Eileen laughed as she pushed to her feet, her eyes twinkling. "Oh, that Philip. He couldn't take better care of me if he were my own son."

Ben's warm smile sent Angela's heart pattering even though it was aimed at Eileen. "I know he thinks the world of you." He paused, rocking on his heels, then took a hesitant step toward the elevators. "Well. . .I'd better go. Pizza's getting cold, and I'm expected."

"Bye, Ben!" Eileen called, waving a pudgy hand.

Alma added, "Have fun with Kent!"

The moment the elevator doors closed on Ben, Angela wheeled on her aunt. "Aunt Eileen! Why didn't you tell me you knew Ben?"

Eileen sat back down, shrugging. She wore a look of innocence. "How was I to know the Ben you were talking about is the same Ben I know? There are a lot of Bens in the world." Her sparkling eyes gave her away even before the giggled snort blasted out. "Of course I knew you were talking about Ben Atchison. What other Ben works at New Beginnings? He's a wonderful young man, and I'm tickled pink you two have formed a friendship."

Angela collapsed against the back of the couch. "I'd hardly call what we have a friendship. . .yet." Her heart gave a hopeful flutter. "But—" She leaned forward, suddenly eager. "Tell me everything you know. Who is he meeting here? This Kent—is he an uncle?"

Alma shook her head, her wrinkled face sad. "No, honey, not an uncle. His cousin. A young man not much older than you."

Angela shook her head as understanding dawned. These apartments housed retirement-age individuals except for those few apartments set aside for the special-needs community. Then that meant. . . She bit down on her lower lip as she glanced toward the elevator doors. Turning back to Alma, she said, "You mean his cousin is handicapped?"

"I'm afraid so." Alma pursed her lips, her face creasing in disapproval. "The result of a drug overdose. He'd been perfectly healthy up to that time." She shook her head, her chins quivering. "Such a waste..."

Angela swallowed. The cookies suddenly didn't set so well. "So—so what's wrong with Kent? What did the overdose do?"

Alma sighed. "Such a tragedy..." She leaned forward, licking her lips.

Eileen patted Alma's hand. "We should be careful not to gossip."

Alma's cheeks mottled with pink. "Oh, well, I certainly wouldn't want to do that...." She reached for another cookie.

Angela felt a little twinge of guilt for encouraging gossip. She'd indulged in more than her fair share of unnecessary talk over the years. But small wonder—Mother was so good at it. However, that wasn't an excuse. Another habit she needed to break. She winged a silent prayer for God to keep her aimed in the right direction; then she returned her thoughts to Ben.

Her heart ached as things fell into place. Kent must be why Ben worked at New Beginnings. He had a personal stake in reaching out to those with disabilities. Something else struck hard, making her heart race. Kent's disability was the result of drug use. *That could have been me.... Oh, thank You, Lord, that I didn't go that far....*

She stood again, forcing a smile to her lips. "Aunt Eileen, thank you for the cookies. And, Alma, I'm so glad I got to meet you."

Alma nodded. "Oh, me, too, dear. You come see me again, will you?"

Angela took the wrinkled hand in her own. The loneliness in the old woman's eyes pierced her heart. "Of course I will." Who would have imagined Angela Fischer making a promise like that to an old lady? Yet she vowed to carry through on the promise.

Eileen rose and embraced Angela. Cupping her face in her sturdy hands, she whispered, "Now you take good care. I'll be praying for you."

Tears flooded Angela's eyes. Aunt Eileen must be thinking the same thing she had earlier—how fortunate it was that she had escaped with little more than a one-year sentence of community service for her drug abuse. Poor Kent served a lifetime sentence....

"Thank you," she said, smiling. "I'll take those prayers."

As she headed for her car, her thoughts drifted to one of the apartments where Ben sat eating pizza with his cousin. How sad. How very sad... She reached into her purse for her keys, and her fingers brushed against something sharp. She withdrew the item—a small, folded square of paper.

A chill struck. She knew what it was. A phone number. For Gary. Dropping her purse, she tore the paper into bits of confetti and scattered them in the gutter. She didn't need that number. She didn't want that number.

But what frightened her was the desire that welled up when she'd remembered what calling that number could gain.

She clenched her fists and vowed aloud, "I'm not doing that anymore!" She snatched up her purse from its spot on the ground at her feet, slammed herself into her car, and zoomed for home as if demons were chasing her.

—◦

Ben pushed a napkin into Kent's fist and teased, "Use that thing, man. You're making a mess."

Kent threw back his head and laughed. He raised the napkin to his face and swished it back and forth in a jerky, awkward movement. When he dropped his hand to his lap, the pepperoni grease had been cleared from his lips and mustache. A bit still shone in the chin whiskers of his beard, but Ben knew he'd get it cleaned up in his shower.

"Good stuff, huh?" Ben asked as he took another bite.

"Ye–es, good. . ." Kent's face contorted as he formed the words. He patted his stomach. "Full."

Again Ben resorted to teasing, a throwback to their junior high days when zinging one another was a sign of affection. "No kidding! You ate three-fourths of that thing by yourself."

Kent's laughter lifted Ben's heart. As boys growing up, they'd been more like brothers than cousins. They'd played on the same Little League team, been members of the same scout troop, and rarely spent a Friday night without a sleepover. They'd had pillow fights and arguments over girls and quizzed each other for spelling tests. Best friends—inseparable. Until the accident that claimed both of their fathers' lives. After that, things had changed.

Ben swallowed his pizza, a lump in his throat making it difficult. If only Kent had known the Lord, he would have sought comfort in prayer rather than in drugs. Ben understood why Kent had turned to alcohol and drug use. The pain of losing a father was a pain too heavy to bear without help. Kent had found his "help" in the most hurtful way available. And it couldn't be changed now. Ben just had to pray that somehow God would use Kent's disability for someone's good.

He leaned forward and tapped Kent's bony knee. "Hey, want to go down to the workout room?"

Kent's eyes lit up. "Go. . .pump iron."

Ben nodded. "Yep. Let me throw this stuff away." He reached for the empty pizza box and crumpled napkins.

"No!" The word burst out, anger twisting Kent's face. "My apartment. I. . . clean up."

Ben raised his hands in surrender, a smart-alecky grin on his face. "Yes, sir! You clean up, sir!" He did his best private-to-sergeant imitation.

The anger faded as quickly as it had flared. Kent laughed. Calm again, he said, "You cook. . .I clean up."

Ben remained seated on the edge of the sofa as Kent gathered the napkins and stacked them in the pizza box. He battled to close the lid, and Ben grabbed his own knees to keep from helping. Ben knew Kent needed to exercise every bit of independence. No matter how hard it was to watch his cousin struggle, he wouldn't interfere.

Finally, after a few frustrated grunts, Kent managed to get the lid closed, trapping the napkins inside. With a triumphant grin, he placed the box in his lap then wheeled his chair to the kitchenette and dropped the box into the waste can.

Spinning around, he crowed, "Ready. . .to pump. . .iron!"

"Got your key?"

Kent patted his jeans pocket.

"Then let's go." Ben opened the apartment door and waited until Kent rolled through before giving it a slam. He poked Kent on the shoulder. "Wanna race?"

Kent's determined scowl reminded Ben of when they were twelve and Ben had issued a challenge. Ben knew Kent remembered little of those days—the overdose had stolen the majority of his memory—but Ben remembered. He knew Kent would lean forward, stick the tip of his tongue out between his lips, and squint at the finish line—in this case, the elevator doors.

"Okay," Ben said, getting into position with a hand on his knee. "Ready, get set. . .and go!"

Ben could have won easily, but he deliberately stayed one pace behind the wheelchair. Kent's raucous hoot of satisfaction was all the reward he needed.

"Aww!" Ben feigned disgust, slapping his thigh. "You got me again."

Kent pointed at him with both index fingers, his face creased in a huge smile. "I got you. . . . I got you. . . ."

Ben thumped his cousin's shoulder. "Way to go, man." He poked the elevator Down button then crossed his arms, pretending to mope. "Well, I'll get you in the workout room. You won't lift more weight than me."

With sparkling eyes, Kent shook his head and raised his fists as if showcasing his muscles. "I will. . .beat you."

The elevator doors slid open. Ben gave Kent's wheelchair a push. "We'll just see about that." As they rode toward the lobby, suddenly Ben wondered about Angela. Would she still be down there? He hoped not. If she looked at Kent the way she looked at the clients of New Beginnings, Ben was fearful of how he would react.

# Chapter 4

"A men."

Angela added her voice to the others who echoed the close of the final prayer. The naturalness of the act gave her a feeling of warmth and acceptance she wanted to savor. Lifting her face to meet Ben's gaze, she smiled.

"I really enjoyed the service, Ben. You were right—this is a great church."

Ben's shoulders lifted in a shrug, shifting his tie. He smoothed it back into place as he said, "The Holy Spirit is here. You can sense it."

"Yes, you can." Angela allowed her gaze to sweep around the room, observing the small groups of chatting congregants. Despite the simplicity of the block building and the essence of grease that lingered in the air, no one seemed in a rush to leave. All appeared at home and comfortable in the makeshift sanctuary.

And although several people had welcomed her this morning with smiles and handshakes, no one had startled at her name. No one pointed or whispered, as she had feared. She couldn't deny being relieved about that. Even though Carrie had prompted her to join a church immediately upon her return from rehab, she had hesitated out of worry. If people recognized her, they might steer clear of her based on her past mistakes. The humiliation of her arrest still hung like a chain around her neck. Being reminded of it by people's reactions added another link to the chain.

But no one had left her feeling uncomfortable this morning. She felt at ease and eager to be a part of the church family. Turning a slow circle, she sought faces from Sunday school, trying to recall names. She hoped the opportunity for friendship existed among the singles her age. Her drug-abuse counselor had encouraged her to form new friendships with people who were not a part of the "partying" scene. She would be more likely to remain clean if she stayed away from users. Of course she had Carrie, but she didn't want to rely on Carrie too much. As a newlywed, Carrie needed her time with Rocky. And Angela needed to broaden her horizons.

"Are you ready to go?" Ben looked down at her, a soft smile in his eyes.

She liked his Sunday face—contented, open. Sometimes at work, she got the feeling he didn't quite trust her. Her heart raced as she realized how much less he would trust her if he knew about her past. Even though she knew total honesty was important in any relationship, she still hoped he'd never find out. The open friendliness would surely whisk away, and she wasn't sure how she would handle that.

They slipped from between the rows of folding chairs that served in place of wooden pews and ambled toward the foyer area, which would have been where the cash register sat when the building served as a restaurant. "I really liked the focus verse from this morning," Angela commented, then frowned, pressing her memory. "What was the reference?" She stopped and consulted the printed program an usher had offered when she'd come in.

"Ephesians 1:4," Ben said. A grin twitched his cheek as he watched her open her Bible and search for Ephesians. "Here." He took the Bible, opened it to the right place, and then handed it back.

"Thanks." Angela grimaced. "I guess I need to get some of those little tab things with the names of the books to guide me."

"No, don't do that." Ben shook his head. "You'll always use the tabs then and never learn to find them for yourself. Try memorizing the order of the books instead."

"Oh, okay. I'll try that." Lowering her gaze to the open Bible, she slid her finger to verse four and read aloud. " 'For he chose us in him before the creation of the world to be holy and blameless in his sight.' " With a sigh, she closed the Bible and hugged it to her chest. "I never really thought about His creating us to be holy before Him."

Ben smiled. "Well, we are created in His image, after all. Sin messes that up though. That's why God sent His Son, Jesus, to die for our sins. It is through His sacrifice that we can be cleansed from all unrighteousness. He makes us holy once again."

Angela blinked at him, awed by his knowledge. "Wow—you've been a Christian a long time, haven't you?"

Ben smiled. "A few years."

"Oh, I hope I'm as smart as you someday!"

He released a light laugh. "Well, Angela, one thing you'll find out." He put his hand on her back to guide her toward the door. "No matter where you are in your Christian journey, there's still a lot to learn."

Angela nodded. Carrie had said pretty much the same thing. That's why it was important to attend church, for the opportunity to continually grow. They left the air-conditioned building and walked across the balmy parking lot to Ben's truck. "I have a lot to learn in many areas, I'm afraid," she said.

He opened the door for her. "What areas?"

Angela climbed in then waited for him to settle behind the steering wheel before answering his question. "Well, for instance, you. . . I was so surprised to see you at Elmwood Towers yesterday after work. I didn't know you had a cousin who lived there."

Ben shot her a sharp look. "How did you know I was visiting my cousin?"

Angela waved good-bye to a couple of people as the truck pulled out of the parking lot. She looked back at Ben. "My aunt—Eileen Cassidy, remember? She told me your cousin lives there."

Ben nodded, his lips set in a grim line. Then he took a deep breath, and his expression cleared. "I really like your aunt. She's a spunky lady with a big heart. On which side of the family is she related?"

Rebuffed, Angela explained her family tree, but beneath her words, her thoughts raced. *Why did Ben change the subject when I asked about his cousin? Could it be he's shamed by what his cousin did?* Her heart twisted painfully in her chest. If he could be ashamed of his very own cousin, he would certainly feel even more animosity toward a stranger. She carefully guarded her words as Ben drove the familiar streets toward her family's estate.

It was best that Ben never found out she had been arrested for drug use.

⎯⎯☙⎯⎯

Ben battled guilt as he listened to Angela, her voice halting at times, share about her relationship with Eileen Cassidy. He hadn't switched gears out of anger, but he suspected by her quiet demeanor she felt as though he were angry. Protectiveness toward Kent welled up again.

Kent had suffered so much rejection since the drug overdose. His own mother and sister had little to do with him, furious at him for wasting his life. His friends had all abandoned him. What good was he to them, trapped in a wheelchair, unable to join them at their parties? Even strangers on the street shied away from him. Ben knew how much those rejections hurt Kent, and he wouldn't willingly put Kent in the line of fire for more pain.

Angela's discomfort around the clients at New Beginnings made it clear how she'd react to Kent—and Kent wasn't stupid. He recognized when people avoided him. Despite his other handicaps, he was still fully capable of feeling. The less Angela knew about Kent, the better. Ben would not give her the opportunity to hurt his cousin.

He stopped the truck along the curb and shifted into Park. He looked at Angela, and the yearning he'd seen in her eyes last Friday, right before he invited her to church, was there again. It took him aback, and he found himself opening his mouth and blurting out a second invitation.

"Did you catch the announcement about the potluck dinner before the evening service? If you'd like, I can swing by and pick you up."

Angela's gaze shot to her lap. She clenched her fingers on her Bible. "Potluck. . . That means everybody brings food, right?"

Ben chuckled. "Well, yeah. Then we all share it."

She took a deep breath, her gaze still down. "I'd probably better not then."

What was bothering her now? Determined to make up for his earlier evasiveness, he assumed a teasing tone. "Why? Don't you eat?"

She turned her face slightly to look at him. Worry and uncertainty showed in her eyes. "I—I can't bring anything."

He could make no sense of that comment. "Why not?"

A huge breath huffed out, and she flipped her hands outward. "I can't cook!"

Ben burst out laughing. "You're kidding, right?"

She glared at him.

His laughter died. "You really can't cook? But—you're what—twenty-one, twenty-two?"

"Twenty-three," she said grimly. "And I know how pathetic it is, but. . ." She paused, biting down on her lower lip for a moment. Finally she sighed and admitted, "Ben, I never had to do much of anything in the way of chores while growing up. We've always had servants. Mother said menial chores were beneath us, and Dad insisted that's what he paid the maid and cook to do. So, I just haven't learned."

Ben stared in amazement. Her comments sure explained a lot about her standoffish behavior at work. But never having chores was beyond the scope of his understanding. He and his sister had been responsible for household duties from an early age. Especially after Dad died, Mom had depended on them to help out. And now that he was grown, he appreciated it. He lived alone, but he could take care of himself, cleaning house, doing laundry, cooking—and not just dumping soup from a can—real cooking.

"Well. . ." He scratched his head. "I tell you what. I'll bring the covered dish, and you just. . .come."

Her jaw dropped. "You can cook?"

He managed to swallow his laughter. "Yeah. I make a mean enchilada casserole with chilies and onions and lots of gooey cheese. Sound good?" He was amazed how important it had become to put her at ease.

Her lips quivered into a weak smile. "It does sound good, but. . ." She tipped her head, her curls spilling across her shoulder and catching the afternoon sun. "Are you sure it's okay to go and not bring anything?"

He grabbed the steering wheel with both hands before one sneaked out and captured one of those spiraling curls. "Perfectly okay. So. . .do you want to go?"

A full smile lit her face. "Yes, I do. Thank you."

Ben nodded. "Okay then. I'll be back a little before six. See you then."

She thanked him again and scooted out of the truck. He watched her bounce up the walk, swinging her purse. She paused on the porch, turned around, waved, and then disappeared inside.

Ben sat at the curb for a few minutes, drinking in the ostentation of the brick and mortar two-story house. He'd been in too much of a rush this morning to really look at it, but at close examination, it was incredible. Pillars extended from the bricked porch floor to the second-story roof. At least three chimneys stretched toward the sky. The garage behind it could easily hold four vehicles.

He craned his neck, his eyes widening. Was that a pool house?

He shook his head, curiosity overflowing. A huge house, servants, the silver rocket. . . Why was someone who obviously had no need to work filling a minimum-wage position at New Beginnings? There was more to Angela Fischer than met the eye. Suddenly Ben was determined to get to the bottom of her secrets. Maybe this evening would help shed a little light on things. . . .

# Chapter 5

Angela glanced up from the dishwashing station when she heard the tinkle of the bell announce a visitor. She looked toward the door, and an involuntary gasp accompanied the tensing of her body. The visitor was hers—Officer Brighton. He held a brown paper bag at his side. Angela's heart flip-flopped in her chest.

"Angela? Are the cups done?"

Angela, flustered, turned back to Steve. The man pointed to the cups stacked in the dishwashing tray. She gave a quick glance at the cups lined up in the plastic tray and pushed her lips into a smile.

"You did a great job, Steve. You filled all the slots. Now can you check to be sure all the cups are upside down? Remember, we don't want them to fill up with water."

Steve beamed. "I will check."

"Thanks." She gave his back a pat, her gaze on the officer who remained just inside the door, scanning the room. A movement to her left captured her attention—Ben leaving his desk to welcome the visitor. Angela began inching away from the dishwashing area. "Steve, you check those cups; then you can start on the silverware, okay?"

"Okay, Angela!"

Angela paused long enough to make sure Steve would follow her directions, and then she darted across the room and cut in front of Ben, bringing him to a halt. She offered what she hoped was a natural smile. "It's okay, Ben; it's for me. I'll get it."

Ben scowled briefly, glancing at the officer, but he nodded and returned to his desk.

Angela hurried to Officer Brighton. Weaving her fingers together, she pressed her hands against her jumping stomach. "Hello. I didn't expect to see you here."

The man glanced at his wristwatch, his face impassive. "The records we have indicate you are entitled to a midafternoon break. Is this not the case?"

"Yes, I do have a midafternoon break, so I could be free for a few minutes." Angela shot a nervous look over her shoulder. Sure enough, Ben was watching.

"Very well, then." He lifted the paper bag. "Take this, and—"

Angela slipped her hand through the officer's elbow to interrupt him. "Come with me." She guided him to the break area where tall partitions shielded them from view.

He frowned and pulled loose the moment they rounded the corner. "Miss Fischer, I—"

"I know why you're here." Angela blinked rapidly as nervousness churned her middle. She lowered her voice to whisper. "It's the random drug test, right?"

He nodded. Holding out the bag again, he boomed, "If you will just—"

Angela whammed her finger against her lips. "Shh!" She darted to the partition and peeked out. Everyone appeared busy except Ben, who peered in the direction of the partitions with a puzzled frown on his face. She zipped back to the officer.

"Officer Brighton, the only person who knows I'm here on community service is the owner. I—I don't want the others to know. Especially—" She stopped herself before she blurted out Ben's name. *Why is it so important for him not to know?* Her heart pattered. She knew why. His friendship had become very important to her in the short amount of time she'd known him. She didn't want him to be disappointed in her.

She clasped her hands beneath her chin and gave her best pleading look. "Please, can't we do this later? I promise I won't leave work. You can pick me up and take me wherever you need to get the test, but I just can't do this here."

"Miss Fischer, the purpose of a random test is—"

"I know, I know, to catch me off guard, which you've certainly done." A nervous giggle burst out, which she muffled by clapping her hand over her mouth. When she felt she had control, she leaned toward the officer and lowered her voice to a rasping, fervent whisper. "But I won't be any less off guard at five thirty. Oh, please, don't make me do this here!"

"Miss Fischer, I'm sure you understand there are procedures we follow to be certain the test is accurate. If I leave now, after having notified you that you will be tested today, the results can be skewed."

Angela wasn't completely sure she understood everything he'd said, but his meaning came through. He didn't trust her. She felt her cheeks fill with heat, humiliation striking. But then why should he trust her? She'd used an illegal substance. She deserved his suspicion. But it didn't make it any easier to bear. God may have forgiven her, but men...?

Lifting her chin, Angela met the man's gaze. "Officer Brighton, I know I made a huge mistake. I'm sorry for it. At the time, I wasn't a Christian and I didn't much care if I did wrong things. But now I have Jesus in my heart, and I don't want Him to be disappointed in me. I'm not perfect, but I'm trying very hard to do what's right." She swallowed. "You don't have any reason to believe me, but I'm being honest when I tell you I won't do anything to make the test skewed. Please let me do this after work."

The officer stood for a long time, his face set in a firm scowl, looking directly into her eyes. Angela held her breath, waiting for him to make his decision. Her thoughts begged, *Please, please, please. . . !*

Finally Officer Brighton released a sigh. "Very well, Miss Fischer. I will return at five thirty and escort you to the police station."

Angela thought her legs might collapse; the relief was so great. "Oh, thank you!"

"But make sure you're here and ready to go." He moved toward the gap between partitions, but before exiting, he turned back. "You'd better be honest with me. The judge will not take kindly to fraudulence."

Angela wondered briefly how one could be fraudulent with a drug test, but she didn't ask in case he thought she wanted the information for future reference. Instead she gave a brisk nod, meeting his gaze with an earnest look. "I understand. And I promise"—she held up her fingers, Boy Scout–style—"no fraudulence."

He gave her one more sharp look before striding out of the break area and heading for the door. She followed on his heels, a smile plastered on her face, her gaze on the back of his shirt. She felt as though everyone in the room was watching her, but she refused to glance around and confirm the feeling.

At the door, she chirped in a loud, cheerful voice, "Good-bye now! Thanks for stopping by! I'll see you later!"

The look on his face communicated clearly he thought she'd lost her mind. But he didn't say anything. He just stepped out the door.

Angela pressed her forehead to the closed door for a moment, bringing her erratic breathing under control. And when she turned, her gaze collided with Ben's. Immediately her heart kicked into double time. She straightened her shoulders, flashed a smile, and wiggled her fingers at him in a ridiculous semblance of a wave. Then, with a deliberately bouncy step, she headed to the dishwashing area to check on Steve.

Ben's gaze nearly bore a hole through her back.

Ben checked the hourly schedule for the clients at the recycling center for the third time, and it still didn't make sense. Not because the schedule was wrong, but because his focus was somewhere else. He pushed the schedule aside and released a huff of annoyance. Rarely did he have trouble staying on track at work, even though his desk sat in the middle of the various centers, surrounded by activity and voices. So why today?

His gaze found Angela at the corner table with three other clients, instructing them in the skill of wrapping cloth napkins around silverware. The fluorescent lights glinting off her curls gave her an angelic appearance. A smile yearned for release, but he swallowed it. Another jolt of—something—struck him, and he forced his gaze to the desktop, his thoughts churning.

He had fought the urge all afternoon to corner Angela and ask about the man who had visited. As her supervisor, he had a right—technically speaking. Visitors were frowned upon during working hours. But, in her favor, she had used that brief visit as her afternoon break and had worked through the scheduled break, so he couldn't accuse her of taking advantage.

Still, who was the man? Her familiarity with him was obvious, the way she'd taken his arm and escorted him to a private area. The giggle he'd heard had created a knot in his gut. Angela hadn't mentioned a boyfriend. He shook his head. What difference did it make if she had a boyfriend? Was he jealous?

That question brought his gaze up to connect with hers once more. He'd made a determination to mentor Angela both at work and in her Christianity. It wasn't supposed to go deeper. Yet, somehow, in the course of seeing her every day at work and sitting with her in church, she'd managed to weasel into his heart.

He jerked backward, his chair springs complaining with the sudden movement, and shifted his gaze to the ceiling. *Lord, You're going to have to direct me here. Angela is a Christian, and I do find her attractive, but there are a lot of differences between us. What is Your will concerning our relationship?*

He didn't receive an instant answer to his simple prayer, but that didn't bother him. He'd learned over the years that God had His own timing. Ben could wait for his answer because he knew eventually it would come and it would be best for him. The bell hanging above the front door sent out its tinkling ring, bringing Ben from his chair. The bus driver for Steve and Doris had arrived.

He spent the next thirty minutes seeing clients out the door, bestowing hugs and high fives, and visiting with parents and caretakers about the progress being made by clients. This was one of Ben's favorite parts of his job—seeing a mother's face light up with pride in her adult child's accomplishments as she realized the child would be able to take a job, earn a wage, and function like any other contributing member of society. Ben loved his work, the opportunity to serve and bring positive changes into people's lives, and he felt the curiosity about Angela's mysterious visitor melt away as he went through the end-of-day routine.

But when the last client had gone and the employees were filtering out the door, Ben walked to the break area to retrieve his refillable soda cup and found Angela at the table, head low, shoulders slumped. Her dejected pose brought an immediate rush of concern.

Sliding into the seat beside her, he touched her arm. "Angela? You okay?"

She glanced at him. Tears glinted in the corners of her pale blue eyes, bringing out the deeper ring of gray blue around the irises. She shrugged. "Not really, but. . .I will be."

"Something happen with one of the clients? I can help you with that."

A shake of her head brought shimmering motion to her hair. "No. Nothing like that. The clients are great. I think we're learning to work well together."

Ben nodded. He agreed. He had seen subtle changes in Angela's behavior around the clients. She still had a ways to go to be completely at ease, but she wasn't shying away from them now; she also didn't seem as stilted as she had the first few days. He processed her answer. If she wasn't upset about something with one of the clients, there were only two other options.

Either he or her visitor had upset her.

"Have I done something to upset you?"

Her head jerked up, her startled gaze meeting his head-on. "Oh no! You've—you've been wonderful, Ben. So patient. . ." But the tears plumped and spilled down her cheeks.

He fought the urge to push his fingers through her hair and draw her to his chest in a hug. She looked as though she could use the comfort. But a hug would be well beyond the bounds between employer and employee, mentor and mentee. He linked his fingers and rested his hands on the tabletop. "Then what is it?"

She seemed to search his face, creating a tightness in his chest. Her lips parted, as if ready to share, but then she clamped her jaw shut, shifted her gaze, and swept the tears away. "Nothing."

Ben forced a soft chuckle. "Now, I learned from growing up with a sister that females can be a little erratic with their emotions, but not even my sister cried over nothing. Are you sure there isn't something wrong?"

Angela kept her gaze aimed forward, giving him a view of her sweet profile. The curve of her jaw, framed by the tumbling curls, became more appealing by the minute.

"I just have to go somewhere—with someone—and I'm a little nervous," she finally said.

Her voice was so soft Ben had to strain to hear her. An image of the man who'd shown up earlier filled Ben's head. He curled his fingers around Angela's arm and gave a gentle squeeze. "The visitor from today, is that the 'someone' you mean?"

She still wouldn't look at him, but she nodded.

Ben felt something rise from his gut. Not quite anger, but certainly a strong emotion. "Has he threatened you in some way?"

Again her gaze spun in his direction. Her wide eyes expressed shock. "No! Nothing like that!" Then she lowered her gaze again, twisting her fingers together in her lap. "There's no threat at all. Don't worry."

Her flat words did little to assure Ben. Yet he could see she wasn't going to share anything more. He still held her arm, and he moved his hand to the back of her chair. Her curls brushed his fingers. "Angela, would you like me to pray for you?"

The tears returned, filling her eyes and bringing a luminance to the unusual irises. She nodded. "But I have to go." Shooting from the chair, she snatched up her purse and zipped around the partition. Moments later, Ben heard the bell tinkle and the door close.

He remained at the table, questions spinning through his head. He had no idea what had upset Angela, but he decided it really wasn't important that he know. God knew, and that was enough. He'd offered to pray, and he would follow through on it. Lowering his head, he closed his eyes and shared his concerns with his heavenly Father.

# Chapter 6

Angela rapped her knuckles against the door leading to Aunt Eileen's apartment and groused to herself. *Twenty-three years old and having to be babysat! It is beyond embarrassing.* Yet the judge's terms of her probation were firm: For the duration of her sentence, she must be monitored by a responsible adult or be placed in a detention facility.

With her parents' decision to take a month-long cruise, Angela needed someplace to go. Neither of her older sisters expressed enthusiasm about her joining them, but Aunt Eileen had cheerfully agreed to having a lengthy visit. At least, she conceded as she raised her hand to knock a second time, Aunt Eileen was fun. If she had to be babysat, Aunt Eileen was top choice as sitter.

The door swung open, and Aunt Eileen greeted Angela with a boisterous hug. "Come in! Come in!" She pulled Angela through the door and gave it a push to close it. "Sorry I didn't get here sooner. I was cleaning the shower."

Angela grinned. A towel was slung around Aunt Eileen's neck, and a white smudge of some sort of cleaner decorated her left cheek. "You don't have to go to extra trouble for me."

Aunt Eileen waved a hand, shooing away Angela's words. "Nonsense! Old ladies clean. It's no extra trouble. Besides, I had to get all of Roscoe's hair out of there. He likes that rug in front of the sink for some reason." She chuckled and leaned down to scratch under the chin of the huge yellow and white cat at her feet.

"Well, okay then." Angela looked around the small living room. The apartment was so plain compared to her own home, yet she felt at ease here. Welcomed. She sighed, suddenly glad she'd come. "Where do you want me to put my stuff?"

Aunt Eileen took the suitcase from her hand. "In the second bedroom." She headed for the hallway, and Angela followed with Roscoe twisting around her ankles. Aunt Eileen continued. "I use it as a sewing room, but I borrowed a twin bed frame and mattress from someone at church. Nothing fancy, but it'll do in a pinch."

Angela stepped into the room. Aunt Eileen had draped the mattress with a multipatched quilt. The curtains were open, allowing in a shaft of sunlight, which highlighted the bright red and blue patches. She sat on the mattress and gave a little bounce while her gaze took in the sewing machine crunched in the corner beside a stack of plastic bins that overflowed with rolls of fabric and sewing notions. Something that appeared to be a half-finished quilt face lay across the end of the sewing machine table.

"Are you sure I won't be in your way in here? It looks like you're in the middle of something."

Aunt Eileen walked over and patted the bulky folds of fabric. "I am. But it'll keep. I can quilt anytime. But time with you? That's a precious commodity."

Mixed emotions mingled in her chest at her aunt's words. Not even her parents seemed to treasure time with her. She rose and gave Aunt Eileen another hug. "I love you, Aunt Eileen."

Aunt Eileen's chuckle sounded. "Aw, sweet girl, right back atcha. Now"—she set Angela aside—"I bet you've got more stuff to bring up, right?" Her eyes twinkled.

Angela laughed. How well Aunt Eileen knew her! "Well, a little, I guess."

Another chuckle let Angela know Aunt Eileen understood the meaning of "little" where any of Angela's family was concerned. "You can slide your empty suitcases under the bed, and I put some extra hangers in the closet for you. Sorry there's no dresser in here. Will that shelf do?"

Angela spotted the laminated, wood grain–printed shelf tucked at the foot of the bed. Spartan compared to her matching chest, mirrored dresser, and armoire in her bedroom at home. But she smiled and said, "Sure. It'll do fine."

Aunt Eileen crossed her arms, her brows coming down for a moment. "You'll have to go out to your car again anyway to get the rest of your things. Can I talk you into making a delivery on the way?"

"A delivery? Where?" Angela trailed Aunt Eileen to the kitchen where she withdrew a whipped topping container from the refrigerator.

Plunking the container into Angela's hands, she said, "Remember Alma? She hasn't been eating so well since she left the hospital. She says nothing tastes good. But she loves my pistachio pudding salad. I thought maybe this would entice her to eat."

Angela shook her head. "Aunt Eileen, why are you so nice and Mother is—?" She broke off, unwilling to insult her mother even if it was deserved.

Aunt Eileen smiled and gave Angela's hand a gentle pat. "Your mother is nice. She just has a different way of showing it."

Angela grimaced.

Aunt Eileen pulled her brows into a frown. "Think of all the good she does in the community. All the committees she heads up and organizes. Aren't those nice things?"

"Well. . ." Angela shrugged. "I suppose they are. But somehow it's not the same as doing little things, like sending pistachio salad to someone who doesn't want to eat."

A chuckle sounded. "Those people who benefit from the fund-raisers probably wouldn't agree with you."

Angela chose not to argue. She headed for the door. "I'll take this over; then I'll be right back."

Aunt Eileen laughed. "Oh no, you won't! If Alma gets you in that apartment, you'll be there for a while."

Angela grinned.

"But don't worry about it. There's nothing in your trunk that will spoil, is there?"

"Of course not."

"Good." Aunt Eileen gave a brusque nod. "Then just enjoy the visit. Spread a little sunshine. It'll do you good." She ushered Angela out the door.

Forty minutes later, Angela finally managed to work her way from Alma's kitchen to the front door. Her hand on the doorknob, she sent a big smile and offered a promise. "I'll be here a whole month. I'll come see you again, okay?"

Alma's face drooped. "Please do. I so seldom have visitors. . . ."

Angela followed an unfamiliar impulse and wrapped Alma in a warm hug. The spindly arms that clung back brought a rush of satisfaction through Angela's heart. It felt good to give. Really good. How she wished she'd learned that long ago.

Back in the hallway, she headed to the elevator, humming to herself. She pushed the DOWN button, and within seconds, the doors opened. Her tune ceased as her gaze fell on a young, bearded man in a wheelchair in the middle of the elevator.

"Oh!" She hesitated. "Is—is there room in there for me?"

The man grunted, but he pushed on the wheels of the chair, moving himself backward. Angela stepped past him to lean against the far wall. The doors slid shut, sealing them inside. The man's curious gaze fixed on her.

"Who. . .are you?" he asked. Although the words were somewhat garbled, Angela understood him.

She offered a smile. "I'm Angela."

"Why are. . .you. . .here?"

Her smile broadened. *Snoopy, isn't he?* "Oh, just visiting a friend."

"Who?" The word came out like a bark.

"Alma Andrews." Angela paused, tipping her head. "Do you know her?"

The slight nod gave his answer. The doors slid open, revealing the lobby. Angela gestured toward the opening, but he stuck out his jaw.

"Lad—ies first."

Angela's brows shot up in surprise. A snoop, but a gentleman nonetheless. With another smile, she edged past him then kept her hand on the door casing until he brought the wheelchair through. The man continued to eye her.

"You. . .go home. . .now?"

Angela wondered if he were trying to get rid of her. "No, actually I'm going to collect some things and head to my aunt's apartment. Eileen Cassidy. Do you know her, too?"

"Eileen is. . .my friend."

Somehow that didn't surprise Angela. "Well, then I'll probably see you again. I'm staying with Aunt Eileen for a while."

"Why?"

Angela decided that really was none of his business. But she smiled and said, "Just because." Standing beside his chair, she said, "Now I need to ask you a question. You know my name. What's yours?"

"K–ent."

"Kent. . ." Angela took an involuntary step backward. Ben's cousin. The one who suffered brain damage after a drug overdose. Sweat broke out all over her body. Swallowing, she forced her lips into another smile. "It's very nice to meet you."

He nodded. "I see you. . .later." Without another word, he caught the rubber of his wheels and gave a push, rolling in the direction of the lobby.

She stood for a long time, looking after him. Sympathy brought tears to her eyes. Despite the beard that covered the lower portion of his face and the dullness of his eyes, she could tell he was a handsome man. His arms showed evidence of strength, although his legs seemed thin beneath the loose denim of his jeans and his hands had appeared clumsy. To think he had been hale and healthy and that a foolish choice had wrought this permanent change.

Then another thought struck. Although initially uncertain, she had slipped into an easy conversation with him. Time with the clients at New Beginnings was obviously making a change in her heart. She hummed again as she headed for the outside doors. She hoped she'd see Kent again, and she'd be sure to give him a big hello when she did.

⁓ఁ

Ben balanced three boxes of Chinese takeout in one hand and pressed the HANDICAP button with the other. Pizza last week, Chinese this week. Both were favorites of Kent's, so Ben alternated between the two, throwing in the occasional deli sandwich. The doors to Tower Four opened, inviting his entry, and he shifted the items into both hands as he passed through.

He headed toward the elevators, but a tinkling laugh caught his attention. Shifting his gaze to the lobby, he spotted the unmistakable curly auburn hair of Angela Fischer. And next to her, in his wheelchair, sat none other than his cousin Kent.

Kent sniffed the air. He shifted in his chair, searching, and his face broke into a huge smile. "Ben! My. . .friend!"

Ben moved on shaky legs toward the pair. "Hey, Kent." His gaze met Angela's. Her cheeks sported a pink blush. "Angela."

"Hi, Ben." She rose, her fingers linking in a now-familiar gesture of uncer tainty. "I see you brought supper. Kent said you would."

Ben's gaze bounced between the pair. "Yeah. It's our Friday routine."

"That's what he said." With a light giggle, she added, "And here I though you were this great cook. But you only bring Kent takeout." She nudged Kent shoulder. "Is that because you're afraid he'll try to poison you?"

Kent's raucous laughter filled the room.

Uncertain how much longer his rubbery legs would hold him up, Ben move to the sofa and leaned against the back. Angela. . .and Kent. . .chatting. Teasing At ease. He'd been so afraid of letting her meet his cousin, yet it appeared the were very comfortable with one another. The wonder of the moment was mor than Ben could comprehend.

She pointed to the cartons in his hands. "At least it looks like you brough something good."

"Chinese," Ben contributed, then felt like an idiot. Of course it was Chines What else would go into these little white boxes with the red squiggle on th side?

Angela's smile swung in Kent's direction. "What's your favorite Chines food?"

"Beef. . .and broc. . .broc. . ." Kent made a horrible face then spat, "Broc'li!"

Angela laughed softly and gave Kent's arm a pat. "Wonderful choice. Yo get your protein and your vegetable that way."

Kent beamed while Ben stared in amazement. Angela—teasing with Kent. H hadn't realized how much she had changed in her brief weeks at New Beginnings.

"Well." Angela stepped around the sofa. "I'll go and let you two eat. I'll se you later, okay, Kent?"

Kent nodded his shaggy head, his eyes glowing. "I. . .see you later. . .An–ge–la."

"Bye, Ben." And she slipped out the door.

Ben stared after her, the cartons in his hands nearly forgotten.

"Ben."

Ben shook his head, trying to pull his scattered thoughts together. Angel was visiting with Kent like she'd visit with. . .anybody. He wished she'd stuc around a little longer and visited with him.

"Ben!"

The sharp note of frustration in his cousin's voice finally caught Ben's fu attention. He turned to Kent. "Yeah?"

Kent pointed at the cartons. "I am. . .hun–gry."

"Yeah. Okay." Ben straightened and adjusted his hands for a better grip Walking alongside Kent's wheelchair as they headed for the elevators, he said "How long have you known Angela?"

Kent's shoulders raised in a brief shrug.

"But she's your friend, huh?"

Kent's smile turned knowing. "An–ge–la. . .is pretty."

Ben swallowed. "Yeah. . ."

"She is my. . .girl–friend."

Ben felt as though a rock fell from his chest to his stomach. Apparently Angela had been too at ease with Kent. Remembering times when he'd witnessed her flirtatious behavior, he wondered if she'd exercised some of that with Kent. If so, Kent wouldn't understand Angela was only playing.

He had a big problem on his hands, and it wasn't juggling Chinese food cartons.

# Chapter 7

Ben awakened early Saturday with a headache. He knew he wasn't sick—unless it was sick with worry. Pictures of Angela with Kent had tormented his dreams, and he knew he wouldn't be able to rest until he'd settled the issue of Kent referring to Angela as his girlfriend.

He threw back his sheets and headed for the kitchen, planning his morning. She was staying at Elmwood Towers with her aunt. After breakfast, he'd drive over and talk to her, make her understand she had to be careful where Kent was concerned. Sure, he wanted her to be relaxed and open around those with handicaps, but flirting with them was a completely different thing. The clients had to learn boundaries for behavior. Apparently Angela needed the same lesson.

He ate his scrambled eggs and toast as slowly as possible and extended his shower. No sense in arriving at the Cassidy apartment too early. Angela probably slept in on Saturday mornings. After the shower, he read the newspaper and even watched a few cartoons before deciding it was late enough to go.

Dressed in a pair of khaki shorts and a solid blue polo shirt—a step up from his normal summer's day-off attire of athletic shorts and T-shirt—he drove across town. He found a parking spot in the visitors' area and walked briskly through the courtyard to Tower Three. The air-conditioned lobby felt good after his brief walk in the Kansas summer heat. Crossing to the panel of intercom buttons, he located the one for the Cassidy apartment and buzzed. After only a few seconds, a crackly voice came through the speaker.

"This is Eileen."

He leaned forward and spoke into the microphone. "Eileen, this is Ben. I wondered if I could visit with Angela."

"Just a minute."

The *thwip* indicated the intercom flipped off. Minutes passed while he stood beside the row of buttons, alternately adjusting his collar and tugging the legs of his cargo shorts. *Maybe I should have run an iron over the twill. . . .*

"Ben?"

He'd expected a voice from the intercom, not from behind him. He spun around, banging his elbow on the wall.

"Whoops." A smile teased the corners of Angela's lips. "Sorry. I didn't mean to startle you."

"No problem." He rubbed his elbow and took a step toward her. She'd done something different with her hair—pulled it up in a rubber band where it spilled out like a fountain of shining curls on the top of her head. He liked it. "I didn't expect you to come down. I could've come up."

Her smile grew. "No, you couldn't. Aunt Eileen is mopping floors, and she didn't want you to see her in her mopping clothes."

"Oh, okay. And you aren't helping?"

Angela sighed. "She won't let me. She says guests aren't supposed to clean."

"Yeah, Eileen can be pretty stubborn."

"I'll say!"

His gaze flicked over her outfit. Although less dressy than what she wore to work each day, she still looked nice in the flowered skirt that fell just above the knee and bright yellow tank top. Not something one would wear to mop floors, he supposed.

"What did you need?" She brought him back to the task at hand.

He drew in a breath. "Let's go sit down, huh?"

A brief, puzzled scowl creased her forehead, but she turned toward the seating arrangement in the large lobby. Her jeweled flip-flops softly smacked her heels as she walked in front of him. She sat at one end of the sofa, and Ben chose the other end.

Facing her, he said, "I wanted to talk to you about Kent."

She settled in the corner and tucked her feet beside her. Her elbow on the back of the sofa, she rested her cheek against her fist. "What about him?"

"Well. . ." Ben scratched his head. "He said something kind of—worrisome—after you left yesterday evening. I wondered if you could shed any light on it."

Her shoulder lifted in a graceful shrug. "What did he say?"

"That you were his girlfriend."

She flashed a smile that lit her eyes. "Oh, that's really sweet."

Sweet? Ben frowned. "To be honest, Angela, it concerns me."

"Why should it?"

Could she really not understand the problem here? Surely she hadn't deliberately set out to mislead Kent. "Did you do something to give him the idea you would be his girlfriend?"

She sat upright, planting her fist against the sofa cushion between them. "What do you mean, did I 'do' something?"

The defensiveness took Ben by surprise. "There's no need to get angry. But you have to understand, while Kent's muscles and mind don't necessarily work like any typical male, his feelings are very much 'normal.'"

"I'm aware of that."

Her words snapped out on a harsh note Ben hadn't heard from her before. His own tone took a firmer quality. "Look, Angela, you can't—"

"I can't what? Talk to him? Be friends with him?"

Ben took a deep breath. This wasn't going very well. "You have to be careful. Kent's been hurt—a lot. Rejection is hard on him. If he thinks you're his girlfriend when you're really only—"

"Leading him on?" She leaned forward, her face inches from his, and nearly snarled. "That's what you think, isn't it?"

Ben hoped his face wasn't as red as it felt. "Well, I—"

Flopping back into the corner of the couch, she flipped her hands outward. "Great, just great. I work so hard at getting over my apprehensions about being around the handicapped, and the first time I feel truly comfortable with someone, I get accused of being a tease."

Ben listened, but he got the impression she was talking to herself more than to him.

Before he could say anything, she swung around to face him again.

"If you want the truth, Ben, I do like Kent. I think he's a pretty nice guy. Great sense of humor, and I can tell he tries hard to do the best he can with what he's got to work with. I admire that. But as for being his girlfriend, no, I didn't tell him I'd be his girlfriend, and I didn't flirt with him. I'm sorry if he got that impression, and I'll try to kindly set him straight when I see him next."

She pointed a finger at his chest. "Because I will see him again. I consider him a friend, and more than that, he reminds me that 'there but for the grace of God, go I.'"

Ben crunched his brows downward. "What do you mean by that?"

Her face flooded with pink, and she shot to her feet. "Never mind. You just remember what else I said. I'm going to be friends with Kent, and you can't stop me!"

Ben sat in openmouthed silence as she thundered to the elevators, her flip-flops smacking the tiled floor. She jabbed the elevator button, stood with crossed arms while staring at the silver doors, and then shot through the opening without a backward glance.

⁓

Angela stomped down the hallway that led to Aunt Eileen's apartment. Who did he think he was, accusing her of leading Kent on? Wasn't he the one who'd put in her evaluation that she needed to loosen up around the clients, to be more natural? Well, what had she done? She'd loosened up, treated Kent like she would any other male she encountered on the street, and now that was wrong, too!

Banging through the apartment door, she bellowed, "I'm back!" She gave the door a slam that probably echoed throughout the entire building.

Roscoe zipped out from under the end table and dashed down the hallway, yellow fur on end and tail puffed to twice its normal size.

Aunt Eileen appeared in the doorway between the kitchen and living room. The knot on the scarf she'd tied around her head stuck straight up like a bow.

Beneath the scarf, her wrinkled face crunched in worry. "Angela, what's with the fireworks?"

Angela stormed from one end of the living room to the other, fists raised, emitting growls of frustration. Aunt Eileen captured her on the second pass and pushed her into the recliner. When she would have jumped to her feet, Aunt Eileen stood in front of her and crossed her arms, feet widespread.

"Uh-uh. Sit."

The firm look on her aunt's face held her in the chair. She slumped back, popped up the footrest, and crossed her ankles. "Fine. I'll sit."

Aunt Eileen gave her one more puzzled scowl before sitting on the arm of the couch. "All right. Spill it."

Angela huffed. "That. . .Ben!"

A smirk twisted Aunt Eileen's lips. "Oh."

Angela huffed louder. "No, not 'oh.' At least not like you said it." Kicking the footrest down, she sat up, put her elbows on her knees, and covered her face. "Why can't I ever do things right?"

"Wait a minute. Back up." Aunt Eileen grabbed one of Angela's hands and pulled it down. "What didn't you do right?"

A grunt of frustration found its way from Angela's chest. "Might be easier to make a list of what I have done right. It would take me all of—oh, three seconds—to name it off." She jabbed one finger in the air. "Coming here while Mom and Dad are away—that's about all I can think of that I've done right."

Although she'd promised to sit, she bounced to her feet again. "But done wrong? Oh boy, can I list those! Hosted all those parties with the sole intention of rattling Dad's cage so he'd pay some attention to me. Ended up with guests who liked using stuff the policemen frown about." She thumped her own forehead with the butt of her hand. "Used the stuff myself. Duh! What is that—three things not done right?"

She began ticking off offenses on her fingers. "Then there's not only using but getting caught, getting sent to rehab, getting sent to community service at a place where I have to relate to people who are completely different than me—and doing it very badly."

"Hold up there." Aunt Eileen remained perched, her gaze pinned to Angela's face. "Why do you think you've done badly? Philip says you're working well there."

Angela stared at her aunt. "He said that?"

Aunt Eileen nodded, the knot on her head bobbing. "Yes, he did. He's pleased with your progress."

"Huh!" Angela thought about that for a moment, but then Ben's evaluation ran through her mind, bringing another scowl. "Well, according to Ben—who is my direct supervisor—I'm not doing things right." Once more, she began to pace.

Aunt Eileen reached out and grabbed her hand, bringing her to a halt.

"Sweet girl, sit down. Please."

With a long sigh, Angela sank back into the recliner.

"Now." Aunt Eileen slid from the armrest to the couch seat. "Tell me exactly what happened downstairs with Ben. You weren't down there more than five minutes. He couldn't have possibly picked you apart in that short amount of time."

Oh, Angela only wished that statement weren't true. She felt tears gather in her eyes, and she blinked rapidly to control them. "Ben told me Kent said I was his girlfriend."

Aunt Eileen smiled, giving a wink and a nod. "Ah, I can see why Kent would want that. You're a very pretty girl."

Angela brushed the comment aside. She didn't feel pretty right now. "He didn't seem happy about it. He asked me what I was doing with Kent—like I'd been flirting with him." She pressed her palms to her chest. "I know I've been a flirt in the past, Aunt Eileen. I did a lot of things that weren't right before I became a Christian, but I'm trying so hard to change, to let people know Jesus is in my heart now."

"Of course you are." Aunt Eileen patted Angela's arm. "I've seen it."

She lowered her hands to her lap, twisting her fingers together. "I thought Ben knew it, that he saw it, but I guess not. I just want to be friends with Kent. I'd like to be friends with Ben, but I don't think he really trusts me. All he sees is this dumb woman who can't relax around people with handicaps. And I just don't see the point of trying if all I'm going to do is fail!"

Her voice fell silent, and Aunt Eileen remained quiet, too, her lips puckered in a thoughtful expression. Roscoe peeked from the hallway, his tail twitching, then made three running leaps to land beside Aunt Eileen's hip. He coiled into a ball and began to purr, his motor a soothing sound.

Angela sighed, her emotions spent. "Aunt Eileen, I'm so. . .alone. Mom and Dad are never around. My sisters. . . They've got their own lives. I'm staying away from my old friends so I don't get myself into trouble, but I really miss them. I miss the fun we used to have. Well, some of the fun. And what scares me is—when Ben accused me of coming on to Kent, I realized the old Angela is still hiding somewhere inside. What if she comes back? What if the need for friendship and fun takes me right back to where I was before?"

"That *won't* happen."

Angela laughed. Her aunt's adamant retort was encouraging, but she wasn't sure it was realistic. "How can you be sure?"

"Because you aren't the way you were before." Aunt Eileen leaned over the armrest of the sofa to clasp Angela's hand. "When you asked Jesus into your heart, He washed you clean. He made you holy. Now you just have to walk like you believe it."

"You mean, I should always be holy? I should never make mistakes?" Angela's heart gave a nervous double beat with that idea. If she were supposed to be free of mistakes, she had a long way to go.

"Now, I didn't say that. Unfortunately, we're humans, and humans aren't perfect." Aunt Eileen paused, her forehead creased in thought. "No, what I mean is, you shouldn't spend your time worrying about what mistakes you might make. You should concentrate on two things. First, you aren't alone anymore. The Holy Spirit is with you, helping you be strong when you feel weak. When you're tempted, you just ask for help, and help will come. The Bible says we'll never be tested beyond our ability to resist. So remember that.

"And second, you've got me. I know I'm no young hipster, and it's not the same as having friends your age to hang up on—"

Angela burst out laughing. "Hang out with, Aunt Eileen!"

The older woman gave a tug on Angela's hand. "All right, all right, so I don't even know the terminology. But I'm here. I love you, and anytime you need something, you can come to me."

Angela thought her heart might melt. The tears returned. "Oh, Aunt Eileen, thank you. I love you, too."

"But just keep this in mind." Aunt Eileen's voice took on a stern undertone. "You don't have to depend on me. If there's a lesson I've learned well over the years, it's that there is One who will never abandon me, never turn a deaf ear, never refuse me comfort, and He's Jesus. Lean on Him, sweet girl, and you'll be fine."

Angela laid her head against the backrest of the old recliner and sighed. "How did you learn all this, Aunt Eileen? How do I get to be as—as comfortable with Jesus as you are?"

A smile lit her aunt's eyes. "Why, same way as with any relationship. Time. Think about your first days at New Beginnings. It was awkward, wasn't it?"

Angela nodded. She had been certain she wouldn't last ten minutes, let alone ten months.

"But what happened?" Aunt Eileen smiled, offering a wink. "You got to know the clients. You formed a relationship with them. And then the awkwardness slowly went away. That's the way it is with Jesus, too. You gotta talk to Him—get to know Him."

Angela nodded, nibbling her lower lip. Prayer. . . Carrie had said that, too. Reading the Bible every day and praying were important things for growing in the Christian walk.

She stood. "Aunt Eileen, I'm going to my room now. I–I'm going to do a little talking with Jesus."

# Chapter 8

Angela rose from her knees at the side of the little bed in her temporary bedroom. Sitting on the edge of the mattress, she released a contented sigh. Aunt Eileen was right—talking to Jesus did make a person feel better. She raised her gaze to the ceiling and added a quick postscript. "I'll talk with You again soon. Count on it."

She rustled around in the half-unpacked suitcase at the end of the bed and located a pad of paper and pen. A list. . . While praying, she'd gotten the idea of forming a list of Christian friends who could be a support to her. She knew she shouldn't spend time with her old crowd. That could prove to be unwholesome. But somehow she needed to replace those relationships. Replacing them with Christian people seemed a wise thing to do.

Flipping the pad open, she wrote CHRISTIAN SUPPORT SYSTEM at the top of the page then began plugging in names. Aunt Eileen's name came first, followed by Carrie and her husband, Rocky. Her boss, Philip, came next. And then her hand paused, the pen nib against the paper. Should she include Ben? He was a Christian, and he'd been a support up until that morning when he'd frustrated her so badly.

Her reaction to him replayed in her mind, and remorse struck. She shouldn't have barked at him like she had. Even if she were angry, she should have kept a rein on her tongue. She knew she hadn't spoken in a way pleasing to God.

Releasing a deep sigh, she contemplated digging her cell phone from her purse and calling him to apologize. Experiences from her past stung her memory. Some of what Ben intimated—her penchant for flirting—was accurate. She'd done so many foolish things. The inability to change them now brought a rush of frustration. Would she pay forever for the mistakes of her past? Although the desire to apologize was strong, the desire to protect herself from further condemnation won out. She didn't reach for her phone.

But she did add Ben's name to her list. At the bottom.

Ben leaned back in his chair and bit down on the inside of his cheeks to keep from laughing. Angela and three clients sorted a stack of clean recyclables, and the confusion of the activity was enough to make a grown man cry. Yet there she was, with her shining head of hair all tousled, directing the chaos as well as a traffic cop directed the noon rush.

"Now, Pete, plastic goes in the middle bin. See? This says PLASTIC. Ketchup bottles are plastic. Yes, I know there's a picture of a tomato on the front just like the one on that can, but see? We have to look at what's under the picture. This is tin." She clinked her fingernail against the can. "And this is plastic." Thunking a finger against the bottle, she demonstrated the differences in the materials. "Do you understand? Now hold up, Jannie, we're not going to start a band here!"

Ben could barely contain his laughter as each of the clients chose an item or two from the bins to *clink* and *thud*. Angela's sweet laughter rang over the top of the noise. Finally she managed to convince everyone to put the "instruments" away and return to sorting. Her smile covered any hint of reprimand, and the clients each giggled, delivering friendly pats on Angela's back to show their willingness to cooperate.

Ben shook his head. How far she'd come. . . . Based on his observations of her first couple of weeks, he would never have imagined her ever settling in. Yet she had, and he realized it was largely due to her commitment to emulate Jesus. He'd observed her attentiveness in church and Sunday school, and her focus during her Bible reading on her break was nearly impenetrable.

Although they hadn't spoken to one another except in passing since his visit to Elmwood Towers almost a week ago, he had continued to pray for her daily. Lifting her in prayer helped him feel connected to her even if she had pulled away.

The bell at the front door tinkled, announcing someone's entrance. Ben shifted his gaze to the door and spotted the center's owner, Philip Wilder, striding through. Philip paused beside the sorting table and visited with Angela for a moment. The beaming smile she aimed at him made Ben's heart lurch. He'd missed having that smile turned in his direction.

Philip laughed at something, gave Angela's arm a quick squeeze, and then walked to Ben's desk. Leaning against the desk's edge, he used his head to gesture toward the sorting table. "They're having fun over there, aren't they?"

Ben watched for another few seconds—long enough to see Pete try to put an empty butter tub on Angela's head for a hat and Angela return the favor—before answering Philip. "Oh, yeah, but I think in the midst of their fun, they're figuring out what needs to be done."

Philip nodded, chuckling, his gaze on the group. "Yes. I'm glad now I followed Carrie's recommendation. Angela's placement is working out better than I had anticipated."

Ben sent Philip a sharp look. "Placement? What do you mean by that?"

Philip gave a start. He jerked his gaze in Ben's direction, and he pulled his lips into a grimace. "It doesn't matter." He turned away, seeming to concentrate on the group at the recycling table.

Curiosity got the best of Ben. He stood and rounded the desk to stand next to Philip. "No, really. What did you mean by "placement"? Our clients go into different placements, not our workers. Are you starting something new?"

Philip blew out a breath. "Ben, really, it's not important."

"It is to me." Ben folded his arms across his chest and looked into Philip's face, even though the other man kept his gaze averted. "If we're starting some sort of new program, training people to work with the handicapped population, I'd like to know that. It will make a difference in how I evaluate their performances."

Finally Philip faced Ben. "You won't need to change how you evaluate performances. We aren't turning into a training center for anyone other than the people with disabilities. I said 'placement' for Angela because she technically isn't a hired employee."

Ben's eyebrows rose. "Isn't hired? You mean, she's unpaid—a volunteer?" His heart gave a lurch. If she were volunteering here, he'd been entirely too hard on her. He owed her a thank-you for her service, not criticism.

But Philip shook his head. "Not a volunteer. She's here as. . .community service."

Ben's jaw dropped. Community service? A judge would make that determination, which meant Angela had broken some kind of law. He glanced quickly at Angela. She handed a cereal box to Jannie then nodded in approval when the other woman dropped it in the appropriate bin. She'd broken the law? He felt his stomach clench.

"What did she do?"

"That, my friend, is confidential." Philip put his hand on Ben's shoulder. "Look, Ben, I wasn't even supposed to let you know her employment here is temporary and court-dictated. I'd appreciate it if you would keep it to yourself. It could alter her relationships with the other employees as well as the clients."

"But is it safe to have her here?" Ben hated himself for asking the question, yet he couldn't seem to stop himself.

Philip released a low chuckle. "If it weren't, she wouldn't be here." He pushed off from the desk. "Frankly, I think it's done Angela a world of good to be part of the staff at New Beginnings. It's given her a 'new beginning' of sorts, too. As I said earlier, it's worked out better than I'd hoped. I call it a God thing."

Ben wasn't so sure about that, but he wouldn't argue with his boss. He nodded, but the thought tormented him the rest of the afternoon. Angela had broken the law and been given a sentence of community service. *What secret is she hiding?*

───

"Pizza again!" Ben announced as he entered Kent's apartment for their standard Friday night get-together.

Kent's eyes lit up. He sniffed the air like a bloodhound. "Pep–peron–i and pep–pers?"

Ben laughed. "You know your pizza. Yep. Added peppers this time." He carried the box to the living room and dropped it on the low table beside the couch. "Want to eat in front of the TV?"

Kent nodded and pushed the chair to the end of the table. With a low grunt, he managed to lean forward far enough to get hold of the remote control. Aiming the black box at the television, he pushed buttons until he located a baseball game. He crowed with excitement. "Home run!"

Ben headed to the kitchen to retrieve paper towels and get a grip on his emotions. Sorrow pressed his chest at Kent's elation at watching the sport he'd once loved to play. Kent had been the champion home run hitter on their junior high baseball team. His mother had taken down the trophy from the shelf in the family room, but Ben knew it was hidden somewhere in the house. He should ask for it, bring it over, and put it on top of the television. Kent might enjoy having it.

He handed a wad of paper towels to his cousin then sank down on the sofa. Although Kent was already munching, he lowered his head and offered a brief prayer of thanks before picking up a piece of pizza. He got as caught up in the game as Kent, cheering for the pitcher and booing when the ump made a poor call. At one point, the camera zoomed in on the scoreboard where, for a few seconds, the score disappeared and was replaced with the image of a pair of spectators—two women wearing baseball caps and waving banners.

Ben whistled and poked Kent with his elbow. "Hey, some pretty girls, huh? What do you think, Kent?"

Kent shook his head, scowling. "An–ge–la is. . .pretty." He grinned. "She. . .is my. . .girlfriend. She visits. . .me."

Ben fought the wave of worry that welled up. Keeping an intentionally light tone, he said, "Oh yeah? When does she visit you?"

"Work. Home from. . .work." Kent chomped down on another bite of pizza. "I see her. . .in lobby."

The worry from earlier in the day magnified with this new information. Apparently she hadn't heeded his warning about Kent's misinterpretation of her intentions. Remembering how she'd spouted her intent to be friends with Kent, he felt his ire grow. *Stubborn woman! Can't she listen to reason?* And now that he knew she'd been found guilty of a crime that warranted community service as a punishment, he was even more concerned about Kent spending time with her.

Since Angela hadn't made Kent understand a relationship beyond friendship wasn't possible, he was left with the difficult task of crushing his cousin. He took a deep breath, prayed for the right words, and tapped Kent's arm.

"Hey, Kent?"

Kent pulled his gaze away from the television and offered a little grunt at the interruption of the game.

"I have to tell you something. . .about Angela."

"An–ge–la?" The expectant look in his cousin's eyes took Ben back fifteen years to seventh grade and the first all-school party. Kent had had a crush on Macie Warren, and he'd sent Ben over to see if she'd go with him to the party. Macie said no, and Ben had been faced with telling Kent the bad news. He could still see the eager hope in Kent's eyes as he'd walked back from the giggling group of girls.

He swallowed. It was just as hard today as it had been back then. "You see, Kent, Angela is a real nice girl, but. . ." He took in another fortifying breath. "She really isn't your girlfriend, is she?"

Kent began rocking in his wheelchair, his face tightening into a scowl.

Ben grabbed his arm to make him sit still.

Kent jerked loose, his scowl deepening. "An–ge–la is. . .my. . .girlfriend," he spat the words.

Ben shook his head. "Your friend, Kent. Your friend, but not your girlfriend."

Swinging his hand, Kent whacked the pizza box from the table. The remaining two pieces flew to the floor, one upside down. "You go!"

The anger tore at Ben's heart. "Listen, Kent, I'm not trying to upset you, but—"

"Go! Go! Go!" Kent repeated the word at top volume, his face red, until his voice sounded hoarse.

Someone knocked on the door, and it swung open before Ben could get up. Kent's resident caretaker rushed into the room. She seemed surprised to see Ben sitting on the couch. "What's going on?"

"Go!" Kent yelled again, pointing a finger at Ben.

The caretaker crouched beside Kent's wheelchair. "Kent, I'll take Ben outside. You calm down, okay? When he's outside, will you be all right?"

Kent nodded his head, his hair flopping. "Ben. . .go!"

The woman stood and grabbed Ben's arm to escort him to the hallway. After closing the door, she said, "What happened in there? I haven't seen Kent that upset in ages!"

Ben hung his head. "I told him something he didn't want to hear." His heart ached. His cousin's fury spoke so clearly of the pain Ben had caused.

"Was it necessary to tell him?"

Ben nodded. "Yeah. I really believe it was."

"Well, from past experience, I know it won't take him long to calm down if we give him some space." She sighed, looking toward the closed door. "I'll stay here and listen. If it sounds as if he's tearing the place apart, I'll go right in. Otherwise, I'll give him ten minutes or so then help clean up the mess he made."

"Okay. Thanks for your help." Ben shoved his hands into his pants pockets.

"Do you mind telling me what you said to get him so upset? I might be able to smooth the waters for you."

"This woman who's staying in Tower Three has given him the idea that she's his girlfriend, and—"

"You mean Angela?"

Ben frowned. "You know her?" Just how often had Angela come around?

The caretaker nodded. "Yes. She's great with Kent. She gets him talking, and they've taken long walks all over the grounds in the evenings. I've never seen her be anything but appropriate with him, though."

Ben stood for a moment, uncertain whether or not to believe her. Maybe he'd misjudged Angela. But there was still the issue of community service. Even if she hadn't been deliberately misleading with Kent, he had big concerns about the reason for her sentence.

"That may be," he finally said, choosing his words carefully, "but somehow Kent's gotten the idea there's more than friendship between them. It needs to be nipped now before he really gets hurt."

"You might be right on that." The caretaker sighed. "As much as I hate to get in the middle of friendships, part of my job is to protect Kent. I'll see if I can keep some distance between the two of them. At least until we can get Kent's feelings sorted out."

Ben heaved a sigh of relief. "Thank you."

The caretaker patted his arm. "Go on home, Ben. It sounds like Kent has settled down. I'll go in and sit with him for a while."

"Okay. Thanks again." Ben waited until the caretaker went into Kent's apartment before heading to the elevators. Riding down alone, his thoughts turned once more to Angela. The caretaker's description of her time with Kent made him regret his subtle accusation, yet at the same time, he still felt uncertain whether or not to trust her with his cousin.

The elevator doors opened to the lobby, and he headed to the doors leading outside, his mind running for ways to prove or disprove Angela's suitability to be with Kent. He'd tried twice to talk to Angela about her life before starting work at New Beginnings. Both times she'd sidestepped his questions and turned the conversation elsewhere. There were many unanswered questions hovering in Ben's mind.

For the sake of Kent's protection, he had to know what Angela had done to warrant a sentence of community service. He needed one-on-one time with her if he intended to uncover her secrets. He slipped behind the wheel of his truck, a decision made. Tomorrow after church, he'd invite her to lunch. Just the two of them.

By the time Sunday afternoon arrived, he'd have his answers. No matter what it took.

# Chapter 9

Ben trotted across the parking area to catch Angela before she climbed behind the wheel of the silver rocket. Amazing how fast she could move through the muggy August heat on those high-heeled strappy shoes.

"Whew, I caught you!" He came to a halt beside the driver's door and grabbed the frame before she could pull it closed.

"Did you need something?"

The apprehension in her gaze troubled him, but he pushed the feeling aside. "Yeah. I wondered if you had lunch plans."

She shrugged. "Not really. Why?"

"Want to go somewhere?" He shrugged, too, feeling as tongue-tied as a nervous teenager. "Grab a bite with me?"

She looked at him for a long time, her expression puzzled, while he squirmed under the silent perusal. Finally she sighed. "I should probably call Aunt Eileen and make sure it's okay."

He waved a hand. "That's fine. I'll wait." He turned his back and pretended not to listen to the one-sided conversation.

"Aunt Eileen? Hi, I just wondered if it would be okay if I didn't come back to the apartment for lunch.... I'm not sure. Ben asked if I'd like to get something with him. No, it probably won't be too late." She laughed softly, causing fresh sweat to break out under his arms. Why did he wish she'd use that soft tone with him? "Sure, I can be quiet when I come in. I know you and Roscoe like your Sunday afternoon nap. Okay, see you soon. Bye."

He turned around in time to see her snap the phone closed, smiling to herself. When she looked up and met his gaze, her smile faded. "Where did you want to go?"

The need to bring the smile back hit him hard. He reminded himself of the purpose of this lunch. "I like that little submarine shop on Fourth and Main. Have you been there?" He knew it wasn't fancy, but the high backs on the booths provided a small measure of privacy. And they had a mean cherry cheesecake—perfect comfort food.

She shrugged again, the curls that fell across her shoulders bouncing with the movement. "That's fine. I'll meet you there." Without another word, she closed her door and started the engine.

He stepped back to allow her passage then jogged to his truck. He chuckled to himself as he turned the key in the ignition. If she drove as quickly as she walked, she'd be there long before he was. Fortunately he was able to pass a vehicle and fall in behind her. They pulled between slanting white lines and got out at the same time.

He double-stepped past her to open the door to the sub shop. The sweet rush of air-conditioning carried a yeasty smell that made Ben's stomach writhe in desire. He noticed Angela draw in a deep breath, too.

They placed their orders at the serving counter, and then he carried their tray of sandwiches, chips, and drinks to a booth tucked in the corner. The sun glared on the large plate-glass window, but the vent overhead whirred, promising to keep them cool.

Ben waited until Angela slid in on one side, tucking her skirt underneath her in a feminine manner. He put the tray down and sat across from her, careful to keep his big feet well back. Once he was settled, he said, "Would you like me to pray?"

She nodded in reply, and he closed his eyes and offered a short blessing. He handed her the paper-wrapped sandwich marked TURKEY/PROVOLONE and took the one with ROAST BEEF/CHEDDAR written on the wrapper. They each opened a small bag of chips and began munching.

After allowing her time to take a few bites, Ben rested his elbows on the edge of the table and said, "So have you lived in Petersburg your whole life?"

Angela blotted her lips with her napkin. "Yes, I was born here." She took another bite.

"Is it a good place to grow up?"

She swallowed, blotted again, and answered, "I suppose. I don't have anything to compare it with. Where did you grow up?"

"A half hour south of here, in Liberal."

"What brought you to Petersburg?"

Ben realized he was getting sidetracked. Again. His intention was to find out about Angela, not for Angela to find out about him. But he couldn't be rude and not answer. He gave her the shortened version. "A job and Elmwood Towers."

At her confused look, he laughed and expanded the information. "I heard about the assisted-living apartments at Elmwood Towers and applied for Kent to move into one. When I helped him move in, I met your aunt Eileen, who told me Philip Wilder was looking for a new manager since she'd given up the position to be a resident caretaker at the Towers." He shrugged. "It was just the kind of job I wanted, and my degree in social services qualified me. God worked it all out."

She nodded slowly.

"Do you have a college degree?"

Her face pinched as though the question pained her, and she set her sandwich down, smoothing the paper wrapper flat against the table. "Yes, I do. But isn't in social services." She didn't offer further explanation.

Ben headed in another direction, one he was certain would open up the door to understanding. "I haven't seen your friend for a while."

She tipped her head. "Friend?"

"Yeah. The man who visited you a couple of weeks ago. . . I didn't catch his name."

Immediately she lowered her gaze, tucking her lower lip between her teeth. He knew he'd hit upon a tender spot.

"Is your relationship with him. . .significant?" His heart pounded while he waited for a response. But he assured himself the thudding evidenced the depth of his curiosity, nothing more.

Without looking up, she said, "Significant but short-term."

The cryptic reply only increased his interest in the subject. He forced a light chuckle. "You know that already, huh?"

She flashed a quick look at him. "Yes. I know that." Sighing, she pushed her food away and raised her chin to meet his gaze directly. "Ben, what's your motive for inviting me here?"

He felt heat climb his neck. If he answered honestly, she'd no doubt run out the door. But he couldn't lie to her and say he had no reason. Words wouldn't form on his tongue. He sat in tense silence, feeling trapped beneath her gaze.

After several long seconds, she released another, regret-filled sigh. "I know what you're trying to get me to tell you. And to be perfectly honest, I'm tired of sneaking around. You want the truth, Ben? Here it is. . . ."

⁓

Angela saw Ben's shoulders stiffen, and it furthered her belief that he'd simply been sitting there, information tucked neatly away, waiting for her to confirm what he already knew. *Okay, Lord, here I go. . . .*

She continued, deliberately keeping her gaze fixed on Ben's penetrating blue eyes. "That man who came to see me isn't a boyfriend. He isn't even a friend. He's my court-appointed probation officer. He came that day to administer a random drug test. I will have at least three more of them before my sentence is up. I have to submit to them because I was convicted of illegal drug use."

Ben's eyebrows shot so high they almost became part of his short-cropped hairline. He did a good job of looking surprised; she'd give him that.

"I was given a one-year sentence, part of which was a requirement to go to a rehabilitation center. I've been through drug rehab, but I have to serve ten months of community service. I'm doing that at New Beginnings." Her mouth felt dry. She lifted her soda cup and took a drink. Ben remained silent, his face unreadable, as she continued.

"You want more truth? My life was hardly lily-white before I got caught. I've done a lot of stupid things, starting in high school. Drinking, skipping school, and—as you've already figured out—enjoying the company of men."

Ben's neck blotched red, and she felt her own face flood with fire as she recognized his interpretation of her confession. She leaned forward. "I never did anything. I wasn't that stupid! But I teased a lot. Enjoyed it, too—the power of it." She released a rueful laugh. "Between my mama's good looks and my daddy's money, there weren't too many boys who weren't interested in spending time with me."

The shame of her past hit again, shrinking her into the seat. She lowered her gaze. "I got my college degree in art history just because I knew it was something that would irritate my dad. He thought it was a waste of time and money. And he was right, because I have no desire to do anything with it. But at least when he was ranting at me, he wasn't ignoring me."

She shrugged, shifting her gaze to peer out the window at the sunshiny day. Watching two sparrows battle over a crumb on the sidewalk, she finished. "And that's why I started using the drugs. I thought maybe Dad would—I don't know—rescue me. That's all I really wanted—a dad to rescue me."

Ben didn't say anything in response. After a few moments of silence, she looked at him. The censure in his eyes stung like a lash. She dropped her gaze to the tabletop so she wouldn't have to see his expression. But it burned in her memory.

Eyes downcast, she finished in a hoarse whisper. "So there you have it, Ben. All my ugly secrets." Suddenly a wave of courage washed over her. Although she had no desire to be subjected to his disdain, she needed him to see her face when she spoke the final truth. She lifted her face and met his steely gaze.

"But you know what? The drug use finally got me what I wanted—Someone to rescue me. Only it wasn't my dad who did it, it was my Father. God rescued me, Ben. I met His Son, and I invited Him into my heart. I've got Him now, and even though I made a total mess of things, He loves me anyway. And I won't ever let Him down by doing something so stupid as abusing my body again."

Ben still didn't say anything. There was something indefinable lurking behind his blue-eyed gaze. Disappointment, certainly, but something else. Something deeper. Suddenly Angela didn't want to pursue it.

"Thank you for the sandwich, but I've got to go." Her dignity in shreds, she slipped from the booth and ran out of the restaurant. As she pulled away from the curb, she saw Ben, still in the booth, staring outward. She blinked to clear the tears from her vision and forced her gaze forward.

Back at the apartment, she nearly ran through the foyer, her heels clicking a rapid tempo against the tile floor. Two residents called hello from the seating area. She raised a hand in a quick wave and charged into the elevator without pausing to chat. She held her breath, her chest so tight she thought she might explode. Not until she'd sealed herself in Aunt Eileen's apartment did she finally release the air she'd been holding.

And tears followed. Rivers of tears accompanied by huge, gulping sobs that doubled her over. She collapsed on the sofa, curled into a ball, and let the torrent run its course. Not since her first night in drug rehab had she cried this hard. She wasn't even sure why she was crying; she just knew the emotions couldn't be held back.

When the tears were spent, she stumbled to the bathroom and used several tissues to clean her face and blow her nose. Her head ached, and she fumbled around in the medicine cabinet until she located a bottle of aspirin. When she'd swallowed two of them with some water, she wandered back into the hallway.

Aunt Eileen's door was cracked open, and through the slit, she spotted her aunt's bare feet sticking out from under a light blanket. Roscoe, at the end of the bed, raised his head and peered at her with round, yellow eyes. He offered a short *meow*, yawned, and lay back down.

Carefully she pulled the door all the way closed, relieved she hadn't wakened her aunt. Back in the living room, she curled in the recliner. Ben's face—with shocked disapproval in his eyes—appeared once more in her memory. Not even when she'd told him the good that had come of her drug-abuse conviction, not even when she'd promised to never use drugs again, had his expression cleared.

Her head throbbed, and she massaged her temples. Closing her eyes, she whispered aloud, "Oh, Jesus, please replace Ben's face with Yours in my head. Remind me that You've forgiven me. Remind me that You love me unconditionally."

Another spurt of tears accompanied the simple prayer. But they weren't tears of anguish. They were tears of gratitude. Because Jesus answered.

# Chapter 10

Ben remained in the booth, too stunned to get up. Only dimly aware of the chatter of other patrons, the hum of the air-conditioning, and the slow-moving traffic on the street outside the window, he sat replaying Angela's words.

She'd used drugs.

She'd been through drug-abuse rehabilitation.

She'd said she wouldn't abuse her body that way again.

He shook his head. Oh yes, she would. How many times had Kent gone through rehab? At least three. And every time, he returned to the crutch of drug use. He was drug free now, but not from choice. He simply no longer had access to people who could provide drugs to him.

Except for Angela.

A part of Ben wanted to kick himself for even thinking Angela might provide drugs to Kent, yet the greater part of him—the part that had learned to protect his cousin—overrode the other. If Angela had used drugs in the past, she knew how to get them. If she knew how to get them, she knew how to share them.

He pinched the bridge of his nose between his thumb and fingers, trying to ignore the memory of her pleading eyes as she'd told him of her acceptance of Christ into her heart. Evidence of growth had been seen in the past weeks, especially since she'd begun attending church regularly. She certainly had the pull of God on her heart. But. . .

Ben hung his head, his chest tightening with the knowledge of how hard the tug of drugs could be. Hadn't he seen it with Kent? Kent had struggled against it, had vowed to give it up, had remained drug free for weeks, even months at a time. . .but always, always he'd gone back to the old habit.

It wasn't as if Ben believed drugs were stronger than God. He knew better. But he wasn't sure Angela was strong enough in her new faith to resist the habit. With wooden movements, he piled the half-eaten sandwiches and crumpled chips wrappers on the tray and carried it to the trash can.

When he got in his truck, he realized he didn't want to go home. The empty apartment held no appeal. He considered driving to Elmwood Towers and seeing if Kent wanted to go for a ride, but the fear of running into Angela made him nix that idea. Starting his engine, he pulled into the street and drove aimlessly. By force of habit, he turned on familiar streets and ended up at New Beginnings.

To his surprise, Philip's motorcycle sat in the parking area behind the warehouselike building. Curious, he pulled in next to the cycle and entered the building through the back door.

Philip looked up from his desk when Ben slammed the door. His face creased into a puzzled frown. "Hey, what are you doing here on a Sunday afternoon?"

"I was about to ask you the same thing." Ben dropped into the plastic chair facing his boss's desk. "Since when do you work on Sundays?"

Philip released a low chuckle and leaned back in his chair. He linked his fingers behind his head and rocked slightly, yawning. "I don't. But my lovely wife had a brainstorm about a fund-raising carnival for the winter Special Olympics, and I needed to check my schedule to see where it could be penciled in."

Ben glanced at the desk calendar in the middle of Philip's messy desk. Every square inch held scribbled reminders. "I assume you discovered you aren't available?"

Another chuckle. "I discovered I'm a busy man—as if I didn't already know it." He rocked in his chair, its squeaky springs loud in the quiet room. "So what are you doing here? I'm pretty sure Marin didn't give you any ideas to pursue."

Ben offered a small grin. "No, although I'll help in whatever way I can. I'm hoping Kent will participate in the winter Olympics basketball game, and maybe some of the wheelchair races in next summer's Special Olympics."

"That'd be great," Philip said. He brought his arms down and draped his elbows on the chair arms. "Angela mentioned he's been visiting the weight room at the Towers, and he's gone walking with her in the evenings after it has cooled down a bit. Sounds as if he's getting out a lot more."

The reminder of Angela spending time with Kent brought a new stab of worry. "Hey, Philip, I'm glad I caught you here. I need to talk to you about Angela." He paused, his gaze swinging through the empty building. It seemed sad and almost lonely with the normally busy stations devoid of clients and absent of Angela's bright hair and beaming smile. Turning back to Philip, he said, "She told me today why she's in community service."

Philip nodded, one eyebrow quirked. "I'm not surprised. I wondered how long she'd be able to keep it from you." He leaned forward, resting his forearms on the desk, and fiddled with a pen. "I've gotten the impression pleasing you has become pretty important to Angela—and not just because you're her supervisor."

Ben pulled his lips into a scowl. "If she'd like to please me, she should stay away from Kent."

Philip's hand stilled on the pen. "Has she mistreated Kent in some way?"

"As far as I know, she hasn't," Ben answered truthfully. "But that doesn't mean she won't."

Philip shook his head hard, a teasing grin twitching. He began rolling the pen beneath his palms. "You're going to have to elaborate on that comment. You just lost me."

Ben puffed his cheeks and blew. "She's an addict, Philip. She uses drugs."

"She *was* a drug user. Past tense." Philip's calm rejoinder did little to reassure Ben.

"I'm not so sure past tense exists when it comes to the addiction of drug use." Ben's heart clenched with his statement. He wished so much it weren't true.

"So you're saying Angela's profession of faith is fake?"

Ben looked sharply at Philip. "Her profession of faith has nothing to do with it."

"Ben!" A brief huff of laughter burst out. "It has everything to do with it."

Unable to find the words to express his thoughts, Ben sat silently.

Philip rolled the pen into a drawer, shut the drawer with a snap, and then linked his fingers together on the desktop. "Look, I think I understand where this concern is based. It's because of Kent, right? The fact that he kept returning to drugs?"

Ben shifted his gaze to the right, away from Philip's earnest face, and nodded.

"So your skepticism is logical. However, you're forgetting that logic doesn't always exist in the world of Jesus."

Ben's gaze jerked back to Philip. "Logic doesn't exist in the world of Jesus? Now *you* elaborate."

Philip shrugged. "How logical is it that a man who grew up bullying and tormenting others would open a business that serves the needs of the very people he used to bully? Yet I became a Christian, and God turned me around."

Ben felt his jaw drop. Philip? Kind Philip, a bully? The picture wouldn't gel. But bullying wasn't an addiction. He shook his head. "It's not the same thing."

"Yes, it is. 'The old has gone, the new has come!' Do you think there are limits on God? Only this thing can fade away, but that thing can't?"

Ben couldn't say he doubted the power of God. Yet, in his experience, a person's powerful desire for drugs could keep that person from leaning on God to resist the need. "I think God has the power to do anything, but I also think some people won't let Him."

Philip sat for a while, staring at Ben through narrowed eyes. Finally he nodded. "Okay. Yeah, I'll concede on that one. People sure can follow a wrong pathway. But"—he leaned forward, his gaze intent—"just because one chooses the wrong pathway doesn't mean they all will."

Ben shifted his gaze away again. Philip's quiet words hit like an arrow in a bull's-eye.

"Give Angela a chance. I've seen so much growth just in the few weeks she's been here. I know you've seen it, too. Can't you trust her when she says she's changed?"

"No." The word came from a throat that felt strangled.

Philip shrugged. "Okay. . ."

The chair squeaked again, and suddenly Philip stepped into Ben's line of vision. Ben met his employer's gaze. Philip's eyes contained no hint of condemnation for Ben's hard stance. Only compassion lingered there.

"Ben, there is a way to ease your fears."

"Fire Angela?" Ben forced a humorless chuckle.

Philip shook his head. "You know we can't do that. She wasn't hired. No hire, no fire." He gave a grin that Ben did his best to imitate. "But we can pray." He pulled a second plastic chair over and sat down, his knees a few inches from Ben's. Folding his hands in his lap, he said, "Marin and I were reading in Ephesians a few nights ago. The topic of holiness is expressed pretty beautifully in that book."

Ben's chin shot up. Ephesians. . .and holiness. . . His minister had spoken on holiness the first Sunday he'd taken Angela to church.

"I'm going to pray for Angela, for her to stand firm in her new convictions. But I'm also going to pray for you—for you to be able to see her as the holy creature God desires her to be." Without another word, he lowered his head and began to pray.

Ben closed his eyes and hunched forward, but the tightness in his chest held back the worries he longed to leave in his Father's hands.

—⌒৹—

Angela consulted the clipboard that held the day's schedule, using her finger to scan the list to locate her name. In the task column across from her name, she read "mopping/table cleaning with Randy, Doris, and Anton." She sighed. Her least favorite tasks, and two of those delegated to her area were brand-new clients, which meant she would have a stressful day. Any change in routine was difficult for many of the New Beginnings clients.

Turning from the assignment board, she headed to her locker, her gaze bouncing past Ben. He kept his head down, just as he'd done the previous two days this week. His rejection hurt more than she wanted to admit.

She couldn't blame him for his disapproval. She certainly deserved it after the poor choices she'd made. Yet Ben's disapproval was harder to bear than any other—even more than her parents'. Their anger and disappointment was largely due to the fact that she had been foolish enough to get caught, thereby causing them embarrassment. Ben's disappointment was directly related to her behavior.

Placing her purse in the locker, she rested her hand on the Bible waiting on the shelf. Through prayer, she'd been able to find comfort for her aching heart each night as she stretched out on the bed in Aunt Eileen's spare room. But during the day, even though she was busy, the ache returned.

Loneliness hit hard. The last two evenings, the caretaker for Kent's floor had turned her away when she'd come to visit Kent. Aunt Eileen was tied up in something with other ladies at her church and had been out. She'd consulted her list of "supporters" and refrained from bothering Carrie. What newlywed wants to spend evenings away from her husband? And she didn't know anyone from the Sunday school class at church well enough to call out of the blue to do something.

So she had been alone. Giving the locker a firmer slam than was necessary, she headed to the cleaning area. The tinkle of the bell announced the arrival of clients, and she greeted those with whom she would be working. Of the three, Anton seemed the most nervous. He hung back, peeking over Randy's shoulder, his round eyes wide behind his thick glasses.

Angela's heart went out to him. She smiled and offered a kind welcome, but he shrank away, making a noise of distress. Angela turned to Doris, the one familiar face among the three.

"Doris, would you like to show Randy and Anton where to find the mop buckets? We'll be scrubbing the floors today."

Doris nodded and looked at the two waiting men. "C'mon, you guys." She waved her chubby hand then scuttled toward the supply closet. With one more apprehensive look thrown at Angela, Anton followed. Randy trailed more slowly, his gait swaying. Angela walked beside him.

She worked with the trio all morning, showing them how to fill the bucket to the waterline and measure the cleaning agent, how to wring the excess water from the mop, and how to push the mop head across the floor. When Anton stepped on the long strings, she reached to assist him. But he pulled away, squeaking in fear.

By the time the lunch break arrived, her temples pounded and she toyed with the idea of asking if she could leave early. Only knowing to gain permission she'd have to talk to Ben kept her from following through.

Despite her best efforts at patience and gentle teasing—things she'd discovered worked well with most clients—she made no progress at all in helping Anton feel comfortable. She nearly wilted with relief when the bus driver arrived to transport him home. She walked her charges to the door and said good-bye to each one, but only Doris offered any response.

At her locker, preparing to go home, her cell phone inside her purse blared out its song. She yanked it out and flipped up the lid. It took a minute before she recognized the number on the screen, but then a rush of eagerness filled her. She pushed the TALK button and squealed into the phone.

"Janine!"

"Hey, girl, long time no see."

Janine's voice, familiar and welcoming, made tears prick behind Angela's eyes. She pulled out a chair at the break table and sat down, cradling the phone against her cheek. "I know. How are you?"

"Ornery—same as always." Janine's laughter rang briefly.

Angela laughed, too. The first genuine laugh in days. It felt good. "Yeah? Well, I suppose the same applies to me."

"What did you do today?"

Angela replayed the monotonous tasks, the unresponsive clients. With a sigh, she said, "I mopped floors and washed tables."

To Janine's credit, she didn't make a smart remark, but Angela could hear humor in her tone as she said, "Sounds like. . .fun." There was a slight pause before she went on. "So, do you have time for your ol' buds?"

Angela licked her lips. She glanced up and, through the break in the partitions, she noticed Ben at his desk, his head bent over his work. Her heart caught. "Yeah. I've got time for you guys. What's up?"

"Todd, Alex, and me are meeting for pizza. Why don't you come? Fill us in on your adventures in Rehab Land." The laughter came again, and Angela ignored the brittle undertone.

"At the Ironstone?" Angela noticed Ben lift his head, and for one brief second, their gazes met. She turned away before he did.

"Yep. At six. Can you make it?"

"Yeah, I can do that. I need to run by my aunt's apartment and change out of my work clothes, though." She had finally resorted to jeans, T-shirts, and sneakers for work, but she couldn't show up at the Ironstone dressed so sloppily.

Janine's snort blasted Angela's ear. "I bet! We'll be there. See you soon." Angela clicked the phone closed and dropped it in her purse. Then she charged out the door.

# Chapter 11

**B**en stared at the closed door, his heart thumping. Although the air-conditioning kept the building comfortably cool, he felt sweat break out on his body.

Who was Angela meeting? She was obviously comfortable with the person. He'd gathered that from the tone she'd used. What he hadn't been able to determine from the lopsided conversation was the purpose of the get-together. Was it possible she was meeting with her drug-using friends?

Ben ran his hand down his face, wondering what he should do. He was Angela's supervisor, not her keeper. Yet he was also her—

Swallowing, he processed where his thoughts were going. Should he consider her a friend? Or something more? He admitted that over the weeks she had worked at New Beginnings he'd come to care about her. His time in prayer for her, attending Sunday school and church together, and their times of conversation had developed an undefined relationship.

As her supervisor, he had no authorization to check up on her outside of working hours. His authority was nonexistent there. However, as a Christian mentor, his concern was not only appropriate but warranted. Didn't the Bible say admonishment in love was a sign of Christian care and concern? Plus, if he took it a step further and considered her a friend, he had a real obligation to protect her. Possibly from herself.

But was there a reason to be worried?

Concern and curiosity wavered at the back of his mind as he went through the closing-down routine of checking the different training areas and locking closets. By the time he'd finished everything, the clock by the back door showed 6:05. Angela had intended to meet her mysterious friend at six. Ben paused, his hand on the doorknob, his gaze on the clock. The *tick-tick-tick* seemed loud in the otherwise quiet warehouse. The clock seemed to deliver a message: *Check-check-check. . . .*

He released a disgruntled huff. He wouldn't be able to rest this evening unless he found out what Angela was doing with that friend at the Ironstone. It would only take a few minutes to run by the pizza place. But it might save him an evening of worry.

He climbed behind the wheel of his truck and headed for the Ironstone. Pulling behind the building, he spotted Angela's silver rocket in the far corner of the parking lot. It sent up a question—was she trying to conceal her presence? He trotted across the asphalt and entered the pizza restaurant.

Lights were dimmed, fat candles sending out minimal light in the center of each table. The room was crowded at the supper hour, most tables filled. He stepped further into the dining area and squinted, his gaze slowly sweeping the room. He knew he'd locate her by her clearly identifiable head of hair. Sure enough, he found her seated at a corner table, her back to the door. As he watched, she leaned sideways to say something to the man on her left, and Ben got a glimpse of a half-empty pitcher of amber liquid. Beer.

His stomach clenched. Alcohol consumption had been Kent's precursor to drug use. Her words from Sunday played through his head, "I won't ever let Him down by doing something so stupid as abusing my body again." Didn't her word mean anything? It was like Kent all over again.

The thought turned his stomach. He took two steps toward the table, his hands curling into fists. She shouldn't be here. He should haul her away. Remove her from the beer and the people and the situation. But then he stopped, taking in a deep breath to calm himself.

How much good had it done to haul Kent out of those kinds of situations? None. Hadn't he learned the hard way that one person couldn't control another person's behavior? Angela would have to decide for herself the choices she was making were wrong. His hauling her away would only lead to resentment, just as it had with Kent. It had nearly ruined his relationship with his cousin.

*I can't go through this again, Lord.* Suddenly he had no desire to stand here and witness her descent into drug use. His chest aching, he turned toward the door.

꩜

"Come on, Angela, you haven't even had a sip." Todd lifted the pitcher and splashed beer into the empty mug waiting at the edge of Angela's paper place mat.

Angela pushed the mug toward the center of the table. "I don't want any, Todd."

Todd snorted.

Janine chided, "Don't be such a stick-in-the-mud. It's light, just like you always wanted. Drink up."

"Yeah," Alex agreed, smirking. "What happened to our party queen? You've become a real dud hanging out at New Beginnings."

The others shared a laugh, adding their own rude comments about New Beginnings' clientele. Images of the clients—cheerful Steve, sweet Doris, bashful Randy—crowded Angela's mind. Protectiveness welled up, and she opened her mouth, ready to spew.

"Quit being a party pooper, Angela. Join us, huh? We've missed you." Janine's comment erased the planned speech from Angela's brain.

Angela stared at the clear, amber liquid. Drops of condensation formed on the glass mug, shimmering like diamonds in the flickering light of the candle. Her throat convulsed. Memories of past times—being in the middle of the action, accepted by the crowd—washed over her. Her fingers twitched as she contemplated reaching for the glass mug.

Planting both palms against the table edge, she pushed her chair backward. "I gotta make a little visit to the ladies' room. Be right back."

She fled the table, her heart pounding so hard she could feel it. As she rounded the corner leading to the restrooms, a movement by the front doors caught her attention. Her gaze jerked in that direction, and she recognized Ben's close-cropped hair and broad back as he headed out the door.

She slapped her hands to her face. Had he seen her at the table with the others? If so, what must he think? Making a rapid turn, she charged after him. She burst through the door, calling, "Ben!"

He looked over his shoulder, and his steps ceased. Turning around, he fixed her with an unsmiling stare. "Angela."

From the look on his face, she knew he'd seen everything. She pointed to the restaurant. "It isn't what you're thinking."

He folded his arms, his brows coming down in a disapproving scowl.

Placing her hands against her chest to force down the wave of guilt, she assured him, "I was just sitting with them. I didn't drink anything."

He still didn't answer. Yet his expression said as much as a lecture.

Anger at his condescending attitude filled her, dispelling any guilt. What right did he have to sit in judgment on her? He had friends, people with whom he could spend time. What did he know of loneliness?

Plunking her fists on her hips, she glared upward. "Look, Ben, I have a right to see my friends. Do you have any idea how much my life has changed? I used to be the center of everything, always involved in small group get-togethers and big parties. People called me to go grab a drink or go shopping or take a drive. Now? Nothing! Not since rehab."

Pointing toward the restaurant again, she continued in a harsh tone. "So I decided to meet some old friends for supper. So they decided to drink beer with their pizza. What difference should that make? It's not like I'm sitting there getting drunk with them."

Ben's stern countenance softened. He dropped his cross-armed stance and slipped his hands into his trouser pockets. When he shook his head, Angela got the impression the gesture was one of sadness. Finally he spoke, his words soft.

"Angela, obviously I can't tell you what to do. You're a consenting adult, and you have to make these kinds of decisions for yourself. But. . ." He lowered his gaze for a moment, taking in a deep breath. When he looked at her again, she sensed pain in his eyes. "But if you would just consider one question before you go back in there: If Jesus were sitting in the chair beside you, how comfortable would you be?"

It was the last thing she expected him to ask. "I—I never thought of it that way. . . ." Would she be comfortable drinking beer if Jesus were sitting at the table? She examined herself and realized she wouldn't feel at ease if that were the case. Shame returned, sitting like a stone in her belly. Aunt Eileen had told her that Jesus would help her resist temptation. Why hadn't she given Him the opportunity to help her?

"It's not that I want to be around beer. Funny"—she wrinkled her nose—"it doesn't even smell good to me anymore." She held out her hands in inquiry. "But what am I supposed to do? They're my friends. Should I tell them they can't have it when I'm around?"

Ben shrugged. "As I said, I can't tell you what to do, only what I would do. And I wouldn't put myself in a position of temptation. Plus, there's a biblical warning about being a stumbling block to other believers. Others, just seeing you there, might be given the impression you think drinking is okay. Is that a message you want to convey?"

Angela's chest constricted. Being at the table with her friends had convinced Ben she thought drinking was acceptable. Did she want others to get that impression of her? She looked at him, ready to tell him how sorry she was, but he spoke first.

"If those people in there are your real friends, Angela, they won't try to tempt you to do something you don't want to do." The earlier disapproval returned in his eyes and his tone, causing a cold band to clamp around her heart. "They'll respect the change in your lifestyle. If they can't do that. . ." His voice drifted off, but Angela knew the end to the sentence.

She released a big sigh. "I didn't know being a Christian would be so. . . hard."

A tiny smile toyed at the corners of Ben's lips. "It's easier when you aren't by yourself." Angling his head to gesture toward the restaurant, he said, "Putting yourself in those kinds of situations is asking for trouble. The Bible warns us not to yield to temptation."

Angela remembered the urge she'd felt to snatch up that glistening mug and gulp the cold liquid. She nodded. "I know, but. . ." But she didn't know what else to say. There were no arguments that made sense, no words that would excuse her from knowingly doing wrong. Setting her mouth in a grim line, she stood silently before Ben, observing how the late evening sun threw shadows on his face. It made him appear stern and unapproachable.

"Well"—Ben pulled his hand from his pocket and jiggled his car keys—"I've got to go. Bible study at church. You. . .take care, Angela." He turned his back and strode quickly to his waiting pickup.

Angela remained at the edge of the asphalt, watching until Ben's truck pulled out of the parking stall and headed toward the street. She had two choices—leave or return to her friends. She thumped her head with the butt of her hand as she realized she'd left her purse under her chair. She'd need to retrieve it.

Stepping back into the restaurant, she took a breath of fortification before returning to the table. Instead of sliding into the seat, she reached under the chair for her purse, fully intending to grab it and run.

But Alex shot her a broad smile. "Hey! You're back! You were gone so long we thought you deserted us. Pizza's here. Better grab some before Todd eats it all."

Todd slapped a piece of sausage and mushroom onto Angela's plate. "Yeah. Come on, sweetheart. You came to eat, right?"

No other mention was made about the beer she'd left to turn warm in the mug. The spicy smell of the pizza was tantalizing—she hadn't eaten since eleven thirty. She was hungry. Eating wouldn't hurt anything, right? The welcoming smiles of her friends lured her into her chair.

She picked up the pizza. As she took the first bite, she realized she hadn't asked God to bless the food. The rock of shame returned, filling her stomach so thoroughly she had a hard time swallowing the bite of pizza. She managed to choke down half of a piece while listening to the others laugh and joke. Some of the jokes made her ears burn. She contributed nothing to the conversation.

Sitting there, listening, she came to the realization that she no longer fit with this crowd. The camaraderie was gone. Why had she thought she could slip back into the old crowd and have things be like they used to be? She wasn't the same person. Her Bible told her she was a new creation. She needed to start acting like it.

Dropping the half-eaten slice of pizza onto her plate, Angela reached beneath her chair and picked up her purse. She opened her purse and withdrew a few bills. "Here." She handed the money to Janine. "For my part of the pizza. I–I've got to go."

"Hey!" Janine's eyes flew wide. "What's wrong? You sick?"

Angela shook her head. She wasn't sick, except maybe sick at heart. And Janine certainly wouldn't understand that. "No, but I can't stay. I attend church—Grace Fellowship—and on Wednesday nights, they have a Bible study. I'm going to miss it if I don't get going."

The two men hooted with laughter.

"Angela—at Bible study?" Todd slapped the table. "Now there's a joke!"

Alex roared, and Janine punched his shoulder to bring him under control.

Angela felt her cheeks fill with heat. Gathering her courage, she said, "It isn't a joke. It's important to me. And, for future reference, I–I'd like to be able to see you guys, but I can't—I won't—be doing any more partying. So if you want to go to a movie or something sometime—"

Todd cut in. "Yeah, kiddo. If a good G-rated cartoon comes to the theater, I'll give you a ring."

Janine giggled, and Alex snorted. The three of them sent smirking grins at one another, enjoying their private joke.

Angela hung her head. Ben was right. These weren't her friends, or they wouldn't try to hurt her this way. Without saying good-bye, she turned and hurried from the restaurant.

# Chapter 12

Ben pulled into the parking lot of Grace Fellowship, killed the engine, but then just sat behind the steering wheel, staring across the wheat fields that faced the church. Angela had gone back into the Ironstone. He'd seen her. After warning her, after encouraging her, she'd turned around and gone right back to a potentially dangerous situation.

*Lord, I can't do this again. I can't watch someone else I love travel the road to addiction. . . .*

He straightened in his seat as the reality of his prayer struck him. He loved Angela. And more than just as a sister in Christ. Somehow his employer-to-employee, mentor-to-mentee relationship had developed into a man-to-woman relationship. But shouldn't the realization that he had fallen in love be a happy one? He didn't feel happy. He felt burdened. And betrayed.

How could God allow him to give his heart to someone so risky? Kent's face appeared in his memory—not the healthy Kent, but the Kent-after-drug-overdose. Loving Kent had been risky, too. But, he argued with himself, loving Kent while he made his horrible choices was different. They'd had a relationship that went back to their babyhood.

But Angela? There was no long-standing relationship, no storehouse of memories years in the making. *Of course I should continue to love Kent. He is my childhood best friend and lifelong cousin. But*—he popped the door open and stepped out—*I cannot invest that much of myself in Angela. It hurts too much.*

As he strode across the parking lot, he sent up another prayer. *Let me love her with Christian concern for a fellow believer, but take the other love out of my heart, God.* He slipped into a folding chair on the outside aisle, closing down thoughts of Angela to concentrate on the Bible study.

The minister announced the passage for the evening's study, then began reading from Genesis 6—God's directions to Noah on the building of the ark. Ben listened, his brows pulled down, wondering what Pastor Joe had in mind.

When he read his closing verse from chapter 7, suddenly Ben understood. " 'And Noah did all that the Lord commanded him.'" A smile tugged at Ben's cheeks as the minister faced the gathered worshippers and asked, "Has God ever commanded you to do something that made no sense?"

Loving Angela made no sense. It promised to get him hurt. He was doing it anyway. But was it something God had designed, or was it just his own heart's desire?

"Think about how Noah must have felt, being told to build a three-story boat—nowhere near a body of water, but right in the middle of the desert—and then fill it with animals because rain was going to flood the earth." Pastor Joe released a light laugh. "I have to tell you, if I'd been Noah, I probably would have been rolling on the sand, holding my stomach, and laughing hysterically. It made no sense!

"Many Bible scholars believe the concept of rain was new. That the earth was like a huge terrarium, with a perfect balance of moisture. If that's true, then the idea of rain falling from the sky was unheard-of and would have been completely incomprehensible to Noah's way of thinking."

He chuckled softly. "I can imagine Noah scratching his head, trying to make sense of these commands of God. Build a boat, one three stories high, right here on the sand. Fill the boat with the male and female of every kind of animal from four-legged beasts to winged creatures to those that creep upon the ground—a daunting task! Watch the sky because clouds will form and dump water enough to flood the entire earth.

"How many questions must have filled Noah's head! Did he ask these questions?" He consulted his Bible, shaking his head. "We don't know. But"—he lifted one finger—"what does that last verse I read tell us? Read it with me. . . ."

A chorus of "And Noah did all that the Lord commanded him" echoed through the room.

Pastor Joe continued, sharing the importance of trusting God to know what was best even when it didn't make sense to the human mind. Ben listened, but at the same time, his thoughts raced, trying to balance his feelings for Angela with what God would command him to do.

*"Pray for her."*

*Yes, Lord, I know I should pray for her.* And he had been—regularly.

*"Pray for her now."*

The urge was too strong to ignore. Closing his eyes, Ben set aside the sound of the minister's voice and began to pray.

—☙

Angela parked her car, opened the door, and swung her feet to the asphalt. But then she sat motionless, half in and half out of the car, debating with herself. When she'd left the pizza restaurant, her feelings were so battered she planned to skip the Bible study and just go to Aunt Eileen's apartment to lick her wounds. Yet, as she'd turned toward Elmwood Towers, something had tugged her heart toward the church.

Now, sitting in the parking lot, aware the study had started at least ten minutes ago, she felt reluctant to disrupt the service by entering late. She lifted her feet, ready to pull them into the car and head to the apartment after all, but that mysterious tug returned.

"Okay, okay!" she mumbled, snatching up her purse and Bible and pulling herself from the car. "I guess if I make a fool of myself walking in late, it's no worse than the fool I've made of myself already at the Ironstone."

She stepped through the church door then closed it as quietly as she could. On tiptoe, she made her way to the sanctuary. Scanning the room, she discovered a spattering of open seats, most of which were toward the front. No seats on the back row were open. She cringed. She did not want to walk in front of anyone and make a spectacle of herself.

Then she spotted several metal chairs, still folded, leaning against the wall near the doorway. Balancing her purse and Bible in one hand, she crept to the chairs and lifted one by the underside of the backrest. She carried it to the far end of the back row and managed to set it up behind the other chairs with a minimum of noise. A couple of people turned to look, but both smiled in a welcoming manner. She smiled back, the tension in her shoulders lessening.

The chair creaked slightly as she settled her weight into it, but she kept her gaze forward, focused on the minister, and hoped no one else noticed the sound. From what she could glean from coming in midway, the topic this evening was following what God asks.

How appropriate. She listened, absorbing the words of the minister as he talked about Noah and his neighbors.

"You see, Noah's neighbors were wicked people. So wicked that God saw no reason to allow them to continue in sin. The Bible doesn't tell us how they reacted to the sight of that huge boat growing in the sand, but if they were ungodly, wicked people, we can surmise they probably gave Noah a hard time. Maybe called him names, asked him if he'd lost his mind."

The minister leaned on the podium and pointed at the listening congregants. "How many of you welcome that kind of treatment?"

Angela shook her head. She'd just experienced it. She didn't like it at all.

"How do you think Noah reacted?"

His expectant face encouraged responses, and several people contributed their thoughts. Angela listened to all of them, but she liked the one delivered in a familiar voice—Ben's—the best.

"I think he turned a deaf ear to his neighbors and only listened to God's voice. How else could he have continued working on the ark for the number of years it must have taken without giving in to the taunting of the crowd and putting his hammer away?"

The minister must have liked Ben's response, too, because he nodded and smiled in Ben's direction. "That's a good point. When the voices of 'the world' surround us, it can be very easy to give in to them, to allow them to influence us.

But if we close them out by focusing on the still, small voice of God, we can be assured of walking the pathway God has chosen for us." He paused for a moment, his face pursing in sadness. "I wonder how many people miss a tremendous blessing because they allow themselves to be pulled off course by the tauntings of an ungodly crowd."

Angela remembered her impulse to return to the apartment this evening as a result of her friends' teasing. She would have missed this lesson and the resulting blessing if she had followed through on that impulse. Gratitude washed over her. *Thank You, Lord, for tugging me here.*

"Now," the minister continued, as Angela leaned forward, eager to hear more, "how do you think Noah was able to do all that God commanded him without getting off course?"

A lady near the front raised her hand. "Noah had a long relationship with God. The Bible says his father also walked with God, so surely Noah had seen faith in action by watching his father."

Angela's heart flip-flopped. She'd not had such influences while growing up. Would that stymie her ability to follow God unconditionally?

"And," the woman went on, "he'd taught his sons to follow God, too."

"What makes you think that?"

Angela could tell by the pastor's tone his question wasn't a challenge but an invitation for the woman to share her thoughts.

"Because God told Noah he could bring his sons onto the ark. I think that means God recognized Noah had passed on the tradition of trust in God to his children."

The pastor gave a thoughtful nod. "Interesting. . . And what that means, if I'm following your train of thought correctly, is Noah had a built-in support system of people who would encourage him to continue work on the ark, even if the townspeople proclaimed it a foolish waste of time."

The woman's head bobbed up and down in agreement.

Turning his attention to the entire congregation, the minister said, "This brings up a good point. We should be strong enough to stand alone if need be. The Holy Spirit can give us the strength to do that, when we ask. Yet how much more secure we feel when we have a body of believers standing behind us.

"Noah had his wife, his sons, and his sons' wives assisting in his efforts. God could have given Noah the strength and ability to do all of the tasks necessary to build the ark and gather the animals on his own, but God allowed Noah's family to contribute." Tipping his head, he raised his eyebrows. "Perhaps we can take a lesson from this and add that God wants us to have the support and assistance of other believers."

Angela hung her head, tears stinging her eyes. The support and assistance of other believers. . . Those words echoed through her head. Who did she have?

Her list on the tablet at home was alarmingly short.

And how would the list grow? She didn't know how to lengthen it. The last name on the list was Ben's, and as much as she wanted him to be a part of her support system, it seemed he found fault with everything she did. Her past mistakes had put a huge barrier between them. Now, because of what she'd done long before she met him, he didn't trust her with Kent, and he didn't trust her to be with her old friends.

If she tried to form a relationship with other Christian people, would they react the same way as Ben had when they learned about the foolish things she'd done? Would they be able to look beyond the old Angela to the Angela she was trying to be with God's help? How she wanted a support system of believers, but she didn't think she could take being turned away time and again when others learned about her past mistakes.

*God, I want a support system of believers. I need help right now. People who will pray for me and help me grow in You.*

Pastor Joe brought the study to an end with a gentle admonishment to trust God to know what's best even if it doesn't make sense. "God's ways aren't our ways, and He sees what is waiting around the bend even when we can't. Let us walk in faith on the pathway He directs, trusting it will always be in our best interests."

He mentioned the prayer needs of the church membership, welcomed a few more requests from the attendees, and then dismissed the people to gather in small groups for prayer. Angela watched as some people rose and left the sanctuary and others shifted their chairs to create groupings. Her heart pounded with the desire to join one of those groups, to be a part of praying.

She glanced around the room, seeking Ben—he would at least be one familiar face. But then she saw him again in her memory, his disapproving frown, and she heard his admonishing words. Joining Ben's group would be a mistake. Why set herself up for more rejection?

So she remained in the corner, separated from the others. Loneliness smashed down on her, bringing the sting of tears. Lowering her head, she closed her eyes. Even if she wasn't part of a group, she could still pray. She sorted through the requests mentioned by the minister, lifting them one by one to the heavenly Father. And when she'd completed the list, her thoughts returned to her own needs.

*Dear Lord, I need. . .friends. People like Noah had with his family, people to support me and help me in the task You've given me. Please, Father, won't You bring some friends into my life?*

Her prayer was interrupted by the touch of a hand on her shoulder. Her heart leaped in hopefulness. Ben?

# Chapter 13

Angela's eyes popped open, and she raised her head, a smile forming on her face without conscious thought. The smile wavered when she found not Ben but Pastor Joe standing beside her chair. She pushed the disappointment aside and greeted the man in a whisper.

"Hello. I—I enjoyed the study this evening."

Pastor Joe grabbed a chair and slid it across the linoleum floor. He placed it next to her then sat down, his gentle smile lighting his eyes. "I'm glad you enjoyed it." He kept his voice low, too. "It's good to see you here on a Wednesday evening. I hope you'll make our Bible study a regular part of your week."

She nodded, eagerness filling her. "I'd like that. I know I have a lot to learn."

The pastor smiled. "Is there a prayer need I can address for you?"

He had a kind face, and Angela found herself feeling very at ease with him. *Surely a minister won't turn away from me if I share my failings, will he?* She searched his face and, seeing only interest, found the courage to share her deepest secrets.

"Yes. There is." She swallowed the nervous giggle that tried to find its way from her throat. "And it's a biggee."

The minister laughed softly. "There's nothing too big for God. What is it?"

"I need friends." Blurted out that way, it sounded childish. And selfish. Thinking about the other requests—a sister who fought cancer, a man who lost his job, a family whose house was destroyed in a fire—Angela felt heat climb her cheeks at her own audacity in requesting prayer for something so frivolous.

But the minister didn't even blink. "You don't have friends?"

Angela grimaced. "Well, I do. . .kind of." She took a deep breath. "You see, four months ago, I had a huge circle of friends. They're still out there, but I don't feel like I can be with them anymore. With those friends, I started using drugs. Then I provided drugs for a party. I got caught, and a judge gave me a one-year sentence. I spent the first two months of the sentence in drug rehab, and now I'm serving the remainder in community service."

Pastor Joe simply nodded. His gentle face showed no shocked recrimination.

Grateful for his acceptance, Angela plunged on. "I became a Christian while I was in drug rehab, and I really want to do things right now. I don't want to mess up. But I haven't found very many people who are Christians who want to be my friend. The drug thing. . ." She sighed, Ben's face once more appearing in her memory. "Well, it gets in the way. And I can't be with my old friends because they still do things I shouldn't be doing now that I'm a Christian. So..." She held her hands out in a gesture of futility. "I'm...alone."

Leaning forward, the minister rested his elbows on his knees. His relaxed position helped Angela set aside the remainder of her worries about rejection. "First of all, let me assure you of one thing—you aren't alone. Ever."

Angela nodded. Aunt Eileen had told her the same thing.

"You have a built-in support system with the Holy Spirit, and He is an ever-present friend on whom you can depend. But"—he smiled—"that having been said, I understand the need for earthly friends. Like-minded people of faith who will not only support you in your Christian walk, but who will also be there to hang out with, have fun with. Fellowship is important, too."

Angela nearly sagged with relief. He didn't think she was being silly! She leaned forward, eager to have her next question answered. "So how do I find these friends? My experience has been that some Christians are so put off by my past, they can't accept me today." It stabbed her heart to say the words, yet they were truthful. She desperately needed this man's advice.

The minister's face pulled into a slight scowl. "I'm sorry you've encountered judgmental attitudes. I understand why people react that way. Sin is difficult to face when you try so hard to avoid it. Yet Christ encourages us to look past the sin to the sinner, to love the sinner in spite of the sin." Tipping his head, he added, "Now, that doesn't mean we blithely accept the sin. We must caution those who walk in darkness that they're choosing an unhealthy pathway. We want to guide them to the light. But we must admonish in love. Do you understand the difference?"

Angela puckered her lips as she considered what he'd said. Was it possible Ben had tried to do what the minister mentioned? Admonish her in love? Perhaps his words weren't so much of condemnation but of concern. Oh, she hoped so! Pastor Joe waited for a response. She believed she understood what he meant, so she nodded.

His gentle smile returned. "Angela, I believe you will discover many Christians are able to love the sinner in spite of the sin. Please don't dwell on those who have chosen to judge you. Forgive them for hurting you and move on. Also, use the experience to help you react kindly to those you encounter with less-than-perfect pasts. That way you're using the experience for good."

Angela hoped she would never make anyone feel as soiled as Ben—whether intentionally or unintentionally—had made her feel. She returned to her original question. "So where do I find these Christians who will be able to accept my past?"

"Well..." Pastor Joe sat up, raising his shoulders in a shrug. "As a matter of fact, we have something coming up that might be just what you're looking for. Wait here. I'll be right back." He rose and strode from the room while Angela waited, licking her lips in anticipation. When he returned, he handed her a folded brochure. "Our young adult singles are traveling to Camp Fellowship, near the Oklahoma border, for a three-day retreat over Labor Day weekend."

Angela examined the brochure while he continued.

"There will be Bible study classes, as well as activity periods with opportunities for small groups to gather and several large group functions. It's a weekend meant to grow young adults in their Christian walks and also to bolster relationships among the attendees. It would be a way for you to get better acquainted with our young adults, and perhaps friendships can be formed that will continue after the retreat."

Angela's heart thumped in hopefulness. "Do you really think it would be okay for me to go? I mean, considering my past. . ."

The man took the brochure and seemed to examine it closely, his brows tugged down. When he looked at her, his eyes sparkled with mischief. "I saw nothing in there that says rehab graduates need not apply."

Despite herself, Angela laughed. "Okay. I'll fill this out tonight and write a check. Thank you for telling me about it."

"You're welcome." Pastor Joe placed his hand on Angela's shoulder. "Angela, being a new Christian is tough. It's like a baby learning to walk—lots of stumbles and scrapes and bruises. But the more you pick yourself up, dust yourself off, and continue to try, the stronger your legs will grow. I'll be praying for you as you get your Christian feet under you."

His image became blurred as tears filled her eyes. His kindness touched her, easing the bruises Ben's censure and her friends' unkind treatment had left on her heart.

"Let's pray right now." He lowered his head, folded his hands, and began petitioning the Lord on Angela's behalf.

Angela listened, his words wrapping around her like a warm blanket, soothing her and assuring her God was listening. By the time he'd finished, she felt certain God had planned for her to attend tonight so she'd learn about the retreat weekend. She could hardly wait for Labor Day to arrive to see what friendships God would provide.

He ended his prayer with an amen and then said, "Just drop the registration tear-off in the office on your way out." He rose. "And enjoy the retreat."

"I will. Thank you." Angela hurriedly filled out the registration form, wrote her check, and headed for the office.

—◌—

Ben lifted his head after completing his prayer and spotted Pastor Joe with Angela, their heads bent in prayer. Relief rushed through his chest. If Pastor Joe were to begin mentoring Angela, he could back off—be relieved of his self-imposed responsibility.

But what if it wasn't self-imposed? What if it was God's prompting that had made him want to reach out to Angela in the first place?

He pushed that thought aside. Surely God wouldn't expect him to go through the heartache of witnessing someone's descent into drug addiction. God loved him too much to put him in a position destined to bring him despair. It was better to allow Pastor Joe to assume mentoring with Angela. Pastor Joe was stronger, better equipped to deal with Angela's special needs.

Rising from his chair, he said good-bye to the members of his prayer group and promised to continue praying for their needs over the course of the week. The others offered their good-byes and moved toward the foyer area, but one member of the group, Stephanie, stopped Ben with a manicured hand on his arm.

"Ben, do you have any needs I can pray for this week?"

Ben looked into Stephanie's brown eyes. In the past, he'd gotten the impression that Stephanie would like more than a casual acquaintanceship, but he saw no hint of coquettishness in her expression. Deciding she was sincere, he nodded.

"As a matter of fact, there is. It's something related to. . ." He paused, uncertain how to phrase things to make sense without giving too much away. Then he realized he didn't need to give Stephanie the details. God knew the details. A simple request would be sufficient. "If you'd pray for God's will in a situation at my workplace, I would appreciate it."

Stephanie didn't pry—just offered a smile and a nod. "I'll certainly do that." Her fingers tightened on his arm. "And you be sure and keep me updated, will you? I always like hearing the praise reports."

Ben quirked one brow, grinning. "Oh, believe me, if there's reason to praise, you'll hear about it."

"Good." She removed her hand, but her smile invited further conversation.

"So did you sign up for the singles' retreat? I'm really looking forward to it. The speaker they've secured is supposed to be very good."

Ben had heard that, too. "Yes, I did sign up. And I'm glad you mentioned it, because I need to remember to put in a request for early leave on the Friday before Labor Day. My boss will need to cover the close-down duties that day."

They continued to visit, discussing the retreat and who all had signed up to go. Then the conversation lagged, and Stephanie glanced around the room. "Oh! I didn't realize we'd been chatting so long. Everyone else is gone."

Ben noticed, too, for the first time that no one else remained in the sanctuary. He hadn't even seen Angela leave. A feeling of regret niggled, but he pushed it aside with a light chuckle. "We'd better clear out. The custodian is probably eager to shut things down for the night."

"Yes." Stephanie fixed him with a sweet smile. "Would you like to go grab a cappuccino or something? Talk a little more?"

Ben groped for an adequate response. Part of him was tempted. Stephanie was attractive, and spending time with her would certainly help remove thoughts of Angela from his mind. Yet he realized accepting her invitation might give her the impression of interest in her, which didn't exist. He wouldn't use her to soothe his own concerns.

"It sounds like fun, Stephanie, but I need to get home. Maybe another time?" He softened the refusal with a smile.

She smiled, too, giving a shrug. To his relief, she didn't appear offended. "That's fine. It was just a thought. You take care, and I will be praying."

Ben walked her to her car and opened the door for her, giving her another good-bye. Her warm smile, accompanied by a cute little fingers-only wave, made him swallow and back away. Why hadn't he noticed before how appealing Stephanie was?

He watched her vehicle pull away before climbing into his truck. As he drove toward home, his thoughts bounced back and forth between the two women with whom he'd conversed privately this evening.

Angela, with her autumn-colored hair and intriguing pale blue eyes.

Stephanie, with hair the color of a walnut shell and dark eyes to match.

Angela, who wore an expression of seeking.

Stephanie, who gave an aura of self-assurance.

Angela, with her questionable past.

Stephanie, with her sterling reputation.

If a person put them side by side in a beauty contest, Angela would certainly come out the winner. But as a potential life's mate? In that contest, Stephanie's attributes were certainly the preferable ones from a Christian viewpoint. Perhaps he would be wise to explore the opportunity of a deeper friendship with Stephanie.

His heart contracted painfully as Angela's image crowded out the one of the other woman. *Now, stop that!* he commanded himself. Hadn't he decided that a relationship with Angela was not beneficial to him? Caring for her only brought pain and misery. He'd traveled the pathway of destruction once before as an unwilling observer. He would not put himself in that position again, no matter how his heart raced every time she came near. He'd just have to set aside those feelings.

"Mind over matter," he reminded himself as he pulled into the driveway of his fourplex. Surely if he distanced himself from Angela, he could forget her.

He shut off the ignition and froze for a moment. Forget her? Did he really believe that was the right thing to do? Lowering his head, he prayed, "God, please forgive me. Of course I don't want to forget Angela. You placed her needs on my heart. I made a promise to mentor her, to support her in prayer, and I will honor that promise. But, God, please. . .her past. . . She can't change it, and I can't seem to change how I feel about what she did. As long as the issue of her drug use is between us, there can't be anything more than a casual friendship. Help me see her in the way You would have me see her. Let me be her friend, her mentor, but please. . .guard my heart."

# Chapter 14

Ben dropped the reports into their file and closed the drawer with a snap. He glanced at the clock and then shook his head at his own impatience. The anticipation was as bad as it had been when he was a kid planning to go to summer camp.

He admitted part of the anticipation had to do with the opportunity to distance himself from Angela for a few days. The past two weeks had been rough, and prayer had been his constant companion. As he'd promised, he prayed for her daily, for her to resist the temptation to fall back into drug use and for her to grow in her Christian walk. But he hadn't watched closely enough to see if his prayers were having any effect. Looking at Angela brought a rush of longing he wanted to squelch.

Rising from his desk, he scanned the area for Philip. Although he couldn't see Philip, he could hear him from behind the partition of the kitchen area, bantering with one of the clients. Ben crossed the room and ducked behind the partition as Angela crossed his path, leading two clients to the washroom to clean up after sorting recyclables. He released his breath in a whoosh, thankful for the chance to hide behind the tall partition and get his racing heartbeat back under control.

Ben waited until Philip gave the client a clap on the shoulder and turned away, signaling the end of their conversation, before speaking. "Philip? I just wanted to remind you—"

"That you're leaving early." Philip grinned. "I know, I know. You've only told me twice already today." Shaking his head, he chuckled. "I'm beginning to think you really want to get away from here for a while."

Ben laughed, too, but he was certain he looked as sheepish as he felt. "It isn't the job. You know that."

Philip nodded. Ben had shared his confusion about his feelings for Angela with Philip and Philip's wife, Marin. Both Philip and Marin were praying for the situation, for God's will to be made known.

Suddenly Philip frowned. "Odd, I just remembered. It seems Angela. . ." His voice trailed off as he passed Ben and headed around the corner, toward the break area.

Ben followed, puzzled.

Philip went to the check-in sheet hanging near the time clock, and he poked the pages with his finger. "I was right. Angela leaves early today, too."

Ben's heart turned a somersault. He broke out in a cold sweat. "Do you know why?"

Philip shrugged. "Something about weekend plans, and she needed to leave two hours early. I had to get it approved through the probation officer, and the approval came in yesterday, just under the wire. She was pretty relieved. Must be something important."

"Yeah, must be." Ben pinched his chin, thinking. When he and Stephanie had talked about those who had signed up for the weekend, Angela's name hadn't been mentioned. In all likelihood, she simply had plans for the long weekend just as he did. The plans didn't have to be for the same thing. Yet, as he tried to assure himself, doubt continued to gnaw at him.

He had to know. Although he hadn't spoken to her beyond casual greetings and farewells since he'd warned her in the parking lot at the Ironstone, he headed out of the break area and went looking for her. His heart pounded as he approached. It doubled its tempo when he tapped her shoulder, and she turned, her face breaking into a smile.

"Ben. Did you need something?"

Unconsciously, his gaze swept across her rumpled hair. Those curls, as always, created a desire to run his hands through the shining locks. He cleared his throat. "Yes. Um. . .Philip mentioned you have plans to leave early today?"

She nodded, and then her face clouded. "I'm sorry. Should I have mentioned it to you, too? Philip didn't say anything when I asked him about it. . . ."

He shook his head. "No, no, clearing it with Philip was the right thing to do. He is the head honcho around here." Her smile returned, but it trembled around the edges, giving her a winsome expression. He stuck his hands in his pockets. "I just wondered if. . .well, if you had specific plans for the weekend?"

Her fine brows came down in puzzlement, and for a moment, he thought she would refuse to answer. But then her expression cleared, and she offered a graceful shrug. "Yes, my plans are quite specific. I'm going on a church retreat."

Ben's heart thudded against his ribs. "Church. . . As in Grace Fellowship?"

Her eyebrows shot high. "Yes! Are you going, too?"

The anticipation melted away to be replaced by a heavy weight of dread. An entire weekend with Angela? Getting through the workdays had been excruciating. What would he do when she was there at breakfast, lunch, supper, and throughout the evening? *Maybe I should cancel my plans. . . .*

He instantly nixed that thought. He'd been looking forward to this weekend for too long to abandon it now. "Yes. Yes, I'm going, too."

"Oh, wonderful! Pastor Joe said it would be a perfect time for me to formulate friendships. You said yourself I needed to make Christian friends instead of hanging out with my old crowd."

She seemed to search his face, and he got the impression she needed his approval. He managed a brief nod. "Yes, that's a great idea. With a dozen different churches sending their singles to the camp this weekend, you should have several opportunities for building friendships." Now why did the thought of Angela forming relationships beyond him make his chest feel tight?

"That's what I'm hoping." She shook her head, making her curls dance. "But I've got a lot to finish up here before I can leave, so. . ."

He got the hint. "Sure. Finish up. I'll—I'll see you later."

He fled to his desk and sat down, fighting the urge to bury his face in his hands. "It's okay," he mumbled to himself as he punched the computer keys to open the budget log. "The campground is big. Lots of people. You'll hardly see her."

"You say something, Ben?"

Philip's curious voice brought Ben's head up.

"Huh?" He hadn't realized he'd spoken loud enough for anyone to hear. Shaking his head, he forced a grin. "No. No, just thinking aloud."

"Oh. Okay." Philip gave him a light pat on the shoulder. "Well, listen, if you need to leave now, I can look over the books."

Ben scooted his chair back and rose. "That'd be great. I do have some things I could do to get ready for the weekend." Like pray for strength to make it through this weekend with Angela only a dormitory away.

"Fine." Philip plunked himself into Ben's chair. "See you Tuesday. And have a great weekend."

Ben yanked his car keys from his pocket. "Yeah, great. . ."

~⌒~

Angela trotted to her car, her steps light and her heart singing. Ben had talked to her! After nearly two weeks of silence, he'd walked up, called her name, and talked to her. The joy that had washed over her in those moments still bubbled under the surface. How she had missed his companionship!

Her constant prayer had been for a restoration of their friendship. She knew she had disappointed him by meeting with Janine and the others at the Ironstone and having that beer on the table. But she'd been working so hard ever since to stay true to her Christian convictions and not do anything that would give anyone the impression that pleasing Jesus was not important to her.

Surely he'd noticed. That's why he'd spoken to her today. She couldn't stop the smile from growing on her face as she considered an entire weekend of activities with Ben. Pastor Joe had indicated the opportunity for building friendships existed. She mentally moved Ben to the top of her support system list.

She climbed into her vehicle, humming. Now that she knew Ben would be there, a feeling of security struck. As much as she had anticipated the weekend, an underlying nervousness had held back full-blown excitement. Being with strangers was never comfortable. But Ben's would be a familiar face, an island of recognition among a sea of strangers.

And with all the opportunities for interaction and joint activities, surely their friendship would grow. When they first met, she'd felt a spark. She longed for their relationship to be as it was before Ben knew about her drug-use conviction. This weekend could prove to be a healing time for both of them. *Oh, please, Lord!* Her heart beat in hopeful double beats.

Since she had said good-bye to Aunt Eileen and put her bag in the car this morning before leaving for work, she drove straight to the church. Several other cars were already there, and two large vans waited by the sidewalk, the back doors yawning wide. People milled around the vans, some with bags in hand.

She parked her car with the others and got out, waving when a couple of people beside the vans waved at her. After retrieving her suitcase, she trotted to the vans. "Hi! Where do I put this?"

A dark-haired woman greeted her with a smile. "We ladies are going on the first van and the guys in the second, so you can put your suitcase in the back of the first one. Here, I'll take it." She took the suitcase from Angela then headed toward the first van. Peeking over her shoulder, she said, "I know I've seen you in Sunday school, but I've forgotten your name."

"I'm Angela." Angela trotted along beside her benefactor.

"And I'm Stephanie." Stephanie put Angela's suitcase with the others, then held out her hand. "I'm glad you decided to join us."

Angela shook Stephanie's hand. "Thanks." She walked with Stephanie back to the milling group of women, her brain buzzing. Something about Stephanie was familiar, but she couldn't place it. She stayed in the group, learning everyone's name and chatting, while more cars pulled into the parking lot and the backs of the vans filled with suitcases.

Not until she saw Ben's pickup pull in did she remember where she'd seen Stephanie before. At Bible study two weeks ago, huddled in a corner with Ben. Jealousy smacked hard, and Angela felt her breath catch. Could it be that Ben had avoided her recently for more reasons than her past mistakes?

She watched him cross the parking lot, duffel bag in hand. He tossed his lumpy bag into the back of the last van, his T-shirt pulling taut with the swell of his muscles. When she glanced at Stephanie, she observed the other woman's gaze following Ben, too.

*Lord, guard my actions.* The prayer came automatically, a recognition of behavior that wasn't pleasing to her Savior. The simple prayer settled her ruffled feathers, and she took a big breath, managing to smile when Ben turned in their direction.

When his gaze fell on her, she saw his steps falter, his grin fade. Then he seemed to shift his gaze to Stephanie, and the smile returned. A pain stabbed through Angela's heart.

Her earlier hopes of establishing a closer friendship with Ben melted beneath the early September sun. Reality crashed around her, reminding her that someone like Ben—strong, steadfast Ben—would never be interested in someone whose past was so shaded.

When he stopped in front of Stephanie, Angela took a step backward, forcing a smile she didn't feel. "I–I'm going to get in the van now. See you all in a few minutes."

"Okay, Angela." Stephanie's bright smile did little to ease Angela's discomfort. "I'll join you in a minute or two."

Angela paused long enough to see Stephanie lift her smile to Ben's face; then she turned and fled to the van. Inside the vehicle, alone with her thoughts, she hunkered into the seat and closed her eyes tight, trying to shut away the image of Ben with Stephanie.

The two had looked right together—both with their long-time Christian lives. Who was she fooling, thinking she was worthy of someone like Ben? She fought tears as shame once again filled her chest, bringing a stifling weight of regret. She allowed herself a few minutes of mourning, of whining silently to God over being stuck in an emotional roller-coaster ride. And when she'd finished, she straightened in the seat and dashed away her tears with the insides of her wrists.

She would not spend this weekend moping. Pastor Joe had said she would find Christian friends who would accept her. So Ben didn't accept her. So what? Ben wasn't the only person who would be at the campground this weekend. There would be lots of other people. She'd just have to set her sights elsewhere. It was time to broaden her horizons, to stop looking at Ben as the only answer to her loneliness.

*Lord, I've prayed for friendships. Pastor Joe has prayed for friendships for me, too. I trust You to meet that need this weekend. Thank You for the people You will bring into my life.*

"Hi."

The greeting startled Angela out of her prayer. She jerked her gaze up to find a smiling young woman standing in the van's open doorway.

"Mind if I join you? I've been on my feet all morning, and I'm ready to sit down."

Angela scooted over and patted the seat. "Sure. By the way, I'm Angela."

"I'm Robyn."

"Nice to meet you."

Robyn grinned, dimples flashing. "You, too."

They began to chat, and thoughts of Ben thankfully slipped into the background as the groundwork was set for establishing a new friendship.

# Chapter 15

Angela swung her suitcase and, with a grunt, managed to plunk it onto the mattress of an upper bunk.

Sitting on the bunk below, Robyn grinned. "Wow! I think we'll call you Muscles from now on!"

Angela looked at the other woman and laughed. Rubbing her shoulder, she said, "I don't think one lucky swing is enough to earn that title. And I hope I'll have enough room to sleep up there with the suitcase, because I'm not willing to wrestle it down until it's time to leave on Monday."

On the bunk next to Angela's, Stephanie stopped rolling out her sleeping bag and said, "If you sleep all coiled up like a roly-poly bug, you'll be fine with that suitcase on the end. Or you could stretch out and use it as a footrest."

Although Angela had tried her best to dislike the dark-haired woman—after all, she had Ben's attention—she just couldn't maintain the feeling. Stephanie was so sweet that Angela found herself drawn to her. On the drive over, with Robyn between them, Stephanie had repeatedly leaned forward and included Angela in conversation. Angela couldn't make herself rebuff Stephanie now.

Forcing a laugh, Angela said, "I think I'll have to sleep with my head on the suitcase. I just realized I brought sheets, but I didn't bring a pillow."

Stephanie picked up one of the plump pillows from her bed and tossed it over. "There you go, with my compliments."

Angela picked it up and hugged it. "Are you sure? You brought two. You must have intended to use them."

With a grin, Stephanie folded the remaining pillow in half, thumped it onto the mattress, and rested her head on it. "This'll work fine."

"Well, then...thanks." Angela swallowed the lump in her throat. It had been a long time since she'd been treated with such unconditional acceptance and kindness by virtual strangers.

Robyn bounced up from her mattress, her eyes sparkling behind the round lenses of her glasses. "Well, now that we're settled, let's head to the cafeteria. Supper starts in another fifteen minutes."

Several others were already heading for the door that led to the hallway. Angela, Stephanie, and Robyn fell in with them. The group laughed and talked as they made their way across a grassy courtyard that separated the dormitories from the main buildings. Angela found herself feeling at ease, and peacefulness washed over her. *Thank You, Lord, for bringing me here.*

Outside the cafeteria doors, a table was set up beneath a green canvas pavilion, and a smiling woman distributed plastic-sleeved name tags printed with each person's name and church of attendance. Each tag also had colored stickers in the upper left-hand corner.

Angela found her name tag and examined it. A blue cross with a yellow rose sticker at its base was on her tag. Robyn's tag had a rainbow in clouds instead of the cross, but she also had a yellow rose. A glance at Stephanie's tag showed a green cross and white daisy.

The three women clipped their tags to their shirtfronts, then got in line to enter the cafeteria.

"I wonder what these are for." Angela wondered aloud, pointing to the stickers.

Robyn shrugged. "Decoration?"

A woman in line ahead of them turned around. Her name tag read: CHARLENE SCOTT, CALVARY CHURCH, SCOTT CITY, KS. She tapped her own symbols. Her flower sticker was a pink carnation. She also had a rainbow, but unlike Robyn's, hers had no clouds. "They'll use these to break us into groups. Sometimes they'll use one of the symbols, sometimes the color. It helps us get to know everyone who is here instead of staying in our own little groups."

Angela nodded and thanked her for the explanation. That made sense. And she liked the idea. The more people she could meet, the greater the opportunity to build her support system.

Once everyone had crowded inside the cafeteria, a man at the front of the room spoke into a microphone. "Welcome to Camp Fellowship, folks. We've got a great weekend planned for you, starting with our opening worship service right after supper. For the moment, check your name tags. We're going to make a seating assignment for tonight's meal."

A murmur went through the waiting crowd as people consulted their name-tag stickers.

The man used the microphone to call out symbols while pointing out different areas in the cafeteria. Everyone moved to his or her directed location as the symbols were called. Angela smiled a good-bye to Robyn and followed Stephanie as she made her way through the crowd to the long tables indicated for those with cross symbols.

A couple of people squeezed between the two women, slowing Angela's steps, and she became separated from Stephanie. Most of the chairs were filled by the time she reached the tables, but an end seat was open at the second table. She stood behind it then looked across the table.

Her heart seemed to forget its purpose when she realized Ben was right across from her. Their gazes met, and Ben's shoulders stiffened. For several long seconds, they stared at each other, and Angela found herself wishing he would smile, engage in conversation, treat her the way he had before she had confessed her sinful past. But he remained silent while a bustle of activity continued around them.

"Shall we bow our heads for prayer?" asked the man with the microphone.

Relief welled when she could break eye contact with Ben. The man led the group in grace. Head bowed, Angela added a quick postscript to his prayer: *Let me have a good weekend of growth and friendship building, Lord, and if it's Your will, please let that friendship list include Ben.*

Chairs screeched on the painted concrete floor as the retreaters seated themselves. Paper plates at each setting held sandwiches wrapped in aluminum foil, a cluster of green grapes, a small bag of chips, and a cup of pudding. Simple fare, but Angela didn't mind.

The man on her left tapped her shoulder. "Could you pass the mustard, please?"

"Sure." She picked up the bottle and handed it over.

The man smiled and glanced at her name tag. "Thanks, Angel."

Angela burst out laughing. Grabbing the corner of the tag, she angled it so he could read the whole thing. "That's Angela. I've never been called an angel before."

The man laughed, too, and Angela heard Ben's soft snort from across the table. She refused to look at him and held out her hand to the man. "And you are?"

He took her hand, giving it a slight squeeze. His eyes were blue, although not as deep in color as Ben's. She liked the length of his blond hair, a little long over his collar and wavy across his forehead. He also had a dimpled smile, which he used to good advantage. "I'm Elliott. Great to meet you."

"You, too."

"I'm a member of Calvary Church in Scott City. How about you?"

Angela glanced at Ben. He held his sandwich in both hands, watching her over the top of the layers of wheat bread and ham. She turned back to Elliott. "I attend Grace Fellowship in Petersburg. I'm not a member, though." Another quick glance at Ben. "Yet."

Ben turned his attention to his potato chips.

"So. . ." Elliott squirted his sandwich with mustard. "Have you ever been to one of these retreats before?"

Angela popped a grape in her mouth. "No, this is my first time. But I've been looking forward to it."

Elliott nodded. "Oh, you'll have a great time. These retreats are very well planned. The activities, the speaker, the music. . . And of course, The Course." He threw back his head and released an ominous *bwa-ha-ha-ha* that brought a round of laughter from the table.

Angela shook her head, her lips twitching with a smile. "And what does that mean—?" She imitated his menacing laugh perfectly.

His grin held approval. "Have you ever been someplace where they've had ropes courses set up?"

Chewing another grape, Angela shook her head. Her curls tickled her cheek, and she pushed the hair behind her ear. "No."

Elliott glanced down the length of the table and raised his voice. "Hey, everyone! Who all has done the ropes course?"

Five people, including Ben, held up their hands. Ben was the closest person with a hand raised, and Elliott turned to him. "You want to tell her all about it?"

His gaze on his plate, Ben said, "Not particularly."

Angela felt color flood her face, and even Elliott paused for a moment, seeming put off by Ben's blunt reply. But he recovered quickly, gave a shrug, and turned back to Angela.

"Well, the most important thing you need to know is all the people who've done The Course are still here and breathing. In other words, they survived." He smirked. "And you will, too." He consulted her tag again. "Hmm, blue cross, yellow rose. . ." He looked at his own tag. "Green cross, orange leaf." A pretend pout puckered his lips. "Well, Miss Angel, we probably won't be in the same group for the ropes course, but"—he winked—"I'll be sure to look you up and see how you liked it."

Angela laughed. "You be sure and do that. Hopefully I won't be the first person to not survive The Course."

As she turned back to her plate, she glimpsed Ben scowling at her. Suddenly he planted his hands against the edge of the table and pushed, his chair screeching against the floor. Without a word, he dropped his napkin beside his half-full plate and headed for the exit.

—⌒♈

Ben stepped outside the cafeteria and sucked in a big breath of evening air. The chatter of voices was filtered by the closed door, but the laughter and teasing could still be heard. He needed silence, privacy, solitude. A chance to convince himself that Angela's flirting with Elliott was no big deal. It would be a very long weekend if he allowed himself to get upset every time she talked to some other man. Half the people here were men, and someone as pretty as Angela would certainly garner attention. *And she sure knows how to respond to it!*

He stomped across the ground, jealousy filling his chest so fully he found it hard to draw a breath. A bench waited beneath a huge elm in the middle of the courtyard. He headed in that direction, determined to sit down and have a serious talk with himself about getting his feelings under control.

When he was halfway across the grass, someone called his name, and he nearly groaned. Spinning around, he spotted Angela trotting toward him, a determined look on her face. He folded his arms over his chest and waited for her to catch up.

"Yes? What do you need?" His tone was more brusque than he'd intended, but his fast-beating heart made breathing difficult.

She crossed her arms, too, and fixed him with a stern glare. "Well, if you really want to know, I need you to stop treating me like I've got leprosy. Truly, is it too much to ask for you to be civil?"

Ben scowled. "I am civil."

She huffed. "Then you and I are using different dictionaries. Civil means—"

"I know what civil means!"

"—polite." She raised her voice, tipping forward and lifting her chin defiantly. "It means being polite, and you were not polite in there. Not to me, and not to Elliott." Releasing a huge sigh, she shook her head, her tousled curls teasing her shoulders. "Ben, I'm sorry if my being here upsets you, but—"

"I'm not upset that you're here," he said, dropping his cross-armed pose and moving toward the bench.

She followed, hovering just behind his elbow. "Then why the gruff reply to Elliott's question? Would it have really hurt you to tell me about The Course?"

He spun around again. "Do you want to know about The Course? Okay, I'll tell you. They have a system of ropes and pulleys attached to tree branches, and—"

"Ben!" She clutched her temples, those autumn-colored waves covering her fingers.

Once more, his hands itched to capture the curls. He plunked his hindquarters on the bench and curled his fingers around the wooden edge of the seat. "What?"

Standing in front of him, she sighed again. Lowering her hands, she wove her fingers together and pressed her hands against her stomach. "The Course isn't important." Her tone turned soft, imploring. "What's important is how we're going to get through three days together here If you are so uncomfortable with it."

*Uncomfortable is an understatement,* Ben thought wryly. The pressure in his chest became unbearable as he forced himself to breathe evenly. "Listen, Angela, it's just..." He pressed his lips together tightly for a moment, battling with himself. Honesty was needed here, but he didn't want to crush her. *Lord, please help me out here.*

"It's just what?" She took a step closer, her intriguing light-colored eyes begging him to explain.

Finally he blurted out, "Every time I look at you, I see you in a hospital bed, tubes sticking out everywhere, just like Kent after his overdose."

Her eyes widened, and she jerked, as if his words had impaled her. "Ben, I told you, I don't use drugs anymore. That isn't going to happen to me."

"But I can't be sure!" He drew his hand down his face. "Do you know how many times I heard Kent say, 'I won't do it anymore, Benny; I promise'... Then days later, or weeks later, or months later, I'd get a call—his mother, begging for help because Kent was at it again. I couldn't trust Kent when he said he'd stay clean, and I can't trust you!"

Tears welled in Angela's eyes, making the darker rim of her irises brighten.

Ben turned away, the sight of those tears creating a stab of pain in his heart. He didn't want to hurt her, yet he had to be honest. His gaze aimed across the campground to the grove of trees at the edge of the property, he finished, "Watching my cousin battle his addiction was the hardest thing I've ever faced. And then, that last time, when he nearly died. . ." He closed his eyes for a moment, grimacing with the remembered pain. "And now, seeing him in a wheelchair, knowing he will never be the same because of the drugs. . ."

"But, Ben." She touched his shoulder, her fingertips quivering. "I've told you and told you. I'm finished with drugs. I'll never use them again. I promise you that. Why can't you believe me?"

He jerked away from her touch, his shoulder tingling where her fingers had brushed. "I can't believe you because I've seen the stranglehold of drugs! Kent was a strong man, but he couldn't resist them. You—you're. . ." To his frustration, words failed. He leaped to his feet, facing her. "I can't do it again, Angela. I won't do it again. I will not watch someone else I love fight a losing battle against drug addiction." Pointing at her, he grated, "So I'm going to keep my distance, and you've got to help. Stay away from me, Angela. Please, just. . .stay away."

The tears broke free of their perch on her thick lashes and trailed down her cheeks. Ben released a muffled moan and spun from the evidence of her distress. A distress he'd caused. He brushed past her and charged to his dorm room. Shutting himself in the quiet room, he sank onto the edge of his bed and buried his face in his hands.

*Lord, I didn't want to hurt her. Forgive me for hurting her, but I can't go through it again. I wish I'd never come here.*

# Chapter 16

Angela watched Ben storm across the grass toward the dormitories. Tears rained down her cheeks, but she made no sound. Her chest ached with the effort of containing her misery, yet she wouldn't give him the satisfaction of reducing her to sobs.

He loved her. She'd heard him say he couldn't watch someone else he loved fight a losing battle against drug addiction. He loved her, but he didn't trust her. She couldn't understand love like that. Shouldn't love and trust be synonymous?

As she stood beside the bench, a flutter of activity captured her attention. People spilled out of the cafeteria, moving en masse toward the worship hall. She should go, too, but her feet remained stubbornly still. Two people separated themselves from the throng and jogged across the grass toward her. Stephanie and Robyn.

Turning her back, Angela wiped away her tears with trembling fingers. Just as she turned around again, the pair came to a halt a couple of feet away from her. Their smiles faded when they looked into her face.

"Hey." Stephanie stepped forward and touched Angela's shoulder. "What's the matter?"

Robyn moved closer to put her arm around Angela. "I saw you charge out of the cafeteria after Ben. Is everything okay?"

Angela shook her head. "No. Everything is most definitely not okay. I need to go back to Petersburg. Is there any way I can get a taxi to come out here or something?"

Robyn and Stephanie exchanged looks. Stephanie spoke. "Angela, a taxi all the way back to Petersburg would cost you an arm and a leg. Come here." She guided Angela to the bench and gently pushed her onto the seat. She and Robyn squeezed in on either side of her. "Now tell us what's going on. Maybe we can help."

Angela looked from woman to woman. Even in the muted light from electric lamps at the top of poles, she could see the genuine concern on their faces. She had prayed for friends. Had God sent Stephanie and Robyn to fill that need? With a deep sigh, she sent up a silent prayer for their understanding then forged ahead.

"The problem is, I did something, several months ago, before I became a Christian. Ben knows about it, and it's. . ." She swallowed. "It's causing big problems."

Robyn put her hand on Angela's knee. "Do you mind telling us what you did?"

"I used drugs." She blurted the words out then searched their faces for their reactions. Neither pulled away or showed shocked disapproval. Relief flooded her, and she gained the courage to tell everything. She left out no details then finished with, "I'm a Christian now, and I've promised God I'll never use drugs again. But Ben doesn't believe me. He—he said he loves me." She glanced at Stephanie, fearful of hurting the other woman's feelings. "But he doesn't trust me. Not at all. And he asked me to stay away from him. That's why I've got to go back to Petersburg. I saw his name tag. He has a blue cross, too. I won't be able to stay away from him."

The trio sat in silence for several minutes. A frog croaked somewhere in the distance, and the breeze rustled the drying leaves overhead. From the sanctuary, a piano began to play, and voices answered the accompaniment. The gentle sounds of the evening wrapped around Angela, enveloping her in peace. She had shared her deepest hurt, her worst sins, and these two women hadn't gotten up to walk away. They remained, their presence a breath of Jesus to Angela's aching heart.

Finally Stephanie spoke. "I don't know how well Robyn knows Ben, but he and I were on a committee together last year at church. My impression of him is that he's very devoted to his faith." Putting her arm around Angela's shoulder, she offered a one-armed hug. "I'm sorry he hurt you. I would imagine he's hurting, too, and his pain is making him behave in ways not typical."

Angela wanted to believe that, but his withdrawal had been so complete after her confession of drug abuse. She sighed. "So what do I do? Do I stay, or do I go?"

"Well, you don't go!" Robyn shifted slightly on the bench, her knees banging into Angela's. "We've just barely gotten acquainted! And I'd like to get to know you better."

"You would? Even after I told you—"

"What's past is past," Robyn said, her voice firm. "No one's perfect, Angela. We've all made mistakes, and in God's eyes, sin is sin. There aren't various levels, with one sin being worse than another. Sin is just. . .wrong. And my judging you for something you did before you became saved would be just as wrong as you continuing to use drugs now that your body is a temple for the Holy Spirit."

Gratitude welled up in Angela's heart and spilled over, bringing a fresh rush of tears. "Then you'll still be my friends?"

"Of course we will!" Robyn and Stephanie chorused together then giggled.

"Still, maybe it would be better if I left. Ben—" Angela started.

"Ben has to answer for Ben," Robyn inserted.

"I agree," Stephanie added. "Ben wanting to keep his distance is Ben's problem, not yours. And to be honest, his problem isn't going to be solved by you leaving. That will just make it easier for him not to face it. No, I think you should stay, enjoy the weekend, and let Ben solve this for himself. If he isn't comfortable around you, then he can make the decision to leave."

Angela looked back and forth, her heart swelling. God had answered her prayer already. True friends! Only true friends would be this supportive. Tears distorted her vision, but she blinked, sending them away. Slapping her own knees, she said, "All right then. I won't run away. But. . ." She bit down on her lower lip. "Could we pray about it? Because it's going to be very tough for me to face him in these group activities with this issue between us."

"Of course." Stephanie took one of Angela's hands then stretched the other hand toward Robyn. Robyn took Angela's free hand, completing the circle. The three lowered their heads and asked God to work His miracle in restoring peace for both Ben and Angela.

─◌

"You'll be okay, Angela." Bruce, the camp activities' director, shielded his eyes with his broad palm as he peered upward at Angela. "The rigging is secure, and I'm acting as anchor. I outweigh you by at least. . .oh, ten pounds."

Angela giggled from the square wooden platform in the tree branches a good twenty feet from the ground. Stocky Bruce outweighed her by at least a hundred pounds, but she appreciated his humor. Her heart pounded so hard that she was certain it would burst from her chest.

"And of course we've got muscleman Ben holding the other rope, so you've got nothing to worry about."

Angela glanced from Bruce to Ben. Ben didn't look at her, but she saw the whiteness of his knuckles as he gripped the taut rope. No matter his feelings toward her, he wouldn't let her fall. She knew that.

"So. . .are you ready?"

Angela looked ahead to the next tree. The ropes course led through six trees, weaving between branches, always well above the ground. She patted the sturdy straps of the rappelling rigging and drew in a breath of fortification. "I'm ready!"

"All right then. . .let go!"

Squeezing her eyes tight, Angela released the branch and coiled her fists around the thick shoulder straps of the rappelling gear. She felt herself whiz through the air, and an involuntary shriek left her lips.

"Open your eyes!" a female voice from the ground encouraged.

Angela peeked one eye open in time to see the rush of branches coming at her. She released another yelp as her feet connected with the second platform. Grabbing hold of a branch, she panted, blood rushing to her head.

The group on the ground applauded. "Woo-hoo, Angela! One down!"

Angela laughed and made a shaky bow from the platform. Those with blue crosses on their name tags laughed at her theatrics.

"See? Nothing to it!" Bruce hollered. "Ready to go again?"

Angela held her breath and gave a nod. She forced her eyes to remain open this time, and the exhilaration of the ride expressed itself in a burst of high-pitched laughter. Her feet on the third platform, she exulted, "Oh, this is fun!"

Laughter rose from the group. She glanced at Ben. A grin twitched his cheeks. Her own smile grew with the small signal of his pleasure.

"Then let's keep going," Bruce called. "No stops at platform four, just straight on to five, okay?"

"Okay!"

Angela finished The Course, her heart racing, but not from fear. Bruce had explained the purpose of the ropes course was to practice letting go and letting God keep a person secure in an insecure world. Sailing through the air, depending on Bruce and Ben to keep her safe from falling, Angela experienced in a tangible way the upholding hand of God. *I trust You, Father, to never let me fall back into the habit of drug use ever again,* her heart promised as she allowed Ben and Bruce to lower her to the ground.

The moment her feet touched the leaf-scattered grass, the blue-cross group rushed forward, patting her back and offering congratulations. She sent smiles through the group, but as she turned, she caught a glimpse of Ben standing well back, his face impassive.

Her heart lurched, her elation faltering. But then she squared her shoulders and made another silent promise. *I won't let Ben's attitude defeat me, Lord. You are all I need for happiness. Thank You for never letting me down.*

⁓

Ben looked across the bonfire to Angela, who sat between Stephanie and Elliott. The man had been like a leech during every free period today. But, he acknowledged, Angela hadn't given him any extra attention. Her flirtatiousness seemed to have been put on hold for the weekend.

Now she held a stick with marshmallows attached over the flame, turning it with a look of concentration on her face. The firelight danced on her tousled curls, bringing out highlights of gold and red. The shadows emphasized the delicate curve of her jaw and the height of her cheekbones. In the flare of the fire, her eyes took on a new luminance, as if lit from within. His heart lurched. Her beauty was like a knife through his chest.

He stifled a groan. This day had been so difficult. Their common symbol put them in nearly every activity together, making separation impossible. Despite his efforts to focus elsewhere, time and again his gaze had followed her. Images from the day replayed like slides on a private movie screen: Angela listening with rapt attention to the speaker, her head bent in silent prayer during quiet time, her elation as she ended the ropes course. And now, her sweet face tipped toward Elliott while fireglow lit her features.

Turning away, he tried to involve himself in conversation with the people sitting nearby, but he couldn't concentrate enough to contribute. With a sigh, he looked back across the flames, his eyes unconsciously seeking the cause of his conflict.

But she wasn't there.

He gave a startled jerk, sitting up straight and searching the area. The only light came from the massive bonfire, so he nearly missed the shadowy figure slipping between trees at the edge of the clearing. Had it not been for the flash of fire in her spiraling curls, he might not have recognized the figure as Angela.

Planting his palms against the log that served as his seat, he nearly lunged to his feet. But Bruce stepped in front of Ben, stopping his movement.

"Hey, gang, anyone have a suggestion?" Bruce patted the guitar that hung around his neck. "Let's sing some praise songs, give God the glory for providing such a beautiful fall evening."

Song suggestions were thrown out, and Bruce strummed, accompanying the voices. Ben sang along, but his participation was halfhearted at best. His gaze remained on the spot where he'd seen Angela disappear. Half an hour slipped by, and still she hadn't returned. Worry pressed at him. Could she have gotten lost? The campground was fairly large, and in the dark, in the trees, a person could get disoriented.

Leaning to the person seated next to him, he asked, "Hey? Do you know if anyone has a flashlight out here?"

The man nodded. "Yeah. Bruce's wife, Lorraine, brought a few of them in case people needed to get back to the dorms."

"Thanks." Ben rose and made his way to the back of the gathered campers to Lorraine. She willingly reached into a burlap bag and withdrew a flashlight at Ben's request. After thanking her, he circled around the group, moving cautiously over the shadowed ground.

He waited until he was in the trees before turning on the flashlight. The beam shot ahead no more than five or six feet, but it was enough to guide his progress. Watching the play of light on tree trunks and on the uneven, leaf-covered ground, Ben thought of the Bible verse in Psalms about God's Word being a lamp for man's feet and a light for man's path. The light only uncovered a path a few feet ahead—far enough to take three or four steps—but limited the vision of the entire path. He had to trust that the beam would continue shining as he made his progress, giving him enough light to continue.

*God, it's like that in life, too, isn't it? You don't allow us to see the whole pathway, but You provide the illumination needed to make today's progress.* His throat convulsed. *I don't know what lies ahead for Angela and me, but I want to trust that You have good things in store at the end of the road. Please let Your light keep shining. . .for both of us.*

A voice startled him, bringing his prayer to a close. He froze, straining to listen. At first he couldn't make out words, only tones; but then the voice raised, and he recognized not only the speech but also the speaker.

"Give that to me right now!"

Angela, making a demand.

Mumbled voices answered. Their words were unclear, but the growling tones indicated anger.

Ben stumbled forward, his heart pounding. The bouncing beam of the flashlight turned the trees into lunging monsters, but he kept going, determined to find Angela and protect her from—what? He didn't know. He only knew he had to get to her quickly.

The voices grew louder, an obvious argument ensuing. He let the sound guide him, his heart pounding harder with each step that brought him closer. He burst through several scrub bushes into a small clearing where a minuscule campfire sent out a weak flicker of light. Angela stood on one side of the fire; three people faced her from the other side. All four jumped and spun toward him as he charged onto the scene.

"What's going on here?" Ben swung the beam of the flashlight across the row of faces opposite Angela. He didn't know any of them. They were young, teenagers probably.

When they spotted Ben, one hollered, "Let's go!" They took off through the trees.

Ben started after them but changed his mind. He didn't care about those boys. He'd come out here for Angela. Turning back, he saw her trot around the campfire and bend down to pick something up. The flashlight aimed at her, he approached, his brows crunched. "What is that?"

She held it against her side for a moment, her face pale. Slowly she raised her hand, and Ben angled the flashlight beam on a plastic-wrapped bunch of crumpled brown leaves. Marijuana. *Oh, Lord, no...*

He lifted his gaze from the packet to her face. Her wide eyes told everything he needed to know. He'd interrupted a drug deal.

"Angela..." He shook his head, the disappointment sagging his shoulders. "How could you?"

# Chapter 17

Angela took a stumbling step forward. The look of betrayal on his shadowed face stabbed her heart. "Ben! It isn't what you think!"

"What am I supposed to think?" he grated, his teeth clenched. "I come out here, worried about you, and I find you—I find you. . ." He released a groan.

She grabbed his arm. "Ben, I didn't come out here looking for drugs. I was just walking, thinking, trying to make sense of you and—" She stopped. There was no "you and me" where Ben and she were concerned. Drawing in a breath, she continued. "I saw the campfire, and I wondered who was here. I found those boys getting ready to make joints."

"So you decided to join them."

How his words stung! "No! Ben, listen to me. When I saw what they were doing, I tried to stop them."

Ben jerked his arm free, his gaze accusing. "I heard you asking for the marijuana, Angela. I heard you."

"Yes, I asked for it!"

"Well, if you weren't planning to use it, why did you ask them to give some to you?"

Frustration welled. How could she make him understand? "I didn't want them using it, making the same mistake I did, so I asked for it. Not for my use, but just to take it away! Ben, you have to believe me!"

But he shook his head, backing away from her. "Once a drug user, always a drug user. You just couldn't stay away from it."

His withdrawal hurt worse than anything she'd experienced before. Her chin quivered with the effort of holding back tears. What had she decided about Janine, Todd, and Alex? If they were her friends, they wouldn't choose to hurt her. The same applied to Ben. He claimed to love her, yet all he did was hurt her. She couldn't stay for one more minute in his presence.

"Fine." She shoved the packet of marijuana into her jacket pocket. "You don't want to believe me? That's fine. I've done everything I know to do to prove I've changed—to prove I'm not Kent and I won't keep using drugs. But you don't want to believe me! You'd rather go on thinking the worst, never taking a chance, never admitting that maybe—just maybe—you could be wrong."

Throwing her arms outward, she released a huff. "Okay, don't believe me.

Stephanie is right. It isn't my problem, Ben; it's yours. And you're just going to have to deal with it." She spun and headed for the trees.

"Angela!"

Ben's angry voice didn't slow her steps a bit.

"Angela, it's dark! You'll get lost! Come back here!"

"I got myself out here; I'll get myself back!" She didn't even turn around, just forged forward, her hands outstretched as she groped her way through the gray gloom. She heard Ben's muffled voice, but she ignored him and continued her halting progress.

Leaves crunched beneath her tennis shoes, the noise an assault to an otherwise peaceful night. She stomped along, determined to put as much space between herself and Ben as possible. Her chest ached with the desire to cry, but she set her chin and held the hurt inside. He'd made her cry for the last time. No more!

After stumbling noisily forward for several minutes, she paused and listened. No footsteps followed her. Huffing from the effort of moving quickly through the dark, she leaned against a tree for a few moments of rest. She slipped her hands into her pockets, and she encountered the marijuana. The plastic bag crinkled beneath her palm, bringing a rush of memories.

The remembrance of past times—filling her lungs with smoke, experiencing the sensation of floating, being part of a circle of acceptance—brought a flood of desire. Ben already thought she was a user; why not prove him right?

It would be so easy to make a joint. The little squares of paper were scattered all over that area where she'd surprised the boys. She could sneak back there, circle around so Ben wouldn't see. A few draws on a marijuana joint would wash away the pain Ben caused, wash away the feeling of failure, and carry her to a height of pleasure. Her fingers tightened on the packet as a war took place in her heart.

Then she remembered another sensation of floating. Today, on the ropes, gliding from tree to tree while trusting Bruce and Ben to keep her safe. Bruce's words filled her head. *Let God hold you up.* Dropping to her knees on the leaves, Angela lowered her head and poured out her heart to God. She begged Him to remove the desire for drugs once and for all. Then she thanked Him for the opportunity to prove her promise was sincere. Finally her thoughts turned to Ben.

"God, I don't know what to do about Ben. I love him, but loving him hurts too much. You can take the desire for drugs away. Please take the desire for Ben away, too." She remained on her knees for several more minutes, absorbing the peacefulness of one-on-one time with her heavenly Father. The chill from the ground made her shiver, and she rose clumsily to her feet. Raising her face to the star-studded sky, she whispered a "Thank You" for God's endless presence, and then she continued her progress toward camp. Before long, she spotted the glow of the bonfire and heard voices raised in song.

There was one important thing left to do. Her heart pounding, she made her way out of the trees. She glanced over her shoulder. Ben was still back there somewhere. Her heart ached. As much as she still loved him, his actions had proven he would never trust her. Trying to win Ben's approval was a losing battle—one she no longer had the energy to fight.

"Good-bye, Ben," she whispered, then walked slowly to the group gathered around the bonfire. She looked for Robyn and Stephanie and located Stephanie first. She worked her way through the group to Stephanie's side and crouched beside her. Tapping the woman's shoulder, she whispered, "Stephanie? I need to make a phone call. Could you come with me, please?"

Without a word of question, Stephanie rose. The pair walked in silence to the dormitories.

—❧—

Ben made sure the small campfire was completely extinguished before turning back toward the group. His steps felt heavy, labored, and he knew it had nothing to do with the late hour and tiredness from a busy day. The weight of Angela's betrayal wore him down. Once a drug user, always a drug user—isn't that what he'd said? Yet seeing it proved true hurt more than he had imagined. His journey through the trees seemed to take hours—hours of painful reflection.

All of the pleasant images from the day now disappeared, replaced by the sight of Angela standing, shamefaced, with a packet of marijuana in her hand. He shook his head, a feeble attempt to clear the image from his memory, but it remained, permanently imbedded in his mind. And she had taken it with her—stuffed it in her jacket pocket and stormed away.

He replayed that moment of her slipping the marijuana into her pocket over and over. If only he could change the scene. Why hadn't he leaped forward, snatched the packet away from her, and flung it into the fire? Instead he'd stood there stupidly and let her walk away with it. Which meant Angela was now in possession of marijuana.

Drugs were in violation of camp rules—a cause for immediate dismissal. One word to the campground administrator, and Angela would be sent packing. More importantly, drug possession was a clear violation of her parole. If he contacted her parole officer, her community service would end immediately. She would serve the remainder of her sentence in a detention facility.

His feet scuffed through dried leaves and pine needles as he moved forward, the beam of the flashlight bouncing ahead. He stared at the beam, his thoughts tumbling haphazardly through his confused mind. The remainder of the weekend would be less stressful for him if he didn't have to see her. One word—just one word—and she'd be returned to Petersburg in disgrace. His chest contracted painfully. Could he do that to her even if it meant having the weekend free of her presence? What a price to pay for his own comfort.

And if he told the administrator, Bruce would contact the authorities. Drugs were illegal. Bruce would be obligated to tell. Then Angela wouldn't be at New Beginnings anymore. That wouldn't necessarily be a bad thing, he told himself. How much easier work would be if he didn't have to see her, be tortured daily by the rush of love and desire that struck with every glimpse of her. Surely if she weren't a part of his everyday routine, he would be able to free himself of the love that had grown for her. Or would he?

The wavering flashlight beam swung back and forth, illuminating the path. His thoughts swung back and forth, illuminating nothing. *Turn her in—it's the right thing to do. Don't turn her in—it's a selfish thing to do.*

He wanted to do the right thing, but the right thing for whom? Turning her in would solve his own problem of having to see her every day. Not turning her in, while giving her a temporary reprieve, would only enable her to continue in drug use.

So turning her in was right for both of them. . .wasn't it?

"Lord, what do I do?" He spoke the words aloud, his anguished thoughts causing his stomach to churn.

Voices and soft laughter drifted through the evening air. He was nearly back to the bonfire. He had to make a decision.

What if he left it to chance? His heart thudded at his own variation of Russian roulette. If he spotted Bruce first, he'd turn Angela over to him. If he spotted Angela first, he'd try to find another way to set things right.

He reached the clearing where people were picking up napkins and crumpled Styrofoam cups, dashing the bonfire with water, and preparing to go back to the dormitories. He scanned the crowd, but he didn't find Angela or Bruce. His heart picked up its tempo. Had she sneaked back to the dorms to make a marijuana cigarette? The smell would certainly alert everyone. He needed to find her, warn her.

That impulse convinced him he didn't want to turn her in. Although he knew it was wrong to keep secret what he'd discovered, a part of him wanted to give Angela one more chance. One more chance to do the right thing. His breath came in spurts out of his nose as he trotted past the groups moving slowly toward the dormitories.

He prepared an ultimatum as he hurried to locate Angela. If she would give him the marijuana, he would dispose of it and keep it secret. But he would make sure she understood if she chose to purchase drugs again, she was on her own. He wouldn't interfere a second time. This would be a one-shot deal. He hoped she'd take it.

As he neared the dorms, beams from a pair of headlights appeared on the lane leading to the campsite. Ben's steps slowed as the car rolled to a stop directly in front of the women's dormitory. His heart skipped a beat when he recognized the insignia on the driver's door. A sheriff's vehicle.

Someone had already discovered Angela had marijuana! So his ultimatum wouldn't be offered after all. Relief and regret mingled in his chest. Though greatly relieved he hadn't had to be the one to make the call, he regretted that it was necessary at all. If only he'd been wrong. If only she hadn't gone looking for drugs tonight. . .

He stopped, watching as the officer turned off the headlights and stepped out of his vehicle. "Hey, what's going on?" someone behind him asked. The others had caught up and stood in small clusters on the grass outside the dorms.

Ben didn't answer. He wanted no role in Angela's downfall.

The sheriff, standing in the *V* of the open car door, rested his forearm on the top of the vehicle and called, "I'm looking for Angela Fischer."

A mumble of voices sounded behind Ben. His heart twisted in sympathy. How humiliating for her to be summoned this way. He longed to protect her, yet he knew he was powerless. She'd made her choice. Just like Kent, she'd have to suffer the consequences.

The dormitory door opened, throwing a splash of light across the concrete sidewalk. The glint of gold in her tangled curls resembled a halo. "I've never been called an angel," she'd said at supper the night before. Ben's heart ached.

He watched her straighten her shoulders, tossing her gilded curls. "I'm Angela."

# Chapter 18

The sheriff turned toward Angela as the crowd surged forward, curiosity driving them closer to the action. Whispered questions and suppositions floated through the throng, but Ben shut out those voices and concentrated on the sheriff.

Angela met the man halfway between the car and the dormitory. A circle of light from an overhead lantern illuminated the pair, showing the sheriff's stern expression and Angela's pale face. She extended her hands toward him, palms up. Ben held his breath. Did she expect the sheriff to handcuff her? But then he saw that her hands weren't empty. The bag of marijuana rested on her open palms.

"Here you are." Her voice was strong, carrying over the mutters behind him.

Another flurry of voices broke out.

"What is it?"

"I think it's some sort of drug."

"Where would she have gotten that?"

Ben took a step forward, an attempt to block the voices behind him. He needed to hear the sheriff and Angela.

The sheriff took the packet and turned it over in his hands, a scowl pinching his eyebrows. "Well, you were right. It certainly appears to be marijuana."

Ben's jaw nearly dropped. Based on the sheriff's words, Angela must have alerted him herself. But she wouldn't have done that if—

The sheriff continued. "Is this all of it?"

Angela's shoulder lifted in a slight shrug. "I don't know if there was more. This is all they dropped."

"Dropped?"

"Yes, sir. When the boys ran off, they left this behind. I just picked it up."

The sheriff reached into his breast pocket and removed a small pad and pencil. He flipped the pad open and looked at Angela. "How did you happen to join these boys?" The sheriff's sharp tone made Ben cringe, but Angela straightened her shoulders and faced the man squarely.

"I was taking a walk, doing some thinking. I had no idea anyone else was out there when I started my walk. I heard laughter and saw a fire. I was curious, so I approached them. It was just. . .coincidence."

"So you had no intention of using the drugs?"

Angela's gaze flitted briefly to the listening crowd. Her face looked pale, yet there was a calmness in her eyes that spoke of strength. "To be honest, sir, when I saw what they had, I was tempted. There was a time when I found a release in drugs. But I'm not that person anymore. I made a promise to God that I would never use drugs again. I intend to keep that promise."

The sheriff gave a brusque nod. "And you don't know who these boys are?"

"No. This is my first time at Camp Fellowship. I'm from Petersburg, and I don't know any of the local families." Her face crunched for a moment, her head tipping to spill curls across her shoulder. "I got the impression from their behavior, though, that the boys had been at that location before. They seemed familiar with the area."

Ben felt his heart beat in his temples. Thinking of the campfire he'd extinguished, he realized Angela was right. The amount of ashes within the circle of rocks, and the scattering of old cans and bottles in the little clearing, indicated more than one party had taken place out there.

"Could you find the clearing again, if need be?"

"Yes, sir. I believe so."

Ben nodded. He could help.

"Do you suppose you could give a description of the boys?" the sheriff asked.

Angela's face pinched into a thoughtful frown. "It was pretty dark, but I think I could. It might not be very accurate, though."

The swell of voices behind Ben started again, covering the descriptions Angela provided while the sheriff wrote on the notepad. The sheriff finished his scribbling then looked at Angela again. "While I appreciate you calling this in, your past history does give me reason to question your lack of involvement."

Angela nodded, her head low. Ben's heart ached at the dejected, shame-filled pose. It ached more when he realized he'd treated her just as the sheriff was now.

The sheriff asked, "Were any other campers around who could substantiate your story?"

Without a second thought, Ben stepped forward. "Sir." He waited until the sheriff looked at him. Angela didn't move. "I was out there, too."

The sheriff angled his pen against the pad. "You are?"

"Ben Atchison." Ben stated his address and telephone number.

"And you were at the scene?"

Ben clarified. "Not at first. Angela went out on her own. But when she didn't come back to the bonfire, I got worried. I thought maybe she'd lost her way in the dark, so I went looking for her. Before I came upon the clearing, I very clearly heard her telling someone to give her the marijuana."

He looked at Angela, wishing she would meet his gaze, but she remained silent with her eyes downcast. He went on. "She didn't ask to use it; she just told them to hand it over. When I reached the clearing, I saw the three boys run off into the woods. They dropped the marijuana before they left."

The sheriff wrote a little more, then flipped the pad closed and slipped it into his breast pocket. "Thank you, Mr. Atchison." Turning back to Angela, he said, "Miss Fischer, I will contact your parole office to let him know what transpired this evening. He may need to ask you a few questions when you return to Petersburg."

Angela finally lifted her head and offered a small nod in reply.

For the first time, the sheriff lost his stern expression. "I'm sure this was a difficult decision for you, to call me, knowing the possible repercussions. I appreciate your making the call. Obviously we don't want our local youth involved in drug use. Hopefully we'll be able to identify these boys and get them some help."

"I hope so, sir." Her voice sounded weak, its former firm tone wilting.

The sheriff strode to his vehicle and drove away from the camp while several people pushed forward, surrounding Angela. Their words of praise for her actions filled Ben's ears. After a few minutes of excited activity, they began to wander into the dormitories, leaving only Angela, Stephanie, and Robyn waiting under the light of the lantern. When Angela's gaze shifted to meet Ben's, Stephanie and Robyn exchanged a look behind Angela's head.

Stephanie said, "We'll turn in now, Angela."

"Yes, but holler if you need anything," Robyn said, shooting a brief glance in Ben's direction.

He hung his head. The women had cause for concern, based on his past behavior. He hoped he could rectify that now. He waited until Robyn and Stephanie shut the dormitory door behind them before whispering a simple question.

"Need a hug?"

Angela gave a start. Had she heard him correctly? The tender look on his face proved she hadn't misunderstood. And a hug was exactly what she needed.

She took one hesitant step toward him, and he closed the gap with three firm strides. She flung herself into Ben's embrace. His arms closed around her, holding her securely against his chest, and she pressed her cheek to his collarbone as tears stung behind her eyes. How she'd needed this hug! And to have it come from Ben. . . She thought her heart might burst from the emotion that pressed upward.

She allowed the warmth of Ben's arms and his heartbeat beneath her ear to soothe away every worry of the last several minutes. How she'd feared the sheriff would refuse to listen to her explanation, would simply haul her away in disgrace. Her knees still quivered slightly as the tension slowly drained away. She replayed words of congratulations and approval from the other campers at her courage, but as much as she appreciated the support of the others, what she really needed to know was what Ben thought of her now.

Reluctantly she pulled away. His hands slipped from her waist as she took a step backward and lifted her face to meet his gaze. "Thank you for the hug, Ben. I—I needed it."

His sweet smile—the smile she'd longed to see for so long—made her knees go weak again. But not from anxiety.

"You're welcome."

She swallowed the lump that formed in her throat. "Could—could we talk?"

"I think we should." Ben stretched out his hand, pressing his palm to the small of her back. A tingle traveled from her spine to her hairline, prickling her scalp. Without a word, he guided her across the shadowed landscape to the bench in the middle of the courtyard. They sat, one at each end of the bench, with a gap between them. Angling her knees toward the center, she faced Ben.

The overhead tree branches, waving in front of the lantern, cast speckled shadows across Ben's face, but she could make out his expression. None of the recrimination of previous days remained. Her heart thudded in a hopeful double beat.

"Ben, I want you to know that everything I told the sheriff was true. I didn't go out to that clearing to make a drug deal. I just happened upon those boys, and I tried to take the marijuana away from them so they wouldn't use it. And when I told him I never intend to use drugs again, I meant that, too."

He opened his mouth, but she held up her hand, stilling his words. She had to be completely honest with him. She wanted no secrets between them to create problems in the future—if they were to have a future.

"Out there, alone in the trees, I thought about opening up that marijuana and rolling a joint. It would have been so easy. No one was around, and I knew from past experience the marijuana would give me a few minutes of escape. My heart was aching, and a part of me really wanted that escape."

She kept her gaze pinned to his, determined to tell all. "But something stopped me. I realized I no longer wanted drugs to be my support system, my escape. I only wanted God. I asked Him to help me resist the desire for drugs, and He answered, Ben. He took the desire away. I know I won't ever do drugs again. The need for them is gone. I have all I need in my relationship with Him."

For long seconds they sat without speaking, enjoying the gentle lullaby of dry leaves rattling in the evening breeze. Ben's gaze didn't waver from hers, and none of the reproach she'd seen before flashed through his eyes. Gathering her courage, she went on. "There's one more thing I need to say." She paused, drew a deep breath, and released it slowly. Looking directly into his dark eyes, she said, "I love you, Ben. And I know you love me."

The muscles in his jaw clenched, and his Adam's apple bobbed in a swallow.

"How do you know that?" His voice sounded husky.

"You told me yesterday when you said you couldn't watch someone else you loved walk the path of drug addiction. So I know you love me." Leaning forward, she placed her trembling hand on his knee. "But, Ben, loving me isn't enough. You have to be able to trust me, too. Love and trust go hand in hand, and if one is missing, there can never be unity."

Pausing, she took another slow breath to bring her erratic heartbeat under control. She feared the answer to the next question, yet she had to ask it. "Do—do you think you can ever learn to trust me when I say I won't use drugs again?"

Ben turned his face to peer across the grounds. A pulse in his temple spoke of his inner battle. Angela held her breath, waiting, praying. Finally he brought his gaze around to meet hers.

Placing his hand over hers, he linked fingers with her. "Angela, what you did tonight took so much courage. Calling the sheriff, telling him you had marijuana in your possession. . . When I think of what could have happened to you. . . You could have been picked up and taken to jail without being given a chance to explain. Yet you took the chance because you knew you were innocent."

Tears glinted in his eyes. "I'm so proud of you. And your actions proved to me your honesty when you say you won't use drugs again."

Angela released the breath she'd been holding in a *whoosh* of relief. She nearly melted, and Ben's arms stretched out, capturing her and drawing her across the bench to hold her snugly beneath his chin. Cradling her in his arms, he went on in a tear-choked voice.

"I'm so sorry I doubted you. I let what happened to Kent put blinders on my eyes. I've watched you over the past weeks, and I've seen so much evidence of growth. That verse in Ephesians, the one about being blameless and holy in His sight?"

She offered a slight nod, cuddling closer, secure within the circle of his arms.

"That's what you are, Angela—holy. Jesus washed your heart clean when you invited Him in. He sees you as holy, yet I refused to see it. Instead I deliberately focused on your past. My fear of being hurt again built a wall around you that wouldn't allow you to shine. I know I hurt you with my harsh words and judgmental attitude."

Pulling back slightly, he cupped her chin and lifted her face so he could look directly into her eyes. "Can you forgive me?"

Angela smiled, her lips quivering as she battled tears. "Of course I forgive you." Saying the words brought a rush of relief so great, Angela wilted against his chest once more.

His lips touched the crown of her head. "Thank you."

Still nestling, Angela shared a private thought. "When I first met Kent and found out his disability was the result of drug use, I felt so. . .grateful."

Ben's hands rubbed up and down her back. "Grateful?" His breath stirred her hair.

"Yes. That could have been me, if I hadn't gotten caught. He reminds me of where I might be if I hadn't allowed God into my life. When I've been tempted to go back to drugs, I've thought of Kent, of how his life has changed because of his choices, and it's helped me choose more wisely."

"Oh, Angela. . ." The words came out in a sigh, and she felt his hands still as he pressed his lips to the top of her head.

Shifting slightly, she looked up at him. "Are you offended?"

"Offended?" He smiled, but she saw a glimmer of tears in his eyes. "No, my sweet Angela. You've given me hope that Kent's life isn't wasted. He still has a purpose. God used him to help you choose to stay clean." He shook his head, still smiling. "Thank you for telling me that."

She snuggled again, her eyes closed, breathing deeply to inhale the scents of the moment—damp earth, dry leaves, and the musky scent of Ben's skin. It was a potpourri she wanted to remember forever.

When Ben spoke again, the rumble of his deep voice vibrated beneath Angela's ear. "You've shared with me. Now let me share with you." Taking hold of her shoulders, he gently pulled her from her nestling spot. His fingers caressed her upper arms as he gazed into her face.

"You said love and trust go hand in hand. You're right. I've loved you for weeks, yet I withheld my trust. But no more. I promise you, Angela, from this moment forward, I will never again question your honesty. I will see you as Jesus sees you, as a new creature, holy and blameless in His sight."

His features swam as tears filled her eyes, and she blinked, swallowing as happy sobs pressed for release.

"He has cast your mistakes far away, and I promise I will not allow those past mistakes to impact the way I view you today. You are beautiful, Angela. Beautiful, pure, and holy. I love you, and I trust you."

She felt the spill of warm tears down her cheeks, but instead of reaching to brush them away, she reached for Ben. He captured her in his arms, drawing her near once more. His lips met hers, warm and tender.

Laughter rang from within her—joy-filled and healing. "Oh, Ben, I love you so much."

Cupping her cheeks, he pressed his forehead to hers. His whisper melted her heart. "Do you believe me? Do you trust me to keep my promise?"

"Oh yes. No broken promises. Not ever."

Ben sealed the promise with another kiss.

# Epilogue

Ben gave Kent's bow tie a quick tug, straightening it beneath his cousin's chin. With a smile, he said, "Wow, you look pretty spiffy there, cuz."

Kent's smile lit his face. "I am. . .best man."

Ben chuckled. "That you are, Kent. That you are." When they were fifteen, the year before their fathers' deaths, the boys had made a pact to stand up for one another when they married. It pleased Ben that, despite Kent's challenges, the promise was being kept.

The glow in Kent's eyes convinced Ben his cousin understood the significance of the event. And, thankfully, over the past three months, Kent's relationship with Angela had developed into a warm friendship. No jealousy lurked in Kent's eyes, only pleasure in his role in the wedding. It was an answer to prayer.

Ben walked to the mirror hanging near the door of the small room where he and the groomsmen readied themselves for the ceremony. Looking at his reflection, he had to smile. When he'd first spotted Angela at New Beginnings, would he have imagined meeting her at the head of an aisle while dressed in a black tuxedo and turquoise bow tie? Not in a million years. . .

Unlikely, he decided. That's what it was. Unlikely. Unlikely that he could fall in love with a former drug-abusing rich girl who didn't even know how to cook. Unlikely that a woman uncomfortable around those with disabilities would fall in love with a man whose life's call was to work with disabled adults.

Even though Angela was the opposite of what he had thought he was looking for in a wife, the love in his heart was so strong and so right. Unlikely didn't matter a bit when it came to God's will. They were perfect for each other. He knew that from the depth of his heart.

Eagerness built to go to the sanctuary, to fill his senses with the image of his bride coming down the aisle. Keeping with tradition, she had adamantly refused to allow him so much as a peek this morning.

"It's bad luck!" she had insisted last night after the rehearsal.

"But wouldn't it be good to take pictures before the ceremony?" It made sense to him to get all the picture snapping out of the way ahead of time.

But she had shaken her head, making her curls bounce. "No, Ben." Stepping into his embrace, she had peered up at him with serious eyes. "I want our first look at one another tomorrow to be in our wedding finery. I want to cherish your expression when you see how I've tried to please you with my appearance."

346

He had chuckled softly, certain she could come marching down that aisle in a pair of worn-out blue jeans and holey T-shirt and it wouldn't change how he felt about her. But instead of voicing that thought, he'd promised, "Okay. No peeks before the ceremony." Then he'd tapped the end of her nose and teased, "But it'd better be worth it."

She had tipped up on her toes to give him a quick smack on the lips. "Oh, I promise. It'll be worth it."

He smiled again, imagining her in the room next door, primping, teasing her curls into place, adjusting her gown. . . His stomach clenched. How much longer would he have to wait?

Spinning from the mirror, he glanced at his wristwatch—his wedding gift from Angela's parents—and heaved a sigh of relief. It was time. He marched over to Kent and took hold of the handles on his wheelchair. "Ready to go?"

"Yes. Let's. . .get married."

Ben laughed. "You got it."

—⊙—

Angela sent a quick glance down the length of her gown of snowy white. Seed pearls and sequins formed delicate swirls on the unblemished backdrop of satin. She touched the beaded band at her throat and felt her pulse racing.

Turning to her father, she whispered, "Is my hair okay? Everything still intact?"

He pulled down his brows, seeming to examine the elaborate twist held in place with pearled pins. She had deliberately pulled a few stands free to fall in spiraling curls along her neck and cheek. Her father tugged one of those free curls, smiling as it sprang back into place. "It looks okay to me." Then his lips tipped into a smile. "You look beautiful, Angela. Simply radiant."

"Oh, Daddy. . ." If everything went wrong during the wedding ceremony, her father's words were enough to make up for it.

The lilting melody of Bach's "Arioso" drifted from the sanctuary, and Angela sucked in a breath of eagerness. She whispered, "Daddy! It's time!"

His fingers tightened on her arm, his smile warm. "Are you sure you want to go through with it?"

"Daddy, please!" She giggled, pulling at his arm. Her father had asked her that question at least four times already, but she wasn't offended. For the first time in her life, her father was taking a genuine interest in her. Even though she had insisted on being married in unpretentious Grace Fellowship instead of the huge church downtown, even though she had chosen a man of moderate means instead of a man of wealth, even though she had chosen a simple ceremony followed by cake and punch rather than a grandiose celebration, her parents had agreed and supported her. She and Ben had every confidence that eventually their witness, combined with Aunt Eileen's, would win her parents to the Lord. Angela had never been happier.

"Okay," her father chuckled. "Let's go."

They stepped through the door as the guests rose in honor of the bride. Ben was hidden from view until Angela turned the corner at the foot of the center aisle, but when she got her first glimpse of her groom, she released a gasp of pleasure.

*Oh, Father God, thank You for the gift of this man.* The sparkle of joy in Ben's deep blue eyes drew Angela like a magnet, and she sped her steps instead of staying in time with the gentle flow of music. She read in his eyes a silent message: *You were worth this wait.*

She answered with a smile of her own: *You're everything I've dreamed of.*

Facing the minister, Ben's warm palm on her spine, Angela drank in the message based on First Corinthians 13. When the minister said, "Love believes all things. . ." she felt Ben's fingers press against her flesh. She flicked a brief glance at him, assuring him she made the same promise.

When she spoke her vows, her voice catching as emotion filled her throat, she offered a silent prayer to God to honor Him by keeping every pledge made to Ben on this day.

Tears coursed down her cheeks when she was finally able to lift her face to receive her first kiss as Mrs. Ben Atchison. Ben cupped her cheeks, his thumbs along her jaw. She clasped the backs of his hands and smiled through her tears.

She whispered as the guests broke into applause, "To God be all praise and honor."

"Amen," Ben whispered in reply. His lips captured hers once more, delivering a promise of wonderful things to come.

# A Letter to Our Readers

Dear Readers:

In order that we might better contribute to your reading enjoyment, we would appreciate your taking a few minutes to respond to the following questions. When completed, please return to the following: Fiction Editor, Barbour Publishing, Inc., P.O. Box 719, Uhrichsville, OH 44683.

1. Did you enjoy reading *Kansas Weddings* by Kim Vogel Sawyer?
   ❑ Very much—I would like to see more books like this.
   ❑ Moderately—I would have enjoyed it more if _____
   _____
   _____

2. What influenced your decision to purchase this book?
   (Check those that apply.)
   ❑ Cover        ❑ Back cover copy        ❑ Title        ❑ Price
   ❑ Friends      ❑ Publicity              ❑ Other

3. Which story was your favorite?
   ❑ *Dear John*                    ❑ *Promising Angela*
   ❑ *That Wilder Boy*

4. Please check your age range:
   ❑ Under 18        ❑ 18–24        ❑ 25–34
   ❑ 35–45           ❑ 46–55        ❑ Over 55

5. How many hours per week do you read? _____

Name _____

Occupation _____

Address _____

City_____ State _____ Zip _____

E-mail_____